WOMAN
of an
UNCERTAIN
AGE

Praise for *Woman of an Uncertain Age*

"In her debut novel, India-born, New York-based journalist Malhotra vividly portrays aspects of Indian immigrant life in the United States." — *Library Journal*

"*Woman of an Uncertain Age* is a resounding 'Yes!' to everything that can go right, all that's worth saving and whether life still wants to surprise us. In the intelligent and sensuous Naina, Priya Malhotra has given us the propelling verve of a classic Terry McMillan character with the multicultural tack we love Bharati Mukherjee's Indian American women for. An American story, a New York story, a grown woman story . . . Here is a novel to represent these high times of new life and reopenings."
— Kalisha Buckhanon, author of *Speaking of Summer*

"A poignant and yet witty account of a woman in her fifties grappling with her past, her at times inappropriate desires, and her life as a single widow. *Woman of an Uncertain Age* is a delightful and surprising read." — Helen Benedict, author of *The Good Deed* and *Wolf Season*

"In *Woman of An Uncertain Age*, Priya Malhotra has deftly woven a complex novel that will draw in readers through her beautiful prose, vivid imagery, and memorable characters. I found myself mesmerized by every step in the plot while identifying with every character's trait, choices, and whims. Even the ones I found challenging, they challenged me in a way that made me a better reader, thinker, and ultimately, human."
— Reema Zaman, author of *I Am Yours* and *Paramita: A Dystopian Matriarchy*

"With a poet's sense of lyricism, a painter's sense of color, and a novelist's sense of story, Priya Malhotra pushes her language to ever greater heights, teetering at the edge, but always pulling back in time. To me, *A Woman of an Uncertain Age* is about loneliness and longing, about acceptance and understanding, about the strangeness of existence, especially for Naina, who grew up in India but now lives in New York, all caught in an intoxicating range of metaphors, yet told with an honesty that cuts to the bone." — Birgitta Hjalmarson, author of *Fylgia* and *Artful Players: Artistic Life in Early San Francisco*

"Priya Malhotra writes with style and verve. *Woman of an Uncertain Age* is acutely observed and ably brings to the fore the particular anxieties and challenges of ageing, immigration and finding love in the most unexpected of circumstances." — Pallavi Aiyar, author of *Smoke and Mirrors: An Experience of China* and *Orienting: An Indian in Japan*

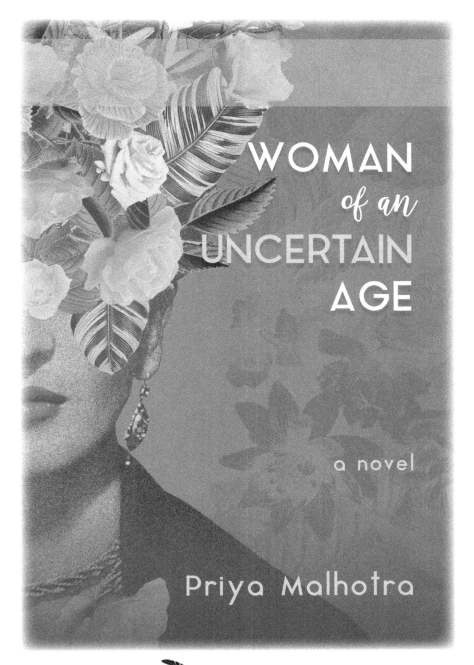

WOMAN
of an
UNCERTAIN
AGE

a novel

Priya Malhotra

Bink Books

Bedazzled Ink Publishing Company • Fairfield, California

978-1-949290-90-5 paperback

Cover Design
by
Desiree Feldman
and Vandana Jain

Bink Books
a division of
Bedazzled Ink Publishing Company
Fairfield, California
http://www.bedazzledink.com

ACKNOWLEDGEMENTS

This book is for my husband, Pran Singh, without whose support it would have never been birthed. His generous support of my creative work and steadfast belief in it were invaluable and, for that, I'm deeply grateful. Pran is the persevering type, so even on days when the manuscript felt like a sinking ship, he would never let me drown in my woes and always urged me to carry on.

This novel would have also not seen the light of day without Jennifer Lyons, my extraordinary literary agent, ally and friend. It is thanks to her that I believed my work had merit and even when the rejections kept coming, her support and enthusiasm of my book never wavered. I'm so so thankful for you, dear Jennifer. You've been a beacon of light for me. The fact that you, who have worked with luminaries such as Jesmyn Ward, the first woman and African-American to win the National Book Award for fiction twice, Gabriela Mistral, the late Chilean poet and first Latin American to win the Nobel Prize for literature, and Oscar Hijuelos, the late Cuban-American novelist and first Hispanic writer to win the Pulitzer Prize for fiction, chose to work with me is truly an honor.

I'm also extremely thankful to Bedazzled Ink, my wonderful publisher and true advocate of women's voices in literature, for publishing my book. Dear C.A. Casey, you're such a thoughtful editor and marvelous human being. A big thanks also to Lorna Owens, a fabulous editor, for her excellence in shaping my unwieldy novel.

I owe so much to Shelly Bahl, my dearest friend and artist, who helped me with all the details regarding the art world, patiently read countless drafts and always offered insightful feedback. Kiri Blakeley, my dearest friend and wonderful writer, thank you for being such an immense source of support and inspiration to me. Also, a huge thanks to Birgitta Hjalmarson, my dearest friend and fantastic writer, for introducing me to Bedazzled Ink, her ceaseless encouragement, and superb proofreading assistance.

I'm deeply indebted to Dr. Urmilla Khanna, my late aunt and former professor of English literature, for inspiring a love of literature in me at a very young age. I also wish to thank Pramilla Malhotra, my mother, Vikram Malhotra, my brother, and Parveen Samra, my sister-in-law, for their steadfast support of my work.

Finally, a big thanks to all my family and friends for their sustained encouragement and interest over the years, particularly Geetika Tandon, Sangeeta Mehta and Ruchira Chaudhary. Thank you all.

Priya Malhotra

PART ONE

CHAPTER ONE

WHEN NAINA, A slender twenty-one-year-old with shiny black hair that touched her hips, and plush lips that, as her family constantly reminded her, were always parted as if she were about to ask a question, left New Delhi to move to New Jersey after marrying Harish in 1974, she was unusually calm compared with other distraught brides who couldn't bear the thought of leaving their homes and families to go off to a foreign land.

At the airport in Delhi, in the middle of the night, she hugged her parents tightly but did not cry or constantly turn back to look at them as she headed toward her flight. She was going abroad for the first time, and sitting on a plane for the second time in her life. She was going to a place she knew little about: America, which was, at that time in India, a far-off and unfamiliar place. It wasn't like going to England, which she could easily conjure up with images of places like Buckingham Palace and Mayfair, people like Mr. Darcy and the Brontë sisters, and food like bread pudding and caramel custard. She already knew about British towns called Birmingham, Manchester, and Oxford—but what of Birmingham, Alabama; Manchester, New Hampshire; Oxford, Mississippi; and the clump of six states in the northeast that Americans called New England? These were places she had never heard of.

Although she didn't know much about the country she'd soon be calling home, she'd definitely heard about this legendary city called New York, teeming with skyscrapers and ritzy areas called Park Avenue and Fifth Avenue. It was the city of *Breakfast at Tiffany's*, *The Age of Innocence*, the city where the sky talked to the earth, the city that the *Illustrated Weekly of India* described as the "vampire kingdom of greed and capitalism." And New York was where she would land, late in the afternoon at JFK, still wearing her chura, the red-and-white wedding bangles many Indian women customarily wear for a month after marriage.

It was a chilly day in April and she was wearing a light brown sweater and her father's tweed coat, a tan-and-red coat from England two sizes too big for her, but the warmest garment anyone in the family owned. Her husband Harish also wore a coat similar to hers, except that his was brown and black; he had thrown it over a pure lambswool black sweater, a thermal undershirt, and a thick scarf whose tassels had irritated her nose while she tried to sleep on the airplane. Harish had tried to get her to wear more clothes, to "layer on" as he liked to say, but she hadn't listened, never imagining the biting cold that would greet her.

The cold was the first thing that jumped at her when they exited the airport, the kind of chill that ripped through her clothes and plunged her into an agonizing delirium. As they waited for a bus to take them to Port Authority, it was then that Harish first held her hand in public—one of the few times in their thirty years of married life to come. Despite the freezing temperature, that public display of affection had excited her. His hands were long and supple, and he held her hand with a modicum of firmness, but she wished he'd squeeze it tighter, much tighter. They sat on a bus and she was astonished by the power of the heating system. It was her introduction to the supremacy of machines in this country. Before she knew it, she was warm again.

The bus was now going over the   Bridge, and she saw the fabled skyline of Manhattan, draped in a twilight mist that softened the sharp contours of the majestic buildings. Her heart beat faster. The city looked like an emperor—haughty, invincible, and heroic. She was mesmerized.

But Manhattan vanished as fast as it had appeared once they changed buses at Port Authority and were off to suburban Montcrest, a New Jersey town full of drab, nearly identical Dutch colonial-style homes and large, long cars parked in driveways, like sentries on duty. It was the place where Naina would spend the next three decades of her life.

NEVER, IN ALL those years, had she imagined she might one day live in Manhattan, Naina thought as she shut her apartment window so she wouldn't have to hear the dry cleaner and his wife arguing in Cantonese. Their bickering was really intolerable. It was, after all, Sunday. Those two could yell for hours with no consideration for anyone near them. She supposed that was what one had to endure to be in Manhattan, a small price to pay. Still amazed to find herself living in the greatest city in the world, she felt a shiver of excitement run through her. But the feeling quickly passed with the sound of a fiendish howl, as if the ten-headed demon Ravan was convulsing in the netherworld.

It was an ambulance on the street below. She covered her ears. Why did they have to be so loud? And if they had to be, why couldn't they have a more melodious tune?

Again, the phone rang, the fourth time that day, but Naina, who would have ordinarily considered it rude, let it go to voicemail.

Although it was almost two o'clock on a gray Sunday afternoon in April, she was still only half-awake, unable to muster the energy to get up. She lay sprawled on her bed, under the white comforter, looking at the short, untidy pile of birthday cards that waited for on her nightstand. Languidly, she picked one up.

"You don't get dumb and old as the years go by, YOU just get SMART, SEXY, and BOLD" screamed a little white card with thick black lettering, which looked

poised to pop off the paper. "*Wild, witty, and wise, a woman in her fifties is a man's most treasured prize*" proclaimed a red-and-gold card that Naina immediately knew had to be from Shona, the optimistic chatterbox who, despite her efforts for almost twenty years, had enjoyed little success with men. "*Age is sage, and knowledge is power, so let the GOOD TIMES ROLL!*" declared another card with Elvis Presley on its cover. But the most unforgettable card, a pretty looking thing with lots of pink roses, was from Karen, her daughter Amaya's friend. "*You've touched so many lives, made so many friends, gained so much wisdom, and known so many joys and sorrows. These are all wonderful, beautiful reasons to celebrate.*" Was this a preview of what Karen might say at her funeral?

Naina smiled wryly as she read the cards that invariably referred to this magical fountain of wisdom that apparently sprung from her. She heard the rusty cast iron radiator hissing away like a spurned diva and the maddening sounds, three floors down, of the dry cleaner and his wife who were still arguing. That tremulous feeling leaped within her again. She was certain of very little, and as far from possessing any sagacity as she had ever been.

Of course, that had not always been the case, and even though she had acquired a distaste for her former life, sometimes she couldn't help being nostalgic for those days when she felt so sure of everything—days framed by predictable domestic rituals. At times, she did fret over little details but never saw or, if she did, never admitted, even to herself, to the blemishes smearing the canvas of her life: the layer of dust turning the emerald green into a moldy green; the cobweb of tiny rips making the majestic purple look like a sad, shriveled eggplant; the weathering of the shining red to the hue of an Indian bride's clothes faded in the sun.

Her headache worsened and she forced herself to get up to take a couple of aspirins. She knew the culprit had to be those pale white drinks in those thin glasses she'd downed at some hazy point during the previous night. What were they called? Something that began with a *sh*. The letters arduously came together to form a word. Sho . . . ts. Yes, shots. Some kind of shots that sounded like military offensives. Kamikaze shots. That was it. Kamikaze shots. They were just as lethal as their name implied, and she regretted having consumed them without restraint. She should have been more careful. Stuck to wine. Not listened to Alannah's *have just one more.* Her body was no longer young and as forgiving as it might once have been if put to the test. Now, like an accountant, it registered every indulgence, made her pay for every bit of carelessness. She decided to take a third aspirin just in case two did not do the job.

Her birthday party the night before had ended up being much more excessive than she had anticipated, but in retrospect she knew she should not have been surprised—considering it had been Alannah, her young friend, who had organized it. A thirty-five-year-old firebrand artist, Alannah thrived on excess and spectacle. She was a woman whose enterprising efforts intensified whenever she sensed she was drawing someone out of some supposed state of deprivation and repression. The theme of the party was "Arabian Nights," and it was held in a lush orange-and-green room in Houri, a hip Moroccan restaurant in the East Village. Like many places on Avenue C, in the first decade of the twenty-first century, Houri—which means "alluring woman" in Arabic—was on the ground level of a dilapidated brick building that still had traces of graffiti on its walls and an air of having once been a place for rough, illicit exchanges. But when you entered it now, you were immediately transported to a decadent paradise that seemed a world away from its questionable earlier life, and from its rundown neighborhood—the depressing-looking deli opposite it, the crumbling pavement outside, the leaky air conditioner wobbling in a window on the third floor of the building next door, on the verge of falling prey to the force of gravity at any moment.

Even though the East Village, once known for artists and beatniks, had long undergone gentrification, these were the vestiges of a bygone era full of sex, drugs, and rock 'n' roll. To Naina, who had moved to the city from her large suburban home in central New Jersey a year-and-a-half before, no place in New York felt as exciting and edgy as the East Village. In Jersey, there was space and more space and nothing of consequence to fill it, and in the East Village, there was so much energy and electricity that it spilled out of the tiniest gaps, rattling doors and walls, threatening to break man-made enclosures.

A glittering curtain of red, gold, and blue beads led you from the restaurant into a cozy party room where there were sofas upholstered in the fiery red-orange of an equatorial sunset, plush cushions adorned with an elaborate pattern of green and gold, and walls hidden behind sheets of fluttering gold silk. Several hookahs sat on small mosaic tables, and delicate coils of apricot, apple, and spice-flavored smoke swirled and swayed as people puffed away, filling the room with beautiful misty patterns.

There had been about fifteen or sixteen people at the party, the majority of whom Naina had not known for more than a year or so, and some she was meeting for the first time. The only ones she considered to be real friends were Alannah and Mara, a forty-two-year-old self-help writer obsessed with everything yoga and new age, and Rob, a tabla player from a yet-to-be signed fusion band, who looked like a big bird as he waved his tattooed arms around while talking incessantly.

Rob had gray hair and a sagging face that made him look much older than his thirty-nine years, but his ebullience and constant use of the phrase "that's cool" made him seem a whole lot younger. He gave her an orange-and-black idol of the fierce multi-armed Hindu goddess Kali as a birthday present, something he had bought during his biweekly visits to Jackson Heights to eat samosas.

"Nains," he said (he was the only person in the world who had ever called her Nains), "Kali kicks ass, let me tell you. I mean that woman can create, that woman can destroy. That's cool. It's so cool. And all we're stuck with here is the boring Virgin Mary, *boring*. Immaculate Conception. Gimme a break. Now, Kali, she's hot, she's totally hot."

"Thanks, Rob, thanks so much," Naina said, thinking how ugly the idol was. "This is wonderful." She gave him a tentative hug. "But we should be kind to the Virgin Mary. She's sort of soothing and nice even if she isn't as interesting as Kali." That part, she meant. She had always liked the Virgin Mary, much more than she had ever liked Kali.

"C'mon, Nains, that's your Catholic School education talking. That's what they drill into you. Love the Virgin Mary. Believe me, I went to one too, miles away from you though, so I know."

In order to beef up the crowd at the party, Alannah had invited three or four of her own friends Naina had never met before. One was Iris, an exceptionally tall woman with pointy features, a freelance curator and art writer who exuded the kind of humorless overconfidence that made Naina want to run and hide in some remote recess of herself.

"So I went to see the new John Currin show at Andrea Rosen," Iris said after she had greeted Naina with a "hello" and "happy birthday" in a manner that suggested that such banalities were not worthy of her time. "I didn't think his work could get worse, but he surprises me every time. He's such a lightweight and gets more misogynistic as he gets older." She vigorously shook her head and exhaled loudly. "God, he just bothers me so much . . ."

Naina didn't know how to respond because, even though she now worked as an assistant at an art gallery in Chelsea, she barely knew anything about Currin except that he was a famous artist known for painting distorted images of women with large breasts. She, did, however, know the Andrea Rosen Gallery, one of the most renowned galleries in Chelsea, and had gone there to see the colossal, dense installation of British artist Matthew Ritchie a few months before.

"I haven't seen that show yet. But, did you see the Matthew Ritchie show in December? It was magnificent."

"You think so?" Iris shot back. "I thought it was so lame, so lame . . ."

Although Iris did not, at any point in the evening, appear to be enjoying herself, she stayed until the party ended at three a.m., drinking one glass of white wine after another.

That image of Iris now crystallized into a hard-edged shape as Naina looked out at the distant, fog-swaddled spire of the Chrysler Building. Thankfully, her headache was getting better.

Then there was Andrew, Alannah's soft-spoken English teacher friend. He seemed much nicer than Iris and had brought her a lovely bouquet of pink chrysanthemums—big, bulbous flowers like those in her garden in India. Naina guessed he was a couple of years younger than Alannah, maybe thirty-two or thirty-three, and probably didn't know anyone who had children, judging by his look of surprise when Naina said something about Amaya's slender span of interest when it came to literature.

"You have a daughter?" he said as Alannah came up to them, bringing Naina another drink.

"Not just a daughter, but a son as well," Alannah interjected.

"Wow . . . how old are they?"

"Four and twelve," Alannah said with a grin. "She looks great for that doesn't she?"

Andrew seemed to believe her until Naina corrected the lie, telling him her daughter—the girl in the charcoal gray dress with shoulder-length black hair engrossed in conversation on the far side of the room—was twenty-eight and her son was twenty-six. At that point, both his eyes and mouth widened, making his face look like a misshapen pretzel with deep hollows. Naina surmised his reaction wasn't because she looked so young, but because no one in his universe was likely over the age of thirty-five. It probably hadn't even occurred to him that a friend of Alannah's could be so much older. It was funny, after that, his tone toward her changed; he became more respectful and after a few drinks, even took to calling her "Ma'am." While she never said anything, she had yearned to tell him that being in one's fifties wasn't as old as he might have thought, that she too had once seen fifty-two as surreal as death, that just because she had grown children and was maybe old enough to be his mother, did not mean there was a huge gulf between them.

The most unsettling moment of the party for Naina was when Karen walked in. The young woman was Amaya's childhood friend who had transformed herself into a trendy-looking journalist from the chubby, chatty blonde girl she always remembered sniffing jars of spices in her kitchen. After they gave each other a quick peck on the cheek, she felt as if Karen was looking at her with the probing eyes of a reporter, trying to reconcile the image she had of Naina with the one facing her—a fifty-two-year-old woman in a long, sleek black dress with two slits on either side; a tummy shaper underneath; and knee-length, three-inch stiletto heel boots. At that moment, Naina felt exposed, as if she were wearing a transparent dress through which her daughter's friend could see every droop in her flesh. The last time she had seen Karen, her stomach was looser and had a small, visible bulge.

Before Karen thought she was a fraud, a farce, a fool, Naina yearned to get away, but she could not be so rude to Amaya's friend.

"Mrs. Mehta, happy birthday," Karen said, her bewilderment conspicuous. "You look marvelous—my gosh—you seem like such a New Yorker now."

"Uh . . . thanks, Karen."

Karen's eyes felt like they were peeling away layers of her skin. Skin that felt as thin and flimsy as paper.

"So . . . so very glad . . . you could make it. Especially . . . especially . . . since you're here . . . I mean . . . visiting New York . . . for such a short time . . . Very . . . really nice of you. So . . . how are . . . sorry, I mean . . . how is everything with you in D.C.?"

"It's good, thanks. Have you been in touch with anyone from Montcrest lately? Oh, by the way, you probably already know this, but I recently spoke to someone who told me that Rishi Nambiar had gotten into Stanford, but his mother didn't want him to go that far away, and I also heard that the Sharmas are completely freaking out because Puja has decided not to go law school but wants to study music therapy . . . isn't that awful? Of all the people in the world, I never thought the Sharmas were that conservative, but you probably know better— Gosh, Mrs. Mehta, you look so great. I can't believe it. I'm sorry, I didn't mean it like that, you always looked good . . . you know what I mean."

Naina smiled weakly, muttering something vague about being too busy with her new job to keep in contact with everyone in Montcrest. Through the beaded curtains, she saw Rita, an arts administrator acquaintance, and Danielle, whom she had once met at an art opening of a Czech installation artist, walking in. Relieved, she excused herself and rushed off to greet her two new guests, grabbing another glass of red wine on the way.

Toward the end of the party—somewhere between one and two in the morning—two Lebanese belly dancers dragged Naina to the floor and made her rhythmically jiggle her hips in concert with theirs. As the alcohol and the swaying of her body took over, everyone and everything around her—shimmering and multi-hued under the colored lights of the Moroccan lamps—seemed magical, and she ended up dancing somewhat provocatively, drawing loud claps and hoots from her guests. She had surprised herself—and by that point in the evening, every surprise seemed like a good one, so she danced alone for an entire song, swept away by her own performance.

Now, standing in her apartment kitchen, with the demonic howls of the ambulances again piercing her eardrums and scattering her consciousness like beads of a necklace coming apart and dashing in different directions, she felt veins of embarrassment course through her as murky images of herself dancing bobbed inside her head. How silly had she looked? What must have everyone thought? At least, Amaya had not seen it since she had left the party by midnight with Karen. Naina pressed her fingers against her ears and closed her eyes. Finally, silence, that sublime wisp of calm she experienced only in brief spurts in New York, came.

Naina pulled out two bags of a strong peppermint tea she had recently discovered near Union Square. Her rattled thoughts gathered again, like beads of a necklace being slowly restrung with a needle by Ramchand, the bony, shaggy-haired man who used to sit cross-legged on a tattered beige cushion at Ashoka Jewelers, the dusty and crusty jewelry shop in Old Delhi her mother always went to.

She wondered what Karen must have thought of her. The shock on Karen's face had been obvious, but she suspected the full strength of her feelings had not made it to her face. Had she *really* changed that much since the New Jersey days? Yes, her hair was now shorter and more layered; she had given up her rich burgundy lipstick for a shimmery, subtler red; she had her eyebrows done regularly and had started going to the gym a couple of times a week—but that much?

Still, whatever changes had occurred in her physical appearance had to be small in comparison with the changes inside of her.

She switched on a Beatles CD as she waited for the tea to cool down. She absolutely adored the Beatles and had done so ever since her college days in Delhi when she fell in love with John Lennon.

For most of her life, Naina felt certain about what would come next, the anticipated rituals of life unfolding themselves with remarkable timeliness. An arranged marriage at twenty-one to a doctor, two children shortly thereafter, the joys and annoyances of raising children followed by the inevitable sadness of letting them go to forge their own way in the world. Yes, there had been a few things she might not have foreseen had she been given a crystal ball when she was younger, like becoming the associate director of a women's health organization in New Jersey or taking several art history courses at Rutgers University in her forties. But nothing hit her with its unexpectedness like Harish's death at the age of fifty-three. He had been a healthy man with no history of heart disease or problems with cholesterol; yet, he had been the one who collapsed and died while performing a colonoscopy on a patient.

She sat down on her couch and buried her face in her hands as the memory of her husband's dead body—so utterly helpless and heartbreakingly pure as it lay in the casket before it was taken to the crematorium—ambushed her. It had been over two years since Harish had died, and while there were days when she did not think of him (that fact did make her feel guilty), that final image still had the power to make her shudder—as if she were suspended in the throes of an unknown limbo.

She was, of course, stricken with grief over her husband's untimely death, but it was more than that. She was so profoundly mystified by this abrupt bend in her life that it punctured her soul, severing it until it never returned to its previous composition.

How could this have happened to her? She had always pictured them as husband and wife reading the newspaper every morning until their eyes could read no more, looking after their grandchildren when their children went off on holiday with their spouses, and reminding each other to take their pills as their memories dulled with age. This vision of the future had seemed as clear to her as an often-traveled road on a sunny day. There was no rational way to explain her belief in this sort of predictable contentment, but when a woman married an educated, well-paid man who had properly been vetted by her parents, security—lifelong, uninterrupted security—was promised in exchange for entrusting your life to a virtual stranger.

At least that was how she had understood the deal—though she had never put it into words until after her husband's death when her thoughts curled inwards, burrowing into murky, cobweb-filled areas. Before he died, that assumed and unspoken bargain had been kept. But, then, it fell apart, suddenly, senselessly, and she felt as if the bricks that held her life together had been jerked out of place, turning her existence into something vulnerable like a cheaply constructed house in an Indian village, trying to keep upright in the rain, thunder, snow, lightning, or anything else that decided to strike it.

She got up and poured her tea and did not add any sugar or milk as usual. If Harish had been there, he would have discouraged her from drinking it like this. He preferred his with lots of milk and sugar, diluted to something that barely tasted like tea. She could imagine his tall, lanky frame swimming in a polo shirt too big for him, his long legs covered in slim, dark-colored slacks, and his pointed, bony feet engulfed in a pair of Clark's brown leather sandals; he would be standing against the kitchen counter and adding more milk to his tea.

Just thinking about him, she became soft with tenderness.

"Why don't you add some more milk?" Harish would invariably ask in his low-pitched, gentle voice that had the effect of a salve. Of all the things about her husband, it was probably his voice she missed the most.

"Then I can't taste the flavor of the tea, you know that," she would always reply.

"I know, I know, I just don't understand how you can drink it like that. Okay, I won't ask anymore."

But inevitably he would ask her again.

There were so many things they knew about each other after so many years. She knew he liked his lamb roganjosh extra spicy with roti, his chicken curry mild with rice, his pastas without any Parmesan cheese, his yogurt always plain, and after dinner; she could tell from his facial expression if he wanted to stay longer at a party or not, from the tone of his voice which nurse he was speaking to; she could see the question marks darting in his small brown eyes when she said or did something he did not understand, the currents flickering in his brain warning him against questioning her at a particular moment.

He knew by the look on her face when she did not like someone, the right moment to interrupt her when she was reading, by the way she clutched his arm that she had had a bad dream—after which, he knew all she needed was for him to say "it's okay, it's okay" in his reassuring voice and to massage her forehead, and she would fall asleep again.

But he never knew what her bad dreams were about and she never knew what caused him to stare blankly at nothing when he'd wake up in the middle of the night, at least a handful of times every month. She had asked him, but he brushed her off. "Nothing, nothing," he would normally say. But there was something about his gaze in the dark, the specter of something undefinable hovering in his bony face. Was it actually there or was she imagining it?

There were so many things they did not know about each other.

She went to sit on her sofa and sip her tea, the unadulterated flavor of mint swirling in her mouth like a salubrious spring. Suddenly, she felt glad not to have to defend how she liked her tea to anyone. It was one of many benefits of living alone.

Had she been attracted to Harish, she wondered, now surrounded by New York women who constantly examined the question of attraction. Yes, she had found him sort of appealing, and wanted to be touched by him, particularly in the early days. But whatever was there was never rekindled, and, in the later years, there had been little amorousness left in their marriage.

Recently, Alannah had asked her why she had been so confounded by Harish's death. She understood her friend being devastated, but why the huge bewilderment? Naina thought about it and then said, "Why are people stunned when a sick or healthy loved one passes away even though they know countless people die all over the world every single day? Death is one of those things where inevitability never protects you from startlement." Still, even as she said it, she again felt how naïve her reaction to Harish's death had been.

A few weeks after he died, Naina moved into the guest room, hoping she might be able to get some sleep there. But she would invariably wake up at three in the morning, make herself a big kettle of peppermint tea, put on her favorite Ella Fitzgerald CD, sit in the rocking chair, and stare at the meandering floral pattern on the crumpled bedspread. She would ponder over existential questions like the meaning and purpose of her life, questions whose answers she had always figured lay somewhere in or around the palm of her hands and so had rarely given them any real consideration. Whenever she thought about them, it was just as an intellectual exercise where she may have prodded the edges but did not probe further.

But at fifty years of age, those assumed answers had seemed to have dissolved into sand and flown away from her hands. She had pictured herself stranded in an eerie void, like someone stuck on a lone highway at night, and because she was slightly afraid of driving—even after so many years—that image had terrified her more than most.

She took her last sip of mint tea and put the cup on her rectangular glass-top coffee table, which she had chosen because of its bamboo-pole legs and because it was neat and compact for apartment living. Paul McCartney's voice came through the speakers. *There will be an answer, let it be.* Really, she wondered. Will there be an answer? When? Where? How?

An hour later, she glanced at her watch. It was past five o' clock. Oh my goodness. It was so late. In a couple of hours, she was meeting Amaya and, for the first time, her half-white, half-Indian boyfriend, and she had yet to shower and dress. There was no more time to sit and ponder. She had to step out of her mind quickly, a skill she'd never quite acquired. But New York life demanded that she learn it.

Naina picked herself up from the sofa, stretched out her arms, and forced herself to hasten the pace. She went to her closet and took out a bunch of clothes. What to wear to such an occasion? She wanted to look like a proper mother of a daughter just a few years shy of thirty, but she didn't want to look like a fuddy duddy aunty either. She threw another set of clothes on her bed, feeling her hands twitch. Meeting her daughter's boyfriend. How odd. What a strange thing to be doing.

First, she tried on a high-waisted black-and-white dress, but decided against it because it brought too much attention to her breasts. Then she tried on a pair of jeans and a black cotton sweater but rejected that because it looked too casual. She settled on formal black pants and a caramel-colored sweater with some delicate embroidery around the neck and cuffs. And what about the shoes?

She spotted her pointy black boots from last night's party standing on the floor—they looked awake and alert, as if ready to dance again with abandon, ready to take long strides, ready to trespass boundaries. She would wear those boots. Meanwhile, a strange restlessness and trepidation scurried about inside her in haphazard streaks.

CHAPTER TWO

AS NAINA HURRIEDLY walked toward the subway, she noticed something new in her Murray Hill neighborhood—a blinking blue-and-red sign saying THAI MASSAGE—CALM, CALM, CALM above a blindingly bright Chinese restaurant. It was not there two days earlier—the pace of change in New York was so disorientingly rapid.

Jai was the first boyfriend Amaya had ever really sounded serious about and Amaya had told Naina that she would really like him—he liked the arts and Gabriel García Márquez was also one of his favorite authors. At least they would have something to talk about. She wasn't used to meeting her children's boyfriends or girlfriends. Unless it was a serious relationship, possibly one leading to marriage, Indian parents weren't generally expected to engage with their children's partners. She wondered if her daughter would be getting married in the near future. Being a mother-in-law would make her feel really old.

Naina walked down the subway steps, her movements now slower. She kept telling herself the evening would go fine. It was perfectly normal to meet her daughter's boyfriend. And it wasn't like *she*, of all people, was conservative by any means.

In the middle of the platform, she saw an older man wearing tattered black jeans and a purple bandanna on his head. He had a big guitar strapped against his shriveled body and sang with vigor.

"But I'm sad to say I'm on my way . . ." he squeaked in a high voice, his rendition of Harry Belafonte's "Jamaica Farewell"—so distant from the original that it was virtually unrecognizable. Yet Naina gave him two dollars, double the amount she normally gave most subway musicians. She always tried to give something to the musicians trying their luck in the teeming, throbbing parallel world beneath the ground of New York City. She stood a few feet away from him, allowing the words, if not the melody, to take her back to those Christmases at Delhi Gymkhana Club when the parents of her friend Reena used to sashay to Harry Belafonte's songs.

She had always been a little of jealous of Reena for having such modern parents. Reena's mother used to have her hair up in a stylish bun, wore chiffon saris with sleeveless blouses, and slow danced with her husband, an elegant man who wore a rose in his lapel and spoke English in that nice, crisp accent Naina believed it was supposed to be spoken in.

It had been more than twenty years since Naina had heard anything by Harry Belafonte, no matter that it was in a mutilated form. She smiled to herself.

She thought about how the subway was one of her favorite things about New York, even in the summer months when it was like an oven to most people. She enjoyed walking down the worn steps and entering the chaotic world of the New York underground where a colorful mosaic on a wall or pillar brightened a dilapidated platform, and cute kids would try to sell M&M's for some vague but good cause. With its unmistakable brew of smells of every type of sweat, body odor, and perfume, the subway reminded her of India—the only other place she knew where so many bodies and their secretions came in such close contact.

When her train finally groaned its way into the station, it was unusually empty for seven in the evening on a weekend. There was just a tiny old lady who kept hitting the floor with a stick and muttering incomprehensibly, and a young woman in braces who kept yelling in what sounded like Russian at the small girl with her. As Naina sat down at the far end of the car, she thought of her life in Jersey, and was once more beset by the idea that it had been like that of a hamster on a wheel. Again, she felt that jab of regret. The grittiness of the subway, and of New York in general, seemed real in a grownup sort of way—not like the fairytale sweetness of the manicured lawns and houses in the suburbs. At the next station, the train stopped for a few minutes, without any explanation, and a group of Indian families rushed in just before the doors closed. One of the women, extremely tall with a sallow face, pointy chin, and dangling silver earrings, reminded her of Sheela, a former neighbor in New Jersey. Was that her? Naina looked to her right to see if she could discreetly change cars. And then she took a second look at the woman and realized she was not anyone she knew. How silly could she be? Why would Sheela, who loved her Lexus and hated Manhattan, be in a New York City subway, holding a five- or six-year-old child on her lap when her youngest was already in college?

"Do you know who this is, beta?" the sallow-faced woman said to the little boy, pointing to another woman in jeans and a heavily embroidered kurti.

He shook his head.

"This is Mala Aunty. She is Akshay's mami. She has just moved to the U.S."

"So, who is this, beta?" a mustached man said who appeared to be the boy's father. "Let's see if you remember."

"Maalaaa," the boy replied.

"No, Rohit." The sallow-faced woman lightly slapped the boy on his leg. "Don't you have any respect for your elders? Taking their name like that. Bad boy. It's Mala Aunty. Mala Aunty, okay. Understand?"

"Sorrreee," the boy said, looking down. "Sorreee, Mala Aunty."

Naina rolled her eyes. She was thankful it wasn't her being called aunty. She hated being called aunty, the all-purpose, ubiquitous moniker Indians used to refer to any lady significantly older than themselves. In her only notable act of rebellion during her early years in Jersey, she had insisted on being called Mrs. Mehta or even Naina by her children's Indian friends. Maybe even *tia* or *tante*, which meant aunt in Spanish and French respectively, or even *teta*, which meant aunt in Czech—any of them would have been acceptable, but not *aunty.*

When she thought of the word *aunty,* she imagined someone stout, round in the middle, in a sari with dyed black hair. Someone, in short, like her mother. Becoming an aunty, in the recesses of Naina's mind, was to become someone who was never admired but commanded the sort of sterilized respect that all mothers automatically received. An aunty was someone who dreamed of nothing but the joys of her children, someone who only spoke of pleasures in the past tense. Naina would have preferred to be called didi, as in older sister, commonly used to address younger women, because didis could still be young and fresh; didis could still have suitors; didis could still have richer futures than pasts—but she never suggested being called that, fearing such a request might be seen as too outlandish.

She had been surprised by how much controversy her request to be called Mrs. Mehta or Naina—something so simple—generated. Indians found it bizarre. This would confuse the children further, they said. How were they to explain to them that all Indian mothers were to be called *aunty* except for her? While Harish and others repeatedly tried to persuade her to let children call her aunty, Naina refused to give in, offering no explanation except that she just didn't want to be called *aunty* and that was all there was to it.

"But, Naina, this is how we address people in our culture," a neighbor had said during a dinner. "What is the big deal? Are you ashamed of our Indian ways or what? Maybe you'll want to be called Mrs. Met or something like that next. We are Indians, we should be proud of our culture . . . we have a great, ancient culture. We're not like those hamburger-eating types who have no respect and will call their dead grandmothers by their first names also."

"But I don't see how being called aunty is so Indian," Naina had countered. "The only reason we use it is because we learned the word from the British."

"Thank you *sooo* much, Maalaa aunty—" The sound of the boy's voice brought Naina back to the present.

The mustached man and the sallow-faced woman beamed.

"See, our children have respect," the mustached man said, nodding to Mala. "Not like in this country."

Amaya's boyfriend just better not call her aunty.

AMAYA AND JAI were waiting for Naina at Masala, an Indian restaurant filled with dramatic posters of Bollywood films from the seventies and the eighties. Initially, she didn't see them, but then she spotted Amaya at the back of the restaurant, laughing with a man. They were sitting in front of a freakish poster of Bollywood star Amitabh Bachchan dressed in a red robe with his hands up in chains. It was from the movie *Bandhe Haath* (Tied Hands), released in 1973, a year before she left for America. She remembered hating the film, one of only a few Hindi films she saw a year.

She gingerly walked toward them. How awkward was this going to be?

When she saw Jai, an unconventional-looking man with a wide face, splayed nose, and cheeks covered with scars—likely left by scratching pimples during his adolescent years—an inexplicable sensation shuddered through her. Jai was a grown, seasoned man. His years were etched in the marks on his face, in his deep-set chocolate-colored eyes framed by long eyelashes that hinted at more fire than his elegant demeanor and distinguished-looking wavy black hair flecked with gray suggested. He looked his age, forty-one, more than a decade older than Amaya—too old for her daughter, not to mention hardly a decade younger than she was.

Of course, she knew her daughter, sensible, mature, and a psychotherapist to boot, would be with a grown man. But Amaya, radiant in a form-fitting red sweater dress and dangling red-and-gold earrings—different from her standard outfits in dark shades of blue, gray, and brown—looked so much like a girl. An adult, a professional, but still a girl. The only other boyfriend Amaya had ever introduced her to, years earlier, had seemed so boyish in comparison that it did not seem obvious that he and Amaya were a couple. But with Jai, that fact stared right at Naina, making her want to turn away from the glare.

"Mom, this is—" Amaya said.

"Hi, Naina, it's a pleasure to meet you." A smiling Jai extended his hand toward hers lying listlessly at her side. "I'm Jai, as you probably know. And belated happy birthday. I heard you had a spectacular party."

Jai emitted an air of effortless confidence, as if few doubts assailed him. Naina slowly held out her hand and smiled feebly. She saw that his fingers were long and sculpted. He firmly shook her hand, the butteriness of his skin livening the fibers in her hand. She hadn't expected them to be so soft; he didn't seem like the kind of man who applied lotion on his hands.

"It's . . . very nice to meet you as well . . . Jai." Thankfully, he didn't call her aunty.

"I can see where Amaya gets her eyes from," Jai said, as Naina self-consciously took off her coat and sat down opposite Amaya. "Shapely like almonds."

Naina felt her cheeks turning red. She fixed her eyes on the closed menu.

"We do have similar eyes, but Mom's can turn greenish-gold in the sunlight," Amaya said. "I wish mine could."

"Ah, cat eyes."

"Oh, hardly," Naina said, keen to steer the conversation away from her. "Have you been to this restaurant before?"

She tentatively raised her head. Jai had several fine lines under his eyes, curved downward like cat's whiskers. They looked like signs of character. Amaya, on the other hand, had no such imperfections.

Jai said he had been to the restaurant and the food was very good, and then he initiated polite conversation—the kind that generally accompanies a first meeting between strangers. He spoke about the Bollywood posters adorning the restaurant, the weather, the recent news about an heiress leaving millions of dollars to her cat, and asked some courteous questions about her birthday celebration.

Naina did not say much, just answering questions and making pithy, unremarkable comments. But she was beginning to feel less uneasy. Jai was a seasoned conversationalist, clearly accustomed to smoothing away the lumps that stand in the way of initial conversations.

They ordered their drinks and surveyed the menu. Naina saw some dishes she had never eaten before. She noticed Amaya giving Jai a sweet smile and he responded by interlacing his fingers with hers. Those long, tapered fingers like the strings of a violin. Naina took her eyes off them and focused on her menu again.

"Naina, what would you like?" Jai asked in that assured tone of his, as if he had been everywhere and knew everything. He looked directly at her.

She could not meet his eyes. "I was looking at the Rajasthani safed maas, but it's got so much ghee, cashew paste, and . . ."

"C'mon, Mom." Amaya shook her head, her dangling earrings tinkling like wind chimes in the breeze. "Mom's obsessed with her weight since she moved to New York. And she really has no need to be, as you can see."

"Yes, I can see," Jai said. "You have nothing to worry about."

Naina could feel his eyes on her body and felt awkward and bashful.

"It looks delicious," Amaya said. "If you get it, I'll definitely help you out, and I'm sure Jai will as well. Won't you?"

"Absolutely."

"I think I'm going to get something else," Naina said, the thought of that rich gravy enlarging her body, a body she had worked hard to firm up, into a fat Thanksgiving turkey. "A chicken curry, maybe."

"Oh, c'mon, Naina. You seem like you really want the safed maas." Jai gave her a playful half-smile that enhanced his attractiveness, and his chocolate-colored eyes lit up, making them look like dark amber gemstones. His forearms were raised and his palms were stretched outward, toward her. "And you must know that the only way to get rid of temptation is to yield to it."

Naina laughed—a laugh not too loud but packed with zest, as if all the organs in her body, from head to toe, had been tickled.

"Well said." The tightly coiled springs inside her slackened and she moved her hands, tightly clasped under the table, to rest on her chair.

"So you're a fan of Oscar Wilde?" she asked, a bit more animated.

"Oh no, you mean I couldn't pass that quote off as my own," Jai said, in mock dismay. "You caught me."

Naina laughed again.

"I told you," Amaya said in an assured tone, which had become more pronounced after she started working as a psychotherapist. "My mom has read *everything*."

"What part of India was your mother from?" Naina asked, halfway through her safed maas that was as tasty and fattening as she had expected. She was on her second glass of wine.

"From Bombay. Or Mumbai as they like to say these days."

"Ah, Bombay," Naina said, smiling. "The city of modern women. Not like Delhi where I grew up."

"She was definitely ahead of her time," Jai said. "Very much so. She came alone in the sixties to the US to study."

"Alone in the sixties to America? That's very bold. How did her parents let her come?"

"I don't think anybody could have stopped my mother from anything," Jai said. "My mother was really something. I mean really. She's the spunkiest woman I've ever met."

"That's wonderful," Naina said, feeling a stirring inside her. "So she came here to study and then met your father?"

"Yes, at Tufts."

"That must have been quite a love story," Naina said, the stirring in her flitting around like fine copper sand in a desert breeze. She came close to meeting Jai's eyes, leaned a little more forward, and smiled. "I'd love to hear about it."

Jai gladly obliged. He said his father, Jacob, raised in a secular-leaning Jewish family in Brooklyn, was a man who loved challenges and anything unconventional. He was too much of a philistine and filled with internal barriers to take the leap to become a hippie, but he shared a great deal of their sensibility. He first saw Jai's mother, Meena, sitting on a lawn bench at Tufts, wearing black-and-white striped cigarette pants and a cream-colored blouse with ruffles. Her long, raven hair was simply tied in a ponytail at the base of her neck, unlike the bouffants, bobs, and beehives popular at the time. And she was smoking.

"How do you know all these details?" Naina asked, even more intrigued now.

"My father. He remembers everything . . . Even things we'd like him to forget."

They all laughed. Naina suddenly became self-conscious as she realized she had laughed louder than him.

Jai proceeded to describe how Jacob approached Meena, only to receive an indifferent response. But the man was infatuated and would not give up. He rearranged his schedule so he'd bump into her at the library, where she spent most of her time, the diner or the local pub, which she regularly visited—although she never drank alcohol.

"She never drank, but she smoked and went to pubs?" Naina asked, wanting to soak up all this fascinating information. Most Indian women of Jai's mother's generation would have never smoked in the 1960s. Only a small percentage smoked now. But Meena was clearly no ordinary woman.

"That was her only real vice, my father used to say when I was a kid. She didn't drink, eat fatty foods, or do drugs."

Jai paused as a faraway look came into his eyes. "She needed to smoke, I guess." His voice became softer and less guarded. "To let out all that fire inside her."

A warm knot of tenderness gathered at the center of her chest. All the blood and bones around her heart felt unsteady. She looked toward her near-empty plate, little globs of creamy gravy of the safed mas staring at her. She knew Meena had died of lung cancer more than ten years earlier, but it sounded as if the scars were still there, a faded scarlet, like a dull, inextinguishable flame. She didn't want to say anything more about his mother unless he decided to.

Amaya reached for his hand under the table. Naina looked away.

"Well, my mother kept resisting my father for the longest time because she didn't want to get married," Jai said. His eyes sparkled and the tone of his voice became vibrant once again.

"She wanted to be an archaeologist and discover treasures left by the ancient Egyptians. But my father was a very persistent man and did not give up. He brought flowers to her dorm, found her favorite Indian snacks at a store in Boston, and wrote her haiku love poems."

"Haiku love poems?" Naina asked, raising her eyebrows, the corners of her mouth twitching with amusement.

"It took a while, but my mother fell in love with my father with the same fierce intensity that she had initially displayed to resist him. She was like that . . . veering off to one extreme and then the other. At heart, she was a romantic. My father proposed to her with a sapphire engagement ring since he couldn't afford diamonds, at a concert at Tanglewood . . . that's a music venue in the Berkshires."

A flush of sensations slowly spread in Naina like watercolors across paper. A bashful red blushing, a weightless lavender floating away, a sunny yellow shining. What a romantic story. Her own had been so dull in comparison. She had never felt such fervor for Harish, and her husband had never actually proposed to her. She had told her parents she was willing to marry him and that had been conveyed to Harish's parents.

Jai's parents were engaged for a year before Meena was able to tell her father. As might be expected, he was furious at first, threatening to cut off the family's relationship with her if she went ahead with the engagement. But she did not back down. She said she would get married in America if she had to and if being cut off was the price to pay to marry the man she loved, she was willing to pay it.

"Wow . . . your dad must be a very special man for her to act so bold," Naina said.

"He is . . . sometimes. And sometimes not."

They all laughed. Naina was careful not to laugh too loudly this time.

"What a Bollywood story," Amaya said.

"It is, isn't it? But wait till you hear the rest. It gets even more Bollywood if that's possible."

What a wonderful storyteller Jai was. Listening to him, Naina could smell the apple-scented air of fall on a New England campus, imagine his mother in her cigarette pants and her long, black hair neatly tied back, sitting outdoors with her legs crossed, never allowing anyone to know how cold she really was. She'd be surrounded by a heap of radiant, dead leaves and smoking a slim cigarette. Meanwhile, his father, wearing a big-collared shirt and trousers with a modest flare at the bottom, would be staring at her with adoring eyes, trying to compose another haiku poem to impress her.

The story continued—a Bollywood movie scene indeed. Meena's father was taken aback by such a defiant act from his own daughter. He knew he could not refuse Meena outright, so he came up with another ploy. Jai's grandfather declared that Jacob would have to come to India for a month to prove he was worthy of marrying his daughter, certain that an American man would not be able to endure India for that long. But he hadn't accounted for a key facet of Jai's father's personality: Jacob thrived on challenges.

Jacob borrowed money from his own father for the airfare and stayed in Bombay in a little two-star hotel called Shiva Room and Board with no regular running water.

Meena's father was surprised by how much he actually liked his daughter's fiancé. Soon, the two of them were smoking cigars on the balcony of the family's apartment in Bombay and talking about Churchill, Truman, and Nehru. Both were addicted to the Second World War. Three weeks after Jacob stepped foot in India, Meena's father acquiesced to the marriage and gave Meena and Jacob a grand wedding—at the Taj Mahal Hotel no less.

Jai stopped and drank some water. Naina continued to look at him. When she realized that the story was over, she reached for her water glass, feeling a tinge of disappointment. She was no longer swept up by an exciting story and absorbed by the distinct rhythm of Jai's narrative voice, curving up and down, up and down.

She was back in a restaurant with her daughter's boyfriend, not knowing why she was feeling so unusual and had no words to describe that feeling. She noticed Amaya and Jai holding hands under the table and turned toward a Bollywood poster with the famous actress Rekha wearing sindoor, the vermilion powder traditionally worn in the parting of a Hindu woman's hair after marriage. It was so prominent, a thick red line extending from the top of her forehead to the crown of her head. It looked like a river of blood. Harish had put sindoor on her on their wedding day and she had worn it for some festivals and weddings later on, but she never liked it and neither Harish nor his family had cared. Occasionally, it did look nice though, when she was wearing a red sari and a bindi on her forehead. But now, even on the rare occasion when she wanted to, she would not wear it since Hindu widows did not wear sindoor.

The dessert was served, and Naina noticed Jai's hands again as he picked up his fork and knife. Such graceful fingers—the longest she had ever seen on a man—deftly cutting the apple pie into three slices.

Jai's eyes were on her. She sat up straight.

"Naina, what about you?" he asked. "Did you have an arranged marriage?"

"I did." Naina was not keen to talk about herself. It was so much better to be engulfed by the flow of his words. "I wasn't courageous like your mother."

"That doesn't sound right. Amaya told me you moved to New York on your own after your husband passed on, you live on your own now in Manhattan, a place, as we all know is one of the easiest places on earth to live in." Jai gave her a teasing smile. "Just kidding, obviously . . . and I believe you found a job in the art world, which I imagine is anything but easy."

Naina moved her finger up and down her right earring. "That's nice of you to say, but it's nothing much . . . I've done . . . whatever little I've done . . . at a much later age. It takes a lot of guts to do what your mother did when she was so young."

"Hmm . . . I don't know if I agree." Jai sounded so confident even when he was expressing doubt, his words and tone so contained, nothing ever spilling out. It must be a useful quality to have. "I think it's easier to do bold things when you're young. Because young people are so filled with fire and think they are invincible. But as people get older, they get set in their ways, and are much less willing to take risks."

"I suppose you have a point."

"Of course he does," Amaya said, patting his forearm. "He always has good points."

AFTER DINNER, NAINA walked to the subway, looking back a couple of times to see Amaya and Jai walking hand in hand in the direction of what she guessed was Jai's apartment. For the first time since Amaya left home for college, she felt as if her daughter were flying away. Naturally, they must have a sex life. She was a bit unnerved at the idea. Probably a much better one than she ever had. The image of Jai's distinct, slightly asymmetrical face flickered in her mind. She felt the stirring within her again. Copper sand flying in the desert air.

Suddenly flustered, she tried to chase the unnamed sensation away, shunning looking into it any further.

About twenty minutes later, Naina was in the subway where she spotted a poster for www.mysoulmate.com, featuring a gray-haired, wrinkle-covered woman in a pink, tea-length wedding gown holding hands with a portly, grandfatherly man in a tuxedo. She smiled. They looked so adorable. She remembered something Jai had said about getting lost while driving in Italy when he was there for his father's friend's wedding. After dating a woman for more than fifteen years, Uncle David took the plunge at seventy-one and had a lavish spread at a vineyard in Tuscany.

Only in this country would people in their seventies think of romance and getting married. Her mind drifted to India where she imagined the wedding announcement of two seniors being first met by horrified disbelief followed by self-righteous sneers. She thought of her grandmother's words to her before she got married and how sensible they had sounded at the time.

"There is a time for everything in life, beti," the sprightly seventy-five-year-old had counseled in Hindi, wearing a white sari, which indicated her widowed status. "When you were very young, it was your time to run around and have fun in a carefree manner. As you became older, you had to study more and become a little more responsible. Then, as you became a girl in the prime of her youth, you started to enjoy the pleasures of youth such as your beauty, watching films with your girlfriends, and attention from men, which I know you ignored. But now, you are about to enter the most important stage of life—married life. All carelessness must go now, and you must take care of your husband and your home. Then you will become a mother and have more responsibility that will occupy most of your life. But that is also another phase. Your children will become older and not need you so much anymore and your life will change again. With age, you will become sober. And then, before you know it, you will become an old grandmother like me. But live life according to your age and the stage of life you are in. In our religion, do you know what the stages of life are? You start off as a student, then become a householder, and when you fulfill all those duties and become old, you withdraw from worldly things and concentrate on God."

What a neat trajectory of life Hinduism had outlined, Naina thought as she gazed at the web of lines in the man's face in the online dating site's advertisement. Her own life, too, had been following a straight course until recently when it swerved onto a winding, shaky path, careening from left to right. Her grandmother was wrong. Everyone did not become sober with age. Everyone did not become more knowledgeable. And everyone certainly did not withdraw from worldly things. Maybe earthly pleasures became even more enticing when you realized you had less time to enjoy them. Jai, too, was certainly wrong about one thing. Older people were not necessarily rigid and less eager to take chances. No, not at all.

CHAPTER THREE

A COUPLE OF weeks after meeting Jai, Naina woke up early on a Monday morning with a blithe feeling, as the late spring sun flooded into her bedroom from the big windows, illuminating her plain white sheets with dancing shapes. Ever since she was a child, she had relished the intensity of the sun—much to the chagrin of her mother who feared Naina's skin might become too dark—and she would often play alone in the severe heat of a New Delhi summer afternoon because no one else wanted to be outside.

That spring, the sun had been particularly parsimonious to New Yorkers, and only on this last Monday in April did it appear for the first time in full incandescent splendor, as if trying to make up for previous lapses. Naina sprawled diagonally on the bed and soaked up the sun, her mind entering a delightful state between sleep and wakefulness. There was an air of languor that induced the sort of dreaminess she had regularly indulged in since she was a little girl. Alas, now, because of her job at an art gallery, a regular stream of social and cultural events, and the requirement to read as much as she could about art, there had been less room for reverie. Still, Monday was her day off and she could afford to linger in bed a bit longer. Today, after weeks of running around, she had nothing on her agenda.

Her thoughts drifted to the cleft-lipped Turkish immigrant to South America, Riad Halabi, who owned a store called The Pearl of the Orient in Isabel Allende's book *Eva Luna*. Over dinner, Jai had mentioned the book was good, and afterward, she rushed to buy it. She was surprised when Jai had told her about Turks going to South America, but then, she had never been to South America herself. Or to Africa or Australia or the Middle East—except for a two-day stopover in Dubai. In Europe, she had only been to London and Amsterdam. But she had been to the Caribbean with the family plenty of times, to islands with glittering waters and soft sands so alike she could hardly tell them apart.

She imagined Riad Halabi with a handkerchief, always covering his face to hide his deformity, learning Spanish and peddling wares in South America. And then returning to Turkey, brimming with hope and marrying that slothful, vulgarly sensual Zulema. That Zulema who, despite all her husband's compassion, ended up betraying him by going to bed with his nephew.

Once again, Naina was in familiar skies, suspended somewhere between the sun and the clouds, floating just like she would do on a reed mat at the back of her house in Delhi or while staring at the garden in Jersey. In Delhi, there had never been any music when she dreamed, but during her fanciful flights in Jersey, there was always music. It loosened her thoughts, made them flow like slow-moving streams, and unlocked vivid images from her brain.

With a good deal of effort, she sat up, did a long stretch with her arms, and got out of bed. She was still a bit tired. Oh, the body. The merciless body. Keeping track of *every* year and *every* intemperance. Doling out punishments accordingly, like one of those super strict teachers at St. Therese's Convent School in New Delhi.

Couldn't she ever just forget about her bloody age?

NAINA SWITCHED ON a CD of an experimental rock band called Explosive Beast she had recently bought, a group her tabla player friend Rob had seen perform on the Lower East Side. It was part of her effort to get up to date. Before, she only listened to music by the likes of Beethoven, Asha Bhosle, Simon and Garfunkel, or the Beatles, read books by writers like Charlotte Brontë, D.H. Lawrence, and Anaïs Nin, and knew little about art made after the 1920s. But now, living in New York and being involved in the contemporary art world, she soon learned that some of her tastes were old-fashioned, even sentimental, and that deeply distressed her. Her friend Alannah had called her "quaint" and "charming" a couple of times and although she knew her friend meant the words affectionately, she did not see them as compliments. Even reading *Eva Luna* seemed to broadcast that she lived in the past when she so desperately craved to belong to the present.

Gala, the intern at the gallery, had seen the novel lying on her desk and exclaimed, "Oh my God, you're reading that. I went through an Allende phase when I was a freshman years ago and so did my aunt." Gala had said those words lightly, talking about the book as if it were some sort of fad, like wearing bell-bottoms in the seventies. Naina immediately hid the book in her bag, but Gala's words had spun more fluttering cobwebs of doubts inside of her.

But if Jai had spoken highly of it—the dashing, far-from-old Professor Jai Silverstein of Columbia University—it couldn't be that dated, could it? The notion instantly assuaged her concern.

Explosive Beast, however, did not create the kind of music that made her thoughts flow like slow-moving streams. Instead, their discordant rhythms of guitar chords and drumbeats fused with twitchy techno ripped her thoughts into jagged bits and jerkily tossed them around until her mind felt like a sea gone mad. She had tried so hard to like it, sometimes playing it on tired nights even though it gave her a headache. Only now could she somewhat appreciate its haunting, psychedelic quality. But just for an ephemeral gasp of time.

After ten or fifteen minutes, she changed the CD to classical Spanish guitar by Andrés Segovia. This, she could appreciate wholeheartedly. It was mellifluous and soothing as one note gave way to another like a string of water droplets continuously flowing into a river. Again, her thoughts ambled along smoothly.

She made herself a cup of peppermint mint tea and ate one of the newfangled protein bars for women, filled with dates, nuts, and other things she hadn't had before—like spirulina and chia seeds. The fog of exhaustion was clearing. Age wasn't everything. The body may not be charitable, but it was still somewhat malleable. Even in her early fifties, she still had a good amount of energy, which had only increased ever since she started to work out.

She left half of the bar. It tasted like hard, synthetic grass on her tongue. As she reclined on the living room couch, she saw the sun pouring in through the window like a mimosa-laced elixir, despite the medium-sized red brick apartment building opposite her. This normal New York City view of an apartment complex with its multiple windows often offered glimpses of its inhabitants: an unknown man dancing alone at night, a woman teaching a child to cook. Such a lack of privacy, however, was something Naina still wasn't quite accustomed to yet. But she could always create a view she liked with her mind's eye.

Over the years, Naina had conjured up all sorts of things. She had envisioned a love affair between a Native American woman and a married early settler, and what America might have looked like had the country been settled by the Italians instead of the British and the Dutch. She had imagined what it must have felt like to go around the world undetected like those women covered from head to toe in Saudi Arabia, and what her life would have been like if she had become a hippie whipping up a frenzy in Haight Ashbury.

At other times, especially during dreary winter days, her reveries became more sensual, made more acute by the distance of their realization. She fantasized about the sun caressing her body like a flickering, formless tongue; about rain-drenched mud beneath her feet; about the sweet smell of the frangipani flower she remembered sniffing in summer evenings when she was a girl.

Never, in all those years, had she shared her fantasies with anyone. Not with her mother, who was always consumed with the servants and being the neighborhood busybody; nor with her father, who despite being more of a romantic like herself, was often lost in sentimental Hindi songs or Urdu ghazals; nor with her brother, six years younger than she was, perpetually playing cricket if he wasn't eating, sleeping, or in school. By the time Harish entered her life, her imaginings had become such a private pleasure woven into her mental fabric that it did not even occur to her to share them with him. And in her gut, she knew her husband, though he was a man with a tender face and a gentle disposition, was just like her mother and brother. With their eyes fixed on measurable, palpable goals, they'd have no interest in hearing about some chiffony universe whose link to the real world they couldn't perceive. They would see musings like hers as vain, inane, and if taken to the extreme, insane. A person's mental faculties, as far as they were concerned, were tools to slice the tangible world into manageable, easily discernible chunks.

Amaya was the only one in her family who somewhat understood her. While her daughter could delve into the world of the subconscious, imaginings for her were merely a means to understand the real. Was Jai like that too? Naina didn't think so. Something in his eyes, the light that emitted from those amber irises, told her he could transcend the world of corporeal sensory experiences; that he could delight in the diaphanous beauty of the forest of dreams. She smiled to herself, dangling her feet off the sofa, so she could get more sun on her legs.

A short while later, the sun was overshadowed by a veil of clouds. Naina was annoyed. It had been bright for less than two hours. *The Sun is God*, the nineteenth-century English painter Turner had supposedly said. She craned her neck upward so she could watch the sun, straining itself behind the clouds, from the window. Where had she read that Turner quote? In a romance novel years ago. She recalled how she used to read Mills & Boons in secret as a teenager so her mother wouldn't find out, and when she first came to America, she had been so disappointed to discover that there were no Mills & Boons here. They were only sold in England and in the British colonies, she had been told. So she had to settle on Harlequin Romances which never seemed to be the same without those elegant London settings and refined British English.

Segovia finished playing the guitar and she got up and put on another CD, this time of West African drum music to rouse her from her languorous state. The fast-moving beats seemed to express the amorphous urgency spinning inside her these days. She was not young and not going to live forever.

Her thoughts drifted to how, in her mid-thirties, her fantasy world became larger and more erotic. She'd picture herself as Martha Graham doing some sort of provocative dance, as an alluring pre-Raphaelite damsel with wild tresses posing for a painting, as a Mughal-era courtesan trying exotic positions from the Kama Sutra—which she had embarrassedly bought and stored at the bottom of her underwear drawer. Although she had enjoyed reading about archetypal romantic heroines like Madame Bovary or Lady Chatterley, she had never seen herself as one of them. She had felt some affinity with the characters and sympathy for them, but that was all. Unlike those heroines, she was neither miserable nor desperate, nor had she ever conceived of doing something dramatic or drastic, except in her sojourns to a dream world.

Still, there had been times—quite a few in fact—when she had yearned for a more exciting and glamorous life. But she never could figure out how that could happen without disrupting the familiar rhythms of her daily existence, so vital that they were almost like a second heartbeat, ticking away yet barely heard.

Naina looked around at her apartment, which she had decorated in a minimalist, Zen-inspired style. Normally, it seemed invitingly serene compared with her colorful, elaborate home in New Jersey. But at that moment, the white walls, the tall rice paper lamp, the small shoji screen, and the Chinese scroll painting, felt foreign and pretentious. As she hugged two pillows covered with a delicate bonsai-tree pattern, she shut her eyes, suddenly longing for her roomy suburban home and its red-walled study, which she had done up with Mughal-style miniature paintings, and for her faintly scented plum-colored irises in her large garden. She could never forget that smell—ephemeral, fragile, and sweet. Like a baby. And, sometimes, like a funeral. She loved irises with their long, proud stems and their petals extending outward, curving like the graceful, open hand of a dancer.

Both she and Harish had loved gardens. Harish had been an excellent gardener, which was rare among the Indian men she knew. He knew how to make the best compost by using the right amount of coffee grounds, coffee filters, vegetable and fruit scraps, and dried leaves. It was the coffee grounds that made the compost so good, he would say, as he sipped a cup of coffee. Even good soil needs caffeine to wake up, he would jest.

Harish had generally let Naina decide which flowers to plant. She would drive to a nursery along the Jersey Shore to pick up the seeds—something she looked forward to every year—which she and Harish would then plant together. For almost three decades, they planted crab apples, marsh marigolds, roses, Eastern red columbines, geraniums, tulips, and, on Naina's insistence, jasmine. Harish had told her jasmine would never grow well in New Jersey; Naina, however, refused to listen. She kept watering the plants in the hopes that they would miraculously blossom—but Harish turned out to be right.

It had been so long since she had been in a garden. Too long. Now, the only flowers she saw regularly were the ones at her corner deli. The previous day, she had seen beautiful buttercup-colored tulips hiding under large clusters of roses and chrysanthemums. Tulips had been Harish's favorite flowers and he always paid extra attention to them.

She lay down again and closed her eyes. She saw Harish, in a plaid shirt, casual pants, and a cricket cap, carefully trimming the stems of tulips with his garden shears as he softly hummed. She could never figure out what he was humming, but she thought she could hear strains of ABBA, Boney M, Bee Gees, and Bollywood songs from the sixties. She wished the image in her head were real and she could walk across the garden, watch the sun's rays falling on those tulips and listen to that familiar hum again.

SLAM! It took Naina a second to realize what the noise was. Every weekday morning, usually between eight-thirty and eight-forty, Laura, her neighbor who lived opposite her, would bang her door shut as she was going to work. Strange, the intimacies between strangers in New York City. She knew that the man in the adjacent apartment liked to vacuum after midnight, that the woman who lived above her liked to walk around her apartment in heels, and that the man in the apartment next to the elevator listened to a lot of Rolling Stones. She also knew that Laura's kitchen was always a mess because her exasperated housekeeper had whispered it to Naina in the laundry room. The divulgence hadn't surprised Naina though—Laura, with her untidy hair and food-stained shorts, looked like the kind of girl who wouldn't clean her kitchen. Or be a good neighbor, for that matter.

During her first week in the apartment, Naina had decided to introduce herself to just a few people on her floor because Amaya had told her that New Yorkers didn't believe in being too neighborly. So, she chose the four apartments closest to her own to pay a visit; she got boxes of chocolate chip cookies to give out. It was good to be acquainted with one's neighbors—especially if one lived alone. What if something happened? And as one grew older, that something suddenly seemed not so far-fetched.

Her first stop was Laura's. It was about noon on a Saturday, and she gently tapped on her door. When she heard no response, she knocked louder.

Finally, Laura opened her door with a jerk. "What's the matter?"

Naina had been surprised by the hostility in her neighbor's voice, but she forged ahead, introducing herself as quickly as possible while feeling foolish the whole time. She gave her the box of cookies to which Laura responded, "Gee, thanks" and closed the door. Naina had run back to her apartment. Was this what she had to look forward to in New York?

After calming her nerves, she approached the next two neighbors who were polite but disinterested. However, the fourth door she knocked on was answered by a German businesswoman called Karin who was subletting the apartment; she invited Naina in and talked to her for almost an hour, asking a flurry of questions about where to travel in India and giving her cups of green tea. But Karin went back to Berlin and now, if Naina wanted to share a pot of peppermint tea or borrow a cup of sugar, she had no neighbor to turn to.

"Don't you know a damn thing about how companies are run?" That had to be Laura barking on her phone. It must have been almost eleven o' clock. This was late for her. Thank goodness, Laura wasn't home much. She was one belligerent woman and the sound of her booming voice ricocheting through the hallway caused the walls to tremble.

Silence resumed. The sun had become stronger, lighting every burgeoning leaf on the branches of the tall tree in front of her building, until the tree virtually glowed.

Naina noticed the only object on her coffee table was *Eva Luna* and it gladdened her. There was very little in the apartment that did not belong to her.

To Naina's surprise, she had discovered living alone wasn't the terrifying thing she had always imagined it to be. In fact, on the whole, she rather liked it. When Amaya had pleaded with her to move to New York to revitalize herself after Harish's death, she had suggested they take a bigger apartment and live together. But Naina had refused. When she finally decided to move, she knew it would only work if she lived alone. Still, there were days, like today, when she would have liked to see Amaya spreading peanut butter on her toast, hear Harish making Turkish coffee, or step out of her door and talk to a friendly neighbor.

After moving to New York, Naina had longed to strip away the cotton balls of dreams with which she had insulated herself for so long and embrace the world. And she had, she thought, feeling a tinge of pride. And though it had been exciting, she also knew it had sometimes speared her and made her shrink from the inside. It was, as she told herself, the big city reminding you of your smallness, the closeness to the world giving you no choice but to accurately assess the proportions of things.

HALF-AN-HOUR LATER, Naina felt a stab of hunger and she craved a doughnut. A soft, round doughnut covered with chocolate glaze and topped with powdered sugar. Yummy and so bad for you. No one she had met so far in New York loved doughnuts as much as she did, and the only person she knew who loved doughnuts even more had been Harish, the taste of melancholy becoming bittersweet in her mouth. During the early days of their marriage, he would bring home a big box of doughnuts and the two of them would sit in front of the television watching *Family Ties* or *The Cosby Show* and greedily eat them up. But, as the years went by, Naina realized she couldn't consume scores of doughnuts without turning into a doughnut herself (Harish, on the other hand, had a metabolism that most people would kill for), and began to limit herself. Now, in New York, with the doughnut man just two blocks away, the temptation was much harder to resist. Still, she told herself, she had been relatively good, eating no more than five or six doughnuts a month since she had moved. Plus, the rest of her diet was generally healthy—though she had been drinking more wine than she should.

The image of the doughnut kept calling her until she no longer had the strength to resist. The line in front of the doughnut man—an Eastern European who understood no English except the words coffee, milk, sugar, doughnut, and numbers up to twenty—was unusually short; there were only two people ahead of her, a chatty old lady who was trying to talk to the doughnut man despite him nodding and saying "no Ingles" and a young, curly-haired boy with a short, wide bag from which spilled out books with accounting titles and a black book titled *Goya: Wrestling with Darkness*. The boy was wearing khaki pants and a blue-and-white striped shirt fluffed at the waist, the same kind of preppy look that her son Karan had. But, Karan, an investment banker with a major Wall Street firm in Chicago, would not, under any circumstances, read an art book, she thought regretfully. What was this boy doing with the Goya? Did he look at it after he was done with his accounting books? Or before? Or was it a gift for someone else? Maybe for his mother or his girlfriend?

Goya held a special place in Naina's heart because it was thanks to him that she got interested in art.

Strolling around her neighborhood, eating her doughnut, she remembered the very first time she saw reproductions of the painter's work. *Treasures Forever* was a moth-eaten, creaky bookstore that time forgot on the border of New Jersey and Pennsylvania, and years earlier, she was browsing there when she spotted a coffee table book lying on the floor. The cover had a picture of Goya's painting of the Roman God Saturn eating his own son. At first, she had been a bit unnerved by the devilish face, the frighteningly bulging eyes, the long, cannibalistic tongue, and the partially eaten body of a child. Still, she was curious and picked up the book, quickly wiped off the thick layer of dust with the handkerchief she always kept in her purse, and stared at that image, and then at all the other pictures in the book. She ended up buying the book and left it on the table in her living room in Montcrest. When Amaya opened it, she screamed—something she hardly ever did.

Naina bought other coffee table books on artists like Michelangelo, Raphael, Fragonard, and Rossetti, building up a solid collection of Old Masters over the years. But they were always stored on the top shelf of the tall China cabinet, away from the reach of the children and not in the face of visitors. When she looked at her art books, she sometimes played opera music—something she rarely listened to otherwise—and got swept up by the sumptuous grandeur and high drama of the paintings. It was only later, after her children had gone off to college, that she discovered Edvard Munch, thanks to a program on PBS, and became interested in early twentieth-century painting. She then decided to take some courses on nineteenth century and early twentieth century art at Rutgers University.

Taking the last bite of the doughnut, Naina paused to look at some Chiantis in the window display of one of her neighborhood liquor stores.

She could never forget the comments that a couple of their Indian friends had made when they discovered she was taking courses at Rutgers. One of their sons, an undergraduate at the university, had spotted her on her way to class and couldn't stop staring. Naina pretended not to notice him and scurried away.

"What is this, Naina?" the boy's mother, Mrs. Desai, had said. "Going to college same time as your children? It's an interesting way to fight the loneliness that comes when the children leave the home, isn't it?"

And, Kanchan Nath, known for her collection of gaudy gold jewelry, chimed in, "Naina, you really are too much. Your head will explode if you go around learning so much. I would get a bad headache if I had to go to college at this age."

She had wanted to lash out at them and tell them that maybe a few headaches would do them some good, but the truth was she said nothing, smiling as if she just shrugged off their words.

As she waited for the signal to change from "Don't Walk" to "Walk" on 31st Street and Second Avenue, she overheard two women next to her talking about some show at the Museum of Modern Art.

"I can't believe they would have something so crappy up," one woman said in a high and agitated voice. "I mean it's the bloody MoMA, for God's sake. Jesus Christ, everything is just becoming one giant corporation these days."

"It wasn't always like that, Susie," the other woman said, her voice mellifluous despite her obvious displeasure. "MoMA used to be fabulous. The best of the best. Do you know how long I've been going there? Forty years. Forty years. This awful stuff is what's fashionable these days. This is what they call *contemporary art*. This is what they show at all those biennials all over the place. What's the poor MoMA to do?"

Once the light changed and the three of them crossed the street, the two women turned left, heading downtown, while Naina continued west. Regret needled her as she thought of all the years she had missed in New York. Those two women had been there for all of it, while she, living just outside the city, had not. They must have known Soho and Greenwich Village when it was inhabited by artists and writers instead of yuppies; they may have seen Picasso's *Guernica* at the MoMA just before Tony Shafrazi defaced it in the seventies. They had probably experienced, firsthand, the hothouse atmosphere of New York in the eighties. Why hadn't she come to New York more often? Before she moved here, she used to come to the city no more than six or seven times a year, many of those times by herself since neither Harish nor most of the people she knew liked to come into the city much.

She scolded herself for having been too intimidated by New York City traffic to drive in more regularly, remembering those precious days when she would come in on a Sunday to go to the Met or the Guggenheim, leaving the kids with Harish; she'd drive so slowly that the people behind her would honk at her repeatedly, daunting her further.

Someone like Jai's mother would probably have never been intimidated, the bold lines and bright colors of Meena's image filling up in her head.

"Hello, this is Jai speaking." Naina heard a distinctly South Indian voice utter these words, and she turned in its direction. Of course, she could tell it was not Amaya's boyfriend, but her arms became dappled with goose bumps. She remembered Jai's voice so clearly; it was so tactile, like an entity that existed on its own. It was a shape-shifter, it could unfurl like a rug, compress like a tight fist, rotate like a wheel. She marveled at Amaya's good fortune.

On the corner of 33rd Street and Fifth Avenue, she stood in front of a store selling Peruvian textiles, admiring the dynamic geometric patterns of an orange-

and-blue blanket. She wondered if Jai had been to Peru, a country that intrigued her. His work focused on Middle Eastern immigrants in South America and though she didn't know whether there were any Middle Easterners in Peru, he might have been to the Andean country.

Naina's mood now lifted—the bittersweet melancholy of an Edith Piaf song was morphing into the heartwarming haze of a Julio Iglesias ballad. She imagined Jai in the Inca ruins of Machu Picchu, a small yet unmistakable figure climbing the steep steps alone, awed by the towering majesty of the stone structures around him. She pictured him wearing a shawl, orange and blue with a geometric design, just like the blanket she had seen, the garment adding a sumptuousness to his otherwise tall, lean figure. She had seen several programs on the Incan citadel on the Discovery Channel, and now she could easily envision him going into the Sun Temple and bowing down, his palms and fingers touching the giant slab of rock in the center.

Naina walked away from the Peruvian textile store, far from the quizzical stares of the people inside as she remembered Jai's palms, small, compact, and downy with faint lines. Unlike his face, which was marked by scars, blemishes, and other signs of a life lived, his palms were like a baby's. Barely visible lines suggesting a destiny yet to be written. She could feel the fibers inside her body waking up and moving. Scurrying to the left. Scurrying to the right. Climbing up. Climbing down.

Naina tensed her body to halt this flurry of motion, but soon relaxed it, allowing herself to enjoy these glimmers of pleasure capering around in her.

About twenty minutes later Naina sat on a bench in Madison Square Park. It would be nice to see Jai again. She should ask Amaya if he might be interested in joining them at a concert at St. Patrick's Cathedral. Alannah had given her five tickets for the concert that she had received from a religious uncle of hers—good seats, her friend had said. Of course, it was on Monday, short notice, and Jai must be such a busy man. And wasn't it strange for a mother to be inviting her daughter's boyfriend to something?

No, it was probably all right, she concluded a little while later. As a modern mother, she should get to know her daughter's boyfriend well. He was clearly no passing fancy. And it wasn't like she was some old lady he was being forced to spend time with. He was only about ten or twelve years younger than she was. A speck in time. And it wasn't as if she were going to brazenly ask him herself. Amaya would invite him and only if she thought it was appropriate.

CHAPTER FOUR

GRAND CENTRAL, AS was usual for almost six o' clock on a weekday evening, was packed—even the cavernous space seemed too small to accommodate the hordes of people bustling about. Barely paying any attention to the magnificent structure with its star-studded domed ceiling and gigantic arch windows as she normally did, Naina walked slowly and watchfully through the crowds, afraid she might get knocked over by some man in a suit rushing to get to a meeting, by some frazzled secretary whose Metro-North train had been delayed, by some sleep-deprived worker craving a doughnut before getting on a train to go home.

She clutched an envelope of printing proofs for an upcoming show's catalog handed to her by Alexandra, a graphic designer the gallery often worked with, during their brief, last-minute meeting at the Grand Central Concourse before Alexandra raced off to catch a train to the Hudson Valley. The New York air was dense with the ambition and determination of the millions who commuted here for work. There wasn't a moment to be wasted. Not an opportunity to be lost. That was what she heard in the restless footsteps of the people scurrying about the train station. What a different world it was from Montcrest where more than half of the Indian women had never worked outside the home and almost none had ever made any mark that deviated from the rules. Even their handwriting was neat and decorous. There were no Ls written with loopy loops, no Bs written with bursting bulges, no Os written like oversized oranges. The air in Montcrest too seemed lighter, barely capable of making a dent.

Finally, Naina found a quiet spot near a Starbucks and took off her heels for a few minutes. What a relief. She normally wore heels to work, low Salvatore Ferragamo wedges adding no more than a couple of inches to her five-foot-two-inch frame. But today she was wearing pencil heels because she was going to the concert at St. Patrick's Cathedral. Jai was coming. She smiled. She never thought he would agree to come, yet she had not given her extra ticket away. He had been unsure until Amaya called her this morning and said he would be there. Naina had immediately changed her heels because she expected to go straight to the concert from the gallery. But she had not anticipated a trip to Grand Central to pick up proofs with her feet perched on those blade-thin, mini skyscraper-like shoes for almost thirty minutes on the platform due to an abrupt halt in service of the subway lines she needed.

She just had to sit down for another ten minutes at the coffee shop to give her throbbing feet a little more rest.

STANDING OUTSIDE THE largest Catholic cathedral in North America, Amaya looked her usual psychotherapist self in a tailored black skirt and a white blouse, but Jai looked even older and more distinguished than the last time Naina had seen him. The gray flecks in his hair shone prominently against the black and he was wearing a brown tweed double-breasted blazer. He looked oh-so professorial. He was so tall, well over six feet, towering over both of them like a cathedral unto himself. Her baby, probably about five-feet-seven inches tall with her short heels, looked like such a baby compared with him. She was glad she was wearing her high heels despite the fact that she was still several inches shorter than him.

"Naina, so nice to see you again," Jai said in that same assured tone of his.

She could not meet his eyes. She felt a flutter of excitement in her.

"How have you been?"

"Fine, fine." Naina fiddled with the spider-shaped pendant around her neck.

"That's an interesting pendant. Where did you get it?"

It was a big spider-shaped silver pendant, hardly suitable for someone her age and hardly the right accessory for her elegant Eileen Fisher short, shaped jacket and lightly flared skirt. She didn't want to tell him she couldn't resist buying it off the street from a purple-haired woman who had explained Wicca to her in great detail. She had worn it today because the gallery was officially closed on Monday notwithstanding she was still working on upcoming projects in the space with Susan, her boss. While she couldn't bring herself to wear jeans and a sweater to work like Susan, the spider pendant was her way of adding some free-and-easy flourish to her attire. But somehow, standing next to Jai and Amaya looking so formal and professional, she wondered if the pendant looked silly on her.

"Oh, just the street," Naina said, almost stammering.

"It looks very striking on you," Jai said, his eyes still warm on her neck and bosom. "It suits you." Then he held Amaya's hand. "Don't you think so, sweetheart?"

As soon as they entered the cathedral, Naina quickly handed the programs to Amaya and Jai. As he opened the program, she again took in the beauty of his hands, which she could look at more discreetly than his face. Not a touch of hair on the back of them. His little finger was unusually long, just slightly shorter than his ring finger. Now, sitting so close, she could smell him. He smelled like the mountains. Like Shimla, the Himalayan hill station where her family used to sometimes go on vacation in the summer. Of fallen pine cones that she used to pick from the ground. Of deodar trees with their strong woodsy odor. Of the morning mist veiling the Himalayas. Her skin tingled.

The concert started. She had never seen the interior of the neo-Gothic cathedral before and it was grander than she had imagined. The music bounced around the grand archways, wrapped itself around the pillars, leaped up to those enormous ceilings, and departed the interior of the house of worship to touch those soaring spires outside.

Delight welled up inside her. She noticed that Amaya was concentrating on the music, but the fabric of her soul did not seem to waver with it. As for Jai, she felt so sure the music was rousing something inside him. Something flapping like a bird's wings. Swaying like a garment left out to dry in the wind. Whispering like a mountain leaf talking to the moon.

Amaya interlaced her fingers with Jai's. Again, Naina looked away. Jai unlaced his fingers and tapped four fingers of his right hand on his thigh in fast, repetitive motions, as if he were restlessly playing the piano. Then he turned toward Naina, met her eyes, and smiled. A honeyed gush spread in her, and she could almost feel its warmth and taste its sweetness.

After the concert, they went out for dinner to a French bistro where Jai talked a great deal about France in that lively voice of a storyteller that took Naina out of time and place and transported her to realms of dizzying enchantment. The winding rhythms of his words absorbed her so completely, the waiter had to ask her twice what she wanted to order before she realized he was talking to her.

"Look at Mom." Amaya laughed. "She's totally into your stories. She has the same faraway look on her face when she's reading a novel."

Jai had spent his junior year of college in Paris, living in the red-light district of Pigalle with a middle-aged man called Monsieur Renaud. He was supposed to live with another Amherst student in the Latin Quarter, but that did not happen because of some labyrinthine confusion. Monsieur Renaud was single and generally lived an austere life, reading and rereading books on French philosophy and hieroglyphs at a desk in his dimly lit bedroom. Still his host conjured up fabulous meals: rich pork stews, coq au vins, creamy garlic soups, beef bourguignons, and duck confits. It was one of the best years of Jai's life, a time when he learned the value of aesthetics for the sake of aesthetics, and pleasure for the sake of pleasure.

Jai, sitting opposite Naina, said "pleasure for the sake of pleasure" with emphasis, the words sounding lush and plush in the curving cadences of his voice. He raised his eyebrows and gave Naina a half-smile as Amaya bent down to pick up her napkin, which she had dropped. Once more, Naina could feel her skin dotted with goose bumps.

Jai said he often went for walks in the pre-revolutionary quarter of the Marais, drank too much coffee in the cafes of Montmarte, even felt a stir of religious feeling inside the Notre-Dame, and got to attend a lecture by Jacques Derrida at the Sorbonne. One time, he got locked up overnight in the Victor Hugo Museum and spent the night on the floor of the elaborate Chinese room.

"That sounds so exciting." Naina laughed, relieving some of the tension stuck in her muscles.

"So enough about me," Jai said, as they finished their main courses. "I'm curious to know more about your gallery, Naina. What kind of gallery is it? What exactly do you do there?"

"Well I, well I . . ." Naina shot a conspiratorial glance at Amaya and then tried to figure out the best way, as she sometimes did, to be vague about her role there. The truth was she was a gallery assistant at Red Circle Gallery, a recently opened nonprofit space that showed new and burgeoning female artists—the kind of job typically done by attractive, educated twenty-somethings. Her work mostly involved unglamorous tasks like sitting at the front desk, answering the phone, filing artist submissions, and mailing out invitations to shows.

"I work with . . .well, the executive director," Naina said, in between sips of wine. "The executive director of the gallery, I mean. My role is really non-specific you know . . . you have to do everything when you're in a small organization.

Help put together a show, which is so much work because every detail has to be organized, like making sure the works arrive from the artist on time, they are hung properly . . . I mean hanging is so important, if a work is not hung properly, it can really kill a show . . ."

"Mom does a lot of stuff at the gallery," Amaya cut in.

As she was restively smoothing the fabric of her jacket near her clavicle, Naina realized she must have been rambling. "So, Amaya, how are those difficult teenagers doing?" she asked, keen to get the subject off herself.

Recently, Amaya, who worked at a substance abuse center, had been assigned three new patients, all aggressive male teenagers severely addicted to cocaine.

"I hope you're being careful," Naina added, a small spike of maternal anxiety jabbing her.

Though she was somewhat concerned about the kind of people Amaya was around, the truth was, she did not worry much about either of her children. Amaya had always been a sensible, grounded girl, the kind who always made wise choices. She was like a tree, deeply rooted in the earth with big, wide branches that reached toward the heavens. She was not rickety like her mother.

An image of seven-year-old Amaya in their Montcrest garden on a cloudy day in October came to Naina as she walked toward the restroom. Naina had pointed at the snow-white wispy sky. "Amaya, do you want to learn how to fly when you grow up? That way, you could go far, far, far away, above those candy floss clouds, close to the sun and the sky, just like airplanes do."

"Mommy, can I really fly when I grow up?" Amaya had said, her face all scrunched up.

"Yes, of course, you can. As high as you want, darling."

And then, Amaya had sat up straight, crossed her legs, brushed some of the leaves off her magenta pink dress, looking like an adorable child sage as her expression became intense with contemplation. "Mommy, I have to learn how to drive first if I want to fly. Because when I go so far up, I'll need to have a lot of food because it will take a long time to get to the sky. And so I have to know how to drive to the grocery store first."

In the restroom, as Naina refreshed her lipstick, which had slid outside the border of her lips to create a clownish mustache, she again thought about how lucky Amaya was. With Jai, Amaya's life could be rich and flavorful, like a good beef bourguignon, a delicacy Naina had tasted for the first time just the year before.

"I really would like to see your gallery sometime," Jai said, his voice now lower and deeper, the color of hushed burgundy, the texture of raw silk.

Amaya had gone outside to take a call from a friend who urgently needed to talk. Jai's hands were on the table, just inches away from hers. His eyes were like marbles coated in chocolate gold and his entire attention felt as if it were a thread wound up on the tip of an arrow and aimed at her.

"Maybe I could come with Amaya to an opening," Jai continued.

"Perhaps," Naina said as agitation buzzed inside her like a pack of fruit flies. "Perhaps." She did not want Jai to find out about her lowly role at the gallery. She fidgeted with her hands under the table and cast her eyes down as Jai's gaze remained on her face, like a feathery caress.

After a few moments, she lifted her gaze and softly said, "You are welcome to come to the gallery."

"That would be lovely, Naina," Jai said, uttering her name with an unexpected familiarity. "I look forward to it."

CHAPTER FIVE

THE NEXT MORNING, Naina woke up thinking about France. She envisioned Jai's hands fingering a book by Albert Camus or Jean-Paul Sartre in a bookstore in Paris, walking hand in hand with some Gallic beauty in colored tortoise shell glasses and stylishly untidy hair, the woman both aroused and comforted by the unexpected silkiness of his hands. She pictured them sitting in Luxembourg Gardens on a summer afternoon in T-shirts, his arm casually draped over her shoulders, the coils of fine hair on his forearm brushing against her skin. Then the woman, who was becoming less Gallic and more nebulous in Naina's mind, would kiss his lips, those lean, wide lips with not an extra ounce of flesh of them. Assured like the rest of him.

Now, Naina's whole body was aroused, electric currents doing a haphazard tango inside her. She lay on her side, hugged a pillow, and thought again about how lucky Amaya was. Amaya knew what those lips really felt like, was familiar with his forearm hair on her arms, and held his hands numerous times. And she would continue to do so . . .

Then, like a startling flash of sunlight cleaving into the night sky in the wee hours of the morning, it dawned on Naina that she was thinking about her *own, her very own daughter, having intimate relations with a man.* She sat up straight, slapped her right cheek, and shook her head frenetically. What in the world was the matter with her? This was ridiculous. Who in the world had *such* thoughts about their own children? New York had made her really crazy.

She started to scuttle about her apartment as another idea trickled into her mind. Her imagination was just so vast. She could envision almost anything, regardless of how strange it was. That idea may be odd to most, but not to all. Especially not to many creative New Yorkers who venerated words like "unique," "unconventional," "quirky," and even "freakish." That was all there was to it. Her oddball mind meandered to bizarre places like—um—her daughter's private life. While she didn't really know of anyone whose brain did such things, she felt sure the thoughts of inventive people strayed in all sorts of unspeakable directions.

Plopping down on the edge of her bed with her legs flung apart, Naina giggled to herself. What a wacky, mischievous mind she had.

When she later entered the subway, she pictured a younger Jai, with long, black, wavy hair, immersed in the resplendently impassioned paintings of

Eugene Delacroix at the Musee D' Orsay. A shadowy woman was running her fingers through his hair.

Below a subway poster saying "Poles are for your safety, not your latest routine" stood a young blonde girl wearing a striking ochre-and-black geometric print dress with tan leather boots. The girl's eyes were a glassy blue, her small lips curled in a bored pout, and she leaned against the subway door. Something about her body language seemed to say she did not belong inside the subway. She looked familiar, but Naina could not put her finger on it. The girl squeezed herself into a narrow space on the seat between two mothers with infants, ignoring the infant on her right, who was trying to get her attention.

Naina realized she was the assistant from Robert Goldsmith Gallery, the girl who had rolled her eyes and stifled a smirk when she had asked her if the gallery had any job openings.

The train reached Bryant Park. A few people got out, and Naina could finally see a seat that no one else seemed to be rushing toward. She sat down diagonally opposite the girl. She obviously did not remember Naina. Naina, however, remembered their meeting very clearly and felt a wave of embarrassment at how ridiculous she must have come across.

The morning of their encounter, Naina had woken up very early and had been in no mood to laze around in bed. The early spring sun had been playing hide-and-seek behind the clouds and she had made herself a cup of strong coffee, a departure from her regular peppermint tea. It had been six or seven weeks since she had moved to New York, and her desire to work felt intense. She felt a pressing urge to pursue something in the arts—something she could only do in New York City; something full time—not like her job at Gyan, the nonprofit in Jersey that helped educate South Asian women about health and nutrition. There, she had to hear all those women with their loud, desperate voices, wanting to know whether male gynecologists might rape them, whether an MRI would snuff them out, whether a mother-in-law's stage 3 cancer diagnosis might mean the difficult woman was going to die soon. Naina had been sympathetic to all but now felt she had already done her good deeds.

While routinely reading *The New York Times*, Naina had been thinking, as she often did, how New York was the mecca of the art world and envisaging how exhilarating it must be to be a part of it. Again, she pictured being able to look at paintings and photographs all day, meeting quixotic artists, regularly going to the Guggenheim and the Met, and talking with her colleagues about the world as it should be rather than as it was.

Suddenly another embryonic thought took a more defined form. Could *she* actually be a part of it? After all, she had taken only six courses on art history. And this was New York where everyone in the art world probably had tons of degrees in the subject, years of experience, and lots of connections. Still, what was the harm in trying? At this point in her life, small rejections could do little damage. That realization emboldened her. Not museums though—museums were too big and grand for her—but galleries, the scores of big and small galleries in Chelsea. Might they be more amenable to considering someone like her?

She had no plans, and decided to go to Chelsea, restless and brave spirits urging her to act—*act, act, act now*, they said.

After spending all morning working on her resume—the first resume she had ever created—she ventured down to the converted warehousing district of New York around three in the afternoon. Most of her previous Chelsea gallery visits had been quick—an hour or two before meeting Amaya or in between running errands or trips to museums in the city. But now she found herself thoroughly exploring those streets filled with galleries, cafes, and even auto repair shops from the neighborhood's less-than-glamorous past, all the while hoping—perhaps foolishly so—to find something or someone who might, just might, help her find a crack in the art world through which she could creep in.

But things didn't quite turn out that way. She had been on 22nd Street for less than an hour when a kind of jitteriness crept into her skin, making it quiver from the inside. She saw that Chelsea was ruled by chic, aloof girls who sat at the front desks in the galleries, but looked as if they were poised at an altitude of enlightened sophistication; by scores of men who carried themselves in a haughty manner that screamed more rock star than art dealer; by cool, young boys with mussed-up hair and cargo pants who looked like they were ready to rebel against anything and everything, including the paintings they were carrying; and by clusters of people who assuredly talked about how a work reminded them of another that she knew nothing about.

Once, when Naina had entered an enormous gallery, she skulked around in a quiet corner, a few feet behind a gigantic metal sculpture by an artist called David Smith whom she had never heard of. She looked at her own clothes. She felt horribly dumpy. Her Lord & Taylor black trousers seemed shapeless, her Macy's brown jacket way too bulky, and her sensible black pumps stank of mall-bought. Nobody in this place was ever going to give her—a middle-aged Indian suburbanite with few credentials except for a febrile imagination—a chance. She should just turn around and leave.

But then she noticed the strikingly dynamic sculpture that looked like a giant letter from some unknown script, and she was intrigued. As she eyed the piece made of welded metal, two women in tight pants and boots approached her quiet corner, admired the sculpture from behind, and talked about some person they had just encountered. They did not even appear to acknowledge her presence even though she had just nervously smiled at them.

Naina decided she would stay a little while longer in Chelsea. No one was going to notice her here, chalking it up to the city's penchant for self-absorption. For the next two hours, she tiptoed through gallery after gallery, staying a few feet away from everyone if she could help it. She found the art intriguing and novel, though mostly inscrutable, just like every previous time. But now its allure was enhanced since it was contemporary art, art that was made now. Something belonging to the present moment, not to some storied past.

A half hour before the galleries were set to close, she walked into an unassuming-looking art gallery called Robert Goldsmith. It was on the fourth floor in the back of a building, with small windows through which ugly brown apartment towers could be seen, blocking any possibility of natural light. The entire space was about the size of an average studio apartment in New York or a huge suburban bathroom, the smallest gallery she had been in so far. But the art—minimalist photographs focusing on the architectural details of ordinary buildings—was so beautiful, she felt momentarily uplifted. She plucked up the courage to talk to the skinny, suede jacket-clad girl busily typing away on a computer. Even then, the glassy blue eyes she just encountered struck her as belonging to a real go-getter, the eyes of someone who never lost sight of her target.

"Hi," Naina had said, nervously smiling, realizing she was sounding deferential to someone who was probably younger than her daughter.

The girl had lifted her head. "May I help you?" Her brittle tone suggested that was the last thing she wanted to do.

"Please, yes-yes, please. My name is Naina Mehta. I'm wondering if there are any job openings at this gallery. I have done about six art history courses, and . . . I love . . . I just love . . . this photography exhibit."

"Uhummm." The girl took a long sip of her coffee. "What kinds of courses have you taken and where?"

Naina could no longer look straight at her. She tilted her head downward. "I've taken courses on Expressionism, Impressionism, post-Impressionism, Romanticism, pre-Raphaelite art, and Realism . . . at Rutgers in New Jersey."

The girl's silvery salmon-colored lips tilted upward like fins into a smirk.

"This is a contemporary art gallery, I should let you know. Which means art that's made now, not a hundred years ago."

Naina heard a roaring silence roiling through gallery.

"Do you have a resume?"

By that point, Naina could no longer stand to be in the same room with the girl. *Art that's made now, not a hundred years ago.* The words echoed in her head, making her shrivel with embarrassment. Was she just a trifling wrinkle from the past? She jumped into a taxi and hurriedly left Chelsea, desperate to be alone.

For the rest of that evening, the girl behind the desk at Robert Goldsmith Gallery, and her withering words continued to reverberate in Naina's head. She had been so envious of the girl's self-assurance. Not too long before she too had possibly possessed that compacted air of someone who knows—though hers could have never been as pronounced or obnoxious as that girl's. Any hint of arrogance in Naina had evaporated since she'd concluded she was actually someone who had barely skimmed the surface of life; someone who, even at her age, had yet to put the pieces together.

Would that young woman also wake up one day and be hit by the same shock of reality? Naina hoped not, feeling a ripple of compassion. And, if such a thing were to happen to her, Naina wished it would happen for her early—before she became older and was expected to be omniscient.

And now, a year-and-a half later, sitting across from her in the subway car, judging by the same supercilious look on her face, it seemed the girl had clearly not been hit by anything.

As she thought about it, Jai, too, had a knowing air. But it was a pleasant knowing air. Fragrant and supple.

Two stops later, Naina heard two touristy-looking girls, who were swinging around the subway car's center pole, speaking French. She saw murky images of France again: Jai slowly sipping a Côtes du Rhône as light from Monseiur Renaud's dining table candle flickered over his scars; Jai, dressed in a trench coat, gazing at the stained-glass windows of the Notre-Dame, hoping to catch a glimpse of the meaning of life; Jai, having his hair stroked by the shadowy figure of a woman.

After she got out of the subway, Naina walked faster than usual to Red Circle Gallery. She constantly looked down at the sidewalk for any unexpected cracks— something she still hadn't been able to overcome her fear of. She just knew one day she would be hurrying in heels somewhere and fall into one of the countless fissures, which no one in New York seemed to care enough about to fix.

Today she anticipated a nice quiet day since it was sunny and pleasant, and most people would likely be relishing the weather outside. Naina was looking forward to being in the gallery surrounded by the delicate, intricate drawings inspired by Greek myths from the current show. She felt grateful to have a job related to art even though being a gallery assistant was nothing to brag about at her age. And the way it had come about had been so serendipitous, life again reminding her of its capriciousness.

One week after that disconcerting day in Chelsea, Naina had been browsing through a book titled *The Hindu Approach to Sorrow* at Barnes & Noble when a distinctly middle-aged woman in steel-gray slim-leg pants and a black jacket turned around.

"Is that any good?" the woman had asked.

"Yes, it kind of is, it's an interesting way of looking at things," Naina had replied. She was surprised the woman had spoken to her. No one had ever struck up a conversation with her like that in New York. And this woman looked like a busy, professional type, not someone who had time for chatting.

"Unfortunately, I don't know too much about Hinduism or Eastern religions in general, but I'd like to learn," the woman said. "What's the basic idea of the book?"

"How can I sum it up . . . I suppose it's saying that attachment is the source of unhappiness. That the world we live in is just an illusion. Maya."

"That's very interesting . . . Sometimes I think my whole life is an illusion. Just kidding. Or maybe not . . . Are you a Hindu?"

"Most of the time, I think. Not always a good one though, I have to confess."

Naina and the woman, who introduced herself as Susan Fegel, spoke for a few minutes regarding the concept of maya, about which Naina had tried to sound more well-versed in than she really was. They also spoke about the deaths of family members they had recently endured—Susan had lost her mother about a year before.

Naina liked Susan. She seemed like the sort of person who meant what she said, the sort of person who came face-to-face with the truth rather than pirouetting around it.

At one point, Susan asked Naina what she was doing, and she made some offhand comment about looking for work. Ideally, something related to art although she knew what a fantastical notion that was in this city. Then Susan piped up, saying she was the executive director of a newly opened nonprofit gallery that supported emerging and underrepresented female artists. She had a position open for a gallery assistant, which, to be candid, was an entry-level position with lots of grunt work, but she would be happy to consider Naina if it appealed to her.

A couple of weeks later, she had a twenty-minute interview with Susan and two board members of the gallery, the secretary, and the treasurer. She was asked to comment on two pieces of art and questioned about her experience writing promotional materials and her organizational skills. It had taken three weeks for Susan to get back to Naina, who was on tenterhooks the whole time, but when she finally did, the news was good.

"There's one thing I feel I should tell you," Naina had said before saying yes to the job. "I'm excited, literally thrilled, at the thought of working here but quite frankly. . . I have to be frank with you. . . I'm completely intimidated by everyone in this area. Everyone . . . what can I say, everyone is so young and hip here. As you already know, I'm none of those things . . . I'll probably be the oldest gallery assistant in Chelsea . . . That . . . is quite frightening . . . Also, I don't have the right clothes."

"If I were looking for someone young and hip, I wouldn't have made you an offer," Susan had replied. "I did have a young girl working for me and she took hours to get any damn thing done. I want you here because I think you will be reliable and hardworking. And I'm—did I tell you—I'm a Midwestern girl from Chicago? I'm not crazy about the attitude of this place. It's all a veneer. They're all as frightened and as vulnerable . . . if not more so . . . as everybody else. It's in your head. If you think you're less than others, you'll allow the bluster to make you feel inadequate. As for the clothes, that's an easy fix."

As Naina now entered Red Circle, which was tucked away in the corner of the fifth floor of a building that housed more than twenty galleries, she saw her big-boned energetic boss, in her usual dark pants and jacket, in front of the computer with that resolute look in her small bluish-gray eyes, the consummate career woman who had impressed her in a bookstore more than a year earlier.

Seeing Naina come into the gallery, Susan, who never gushed about any artist's work, glowed with praise about some artist called Anastasia Diamant.

"Don't you think this is amazing work?" Susan said, as she showed Naina images of the artist's abstract black-and-white paintings on a computer screen.

Naina examined the images. She liked being asked her opinion on new submissions. Susan had recently started asking for her input more and more, and once even for help in writing a press release.

"It looks fascinating," Naina replied. "And sort of cryptic. What's it about?"

"She takes fragments of hieroglyphs to create these forms that I just love," Susan said. "Look at those forms over there—aren't they great? Don't they look like writing instruments?"

"They look more like some kind of weapons to me. I do think they are intriguing . . . but don't they feel a bit scattered?" Naina couldn't help wondering if the images resembled herself, tiny bits dispersed all over the place—without a shape to give them coherence.

"But that's what's so great about the works. There's no harmony. It's like she's saying all human history consists of is scraps of disconnected stories and that we individuals are just a jumble of disjointed, competing influences."

"Hmmm . . . I see. Fascinating . . . I don't know. The work just seems . . . what's the word . . . unfinished to me. But of course, that's just my humble opinion . . . I'm so new to this . . ."

"I want you to think about it some more. I love it. Anastasia is based in DC and has had a couple of small shows there, but I think we need to show her here. Before someone else offers a solo show."

Susan stood up and looked at her watch.

"Oh God, it's ten-thirty already. Forget about Anastasia Diamant for now. There's still so much work to do for the Mary Di Russo show, I don't know why I keep forgetting that. I've got to run to the Verizon store to pick up my phone . . . they said it would be ready by ten forty-five . . . so I can actually be traceable again. What did we do before cellphones? I should be back within half-an-hour provided it all goes well. I want you to check for any typos on the Di Russo press release by the time I'm back. Also, can you please follow up with the treasurer?"

Twenty minutes later, after she had completed her tasks, Naina sat ensconced in the quiet of the cozy office that felt like a second home, typing a list of potential donors on the computer. She decided to take another look at Anastasia Diamant's work, and once again, something about the splintered shapes littered across the paintings made her feel uneasy. They were placed randomly, without any design. When she looked closer, the slivered shapes resembled her vision of Jai's scars under a microscope—thin and sharp. What did his scars feel like? Were they rough? Well, these were things for Amaya to know. She shooed that thought away. Hazily, the shadowy woman emerged in Naina's head, tracing Jai's blemishes with her fingers numerous times. Unexamined and unexplained emotions continued to unfold inside Naina like a bale of cloth with a beguiling array of colors and patterns.

The treasurer called with a follow-up question, interrupting her reverie.

After the call, she remembered Jai talking about Monseiur Renaud reading books on hieroglyphs in Paris. Jai had said he had developed an interest in them himself. She wondered what he would make of the paintings.

Then an idea came to Naina, flecking her with eagerness. She would invite Jai and Amaya to the gallery after six, when the gallery was closed and Susan was gone. This way Jai could see the gallery, she could show him Anastasia Diamant's work on the computer, and, most importantly, he would never know how lowly her job really was.

She was about to write an email to Amaya, asking her if she and Jai would like to visit the gallery next week, when Susan rushed back in, ushering in the real world, a world of logic, practicality, and constraints. Now, hesitation quivered within her, and she wondered again if she was being too familiar with her daughter's boyfriend. Was it too much? Was she crossing the line? There were plenty of museums and galleries Jai could visit in New York, and Amaya, with her inordinate amount of sensibleness, might find her mother's behavior batty.

But after lunch, Naina changed her mind again. She was overthinking it. This wasn't some existential dilemma. It was no big deal. She wrote another email, a meandering note filled with *ifs* and *buts*, yet stopped short of sending it. She'd wait until the next morning just to make sure. Re-reading it the following day, she could see the tone of the email was so formal it read as if she were living in Jane Austen's world. So she shortened it, toned it down, and quickly hit send with trembling fingers.

CHAPTER SIX

NAINA GOT OUT of the subway after an unusually light day at work and felt the sway of a breeze. It really was a beautiful evening. The sky was twilight silk. The temperature was a pleasant eighty degrees, and the mild humidity acted like a natural moisturizer on her dry skin. She decided to go for a short walk before picking up some adana kabab at the Turkish place near her apartment.

The weight of the book in her bag squeezed her right shoulder and the discomfort had become worse with each passing day since she had been carrying it back and forth to work and poring over it on the subway for an entire week. The book in question bore the title *Egyptian Grammar: Being an Introduction to the Study of Hieroglyphs*, which she had hoped would become more engaging—if only because the book came from Jai.

Several days after Jai and Amaya had visited Red Circle, where Naina had been in jittery high spirits, the three of them decided to meet at the MoMA. Naina was much calmer and made sure she didn't talk excessively. She was taken aback and delighted when, as they stood next to a fantastical painting by Paul Klee with hieroglyph-like fish and flowers—striking her as being both a visual representation of something enigmatic and a decipherer of signs—Jai handed her a puckered leather-bound book on Egyptian hieroglyphs with a seemingly interminable number of pages. The book's thickness, however, didn't put her off. The fact that he had thought of her—and thought of her enough to bring her the book—filled her with a warm, buttery delight.

"This was one of my mother's favorite books," Jai said. "I thought you might like it."

Since the Paul Klee show, Naina had tried and tried to read the book, but to no avail. Finally, she had to admit she wouldn't be able to read another word without it turning her head into a mess of stringy, scrambled eggs.

Egyptian Grammar, written by a world-renowned Egyptologist and linguist called Sir Alan Gardiner, was as dense and impenetrable as a rain forest, and clearly written for scholars or those seriously interested in decoding Egyptian hieroglyphs. And it was over six hundred pages. It would take her years to get through it—she had no interest in putting herself through that. Of course, she wasn't going to tell Jai. She was going to just talk about the parts she had found interesting. Which was quite a struggle in itself.

Still, Jai had thought of her. That he gave her such a scholarly book, which his mother had loved, surely showed he not only regarded her fondly, but also found her intellectually adroit and engaging. Again, those warm, blithe feelings flowed through her.

It was now past eight at night. What she had expected to be a short walk, turned out to be a real hike. She walked all the way to Union Square, browsed some books at Barnes and Noble, and then headed back to her Murray Hill neighborhood. All the restaurants—Thai, Italian, Indian, and German—squeezed between drug stores, delis, nail salons, and dry cleaners reminded her about what a quirky place New York was. She stood a few feet away from a frame shop, in front a red-and-yellow Mark Rothko poster she had just admired, and noticed she could spot a restaurant in every direction. Restaurants were as ubiquitous to New York as the sky, yet there seemed to be no overarching design governing their location. Like slums in third world countries, they just seemed to pop up wherever they found a spot. Just like her own life now. One without a master plan. Where she wandered every which way like the wind. As the notion of a master plan entered her mind, she started to fidget and tried to clear her head.

She looked up and saw the skyscrapers shooting straight into the sky as if they were tall, gigantic legs, and Manhattan, at that moment, looming like a multiple-legged mythological creature daring the heavens with its vertical might. And if it were a mythical creature, it would be male. But one that could give birth—to new ideas, new trends, new cultures, new selves. It was an incredibly fertile creature. Instead of legs, the skyscrapers could also be male organs like shiva lingams. She softly giggled at the notion and covered her mouth.

Or maybe something less auspicious. Like the Cyclops greedily swallowing humans or the selfish self-gobbling up the altruistic self.

As the breeze picked up speed, Naina thought about sex. She remembered how Harish, even after all those years, had seemed like this perpetual nightly stranger in bed, awkwardly taking off her clothes in the dark or carefully touching her breasts as if he were examining a patient. At the same time, she—especially on those days when she felt particularly amorous—would be busy fantasizing that it wasn't her husband's brittle lips planted on her own, but John Lennon's dew-kissed ones; that it wasn't just the American suburb's eerie nocturnal silence in her ears, but Amitabh Bacchan's deep-throated murmuring; that it wasn't her husband's slim arms holding her, but Pierce Brosnan's brawny embrace. And then, as she heard a couple arguing about almond milk versus soy milk standing outside a high-end deli, she remembered the days when she felt indifferent to carnal desire and her thoughts darted from the grocery list to the weather forecast to the children's homework when Harish was inside her.

NAINA STOPPED AT the Turkish restaurant to pick up her eagerly anticipated charcoal-grilled adana kabab for dinner. Through the plastic bag, she could catch a whiff of its smoky smell. Her lips stretched into a tiny smile. When she had first moved to New York, she cooked every meal, just like she did in Jersey. Where regardless of whether she was preparing Indian food or not, she cooked everything the Indian sway—with a million ingredients and spices. It wasn't as if she had any real objection to takeout, but it seemed like an unnecessary extravagance for someone like her who knew how to cook. Plus, it just felt like something younger people did, like those who lived in her building—groggy-eyed twenty-somethings who craved some solid sustenance after stumbling home from a night of drunken revelry.

But now, most times when she ate in—even when Amaya came over—she would order in from one of the treasured takeout menus she had arranged alphabetically, always making up some excuse about how she had forgotten to shop for ingredients or how the yogurt or tomatoes in the fridge had gone bad, or how she was too tired to cook even if she had had a lazy Sunday. Amaya joked she had turned into more of a New Yorker than most who lived in the Big Apple.

After finishing her adana kebab, Naina took off her blouse and skirt and stood in front of the mirror, wearing the coral-colored bra and matching panties she had recently bought. She held a picture of herself with her giggling girlfriends at her twentieth birthday party at the Royal Restaurant in Connaught Place. She remembered her reputation as a beauty in those days as she looked at the black-and-white photo that showed off her clear skin, sparkling eyes, long hair, and slim body, accentuated by the hot pink-and-green maxi dress she had spent a whopping hundred rupees on. Ever since she was a child, people had complimented her eyes—her grandmother used to say she looked at people as if she were looking into their souls—and it was her grandmother who decided to name her Naina, which in Hindi means eyes. Naina—when pronounced properly as Neh-naa—had a melodious ring to it. Oh, how she missed people saying her name properly in America!

Naina gingerly turned toward the filigreed bamboo-edged mirror and decided she would be very objective in assessing her body, something she rarely did with any degree of concentration. But there she loomed in front of herself, her reflection more remote than intimate.

She started at the top—the parts she was accustomed to looking at.

Yes, her flowing black tresses had been replaced by neat layers of hair that fell to her shoulders. But so much more appropriate for someone her age. Around her eyes, admittedly, she had developed crow's feet and dark circles, but nothing that couldn't be easily disguised with a touch of the right concealer. That tight stomach of her early twenties did bulge a little, but luckily it mostly disappeared with proper shapewear. She cringed when she saw a skein of smudges on the sides of her stomach. She shook her head and sighed. Such was the fate of women. Motherhood meant being permanently and indelibly marked. Even after your children could look after themselves, your body still bore the badge of giving birth decades before.

She carefully scrutinized her belly. Actually, compared to many women with children, her stretch marks weren't that bad. They were tiny, faint lines, not hideous stains that stood out like splotches of cow dung in an Indian village. And her belly was definitely not huge.

She moved her gaze upward again. Thankfully, her eyes had managed to retain much of the luster of years past, and her lashes were still long and thick. Even Jai seemed to have noticed.

After the Paul Klee show, they had stopped for a coffee at the MoMA café. When Amaya went to the restroom, he had leaned across the table and complimented her eyes in that almost bass voice he used when they were alone together.

"You have really luminous eyes. They have a life of their own, and they look out at the world with girlish curiosity."

A flaming heat had saturated Naina's body, igniting tiny sparks between her legs. She stared at her unfinished café au lait, clasped her hands together, and gently tapped her foot under the table. And then, somewhat aware of how unbecoming she might appear, she tried to impede the flood of color inside her, and turn herself black and white, like the color-block dress she was wearing. She swiveled her head to the left as if she were looking to see if Amaya was on her way back, even though she had seen the long lines at the restrooms and was quite sure her daughter would be a while.

Naina raised her head again but avoided any eye contact with Jai. She smiled a thousand-megawatt neon American-style smile, atypical for her, rolled some strands of her hair with her fingers, and somehow found her voice again.

"Thank you," she said. "I haven't been called 'girlish' in a long time."

"But you are girlish. In so many ways."

"I'm not that young, you know. I'm Amaya's mother." She immediately wished to swallow her words up whole, then have her bones rip them apart and bury them in a place inside her where they could never escape. Or better still— burn them on a pyre, like the Hindus did with the dead.

"What does age have to do with it? Girlish refers to a state of mind that has nothing to do with the number of years a person has spent on earth."

When Amaya returned, Jai clasped her hand and his face was awash with the most tender expression. "Honey, you took a long time."

And the stream of blithe, bright color stopped mid-stream, and, in the nether regions of Naina's mind, she felt an inexplicable itch of something. Something that felt like shame.

Now, standing in her coral-colored bra and panties, she remembered Jai's voice, tactile like flesh, caressing the lips, hair, and neck of a shadowy woman, and felt torrid flickers between her legs again.

The shadowy woman had become a regular figure in Naina's imagination, a nameless, faceless outline, an empty silhouette. Like any other shadow, the shadowy woman was created by the obstruction of light, and, in this case, the blocking of the light of truth. A truth so disgraceful, so awful, the shadowy woman was one of the many things that had to be contrived to mask it so it would not bubble up to the surface of Naina's consciousness and create a tempest in its wake.

Despite these stratagems, her feelings continued to inch toward her consciousness and rattle her bones until she kicked them down again. And again.

After spending a long time assessing herself in front of the mirror, Naina suddenly took off her bra. Fleshy breasts, shaped like papayas, with dark brown nipples protruding from them, fell out. She stared at them, taken aback by their unabashed physicality. It had been years since she had actually looked at her breasts, except during the unthinking rituals of washing them in the shower or checking for breast cancer. They seemed like mammalian creatures with a secret life of their own, both attached and detached from her simultaneously.

She examined them from every possible angle, happy to see that despite a little droop, her breasts were still pert. Not "girlish," but not "old ladyish" either.

She stepped back a couple of feet away from the mirror and concluded that except for a bit of excess fat in her thighs and stomach, she didn't look too bad.

Naina changed into her pajamas, brushed her teeth, and took the old photograph to bed so she could study it one more time. Soon, memories of the longing faces of timid young men on bicycles, the whistles of the bolder ones, and the ardent love letters from the anonymous ones came to her. She thought about some of the men who wanted to marry her. There was Mahesh, the balloon-bellied accountant who, in an anxious flurry of words, told her she was even more beautiful than the legendary Bollywood actress Madhubala, in the only private moment they shared during their arranged meeting; Satinder, the gaunt-faced Indian Civil Service officer with a pleading expression that seemed to say he would worship her for the rest of his life; and Mohan, the smooth-talking lawyer who repeatedly called her father to ask the family to reconsider their decision of rejecting him.

Resentment against Harish simmered in her for never telling her she was beautiful or making her feel desirable. Did she waste all the beauty of her youth on a husband who couldn't care less? Was his attitude the reason why, for all those years before she came to New York, her girlhood interest in clothes had slackened? Was he the reason why she hadn't looked at her breasts in years? Or was it her? Had she, during all that time, just become lazy? Had she, as they liked to say these days, "lost touch" with her body?

Naina went back to the mirror and realized, regardless of how hard she tried to console herself, she looked light years away from that old picture and would never look like that again. Time with its unrelenting and unremitting linearity would not allow such a backward leap. While Jai had said she was bursting with "girlish curiosity," he probably thought she looked middle-aged, the idea pricking her like a needle. She could no longer bear to see her reflection.

She paced around her apartment and the shadowy woman appeared again, arching her back, flinging her hair, and opening her lips as the silhouette of a man grabbed and kissed her. The fantasy kept spinning in her mind like a wheel desperate to roll forward.

Perhaps, it was possible. Perhaps it was still possible for someone to stare into her eyes as if they were mirrors of enchantment. Perhaps it was still possible for her to feel lush like a silk Persian carpet. Perhaps, she thought, blushing, it was still possible for her to shudder with pleasure as someone caressed her papaya-like breasts as if they were as luscious as the most pert and perky of bosoms. But how could this happen? When? Where? How?

A few minutes later, her reverie subsided and she was struck by the absurdity of her thoughts.

CHAPTER SEVEN

NAINA WAS RELIEVED as she turned off the lights and locked the door at Red Circle; it was a Thursday and the third day in a row she had to work late because of an upcoming group show. One of the artists had not completed the work she had promised to deliver, and, at the last minute, they had to change the press release and the catalog.

She was glad to finally be in the fresh air after being cooped up for so long. She was also really looking forward to a glass of wine at the Heaven wine bar a few blocks east on 9th Avenue where she and her artist friend Alannah, the organizer of wild birthday parties, would meet a few times a month. Sometimes, Mara, their yoga and new-age obsessed friend also joined them, but tonight she was busy. Naina hoped Heaven would have the Casa Lapostelle Merlot from Chile Jai had introduced her to the last time the three of them had got together. It was earthy, plummy with an aftertaste of something burnt, and absolutely delicious. He knew a lot of about South American wines, and she knew almost nothing. Now, she was beginning to acquire quite a taste for them.

Naina was also eager to find out what had happened with Josh. About a week earlier, Alannah had her second date with him, which she had not been looking forward to at all. Josh was a scientist in a neurobiology research unit at a drug company in New Jersey, and Alannah's cousin had set them up. Josh was supposedly tall, wore round wire-rimmed glasses and very smart, but had the personality of a "pumpkin pie desperately in need of a heap of cinnamon and nutmeg."

To Naina, the world of dating seemed like an ongoing saga—filled with plenty of drama, emotion, and suspense. It wasn't scripted like an arranged marriage where there were only two roads—marriage or no marriage. With dating, there was the possibility of a slew of curious scenarios.

On the street, she saw a young, slender woman eating a long piece of ciabatta bread filled with multiple layers of ham and cheese. It was peculiar to see a slim, well-dressed girl eating something so large and obviously fattening. Naina picked up a menu of a new Middle Eastern takeout place on 25th and 10th and examined it to gauge how calorie-intense the food was. Satisfied, she neatly folded the menu and put in her bag. Mostly, she saw fashionable New York girls eating just wilted leaves weeping in the salads they ate for lunch, picking at them like little birds or rabbits. She smiled to herself as she realized she now studied people with a great deal of keenness, just like when she first came to America.

But now, that keenness was more knife-like, taking on a greater sharpness and urgency.

Naina had observed that a person in New York had to be interesting or important to make friends, that people here were as needy as they were independent, that many women in their forties, fifties, and even sixties had never been married. The latter was the most surprising. She understood one could be divorced or widowed at that age, but never married? Never even lived with someone, as a couple, for any substantial length of time? Still waiting to find the right person?

She also learned that New Yorkers looked down on Jersey and all suburbs, in fact. So whenever someone asked her where she was from, she first said India, which people seemed to be intrigued by, and then, when pressed further, said she had been living across the river before moving into the city. She noticed some people would pay attention to her at the gallery's events because they assumed, given her advanced years, she must have a higher position, and when they discovered she was just an assistant, they would look surprised—though they'd try to hide it. Of course, she would always dodge any questions about what she did by initially saying something vague, like "she worked with Susan"—just as she had done with Jai.

In the beginning, when she was in art-related settings, she had been self-conscious about saying too much since she didn't know that much; but then she realized that if she said nothing, she would never be noticed. And she hadn't come to New York to live like a ghost.

So she made it a point to seriously study contemporary art in the same studious, diligent way she had studied English literature in India and art history at Rutgers. She read a great deal of books and magazines on the subject and went to see as many shows as she possibly could, jotting down notes in the taupe-colored notebook she always carried with her and scribbling reminders about exhibitions she needed to see.

But contemporary art could often be so strange and unfathomable and she was forced to bend, twist, and contort her mind in ways she had never done to get even somewhat close to understanding it. Even so, comprehension often seemed incomprehensible. And unattainable.

Still, she would spend inordinate amounts of time examining images of Damien Hirst's dead and dissected animals in glass tanks from every angle to make sure she wasn't missing anything, Google everything she could find about Tracey Emin to understand why her sensationalized private life qualified as art and ponder over the role of aesthetics and beauty in art when she looked at images of Cornelia Parker's pile of burnt cocaine. Finally, it had all begun to seem less daunting yet still as exacting. Questions just begged more questions.

Her cellphone beeped. She reached into her bag and found a text from Alannah saying she would be fifteen minutes late—which, she knew, meant at least twenty minutes. Alannah acted so Indian in some ways. Always running late and always wanting to share food at restaurants. But her delay meant Naina could stop at the wine store and pick up a couple of bottles of the Malbec Jai had introduced her to.

In New York, Naina had discovered that all the little pieces of knowledge she had collected over the years, even though they never added up to a completed jigsaw puzzle, were finally useful. If she couldn't be important, she could at least try to be interesting. Once she figured that out, she began discussing topics she felt somewhat confident about: the meaning of the mandala to Carl Jung; the influence of Rumi in Bill Viola's work; the origin of the word hysteria; Byron's fascination with the East; and why *Villette* and not *Jane Eyre* was Charlotte Brontë's best book. She made an effort not to sound too much like an old-fashioned romantic, but, at the same time, retain the basic texture of her inclinations since that was what drew people to her. This balance ended up being a clever one although it was not premeditated; it was motivated more by instinct than calculation.

When she made conversation, she peppered it with a light sense of humor and, on some occasions, if she deemed it appropriate and was feeling particularly self-assured, expressed her eccentric side—like the time she told Alannah that she had once written a five-page letter to Merchant Ivory Productions urging them to make a movie out of Wilkie Collins's classic detective novel *Moonstone*. When she never heard back from them, she sent a second letter, longer than the first. And then a third, longer than the second. And then a fourth, longer than the third.

Alannah had been impressed and amused. Like Naina, she also loved Victorian novels, particularly those by William Thackeray and the Brontë sisters. And she liked *Moonstone* so much she asked Naina if she could help her get a real moonstone from India. Naina had laughed. She, herself, had never, to her knowledge, seen a real moonstone in her life.

The other training from Naina's past that proved useful in meeting people was her job at Gyan. While her official title at the nonprofit was associate director, her real role had been one of chief listener. Health-related, child-related, husband-related, in-laws-related, money-related, assimilation-related . . . everyone came to her with their questions and woes, knowing she would not only help them, but soothe them as well.

She had met Alannah during her third month at Red Circle when Alannah had burst into the gallery, like a fire-filled bubble, more eager to vent about how awful the other shows in Chelsea were than look at the art on their walls. Naina was all too happy to listen to another's opinion about the shows. They bonded over Victorian novels, Georgia O' Keefe, and Edvard Munch when they met up for drinks and art openings. And felt a special connection when they spoke about the magnificent psychological corporeality of Frida Kahlo's paintings, which so lushly rendered more facets of the female self than most women were willing to acknowledge within themselves.

Some weeks later, Naina met Mara who had been friends with Alannah for more than a decade, ever since the two had met in a remote town in Peru. After that, they had become a sort of trio Naina still found odd to be a part of.

Rob, her tabla player friend, was the only person she had met in the most unusual way—a way she thought could only happen in New York. She had been sitting in a café near her apartment one day, reading about an upcoming tabla performance by the Indian maestro Zakir Hussain, when a man with tattooed arms sitting next to her said, "That guy's a genius. So cool. Are you going to go listen to him?"

"I'm thinking about it."

He perked up at her response and after a brief conversation about Zakir Hussain, for the next half hour he talked about the Indian-influenced rock band where he played the tabla. And then he told her how vexed his Jerry-Falwell-worshipping family in North Carolina was when they found out he was playing some "Hindoooo instrument that will tempt the Devil." He said those words with such delight, it was almost as if he wished his tabla playing could, in fact, tempt Satan.

To Naina, it seemed that New Yorkers were little pieces that had broken away from a larger superstructure, and she was just one more anonymous piece joining this mass of charged, untethered fragments. For the first time in her life, personal details, such as age, hometown, residence, and marital status that one used to situate people, were so inconsequential. She felt as if she were now a woman with little to define her except herself and envisaged herself in a parallel universe where nothing from the old, familiar universe ever intersected. After more than thirty years of living in the US, she finally felt like she was becoming an American.

She looked at her watch. It was only 7:37. She could walk to the next avenue for exercise. She enjoyed strolling by herself. Unsupervised, ignored, and silent. Walking on the streets, brushing against unknown people; allowing herself to be squished like a roti on the subway by the chests, legs, and arms of strangers; covertly eavesdropping on the tiffs and endearments between people—such impersonally personal closeness she liked. Being solitary in a big city offered her the best of both worlds—privacy and intimacy at the same time.

Her cellphone rang, its dancey Latin ringtone always pleasing her. It was her son Karan.

"Hi, darling."

"Hi, Mom, how are you?"

"I'm good. Just finished work and going to meet a friend. How is your packing going? I wish you had let me come and help you."

"It would have been great if you could have come but only one weekend worked for you, and that weekend was crazy work-wise for me . . . Wait, today's Monday . . . I thought Monday was your day off. *Why* were you in the office today?"

Oh no. Not this conversation again.

"We just have a lot of work to do, Karan. There's a show coming up soon. You can understand that, can't you? Don't you have to work extra hours before a roadshow?"

"I'm twenty-five. It's my time to work hard. Not yours . . . You don't have to do this you know."

"I know, I know. But I want to."

"Financially speaking, Dad left you fine. And I'm not doing too badly myself. Dad would not have wanted you to do this. He always said he brought you to this country for a better life and I'm sure that did not mean doing some secretarial job."

Karan almost spat out of the words "secretarial job." Now, Naina was really infuriated. Her son could be much more of an elitist than his father sometimes. Still, she felt a prick of guilt for saddling him with a mother who made unconventional choices. She did not fully speak her mind.

"Secretaries are people too. Human beings like everyone else. And, I love my job. Plus, I'm not just a secretary. I select some of the artists that get shows."

She knew she was really stretching the truth, but Karan would likely never find out. Or so she hoped.

"And you know I think I can move up the ladder. Susan seems to like me quite a lot."

"And when do you plan to move up the ladder? When you're ready to *retire?*"

She smelled a note of concern in his voice and her annoyance mingled with a wave of affection. She knew that, deep down, he was worried about her, wondering if she had somehow fallen off the deep end.

"I'm fine, Karan, really," she said, buttering her tone. "Seriously, please don't worry about me. But, how are you, beta? Tell me about you."

"I'm excited about San Francisco. Chicago's just too damn cold. But you must come soon, once I'm there . . . maybe you'll be able to come for a real long time if you decide to give up that job of yours. I'm going to rent a place near the water and I know how you like the water."

"Water, that sounds wonderful. I can't wait. I'll be there before you know it, I promise."

"So Nitin tells me that you weren't able to make it to Sheela aunty's party . . ."

"Well, I was . . ."

She heard his Blackberry ringing. The sound of hands clapping.

"Hey, Mom, I just got a call from a client. Gotta run. Talk later."

Naina shut her eyes and felt grateful to that person. He or she had saved her, at least for now, from having to explain to her son, yet another time, that she had been too busy to go to New Jersey to visit her and Harish's old friends. That, of course, was not really accurate and she suspected even Karan knew that, but she couldn't bring herself to tell him the truth. That she had little interest in keeping in touch with all the Indian families who comprised their former circle of friends and acquaintances.

She lost interest in strolling and headed toward the wine bar. She could wait for Alannah there, have a drink, and cool her feelings.

Occasionally, Naina did communicate with their old friends, but never told them she was a gallery assistant. "After such a good position at Gyan, you are running around like a servant for some Jewish woman," she could just imagine Ranjana, from Stern Heights, saying. "That sounds even too low for our kids . . . What's wrong with you?"

Ranjana had a tendency to say these caustic things, which inevitably stung her, but Harish used to tell her she was too sensitive and took everything personally. "Naina, look at the whole person," he would say. "Why do you bother if Ranjana or Neeta makes some remark? They make odd comments to everybody. You know Indians are not politically correct or sensitive like Americans. They just say whatever comes to their mind if they think you are close. And you know they think of you as family. Don't you remember how Ranjana helped you with the kids when you had pneumonia?"

Harish did have a point, she knew—a point she could only grudgingly acknowledge, even now.

She wondered what the women in Jersey must be doing at that moment. She pictured Ranjana eating a chocolate with her afternoon tea, Sarita reading *Filmfare* in her movie poster-filled family room, and Aditi arguing with Samesh about whether they should go to India during Diwali or Christmas. For so many years, although they must have known a hundred-plus Indians in the area, Harish and she had generally socialized with a set of about fifteen or twenty couples. And while she had cordial relationships with most of the wives, she never became close with any of them. It was only in her few relationships, independent of Harish, that she found true friends she was moderately close with, and except for Kalpana, the bookish housewife from Chennai she had met at a book club, they were all non-Indians—such as Cindy, a divorced paralegal who was her neighbor for years until she moved to Phoenix several months before; and Lily, a fabric designer and innkeeper of a bed and breakfast in western New Jersey, who had been in one of her art history courses at Rutgers. In the first few months, after leaving New Jersey, Naina had made an effort to keep in touch with this small group of people. But, gradually, the emails and phone calls became less and less frequent, and, after a while, they had whittled down to just a few times a year—birthdays and holiday greetings in the form of vibrantly colored, singing and dancing e-cards that, despite all their pomp and show, were frugal in their messages.

At least, she thought, walking fast to escape the sudden smell of the sewer, Karan hadn't brought up their house today. The house she had sold before moving in such a fit of desperation that she had not given much consideration to her son's feelings. Her muscles tensed up with guilt. She could see, with less obfuscation and more tenderness now, that Montcrest and the Indian families Karan grew up around were home for him, and home was something immobile and non-negotiable. The way he saw things, like his father and many in their circle, one, never, ever, turned one's back on one's home or one's roots. That was a sign of poor character, crowned by the one of the most glaring of failings—disloyalty.

He would never understand her point of view and that was her cross to bear. Her muscles tightened even more.

Naina knew Karan understood that the city might rejuvenate her, but she also realized that the rest of it confused him: the selling of the house, the rejection of old friends, and the "menial job." Of course, his disdain for her job should not have come as a surprise. When he and Amaya were teenagers, Harish had not wanted them to go and work at Dunkin' Donuts or sell newspapers during the summer like the American kids did. Spend your time studying or reading and not on some useless job, her husband would say.

Now, Naina regretted not contradicting his viewpoint.

A couple of months earlier, in a moment of anger, Karan had said to her, "Is Abhay Patel your rock star now? At least he did what he did at eighteen, Mom."

She had cowered at the implication. Abhay Patel, the son of a neighbor's cousin, had dropped out of high school, legally changed his name to Rick, married a white woman who lived in a trailer, and moved to Austin where he became a nurse's aide. She knew what Karan was saying. That a young kid who turned his back on his roots was bad, but at least it was more understandable. But a mother in her fifties, not to mention his own mother, doing the same was downright disgraceful. What was he to make of that?

It was awful of her to put Karan through this; he must have had to muster up excuses whenever his friends asked why his mother never went back to New Jersey. She sighed as the elbow of a roller skater jabbed her in the shoulder, the brief but forceful contact unusually feeling like an infringement. Although she and Karan were once one in her womb, they were now completely separate individuals, distinct yet forever deeply connected. Wasn't it all right for her to live her own life, no longer immersed in motherhood, in her own way? . . . Wasn't it? . . . But at what cost?

Naina arrived at Heaven, with its exposed brick walls and lots of candelabras. As soon as she took her first sip of the Casa Lapostelle Merlot, Alannah walked in. She saw Naina, and her expression changed from cheerful to concerned.

"What's up, honey?" Alannah asked in her loud, gravelly voice that always made people turn around and look at her. "Did some homeless guy steal your wallet in the subway or somethin'?"

Naina couldn't help grinning. Alannah had that effect on her. Around Alannah, the world seemed like a comical, absurd place.

In a low voice, Naina told her about her conversation with Karan, frequently darting a glance to the next table to check to see if anyone was listening.

"Well, that's just nuts," Alannah said, raising her voice in agitation. "What the hell is his problem? It's *your* life, honey, *your* life. Whether you hang out with a bunch of boring Indians in New Jersey or cool New Yorkers like *me*, is *your* problem, not his. How dare he make you feel bad about moving on with *your* life the way *you* want to? Gimme that phone. Let me give him a piece of my mind."

"It's not so simple, not so simple." Hearing someone else criticize her son perturbed her. "He's a very good boy. He's just . . . just . . . worried about me."

"Sounds to me like he's more worried about what his friends think."

"But doesn't he have a right to be? I'm his *mother*."

"*No way. It's your life. Yours. Not his. Yours. Mother or no mother.*"

Naina emitted a long, deep breath and took another big sip of her Merlot. Alannah's perspective, she knew, was very American. That a person's own wants should always take priority. It was a duty—almost like a religious calling. A calling she had been heeding since Harish's death. Hadn't she gone overboard?

As the evening progressed and the wine flowed, Naina's mood lightened and the conversation turned to Alannah's date with Josh. It had not gone well. Apparently, she had asked him, in an effort to make conversation, how overprescribed he thought psychiatric medications were these days, and he went on and on about how psychiatrists were nothing more than drug peddlers. He listed, in great detail, the side effects of Prozac, Zoloft, and Paxil, but insisted that Xanax was the most dangerous of all medications because of its highly addictive qualities.

"The gentleman doth protest too much," Naina said, giggling. "Sounds like he might be on some strong psychiatric drug himself."

"More like a cocktail of them."

Alannah vigorously shook her head. "Jeez, men are so nuts these days."

"Maybe he needed them to handle you, Miss Alannah. I might have needed a strong cocktail of drugs if I had to go out with you."

"Oh, stop your nonsense. I know I'm a ball breaker but I need someone who can deal with me, not someone who resorts to talking about or taking happy pills to hide."

"So you're not going to give the drug cocktail expert another chance then?"

"Are you nuts?"

"That's possible, but that's a separate matter . . . But people in medicine can be like that sometimes. You should have heard Harish. He could really go on about bowel movements. I don't think he had any sense of how disgusting he sounded."

"So just because you had to put up with a guy who could talk endlessly about shit doesn't mean I have to put up with a guy who goes on and on about bottled smiles."

Soon, they were cracking up.

"But, you've only met him twice," Naina said. "He sounds well-educated, well-behaved, and interested in art. C'mon, he's even heard of Kiki Smith."

"Only twice, honey? How many times did you meet Harish before you decided to marry him?"

"It's not like you have to make a decision to marry him soon . . . we met three times before getting engaged."

"So the dude must have made a pretty good impression, right?"

Naina laughed as she remembered that first meeting: the two of them, shy and embarrassed, sitting on her family's living room sofa surrounded by both sets of parents, exchanging just a few words with each other. She had asked him whether New Jersey was a big or medium-sized city, whether it was true that most Americans owned color televisions, and whether he liked the Beatles. To her delight, Harish had said he did like the Beatles, something she later discovered was only partly true.

He had asked her if she were afraid of sitting in an airplane for hours and looked pleased when she said no. She said she would very much like to be in the air for a long time. Then he had told her that while servants were not common in America, there were myriad household gadgets—vacuum cleaners, dishwashers, food processors, and this amazing device called the microwave oven that could heat up food in just a couple of minutes. Housework really wasn't as difficult as she might imagine. She had sensed a strain of kindness in his voice and that had moved her. When she decided to marry him, just a few days later, it was not because she had felt the sort of giddy love she was used to reading about—that was just not what most Indian girls of her generation expected or based their marital decisions on. Bollywood movies and Mills & Boons novels were filled with stories of rhapsodic love between two people starting out, but real marriages were not. *Marriage comes first, and then love* was an adage she had heard repeated like a chant throughout her life. And tragically, lamentably, dispiritingly, she had not fallen wildly in love with anyone by the time she turned twenty when her parents started introducing her to eligible bachelors.

She had chosen Harish because she felt marrying this seemingly considerate, handsome man whom she felt fairly attracted to was the best course for her. And probably the best option available. Maybe she would fall passionately in love with him? Oh, she had certainly hoped for that. It had been known to happen to others. But not often. Still, there was always a chance.

Also, Harish lived in a foreign country, adding a special allure for someone who had never left India in twenty-one years. And, very importantly, she had a sense he would leave her alone, leave her to swim in the sea of her own imaginings, making rapturous love to her fantasies. But she never told Alannah any of this, suspecting her friend would not understand and feeling too drained to explain.

"Oh, Harish made a terrible impression when we got married. Just awful. He ate with his mouth open, spewing out big grains of rice everywhere, didn't use any deodorant, couldn't even look at me in the eye, and drew a diagram of the digestive system for me."

"Oh, come on, you know I don't believe that." Alannah snorted. "So tell me, how exactly does this work? Do your parents decide for you or do you get to make your own choice about whom to marry from the bevy of men that you meet?"

"Well, I'll start at the beginning. Many Indian houses have a big painting of the elephant God Ganesh near the main door of the drawing room, what you call the living room here, and the eyes of Ganesh are made to slide from the back. So, when prospective grooms enter the house, they can slide the eyes and peep through the slits. They will see the prospective bride dressed in red with lots of gold jewelry, sitting coyly in the living room, and if any of the men like what they see then a meeting is arranged."

"Really? Jesus Christ! No way!" Alannah gasped and her lip-sticked mouth turned into a gigantic hole, like a ravenous, red-lipped batfish. A second later, she realized that Naina was joking.

Naina broke into a fit of laughter.

Alannah continued to press her about how arranged marriages worked and Naina decided that if she did not somewhat satisfy her friend's curiosity, she would not be left alone. So she gave Alannah an abbreviated summary of the arranged marriages in her family. Her grandparents had been just teenagers when they got married before ever seeing each other. But her parents had seen each other, just once before marriage, and if either had had a serious objection, it would have at least been heard by their parents. At least that was what she believed. Both she and her brother had met their spouses a few times before getting married and her brother even got to meet his wife-to-be alone at least seven or eight times before they agreed to get engaged. And yes, a woman, too, had the right to say no if she wanted to and she herself had rejected some men. Like the accountant Mahesh, because his gut looked like a big balloon she said, laughing at the memory.

"So you obviously never slept with Harish before you got married."

They were both on their third glass of wine. Alannah's curiosity became even thirstier and her rounded eyes were like vortexes in a sea, ready to suck in the juicy details of other people's lives.

"What was sex with him like?"

"Oh, come on, I'm not going to talk about that." Naina could feel color surge to her face and cause drizzling, dripping streaks.

"Why not? Why're you embarrassed? You're a woman about town in New York now. Soon enough, I'm sure you're going to be having sex again."

The very thought of revealing her naked body to any other man, allowing him to touch her breasts or enter her body seemed so foreign to Naina that she jerked her head back. "*What*?"

"Oh, don't *what* me, honey. You know it's going to happen at some point."

"My dear, do you know how old I am? I've just turned fifty-two. I've been through menopause. I don't think men are going to be interested in a post-menopausal widow when there are so many tempting twenty-two-year-olds parading themselves like ripe cherries ready to be picked."

"Yes, Grandma. You're fifty-two. And today, that's young. These days people are still kicking into their nineties. Gosh, there's this woman who lives above me . . . she must be in her sixties or something . . . she wakes me up at like seven every Saturday morning because she's making wild love to her white trashy boyfriend. So annoying. And you think fifty-two is old?"

For a moment, Naina tried to imagine her matronly, rotund mother at fifty-two having sex with her father, let alone another man, and could not picture it at all. By that age, pleasures of the flesh seemed so far in the past for her mother that to think of her having sex was as bizarre as thinking of a goat and a gorilla having a baby—even though her mother was a married woman and not one of those unfortunate widows of her mother's, or worse, her grandmother's generation for whom such pleasures were surely impossible.

Times had definitely changed, and she knew that some young widows were now remarrying. But she also knew that many widows were still ill-treated, both in India and the diaspora. Even now, some of those women, especially if they lived in conservative communities, were rebuffed at weddings because they were seen as harbingers of bad luck. And some were compelled still to strip their bodies and lives of all color and pleasure and don only white saris for the rest of their time on earth.

Of course, she was in a fortunate position and would probably never be subjected to such debasement, but she was well aware that Indians still tended to have an old-fashioned view of widowhood—particularly when it came to older widows. She instinctively understood that in the eyes of most Indians, the flames of a husband's pyre were assumed to extinguish a middle-aged wife's bodily desires.

Naina had no energy or inclination to get into all of this with Alannah. So she attempted to change the topic by talking about some Frida Kahlo paintings she had recently seen, but to no avail. Her friend insisted on prying into her sex life.

"Hmmm . . . you won't let that go, will you?" Naina put down her glass of wine as she wondered how to respond, looking up at the ceiling. "Harish was the first man and only man I've ever slept with. I have nothing to compare it with . . . In a way, he was even shyer than I am. He never looked at me . . . naked, you know." She stopped and covered her mouth as the realization of what she had just said permeated her with color. "What are you making me do? I've never talked about this to anyone . . ."

"We don't have to talk about it anymore if it's making you too uncomfortable," Alannah said, her tone gentler now.

Naina sighed softly, turned her head sideways and then looked at the walnut-colored hardwood floor. "We rarely . . . very rarely did anything during his last years . . . But most times, almost always even in the early years, I wanted him to look at my body, look into my eyes, only his eyes would be God knows where and he would just hurriedly touch me before doing the deed . . . And there were times when he just didn't or couldn't do it . . ."

Alannah put her arm around her. "You poor baby. I'm sorry, honey . . . I didn't mean to make you so uncomfortable."

Alannah quickly changed the topic to Amaya's boyfriend. Naina lit up and described Jai in full detail, the color and length of his hair, the scars on his face, his love of Gabriel García Márquez, his knowledge of South American wines.

"All right, enough, enough. You make this guy sound like God's gift to women. Listen, I've been around long enough to know that *no* man is God's gift to men." Alannah smiled, mischief brimming in her heart-shaped face. "Wow, you've spent a lot of time studying this guy. Are you sure you're not into him yourself?"

"Alannah! How could you suggest such a thing?" Naina felt incensed as she squeezed her eyes into tiny, curved gashes. "Amaya is my daughter and he is *her* boyfriend. Never ever suggest anything like that . . . *ever*, I mean *ever*, again. Do you understand me?"

CHAPTER EIGHT

NAINA AND JAI walked toward the fountain in middle of the plaza at Lincoln Center after watching the Film Society's showing of *Heat and Dust*; it was unusually quiet considering the number of events going on that night. They sat on the rim of the illuminated fountain and enjoyed the cool, starless June night. In front of them was the resplendent Metropolitan Opera House with its grand arches, chandeliers, and Marc Chagall murals. Jai looked up toward the somber sky. Naina, still feeling awkward being alone with him, couldn't think of what to say.

She was tingling with sparks of both apprehension and delight moving up and down her body; she eyed everything around her without focusing on anything in particular. He had been so chatty before. She didn't know what to do. Should she suggest they leave? Maybe he had had enough of her company and wanted to be alone or spend time with Amaya or someone else his own age?

She ended up saying nothing and folded her hands in her lap, gently tapping the plaza's cement with her heels and pretending to be absorbed in the surroundings, which were increasingly becoming fuzzy and faraway.

Naina had been thrilled to discover Merchant Ivory's *Heat and Dust*, one of her favorite films, was going to be playing at Lincoln Center. But none of her friends seemed to be free that Thursday night, and when she spoke to Amaya—who was out of town for a conference—her daughter suggested she ask Jai, who was also a fan of Merchant Ivory films.

Naina was surprised. Going out alone with her daughter's boyfriend? Again, she had felt currents of nervousness and excitement.

"Are you sure it's appropriate for us to go out alone?" Naina had said, her words choppy as a flurry of question marks interrupted the flow of her thoughts.

"Of course it is. I think you both know each other too well to be uncomfortable. Why? What's the matter?"

"Oh, nothing, nothing . . . well . . . maybe you can ask him if he would like to join me."

"Oh come on, you can ask him yourself. You are so comfortable around him. Why are you suddenly acting so shy? He's a very special person in my life and I'm really glad you guys get along so well . . . I'm extremely lucky that you are supportive of our relationship . . . I really don't know if Papa would have approved of someone half-Indian and so much older than me. Don't you think so?"

"I guess not," Naina mumbled as a discordant array of drumbeats dimly rumbled at the edge of her mind.

She had typed a short email to Jai, her fingers trembling the whole time. She told herself it was okay to go out alone with her daughter's boyfriend; times had changed and this kind of socializing was not inappropriate. Social norms were being reshaped all the time. In her day and most certainly in her mother's, even having a boyfriend would have been frowned upon. And now, at least among her Indian peers in America, dating was becoming more accepted —but there was a definite bias against dating and marrying non-Indians. A bias she did not share. She was a liberal, free-thinking soul. She and Jai had many common interests and were sort of like friends, so there was nothing wrong with them going out alone. Nothing at all. It wasn't like they were going on a date or anything.

The next morning, Naina had received a quick email from Jai, saying he would love to join her. She read and re-read the email several times, smiling to herself. And then forced her body, which felt so much heavier than her bubbling heart, to go the gym.

Naina paid special attention to her appearance the night of the film, using large amounts of age-defying concealer under her eyes and mouth, and changing the color of her lipstick three times before deciding a rich mauve looked the best. She wore boot-cut pants and a long-sleeved burgundy top with an elaborate geometric pattern. It had a generous V-neck and was fitted around her breasts before floating downwards. Somehow, she liked wearing burgundy around him—it made her feel rich and vibrant.

Jai was only the third man in her life she had ever gone out with alone besides Harish and male relatives. The first was Mario, a happily married Brazilian journalist whom she had got to know through her work at the nonprofit in New Jersey, and the second was Rob, the tabla player, who was, by now, like a younger brother.

She hadn't been able to concentrate on the film. She was acutely aware of Jai's presence, covering her skin as if it were a blanket of heavy dew. All perspective was obfuscated.

"*Heat and Dust*, I hate that title," Jai said, bursting the hush on the plaza. "Summing up India in those reductive words."

"Yes, I suppose you're right." She was glad the silent spell had been broken. "It's an excellent film though."

"Excellent? I find few films excellent. It's a very good film. In my opinion, of course."

"So which films do you find excellent?" Naina lifted her gaze to meet his eyes. Dark chocolate framed by long lashes. Then feeling bashful, she veered her eyes away from him.

The night was getting cooler and Naina had not brought anything warm. She was also getting hungry. But Jai continued to sit on the rim of the fountain, his legs spread slightly apart, his spine arched backward. Naina, who was sitting upright with her legs interlocked a few feet away from him, hoped her shivering wouldn't become obvious.

"Well, let me think . . ." Jai said. "*Blue Velvet* is definitely one of them."

"Aha, I see . . ." She had never seen or heard of the film. "What else?"

"I'd say *The French Lieutenant's Woman* and *Kramer vs. Kramer*."

"Yes, those are excellent films." She was relieved she had seen them and loved them too.

Jai turned his head toward a loud noise. Naina spotted a brown birthmark in the shape of a crescent moon close to the nape of his neck. It was so neatly and perfectly shaped it did not look like a birthmark, which were often blotchy. And it matched the chocolate color of his eyes. It was the most beautiful birthmark she had ever seen. Swirls of pleasure slow danced inside her, reaching down between her legs where they did backflips. She straightened her back and crossed her legs tighter.

After some time, Jai looked at Naina, his eyes appearing to soak in every detail of her face. He held her gaze for a number of seconds, taking Naina out of time, space, and place, plunging her into a zone where she felt something so sweet and strong, like a concentrated essential oil. For those few seconds—or was it a whole minute?—or more—the past and the future smashed into this one extravagant, tiny moment. For just that flash, she didn't care what happened next.

The sudden sound of birds chirping and screeching jolted her, making her jump. It was the sound of Jai's cellphone ringtone, a rather eerie sound. The exquisite moment splintered and the earth, with its myriad concerns, returned. Naina crossed and uncrossed her legs.

Jai glanced at his phone, said excuse me, and then got up to take the call. She felt an inexplicable anxiety and the chill in the air bothered her more. Who was he talking to? Why did he get up to take the call? Would he tell her who it was? What was *she* doing here with him?

Jai returned a couple of minutes later, his lips slanted to form a slight smile. Or was it a smirk? "Sorry about that."

He sat down next to Naina, a little closer than before, and again they sat in silence.

"It's a gorgeous night," Jai said finally. Once more, he looked up toward the blank, bleak sweep of the slate-colored sky. Still not a star in sight. "The temperature is perfect." Then he turned toward Naina, his eyes sweeping over her body. "You're not cold, are you?"

"No, no, I'm fine."

"How about sitting here for a little while then?"

"Uh . . . okay, all right, sure."

Naina shivered even more, hoping Jai would not notice.

A little while later, they heard a high-pitched bark from behind and saw a small, fuzzy brown dog wearing a ruffled pink dress with the words "Mommy Loves Me" embroidered in white on it.

Naina and Jai exchanged smiles, suppressing the urge to laugh as the dog owner, a short woman in neon pink tights and a white-and-pink top, matching the colors of the dog's outfit, was within earshot. The dog then decided to urinate, soiling the pink and white polka dot ruffles at the end of her dress, which covered half her bottom and her tail.

"Oh, Annabelle . . . I've told you so many times to be careful in dresses. *Careful. Careful.* Don't you know how expensive that is?"

The dog looked at her distressed owner while she was talking, and then turned to walk toward the Metropolitan Opera, tugging on her leash.

"No, Annabelle, no. Mommy says no. Your dress is soaked and we've got to get you home. We'll come back to the Opera another time. Now Mommy has to wash your dress before it gets ruined again. And no more pee-pee while you are wearing that."

As soon as the woman and the dog were out of sight, Jai and Naina burst into laughter, stripping away some of the weight of the somber night.

"Ah, the life of a dog in New York," Jai said. "Way better than anything I could ever have . . . If I'm ever to be born again, I want to be reborn as a cute little dog to a wealthy New York woman."

Naina laughed again, but careful not to laugh too loudly around Jai whose own laugh was more subdued. She unfolded her legs and turned slightly toward him.

"I recently read about a new dog spa in upstate New York where dogs can get conditioning milk baths, clay treatments, massages, and yoga classes," she said.

"No way!"

"It's true." She smiled and fiddled with the straps of her handbag. "It's called Shambala Holistic Wellness Center. Shambala is the Buddhist word for paradise, I think."

After some light-hearted banter, they returned to discussing *Heat and Dust*.

"Greta Sacchi is an effortless actress," Jai said. "She was such a convincing British madam looking for love in the arms of an Indian nawab. I wonder if that kind of thing happened a lot."

Strange sensations zigzagged through Naina, and she felt herself blushing. *Looking for love in the arms of an Indian nawab.* His words repeated in her mind, his voice like a caress. Once more, she could feel him on her skin, like a drape of dew, as he sat barely a foot away from her.

Inattentively, Naina looked toward the Marc Chagall paintings at the Metropolitan Opera, struggling to find the right words. "I don't know if it happened a lot. Maybe it did. Perhaps it did . . . For madams stuck with boring British husbands and stuffy colonists, I'm sure an Indian prince must have seemed quite exotic." She brushed her cheek with her ruby-tipped fingers. "You know, I thought it was interesting what Harry . . . he's such a delightful character . . . was saying about women in the 1920s being ready to risk everything for love." Her voice faintly quivered.

Naina swiveled her head toward Jai and saw that bantering upward tilt of his lips that instantly put her at ease.

"You are a hardcore romantic, aren't you, Naina?"

"A hardcore romantic?" She smiled and touched her hair. "How can a person be a hardcore romantic? Isn't that an oxymoron?"

Jai grinned brightly. His scars shone under the fountain's white light, as did his rust-colored shirt He looked extremely handsome.

"These days, being a romantic seems so passé," Naina said, looking toward the New York City Ballet theater.

"Not for you."

She quickly turned to face him. "I guess not for old-fashioned me, right?"

"Come on now . . . actually, it's kind of charming in our times."

"You mean charming like vintage clothing and homemade quilts?"

A FEW WEEKS later, Jai and Naina met up—again alone. An acquaintance whom Naina knew through the gallery had cancelled on her at the last minute, leaving her with an extra ticket for Oscar Wilde's *An Ideal Husband*; she had frantically called everyone she knew to see who might want to join her. But she only got voicemails. Amaya was the only one who returned Naina's call, saying she had to work late.

"Should . . . should . . . I ask . . . Jai?" Naina said.

"Of course," Amaya replied.

Jai did not answer his phone when Naina called, and when she got his voicemail, she found herself dithering and did not leave a message. But she tried him again about an hour later, surprised he picked up.

"Oh, hi, Naina," Jai said quickly, as if he were in the middle of something. "Is everything okay?"

"Hi, Jai . . . I'm . . . I'm so . . . sor . . . sorry to bother you . . . Are you busy?"

"Kind of. What's up?"

She bit her lip. She should have never called.

"I'm sure you're busy but I thought . . . I thought . . . I'd ask anyway. *An Ideal Husband* is playing tonight at the Cherub Theater on the Upper West Side. It's a small theater just a few blocks from you . . . I . . . was wondering if you wanted to go." She quickly exhaled. Finally, the words were out.

"Tonight?"

"Yes . . . I know it's last minute and I'm really sorry about asking you so late . . . But one of my friends dropped out and I have an extra ticket . . . it's . . . it's perfectly okay if you can't come . . . it really is . . . but you mentioned you liked Oscar Wilde and . . ."

"So I'm an afterthought?"

"No, of course not, of course not . . ."

"Hey, I'm not sure about tonight . . . Is Amaya coming?"

"No . . . she's going to be working until at least eight-thirty or nine. I already asked her."

Suddenly, Naina felt terribly embarrassed. He wanted to be with Amaya. He wouldn't want to go out with her again. Why was she calling her daughter's boyfriend? What was she thinking? But they were sort of like friends. Weren't they?

"Well, I'm not sure if I can make it . . . Do you have anyone else to go with?"

"No, but I'll be fine . . . it's okay . . . it's perfectly, really okay . . . please don't worry about it."

Naina could taste grapefruit juice on her tongue, so sour was her mortification.

"Well, let me see if I can get out of a meeting. I do like Oscar Wilde. I'll call you and let you know within an hour."

"DO YOU KNOW, I am quite looking forward to meeting your clever husband, Lady Chiltern?" Mrs. Cheveley said, played by a young sporty-looking girl who walked as if she were wearing heels for the first time in her life. She moved her fan in strong, jerky motions and spoke with a thick Boston accent, the sound of her broad A's prominent. Certainly, a far cry from the charming, sophisticated femme fatale she was supposed to be. "Since he has been at the Foreign Office, he has been so much talked of in Vienna. They actually succeed in spelling his name right in the newspapers. That in itself is fame, on the continent."

I hardly think there will be much in common between you and my husband, Mrs. Cheveley," Mrs. Chiltern said, played by a short, nervous-looking girl who came across like a bewildered teenager rather than the moralistic champion of women's rights portrayed by Wilde. Her Southern drawl sounded more friendly than hostile.

Naina squirmed in her seat, resisting the urge to bury her hands in her face. The play, despite being in a small, little-known theater, had got good reviews. But it turned out to be an amateur production with actors who seemed like students or recent graduates. Her muscles were shrinking and tightening into wooden sticks. Oh, dear God, no! Not this! Jai must be so irritated with her. She had wasted his time. He probably thought she was an idiot. What to do now?

After discreetly reaching her hand toward his and withdrawing it a few times, Naina finally tapped Jai's wrist and whispered, "I'm so . . . sorry, I had no idea the play would be so terrible . . . Do you want to leave?"

"No. I think it's totally hilarious . . . Are you okay?"

"Yes, yes, I'm fine. As long as you're okay." She would have gladly walked out but did not let on.

Throughout the play, Naina touched her face, crossed and uncrossed her arms and legs, and darted discreet looks at Jai. Sometimes he seemed amused, sometimes distracted, sometimes irritated, and sometimes he leaned toward Naina and exchanged raised-eyebrow glances with her. And sometimes, he peered at his phone.

When they stepped out, Naina kept apologizing and he kept telling her not to worry about it. The play, in all its absurdity, had been hugely entertaining.

Naina was ravenous but could not bring herself to mention dinner. Inviting him to the play seemed more than enough.

Fortunately, he brought it up. He asked her if she was in the mood for Thai and she enthusiastically agreed—notwithstanding it was the last thing she wanted because she had had her fill of it over the past two weeks.

"Do you have a favorite line from *The Ideal Husband*?" Naina asked, squished in the corner of a brightly lit restaurant called Tasty Siam.

"No. I can't say I know the play that well . . . But I have a feeling you do." Jai looked at her with that mischievous tilt of the lips, which made him seem much younger and made her feel relaxed.

Naina briefly met his eyes and smiled.

"C'mon, what is it? Pray tell."

"I've been a fan of Oscar Wilde for a long time. Since I was a young girl." She studied her soup, a medley of vegetables, half-singed and drowning in a spicy broth. It was too hot for her to eat.

She could smell Jai again, the cool, invigorating scent of the mountains. Of pine cones and whispering woods. Of sweet peaches and apricots in the Himalayas. Her entire body was in a heightened state and her nipples had turned into hard dots.

"So you must have a favorite line then?"

Naina coyly pursed her lips. "I can resist anything except temptation."

Jai laughed. It was uncanny how many years he shed when he laughed. Those perfectly set white teeth shone and the scars receded from his face. Still, his laugh, always at low volume, seemed to permeate only a part of his heart and soul.

"I, too, can resist everything except temptation."

Naina's face burned and her heart beat faster. The crimson glimmers between her legs were doing an agitated dance. She quickly excused herself to go and make a phone call. As she stepped outside, she saw a couple kissing on the sidewalk. Her nipples were even harder and there was a wetness between her legs. How was she going to go through the rest of the evening? She inhaled sharply and closed her eyes.

She could hear one side of her brain, the barbed, bellowing side that judged her. It was her mother's dictatorial voice and it was spewing fire and hurling names at her. *How could any decent woman let her body react like a whore? Did she have no decency left? She had to stop this. Stop this right now. Before she got two slaps. No, not two, not three. Ten slaps.*

Naina cowered. Her muscles squeezed, making her feel small and scared, and the excitement in her body abated. She couldn't go back inside, not just yet. To distract herself, she decided to pay her mobile phone bill early. A few minutes later, she walked back into the restaurant, determined to carry on the evening properly.

"What happened to you?" Jai asked.

"Nothing, nothing," Naina mumbled as she looked down, her lips quivering, her fingers fiddling with the straps of her bag. "I just had to make a phone call . . . To an artist."

"Are you all right?"

She could barely tolerate the directness of his gaze anymore. It was as if he saw right through her, even the parts she could not see. Did he see something inappropriate? The thought made her nerves jump like a monkey hastily leaping from tree to tree.

"Is there something . . . ?"

"No, nothing, there's nothing, there's nothing," she said, with both force and nervousness.

"Relax, Naina, I was just going to ask you if something was bothering you, but you didn't even let me finish my question."

The waiter came by to take drink orders, and Naina ordered a strong cocktail. A wine would not do tonight. Again, she heard her mother's voice bellowing at her. *Behave properly. Like a good girl. From a decent family. Not like one of those whores Mrs. Thadani's raising.*

The manager of the restaurant came by and gave them each a card. "This is for you." He flashed a wide, saccharine smile that, one could tell, came as naturally to him as breathing. "Enjoy. It's for special customers."

"For special customers?" Jai said. "I wonder what makes us so special."

Naina did not say anything. She was relieved the card provided a distraction. "SPECIAL LIMITED TIME GIFT," the card shouted, a bright purple piece of paper with rainbow-colored lettering. It was a coupon offering twenty-five dollars off a Thai massage at a new place called Die Orchidee Wellness Spa.

She opened her bag to put the card in to throw away later when Jai chuckled. What was so funny?

"You're probably wondering why I'm laughing."

The cocktail was sweet and strong. Her lips trembled less and she tapped her feet on the floor slower.

"This coupon brings back such a funny memory. *Die Orchidee* means the orchid in German. Remember I told you that I'd spent a year in France in college?"

Remember? How could she forget?

Leaning in a couple of inches closer to Naina, Jai said during that year, he had made friends with Stefan, a German student who was living in Paris because his father was a diplomat. One time, his maternal grandmother came to visit them from Germany. Stefan had often told funny stories about how his grandmother, who had been proper and tight-lipped, had become rude and oddly extroverted as old age and mild dementia set in.

Stefan invited Jai to his mother's fiftieth birthday party and Jai took a bottle of champagne for Stefan's mother, and when he met her, an elegant diplomat's wife who spoke English well, he presented the bottle to her, saying, "Happy birthday, Mrs. Schmidt, here is a little gift for you."

"And then, all of a sudden, I saw a woman who I knew had to have been the grandmother. She was pulling her daughter, Mrs. Schmidt, to her side, yanking the champagne away from her, and screaming and pointing to me," Jai said in that distinct narrative voice of his, curving up and down, up and down, transporting Naina out of the tacky, brightly lit restaurant, out of her quivering body, out of the spiraling storms in her head.

"'Polizei! Polizei,' the grandmother yelled, 'get this man out of here, out, out, now, now.'" Jai, his elbows on the table, gesticulated moderately and with a great deal of control as he usually did. "'He wants to kill my daughter. Kill, kill, you hear me?' I was so terrified and embarrassed that I just stood rooted to the spot. Everybody at this elegant party stopped and stared at me, but nobody moved or said anything. Then Stefan, who could be quite the class clown at times, started to laugh."

Naina, fully immersed in the cadences of Jai's voice and his story, imagined a young Jai dressed in a gray pinstriped blazer and fitted black slacks, with some sort of neutral-colored European-man scarf looped around his neck, turning beetroot with mortification—the opposite of the picture of confidence he was today. She felt a lump of tenderness.

"Stefan shouted, 'Everybody, everybody,' and he was holding his grandmother and hugging her . . . she looked like a mad hen with rainbow-colored, disheveled hair . . . 'there's been a big confusion,' he said. 'My friend is not trying to poison my mother . . . gift in English means a present, *Geschenk*. Not *Gift*, poison.'"

Naina broke into giggles, more loudly than she meant to. "That's a great story. I'll be sure never to use the word 'gift' if I'm ever in Germany." The air lightened and flitted around her body. "You really are a good storyteller. Have you ever thought of writing fiction?"

"Oh you flatter me, madam." His dark, amber-colored irises shimmered ever-so-imperceptibly.

After Naina ordered her second cocktail (her last one, she told herself), Jai asked about her family and she talked about them in detail. It distracted her from the way she was feeling and she was pleased he was interested.

She told him, growing up, she mostly spoke English in school, with her friends, and her father. But with her mother it was generally Hindi or Hinglish, a combination of Hindi and English. Her father, who retired as a senior officer in the Indian Railways, generally spoke in Hindi and Punjabi to his wife, sisters, mothers, the domestic help, and the non-English speaking lower ranks of the Indian Railways. She recalled her mother, who spoke good but not excellent English, always knew her husband was upset with her when he spoke to her in English. "Don't be unreasonable," he would always tell her.

As Jai asked questions, his attention to her answers felt like a blazing meteor directed at her, and only her.

And when her mother was angry with her, she would always chastise her in Hindi, and then somehow fit in the phrase "foolish girl." Even in the last conversation they had before she died eight years earlier, she had called Naina a "foolish girl."

Jai laughed. "Foolish girl. That sounds like a good way to make your daughter feel young."

"I didn't need to hear that to feel young," Naina said, annoyed. Did he think she should feel old?

"I'm sure you didn't. I didn't say it right. What I meant to say is that's a way to make your daughter feel like a little kid."

"I had Amaya when I was very young, Jai," Naina said in a low voice filled with unusual familiarity. She flicked her hair to the left. "I'm not that much older than you, you know."

"Not much older, but definitely more youthful. I wish I always felt youthful . . . New York is a stressful city; it can age you quickly."

"You think so?" Naina felt just the opposite; that New York could make you always feel young, but somehow she didn't want to say it.

Soon, Jai asked more questions about her family and wanted to know if they had been affected by the division of India into India and Pakistan, a subject he was very interested in. Naina was glad. Age was a topic she did not want to discuss with him, and few people had shown such interest in her family's story.

Both her parents, Hindu Punjabis, were born in Lahore, she told him. Her maternal grandfather was a prosperous cloth merchant in Lahore while her paternal grandfather was a reasonably well-off bookseller. But like so many other Hindus, they fled Lahore for Delhi during the partition of India and Pakistan in 1947. Her mother's family lost a lot, grieving for the good old days of Lahore until the end of their lives—despite the fact that her grandfather was able to establish himself as a respectable cloth merchant in Delhi. Her father's family was more fortunate. Although they lost their business, unlike her mother's family, they were able to transfer assets like money and jewelry to India, and her paternal grandfather quickly set up a store selling school and college textbooks.

Naina noticed his hands once more as he ate, those slender fingers and compact palms. A charge shot through her own hands, making them tremble, and she had to be very careful not to spill any food. Again, she could hear her mother's clarion voice. *Behave yourself, you stupid girl. Always with dignity. When you behave badly, you don't just disgrace yourself. You disgrace your entire family.*

"So, what was your mother like?"

"My mother was like a lioness." She stopped and took a deep breath. "She was very strict and very no-nonsense. She was the self-appointed guardian of the neighborhood's morals, the critic-in-chief, as my father would call her." Naina sniggered. "She was always right. Always. My father could never overrule her. But he was not interested in overruling her anyway. He was a gentle soul and often lived in a world of his own."

She looked across the restaurant. "His heroes were Jawaharlal Nehru and Mahatma Gandhi and he was proudly nationalistic. You know, he was the kind of man who would rather die than accept a bribe. My father's idealism and my mother's extreme pragmatism was always a source of friction between them."

Images of her father—a tall and thin man with a melancholy expression, sitting alone in the back veranda, spending long hours next to the radio or the big gramophone record player—came to her, bringing with them nameless, shapeless feelings. She wished she had known him better, she said to Jai, who leaned forward and rested one elbow on the table. Her father used to love sentimental Hindi songs and Urdu ghazals and she could picture him slouched on a cane chair, listening to the famous romantic Hindi film song, "Chaudvin Ka Chand" (A Full Moon). *Chaudvin Ka Chand Ho Ya Aftab Ho, Jo Bhi Ho Tum Khuda Ki Kasam Lajawab Ho* (You might be the full moon or the sun, but whatever you are, you, I swear by God, are amazing)

"You know, when he died, after a long illness, fifteen years ago, the radio had been on."

"I'm so sorry for your loss, Naina," Jai said in a low, slow voice. He placed his hand on the table, inches away from hers. "It seems you had very tender feelings toward him and maybe even saw him as a kindred spirit."

Naina nodded. She felt as if Jai understood the import of everything she was saying, knew the thoughts that were compressed into words, and words for the gaps where there were no words. Sweet feelings of gratification slowly mingled with the bittersweet emotions about her father. They sat in silence until the waiter came to ask a question, dispersing the moment.

Naina heard a drumbeat, a powerful drumbeat, pulling her further out of her dreamlike state like an alarm clock. It took her more than a few seconds to register that it was Jai's phone ringing. He had switched the ringtone from the sound of birds chirping and screeching to another jolting sound.

"Hi, sweetheart. How did it go today?" Jai listened for a bit. "Cool. I'm with your mom and listening to stories about your family. Fascinating."

So it was Amaya. Naina looked down at her napkin, a crumpled piece of beige paper with patches of dried-up soup that looked like leprosy.

"I'm sorry, sweetheart. I can't meet you now. It's late and we're just finishing up with dinner . . . I've got an early start tomorrow."

So they weren't going to meet tonight. Naina looked up and then toward a big, beautiful bronze statue of Buddha. It wasn't that late, just a little after ten-thirty. And Jai didn't look that tired. And Amaya couldn't have been more than fifteen or twenty blocks way. Wouldn't a man in love be keen to see his sweetheart whom he hadn't seen for a few days? It was definitely peculiar. Her heart expanded at the thought. And then withered as disconcerting, discombobulating feelings circled around like ominous birds in the subterranean regions of her mind, the process of expansion and contraction repeating itself again and again.

"So that was Amaya as you probably figured out," he said. "She's going out for drinks with some colleagues, but I've got an early start so I don't think I'll be joining them because I know I won't be in bed until well after midnight, if I did."

"Umm . . . are you sure? It's okay if you want to leave . . . I'm sure you want to see Amaya. You must be longing to see her."

"I'm certain. They have excellent desserts here. Especially green tea ice cream. Should we have a look at the dessert menu?"

"Umm . . . okay."

Naina went into the restroom to refresh her perfume. When she returned, thankfully, her half-eaten meal had been taken away.

CHAPTER NINE

NAINA DID NOT see Jai for several weeks. Jai had invited her to a concert, but she declined. Her physical reaction to him had grabbed her by the neck and shaken her more than ever before, and guilt and shame kept splattering away in the underbelly of her mind. She felt her self-portrait—a good mother, a decent person, a moral woman—crumbling, and she continuously fabricated fictions, justifications, and denials, but each one was flimsier than the other, and unable able to bind the picture of herself she held so dear.

Earlier, Naina had tried hard to play down her feelings for Jai, that they were nothing but a deep admiration for him, but now she told herself all sorts of other things . . . Jai was an attractive, interesting man—it would be natural for any woman to feel drawn to him. Just like women felt drawn to famous actors or authors. Since Jai was so much like her, of course . . . of course she felt a great affinity for him. Like her, Jai was someone whose passions were scarlet, which had been muted to a modest pink. Like her, he liked Beethoven, Ella Fitzgerald, Philip Glass, Zakir Hussain, and Cesária Évora. Like her, he liked Gabriel García Márquez, Salman Rushdie, Tennessee Williams, Naguib Mahfouz, and even Emily Brontë. Like her, he enjoyed witty British dramas and a good masala chai. Like her, he loved Frida Kahlo. In fact, he was more like her than any other person she had ever known and she imagined that they were made of the same material—a rich terracotta clay.

It was an affinity, a form of kinship, not love or infatuation or anything like that.

She had had such a sexually unfulfilling marriage, so being around an attractive man sometimes excited her. Unfortunately, wretchedly, dreadfully, that man was her daughter's boyfriend. Still, weren't human beings wired to feel desire? Wouldn't she also be aroused if Hugh Grant or Pierce Brosnan or Zakir Hussain were near her? It was not important who the handsome man was, she told herself, pushing aside the absurdity of her words.

Naina surmised that Jai, even though he seemed to like to go out alone with her, appeared to listen to whatever she was saying as if it was the most important thing in the world, likely saw her as a friend with common interests. Maybe even as a kindred soul.

There was nothing untoward in either of their feelings. Amaya was fortunate to have found such a wonderful man and Naina, as a proper mother, would support her relationship and find joy in her daughter's happiness.

IT WAS A Sunday afternoon in New York and everyone was having brunch outside. Bare backs and shorts were spilling out onto the sidewalks. Men and women were leisurely downing mimosas and coffee, and tempers were flying as people got impatient after waiting for hours to get seated. Even though it was late September, the day felt like summer if it weren't for the fall colors and the crackling rugs of leaves on the ground.

Amaya and Naina had just finished brunch at Plaisirs Negligente, a fancy French cafe on 25th Street and Fifth Avenue, and planned to go shopping. Normally, Naina did not take Amaya to such expensive places or go to them herself, but she said it was a special indulgence for a special daughter. She also told Amaya she would buy her anything she wanted that day. It was her treat.

After buying a couple of black sweaters at Zara (Naina had wanted Amaya to buy one black sweater with a colorful pattern on the chest and cuffs, but Amaya insisted on a plain polo neck), they looked at Anthropologie's window display. Naina pointed to a boho patchwork skirt, telling Amaya she should try it on. Amaya puckered her face in disgust.

"So, I want to buy a birthday present for Jai," Amaya said, looking subtly chic in a black-and-white shift dress that flattered her tall, slim body, a twisted silver necklace, and a high ponytail. "Any ideas?"

"Let's see. Hmmm . . . how about a cologne?"

"A cologne?" Amaya arched her eyebrows and swiveled her eyes in that condescending way that Naina couldn't stand—as if her mother were a trifling child unaware of the ways of the world. "That's so clichéd."

"Well, you know him best," Naina said, hearing herself sounding almost petulant. "I'm sure you'll be able to figure out what's best to buy him."

"Oh, come on. Are you really offended? You're a friend of his, you know him well, and I need your help with this."

Naina pushed away the muddled bubble of feelings that suddenly arose in her. "What about a lamp? I saw some interesting ones in a store on the Lower East Side."

"That's a good idea. But Jai has a lot of lamps in his apartment. And in his bedroom is my favorite. A blue-and-white Chinese porcelain ginger jar transformed into a lamp. It's vintage and has this soft, atmospheric light that I just love."

Naina was quiet as the thought of Amaya in Jai's bedroom, him kissing her bow-shaped lips, and his long, tapered fingers caressing her body, pinched her, making her insides squirm like worms in distress. She turned her gaze toward the traffic and watched a speeding bicyclist with a red helmet impudently going through the red lights. He moved faster than any of the big vehicles and turned into a kinetic blur.

"Mom, where are you?" Amaya teasingly asked, waving her hand. "Lost in some fantasy world again?"

"Oh no. I was just looking at that cyclist going so fast. As if he were the only one on the road. He could get killed doing that . . . It's amazing the risks people take."

"Foolish and dangerous. Not only could he kill himself but others as well."

As they walked around the Flatiron District, vivid, stubborn images of Jai and Amaya kept jabbing at Naina's thoughts. Jai pulling the rubber band off Amaya's hair, him burying his face in her cleavage, his scars leaving an imprint on her body. Her kissing the crescent moon-shaped birthmark close to the nape of his neck, her running her fingers through the small of his back.

Naina's mother's voice bellowed at her. *Stop dreaming. Come back down to earth. Don't be foolish like your father.*

Her breath suspended, Naina lifted her chin, squared her shoulders, and took long, straight steps. She was not attracted to him, she told herself for the umpteenth time. Naina walked briskly to keep pace with Amaya and the pictures in her head started losing color and shape. She talked to Amaya about the awful dress the girl walking in front of them was wearing and then the conversation turned to a new Ethiopian restaurant that had opened in Amaya's neighborhood, and then to the terrible traffic in New York. Briefly, Naina felt nostalgic about the relatively empty, traffic-free streets of New Jersey and Amaya recalled, with a laugh, how long it took to get anywhere in New Jersey when her mother was driving.

"I have an idea for Jai's present," Naina said, as they exited a bakery after indulging in mini chocolate cupcakes. "Maybe not very original, but I think they look great on men. How about a tie?"

"A tie? Hmmm." Amaya wrinkled her forehead, placed her palm on her cheek, and pursed her lips like she normally did when she was thinking. "It's not a bad idea. It actually might even be a good one. Where do you think we can find a good one?"

"Salvatore Ferragamo, they have great ties."

"A Ferragamo tie?" Amaya asked incredulously. "Now what makes you think I can afford *that*?"

"Don't worry about that. Let's go have a look."

"If you say so." Amaya threw her hands up in resignation.

They reached the Ferragamo store, and Naina stood in front of the window display, her eyes fixated on the rust tie with butterflies, dragonflies, and ladybugs flying over it on the odd, elongated male mannequin dressed in a gray suit.

"This is perfect for Jai." Naina pointed to the tie.

Amaya's eyes widened as she raised her eyebrows. "*What?*"

"It's gorgeous. It will look so good with a black suit. I recently saw something similar on a guy at an opening and it looked great."

Amaya sighed and shook her head. "Mom, I have no idea what's got into you. This is so not his type. Secondly, I can't afford it. He's a professor, for crying out loud. Not one of your artsy guys at those openings."

"But, Amaya, he has an artsy look about him and this will so flatter his skin tone. Plus the tie has a sense of humor."

"Mom, Jai doesn't look artsy. I don't know what you're seeing."

"I'm seeing just fine, Amaya. I think he does . . . He could."

"Anything else? There's no way I'm spending a dime to buy that buffoonish tie."

"Let's go in at least," Naina said, holding Amaya's hand. "Maybe we'll find something else. They have women's clothes too."

Naina led her daughter downstairs to the women's section where she headed straight for the perfumes.

"You've got to try this, Amaya," Naina said, after she sniffed a perfume from a strip. "I think it has some jasmine in it."

"God, it's awful." Amaya scrunched up her nose. "So floral and strong."

"It's beautiful. And it smells so nice on you."

"There's no way I'm wearing that perfume."

"But you hardly wear any perfume except for some occasional Issey Miyake, which hardly has any scent." Naina sprayed the perfume on her own wrist.

"I'm not a big fan of perfume. You know that. So when I wear something, I wear something light."

"But a powerful scent keeps a man attracted to a woman. Haven't you heard about pheromones? I'm sure Jai will love this perfume."

"And what would you know about pheromones and what keeps a man attracted? You had an arranged marriage and you've never been with anyone else except Dad."

Naina felt her facial muscles stiffening as she looked at Amaya. "What do you know about what I know? You're talking like I had an arranged marriage where I married some old, ugly man I had never met before in some remote village. And you very well know that was not the case. We met a few times before we got married. And I could have easily rejected him if I had wanted to. Easily." She raised her head. "There were many men who wanted to marry me. But I rejected them."

"All right." Amaya shook her head. "I didn't mean to say you didn't know anything. I believe many men wanted to marry you, but there's no need to be so pompous about it."

"Did you know that your father loved Chanel No. 5 on me?" She heard her voice arching into a smug, diva-like tilt. "People who have arranged marriages are human beings just like everyone else, you know. They also have to keep their partners attracted to them just like everybody else."

Not entirely true, but it was also not entirely untrue. Naina went to find a restroom, still feeling the sting from Amaya's words. Yes, it was true that commitment and loyalty generally outweighed physical attraction in an arranged marriage, and people often had sex and stayed together regardless of whether they felt a strong desire for each other or not. But there were those who felt their hearts flutter for each other for years and years, much longer than the average American couple. Like Sushil and Rachita in Montcrest. And there were those who yearned for something else or were repulsed by their partners and sought pleasure elsewhere. She, of course, would never have done something like that. She wasn't *that* type of woman.

And in contrast with her parents' generation, more Indians today were making an effort to make themselves attractive to their spouses—wearing special fragrances, working out, dressing in a way the other liked, and buying elaborate Valentine Day presents.

But Harish had never bought her a Valentine's Day present. Naina carefully reapplied her mauve lip liner. That had bothered her during the early years of their marriage. On their anniversary and her birthday though, he always bought her a box of Godiva chocolates. The same thing year after year.

Naina walked out of the restroom and found Amaya texting. She decided to test more perfumes. Almost half-an-hour later, Naina held up a blue bottle called Incanto Charms, the first fragrance she had liked, but the one that Amaya had hated.

"Well, if you aren't going to buy it, I think I will," Naina declared.

In the tie section, Naina lobbied again for the rust one with the flying insects. She again offered to pay the two hundred dollars for it, but Amaya would not listen, saying, for the umpteenth time, it was not Jai's style.

"But it will look so great on him. A black suit and this tie—it will look exceptional."

"I know you're an Indian mother and are keen for me to get married and all that, but I don't have to get him such an expensive present you know."

"I'm *not* pushing you to get married, Amaya. I'm *not* one of those Indian mothers. You should know better than that. All I'm saying is that this would look good on Jai." Naina shrugged her tense shoulders. "But if you don't agree, that's fine. It's your boyfriend, your life."

"That's right."

Naina then looked at a purple tie with tiny black bee-like shapes. How about this? Do you like it?"

Amaya audibly exhaled. "It's not bad." She looked at it again. "Well, those shapes are kind of cute."

"Okay then." Naina picked it up. "I'm buying it for you and you can give it to Jai. But don't tell him I paid for it. Darling, you won't regret it, I promise."

When they stepped out of the store, the sun was setting in a semicircle blaze between two buildings, its voluptuous shape and golden apricot hue infusing a feminine aura to the masculine linearity of the tall, neutral-colored structures of Manhattan. They stared wordlessly in admiration, as they always did with sunrises and sunsets. Both found these times magical.

"The earrings Jai bought me were so beautiful," Amaya said as they headed toward Union Square Park. "They were teardrop-shaped rubies . . . what do you call them . . . cabochons . . . and they were in the back of the store, hidden under hundreds of pearl necklaces and he spotted them. Not too expensive or anything . . . well nothing is too expensive in those stores in Cold Springs, but stunning."

"Oh, wow! Wow . . . I'd love to see them. Do you have them with you?"

"No, I don't have them. Why would I carry them around? What a strange question. I'll show you the next time you come over. But I think you'll like them. Jai does have good taste."

"I have no doubt about that . . . Has he ever made you wear them?"

Amaya shot Naina a curious glance. "That's an even stranger question. He put them on me at the store."

"Which ear did he do first?"

Amaya looked really baffled. "Do you think I remember? And what does it matter?"

Amaya was quiet for a few seconds, and then stopped and looked at Naina with narrowed eyes and a furrowed forehead. Her daughter's eyes seemed ominously piercing. Like those of a seer, like those of someone who could see through shadows, strip away the camouflage, and crack open chimeras. Naina wanted to turn into an invisible being and run past the tall buildings, past the clusters of people everywhere, past the lights and the noises to some far-flung place beyond the horizon. But she just stood there, looking down with a trembling mouth and fingers toying with the sculptural wire necklace she had got at the MoMA.

"You know, I've never seen you take such an interest in anyone I've dated before." Amaya's voice was heavy with an unexpected gravity, her eyes still probing. "Not that I've dated much, but still. Now, you want to know where we go for dinner each time, whether it was a candlelight dinner, whether I wore red or bronze lipstick, whether he wore cologne, whether he prefers to see me in dresses or pants, whether he likes my hair tied up or loose, whether we held hands on the subway of all places, for Pete's sake, whether the moon was out when we went for a walk, and God knows what else. What's this about?"

Amaya's words stung, and Naina flinched. What did Amaya suspect? Naina's anxiety spiraled and spiraled and spiraled. Her heart raced; she blinked nonstop; and her hands were clammy as she frenetically fingered the straps of her handbag.

"Now what? Now which nervous land has your mind gone to? And why do you always keep fidgeting with those straps?"

"Nowhere, nowhere, nowhere," Naina replied, forcing a smile, trying to catch the words scattered in her head to form a sentence. "When I was a young girl, when I was a young girl . . ." She closed her eyes and sighed. "When I was a young girl, nobody took an interest in my relationships."

"*You* had relationships?" Amaya asked.

A bolt of anger shot through Naina. "Yes, I, I . . . your ancient, backward mother . . . had relationships. Hundreds. Thousands."

Amaya stared at her, looking exasperatingly bewildered.

"You . . . you know I'm just kidding," Naina said softly, regretting her words, and looping and unlooping the ends of her hair with her forefinger. "What I was saying was . . ." She had to stop her heart from racing, quiet the thoughts in her head that were flapping like clothes drying in the wind, and gather her scrabbled mind. She had to.

"What I was saying was that . . . I was trying to say that when I was young nobody took an interest in what kind of relationship would be right for me, what kind of marriage would make me happy, beyond the usual arranged marriage criteria of decent family and decent job . . . and after I got married . . . nobody ever gave me any guidance or advice or took any interest in my relationship."

Naina stroked the side of her neck, a gesture she would only later learn was something humans did to soothe themselves. "I really want you to be happy in your relationship," she said in a steadier voice. "If I'm a little too inquisitive, I'm sorry about that. I think, I really think, you're with a wonderful man and I just want to make sure I'm there, taking an interest, guiding you. I just want to make sure everything goes smoothly . . . beautifully, perfectly . . ."

"Oh, Mom." Amaya's features and voice softened, and she looked like her little girl again. "You're so sweet to care so much. But can anything in life, let alone relationships, go perfectly?"

"I hope so . . ."

"You are such a dreamer . . ."

They went and sat on a bench in Union Square Park, under the wide branches of a tall tree, near an old lady in a prairie-style dress singing a Norah Jones ballad, the lazy, sultry tune punctuated with the raucous, animated sounds of Mandarin spoken by a large group of tourists.

Amaya looked up at the twilight sky, placing her palm on the left side of her face and squeezing her lips. "I can't help but wonder if you're living vicariously through me because you didn't have the opportunity to date," she said, her tone contemplative.

Again, Naina felt a jolt of fury. She dug her fingernails into her palms. She wanted to say it was presumptive and arrogant of Amaya to think her life was *that* exciting. She had lived through things her daughter never had, and if she wanted to live vicariously through someone, there were so many people in the world, both in fiction and real life, who had far richer lives than Amaya's.

Instead, she swallowed forcefully, hoping to push down the chili peppers of indignation in her mouth.

Then Naina just looked at her daughter, at her oval face with the chubbiness in her cheeks that had not left since childhood, her almond-colored eyes that looked like her own, her little bow-shaped lips that she used to kiss continuously when she was a child, and felt a gooey gush of love, the sort of gooey gushy feeling that only a parent can have for their child. She covered Amaya's hand with her own as they sat in silence.

"Amaya, my darling. I want you to have a wonderful life because you are a wonderful girl. You are my marvelous, mature, sensible daughter. And I love you. But you're all grown up now and you have your own life and I have mine. And I'm quite happy with mine right now. I don't think I need to live vicariously through anyone, not even you."

She teasingly poked Amaya's chest. "So get that thought out of your pretty little head, my dearest."

CHAPTER TEN

"I'M FEELING VERY tired so I don't think I will be able to make it." Naina was lounging on her couch on Sunday morning holding the phone close to her ear.

"Oh c'mon," Amaya said, her exasperation coming through over the phone. "This is the third time you've said that. Listen, I know I was probably a little hard on you the day we did brunch, but you were asking a lot of questions and I guess I snapped a little."

Naina did not respond, not in the mood to get into it.

"Listen, I'm sorry. I know, I really know you want the best for me and I love you." Amaya laughed; a tinny laugh that sounded deliberate. "And I know you're a little bit quirky, but I still love you."

"I love you too, darling. Very much."

"Then you know how much it means to me that you and Jai get along and are friends. Why are you avoiding seeing Jai? He told me he invited you to a lecture the other day, but you said no."

"Well, I'm not interested in living vicariously. I want to live my own life and only my own life."

"Gosh, Mom, you really know how to make a mountain out of a molehill. Listen, I'm sorry I said that. Your inquisitiveness was bothering me and I was just wondering. Now that's not so wrong, is it? To ask a question if something is on your mind. And even if you were living vicariously through me or someone else, what's the big deal? We all live vicariously in some way or another. Books, movies, soap operas, the entire TV, for Pete's sake . . . aren't they all ways to live vicariously?"

"But do you really think I'm living vicariously through you, Amaya?"

"I think you have a very active imagination and can live vicariously through anyone. But it's irrelevant. You, and everyone for that matter, have the right to live vicariously . . . Please do come out with us this evening. Please."

"You still didn't answer my question. Do you think I'm living vicariously through you?"

"No, I don't know . . . no . . . no. Can we please just forget I said that? Just toss it out of your mind . . . Please come out with us to Chailicious in the evening. They have all kinds of masala chais. You will love it. Even for an hour. You know how much yours and Jai's friendship means to me. C'mon, please . . ."

Naina eventually agreed, moved by a strange mix of motivations, both equally powerful, both in conflict with each other, yet urging her to do the same thing. There was the gooey gush of love she felt for her daughter, the desire to hear her tinkling laughter, to hear her voice sound bright and sparkling, not disappointed and pleading.

And then there was the other feeling that charged every cell in her body, made her weak in the knees, and made her starry-eyed and full of dreams like a young girl at the start of a Bollywood romance. It had been nearly six weeks since she had seen Jai. Nearly six weeks of living with a hole in her heart, a hunger in her body, and a thirst in her soul.

That time had stretched and elongated itself, making it seem so interminable that she felt like she would live in this suspended, aching state forever.

NAINA AND JAI started meeting alone again, typically once or twice a month, and generally on Monday afternoons because Naina had the day off, and Jai finished teaching by noon. Amaya generally worked late that day. The first couple of times Jai initiated their meetings, but then Naina started to invite him out.

Even though she found Jai to be a great storyteller, he was someone who did not reveal much about his inner life. But he did tell her he grew up in a fiery, undisciplined home and was an impulsive, punk rock-loving wild child in high school. The trend continued at Amherst, but abruptly ended at the end of his senior year in college when Amanda, his waif-like hippie girlfriend with the moody brilliance of Sylvia Plath, suddenly died. After Amanda's death, he plummeted into anguish, barely graduating from college. Then, he resolved to finally grow up.

He said Amaya was one of the kindest, smartest, and most stable girls he had ever met. He was so impressed when he had learned she worked with those struggling with substance abuse—now that took courage and steadfastness. Naina had done a great job in raising a terrific daughter. When he said things like that, Naina smiled, nodded, and said nothing except thank you.

Now, the lure of Jai felt like a looming force that was much larger and mightier than her. Like an imperial power, this force kept trying to take over her mind and make her think and do as it directed. Which meant betraying the crumbling old country of herself—the honorable mother and woman. The collapsing nation of feminine ideals that was still determined to stay alive and relevant.

Despite the conflict, the two factions were not quite yet at war since Naina had not fully felt, touched, and smelled the truth about Jai as it slowly gathered form and shape, and climbed up toward the surface of her consciousness.

BY DECEMBER, THE holiday season was in full swing, and it buoyed Naina's spirits. Restaurants were shimmering with lights; stores were filled with enticing discounts; tourists with maps jabbered in foreign languages; and the staff at the coffee shop near Red Circle were dressed in Santa hats and antlers. The coffee shop also had a new item that Naina found hard to resist—a pumpkin spice and mocha latte. She first had it sugar free, but it tasted awful. After that, she had it with loads of Splenda.

It was a very busy time, and Naina kept herself as occupied as possible, shunning thoughts of her own quandary. She had to make sure that Red Circle's holiday party went off smoothly, which was a gargantuan task in itself. This year was their biggest—they had eighty people attending, double the number of the previous year. Also, her new-agey friend Mara's first book, *The Creative Goddess Within*, had just been released, its cover gleaming with colorful images of Ix Chel, the Mayan goddess of creativity, magic, and sexuality; Minerva, the Roman goddess of music, poetry, and crafts; and Durga, the Hindu goddess of the feminine creative force. There were lots of launch parties for the book and Naina made sure she attended as many as she could. She was very fond of Mara, who—like her book—was a bit hokey but extremely comforting and entertaining. And then there were endless art world holiday parties that kept her engrossed and up late for more nights than she could handle. Also, Alannah announced that she was trying online dating as a Christmas present to herself, and Naina perked up, keen to follow her dating adventures.

It was also a bit easier for her to avoid obsessing about Jai since, for most of this time, he was away in Argentina where he had to attend a conference and be a guest lecturer at the University of Palermo. However, he managed to take time off as he was able to conduct his classes remotely for a bit. He sent Naina short emails once or twice a week, sharing his experiences in Buenos Aires. He described eating a spicy choripan (chorizo sandwich) in the bustling, cobblestone street-filled neighborhood of San Telmo; discovering an amazing gramophone player in the antiques market; and dancing, to his embarrassment, in a street tango performance in Plaza Dorrego. She would love Buenos Aires, he wrote. The city's vibrancy and joie de vivre reminded him of her own.

Every time, she received an email from him, she was thrilled, but she couldn't help wishing he had said more—but more of exactly what she did not know.

The highest point of the season for Naina was Red Circle's exhibit of paintings by Egyptian artist Anat Hawass. Hawass was the first artist she had lobbied hard for Susan to show, and not only had the art been exhibited, but it also received rave reviews—only the second time the gallery had received such accolades.

Anat Hawass made expressive and lyrical paintings inspired by Arabic calligraphy. Geometric orange flowers flew through cerulean space in one work;

a beehive overflowed with fluttering pink and purple bees in another; and turquoise-and-marigold leaves floated upward, as if they were about to meet the sky in the most riveting of paintings. *Time Out New York* wrote the work "created a poetic dialogue between text and form," hailing Hawass as an artist to watch out for. *Art News* called the paintings "fresh and mesmerizing."

Susan had been so pleased that she had said she wanted to promote Naina. But in light of the gallery's budget, they needed to hit their next fundraising target first.

Before Jai left for South America, Naina wanted to invite him to view the paintings; she was almost certain he would love them, especially since he had fancied his birthday present of the bee-flecked tie and guessed Naina had chosen it. A Monday afternoon when Susan was out would be perfect. But she wasn't able to make it happen.

She planned to ask Amaya to come and see the work when the gallery was open so her daughter could see, for herself, the wonder in viewers' eyes as well as Susan's increased regard of her. Of course, while Jai was still in town, she told her daughter not to bring him with her before the gallery closed at six, a request Amaya said she was baffled by since Naina and Jai were now friends.

Naina smiled to herself as she read and re-read the brief *Time Out* article in her office, still filled with disbelief.

She could hardly wait for Amaya to see the exhibition's reviews and had made sure she had good photocopies. Naturally, she wanted to her daughter to be proud of her, but she also wanted her to see her mother did not need "to live vicariously." Even at her age, she could accomplish things on her own.

The young had such arrogance, as if they were the only ones who had meaningful, interesting lives. Assuming that older people were dying to live through them. The idea infuriated her.

FOR CHRISTMAS, NAINA went to San Francisco to spend time with Karan who, she found, was becoming even more conservative as he got older. He hung out with mostly other Indian men in finance and some preppy American men and spent his free time on weekends playing tennis or baseball, dressed in khaki shorts and Polo shirts. She revealed little of her life to him but did his laundry and cooked for him. She was also careful to pack some of her older, less fashionable attire, wearing clothes he had seen her in before.

One night, at dinner, Karan kept talking about his father, how Harish had taught him everything in life, from baseball to a strong work ethic, and how he was still his hero.

"If I can be half the man that Dad was, I think I'll die happy," Karan said as he sat at the dining table, eating the chicken curry Naina had prepared.

Naina observed the way he slouched at the table, his thin, unblemished face looking so innocent, his light brown eyes filled with tears he wasn't shedding, and she felt awash with maternal love. She got up from her chair and hugged him. "Oh, beta, it will be all right. Even though he's not physically present, you know that he loves you very very much wherever he is."

"Yes, Mom." He hugged her in turn and pulled away from the embrace. "I know I'll be all right, but it's you I worry about. It's just not right, it's just not fair, that you have been left alone so young . . . Without Dad to take care of you."

Naina lowered her head and kept quiet at the pity dousing those words. But that only made Karan more vocal in his outpouring.

"Gosh, I can't even begin to imagine how hard it is for you. You must be so lonely. I want you to know, I really want you to know that both me and Amaya are always there for you, no matter what. We never want you to feel alone. Anytime you want to give up that job of yours you can, you know that."

She pressed her lips together. Why did he always have to say that?

"You know, Mom, I'm doing pretty good money-wise now, so you have nothing to worry about . . . Not that you did before . . . I just want you to be okay."

"Beta, I'll be fine," she said firmly, moving away from him and clearing the dishes from the table. "I miss him, but life has to carry on. I have wonderful memories to live with."

"Why don't you go to Jersey more often? You have so many friends there . . ."

Naina knew any explanation she offered would push her down into a deeper hole. Instead, she turned on the tap in the kitchen sink and washed the pots and pans.

The next night, as they sat on the couch, the Golden Gate Bridge glimmering out of the window, the conversation turned to Amaya.

Karan frowned. "What's Amaya up to? This guy she's dating is like eleven years or something older than her. That's way too much of an age difference. And she tells me you totally approve. What's going on?"

"Eleven years is not too much. Jai is a fabulous guy. He's educated, he's talented . . . Do you know he can play the piano? . . . Well-read, treats her well. She's lucky to have him. What's a few years here and there?"

"The guy will be dead by the time she's like sixty-five," Karan said, his voice dripping with condescension.

"Really? Your dad was only four years older than me and he died when I was fifty."

Karan sat hunched over in silence, and Naina immediately regretted her words.

CHAPTER ELEVEN

SOMETIME BEFORE THE dawn of the New Year, the truth, too vast to be contained, slammed open the door and emerged on the surface of Naina's mind. It was an alien creature with a face half-human, half-cheetah, with ten identical heads like the Hindu demon Ravan and surprisingly shapely claws painted in the softest of mauves. Finally, she saw the truth as clearly and unambiguously as Dorian Gray saw his aging, hideous portrait.

She was in love with Jai. Head over heels. Heels over head. Heart over head. Body over head. Fully, completely, absolutely. She had tumbled into the last place on earth she wanted to be—madly in love with her daughter's boyfriend.

The ground quaked and the self recoiled from itself in horror. Her mother, lodged in her head, jumped out and slapped her face. Once, twice, thrice, four times, five times—too many times to count. Then she spat on her.

Inside Naina, a vile brew of disgust, guilt, grief, and longing churned and churned, making her stomach turn, turning her insides out, turning her outsides inward.

What kind of woman was not a mother first? And foremost? Was such a woman even a woman at all?

Once again, Naina was lost. Once again, there was darkness everywhere and she was stranded in this large, eerie void, searching, grasping. Once again, there were no answers, just an array of questions buzzing and buzzing in her head until she couldn't bear it anymore.

She barely left the house—and it helped that the gallery was closed because of the holidays, and Amaya and Jai, who had returned from Argentina, had gone to the Poconos Mountains to bring in the New Year. As she spent day after day, night after night, pacing around her apartment, she acquired a habit for throwing things. One time, she flung her lip gloss, smearing the bottom of a white wall with a zigzagging blood-hued stain; another time, she hurled her perfume bottle, which broke and overwhelmed her odorless room with a garden-like smell; and still another time, she tossed a conch-shaped ceramic flower vase made by a contemporary artist, decorating her blonde hardwood floor with specks of white.

Often, Naina would look at her physical self, her head and neck securely atop her body, her arms firmly connected to the torso, her chubby thighs seamlessly extending into thin legs, and this cohesiveness would strike her as peculiar. Why couldn't her inner self be like that? If she could embody her mind with paint, her torso would disintegrate across the canvas in a scarlet scatter of stars. And her guts, the most livid shade of purple, would be distended and distorted like Dali's melting clocks.

When Naina finally went out, such as to the grocery store because there had been nothing to eat in her apartment, her mind was so tangled that she could not orient herself to the external world. One time, she walked out of the grocery store without paying; another time she almost got hit by a truck when she didn't mind the *Don't Walk* sign; and a different time, she went to take out her trash in a transparent nightie and didn't understand why her neighbor was staring at her. Once, she did not even notice the burning smell coming from 1B, an apartment on the lobby level—an odor so strong that everyone else who passed through the lobby desperately tried to call the management.

She never wanted to be a bad mother, she never wanted to be a bad mother—the words repeated themselves in her head, an icy, tainted chant.

Naina wrapped a comforter tighter around her as she sat in front of the window. The freezing night was pitch dark, and she watched snow fall in wisps from the sky, a perfect shade of pure white, as if it were a benediction from the heavens. Like a quintessential mother. The mother who, through human history, had always been seen as this hallowed, selfless entity. Always sacrificing for her children—as she had once done.

Naina needed some peppermint tea. She could feel a splitting headache coming on. Oh, how she wanted to just split into unrelated, unrecognizable shards! And how she wanted to keep herself whole with no part divided against the other! She wanted to take a couple of aspirins, but the bottle was empty. She flung it across the room. After putting the kettle on, she returned to the window and stared at the falling snow.

Pure, pristine white. Like a perfect mother. And a perfect Christian bride. And a perfect Hindu widow.

She noticed a lone man huddling in his parka on her street corner like a vulnerable puppy as the snow continued to envelop him and his two pizza delivery bags. He was the only person on the street and looked so defenseless against the elements. Her heart, for the first time extending beyond herself, reached out to him.

She drank her tea in bed, her comforter enveloping her. Again, she thought of Jai: his teasing half-smile that melted years off his face; his lissome fingers inches away from hers at the Thai restaurant, igniting every nerve in her hands; his voice like a caress when he was talking about finding love in the arms of a nawab; and his being so in sync with her when they were at the Spinning Wheel concert. Her heart soared and soared with that heavenly feeling of what felt like love—mind-defying, age-defying, gravity-defying, ethics-defying, self-defying love. Something she had never known before. She wanted to cry.

ALMOST TWO WEEKS later, Naina started going for regular walks on the esplanade by the East River, brisk walks that, despite her warm coat, made her cold to the bone and her muscles ache. Those were windy days, and she would look at the water being whipped the way she whisked an egg for an omelet when she used to cook. It looked as if the water were quivering as much as she was.

She couldn't tell anyone about her predicament. Even her friends Alannah and Mara, as liberal as they were, would probably be flabbergasted by a mother falling in love with her daughter's boyfriend. How *could* she feel the way she felt? It was just too terrible. She was just too terrible, she told herself again and again.

One day, Naina sat on a bench overlooking the East River, cleaning her fingernails, something she normally never did in public. She had discovered some dirt under her fingernails before leaving her apartment and took her nail clippers with her. She gazed at the water and vigorously scrubbed away.

"Lady, I think your nails are pretty clean," a woman said. "If you keep going on, you'll start bleeding."

Biting her lip, Naina quickly put her nail clippers back in her bag and then looked at a homeless-looking woman with dirty, disheveled hair, pushing a cart that probably contained all her worldly possessions.

"Thank you," Naina said. And they exchanged a glance before the woman pushed away.

Naina's mind turned back thirty-seven years to Sister Rosemary, the Goan nun with a wide, lined forehead and a bushy unibrow, dubbed the "fingernail witch" at St. Therese's Convent School. A brick-heavy air of self-assurance used to fill up the hot classroom whenever the nun entered. In her white-and-black habit, with every strand of hair neatly tucked into her headdress, and her big leather sandals, always as ready as a ripe tomato eager to leap into a hot curry, she would lecture a group of primarily Hindu students on moral science. Sister Rosemary began each class by asking the girls to come to her desk, one by one, and show her their fingernails. The girls who had clean nails were told to go back to their desks and the ones who were caught with even a speck of dirt under their nails were made to stand for the whole class period as she declared in her hoarse, scary voice of a Hindi movie villain, "Cleanliness is Godliness. Cleanliness is Godliness, Cleanliness is Godliness . . . Why can't you understand that? I've told you hundreds and hundreds of times and yet some of you don't seem to understand. No, I'm wrong, you do understand, but choose to disobey. Do you know what that says about your character? If you can't be decent enough to do something so small as keeping your fingernails clean, how will you keep your characters and souls pure? How will you respect your elders? How will you remain chaste until you are married? Dirt on your fingernails tells me something about your virtue or lack of it. If you are capable of allowing dirt under your fingernails, how do I know that you will not let dirt sully your character? Today, the world is filled with sinful temptations and your parents have sent you here, to a good Catholic school, so that you will learn to be as pure and virtuous as angels. Next time . . . do you hear me, girls? . . . If I find anybody's fingernails dirty, I will make the whole class stand outside so that the whole school can see what filthy little creatures you really are."

Naina, who generally had clean fingernails, only failed Sister Rosemary's test once and felt so awful about it that she went home and locked herself up in her room and cried for hours. And her mother, predictably, said it served her right.

She got up from the bench next to the East River and headed home. Snow started to fall with an increasing determination, and it looked like it might turn into a blizzard by nightfall. Thoughts of Sister Rosemary's favorite poem, "Angel in the House" by the Victorian poet Coventry Patmore came to her. She remembered the lines the nun would quote over and over again until they were seared in the girls' heads:

> *Strong passions mean weak will, and he*
> *Who truly knows the strength and bliss*
> *Which are in love, will own with me*
> *No passion but a virtue 'tis.*

Strong passions mean weak will. What a ridiculous concept, she thought, suddenly angry. Strong passions meant a strong, not a weak, will. She hurled the nail clippers into the first trash can she saw before bumping into a young man in a suit on 34th Street and First Avenue, the unexpected human touch briefly pleasing her.

AS TIME PASSED, Naina became less discombobulated—or maybe she had subconsciously figured out how to function in the world, constantly flummoxed, just like those who go about their business as if everything was normal after being diagnosed with a disease. But once the holidays were over, she took some days off, citing illness.

When she returned to work, she struggled at first to find her rhythm, but then she jumped right in. The wires that had been entangling her mind at home did not, thankfully, get a strong enough current to cause an outage—unlike the hot summers in India when the electricity would often go off because of the plethora of cooling machines overheating the power grid. The gallery was also the only place where she felt a sense of purpose and where, in comparison with the rest of the city, she felt somewhat intact.

After a while though, things began to change. While guilt and shame continued to agitate her like a flea bite that refused to go away, her other self—

the woman, the self-interested individual, the mortal besotted beyond reason and ethic—started rearing up its head and asserting itself.

Most nights, she'd be alone, drinking a good deal of wine and simmering with an intensity that grew fiercer and fiercer. No matter what, she couldn't deny it to herself. She and Jai were made of the same stuff—a rich terracotta clay, she would think, as a delicious feeling, like the taste of rasmalais—gooey balls of cottage cheese swimming in thick, sweet milk—would flow through her.

But what about Amaya? The other side of her, appalled, would protest and swat away the sweetness, filling her instead with a guilt that tasted as bitter as karela, the bitter gourd she had to regularly eat while growing up.

"Whatever else is unsure in this stinking dunghill of a world, a mother's love is not." The line from James Joyce's *Portrait of the Artist as a Young Man* kept swirling in her head, and although it evoked some tender feelings, she felt a stronger urge to give James Joyce one tight slap.

And then Sophia Loren's words, which she had always found so perceptive, kept Joyce's words company. "When you are a mother, you are never really alone in your thoughts. A mother always has to think twice, once for herself and once for her child."

BY THIS POINT, Naina's boundaries between self-indulgence and self-denial, love and pain, guilt and self-assertion, motherhood and womanhood, were bleeding into each other, creating a strange hodgepodge of shapes and colors, difficult for the mind to comprehend and the eye to settle on.

The child always comes before the parent, Naina's obstetrician had told her when he denied her request for sleeping pills during her second pregnancy. During those days, she would lay awake all night, with a feeling of queasiness that always seemed like it was going to erupt into something, but never did. And there was this itchiness all over her dry skin. It's the law of nature, Mrs. Mehta, Dr. Randolph had said. Your parents put you first. Now you have to put your child first. It's the same in the animal kingdom. Did you know that a female octopus grows weak from hunger when she lays her eggs because she does not leave them to hunt for her own food?

Was she violating the laws of nature? She sank into her pillow with feelings like the bitterest of karelas, drowning out all the lusciousness of the rasmalais.

LATE ONE NIGHT, Naina turned on the music system without seeing which CDs were in there. Again, she paced around her living room. Past eleven o'clock, she could hear the familiar click-clicking, clack-clacking of the stiletto heels of the Russian woman who lived above her—presumably the same woman who looked like a scarecrow with her scant flesh and extravagantly painted-stick face. The sound was jarring, jabbing at Naina's fragile state. She wished the woman would stop, but she knew that once she started her high-and-flighty strut, she would normally continue for at least twenty minutes. But that night, the woman ceased after just a minute or two.

Naina stopped pacing as she realized she had not even thought about whether Jai reciprocated her feelings. She clamped down on her lower lip and struck her thigh with a balled-up fist. What if he didn't feel the same way as she felt and laughed at the idea of the fifty-four-year-old mother of his girlfriend being in love with him? What if he found it ludicrous?

And then she remembered how Jai looked at her when she was talking about her father, the excitement in his voice when he told her he didn't often meet people as crazy about Goya as she was, the way he soaked up what she had to say as if they were the most important words in the world, the way he had run and got her a bottle of Tylenol when she had complained of a headache after watching that horrible production of *An Ideal Husband*, the number of times he had met her alone—no, no, he felt the same way . . . he had to. This sort of connection was so extraordinary and exceptional, it happened to people once in a lifetime—if they were lucky. There was no way it could be one-sided.

Her body slackened, lubricated by the sensuous jasmine-like scent of being desired. Again, that heavenly feeling of love came over her and she soared. But inevitably, her other self stood up . . . in horror, in terror, in mortification. It spat on her, slapped her, and spewed insults all over her.

This strife continued for weeks and weeks, with no resolution in sight. One night, in order to distract herself, Naina asked Alannah and Mara to join her for dinner. As the three of them ate fish tagine at a Moroccan restaurant in Hell's Kitchen, Alannah rattled off a few stories of online dates she had gone on, stories that Naina listened to with great curiosity. One man kept talking about the joys of fatherhood on the first date and another went on and on about how shitty his job was. There was one man she liked, a graphic designer, a hot guy with a wicked sense of humor, but she sensed he wasn't into her.

"How do you know when a man likes you?" Naina asked.

"Oh, you just do, honeybun. To use Mara's language, you just feel the energy." Alannah waved her hands about.

Naina considered that. Yes, she definitely felt the energy emanating from Jai when they were together. Propelling her toward him. Inviting her into his orbit. Inciting her to do things she had never done before. Her body was again dappled by goose bumps and she felt shimmers shimmying between her legs.

DURING THAT TIME, Naina wanted to skulk away from Amaya and Jai. A couple of times, she made up some excuses, but she knew she couldn't continue to do that. So she would meet her daughter for a quick coffee or for a movie where they wouldn't have the opportunity to chat much. But every time they talked, Naina found herself avoiding her daughter's eyes.

One time, Amaya mentioned a friend's cousin who seemed interested in her and had invited her to a movie.

"You must go," Naina said. "Who is he and what does he do?"

"I must go?" Amaya's eyes widened with surprise. "What are you talking about? Have you forgotten that I'm in a serious relationship?"

"Of course not, of course I haven't forgotten. Do you think I'm a hundred-year-old woman with dementia? How could I forget?" She moved her fingers up and down the straps of her handbag. "I just think that, at your age, you should keep all your options open and keep exploring."

"Mom, what's wrong with you? Are you asking me to cheat on my boyfriend?"

"Don't be ridiculous, Amaya." Naina could hear the exaggerated self-righteousness in her voice, edged with the sharpness of her convent schoolteachers and her mother. "I'm just asking you to keep an open mind. Sometimes, the right person may not be who you think he is so just keep exploring. That's all."

Amaya looked stunned. "What's gotten into you? First you go on and on about how wonderful Jai is, and now, for no apparent reason, you hardly inquire about him and are asking me to go on a date with another guy as you nuttily keep touching your handbag. *What is the matter with you?*"

Amaya's forehead crinkled, and she rested her chin on her knuckles as she peered at Naina. Once more, her eyes, with their rapidly enlarging pupils, loomed like a seer's, peeling away the camouflage and prodding open mirages.

Thankfully, Amaya did not say anything, but every second of silence stretched into a vast, shaking space.

"Maybe it's you who wants to date," Amaya said. "And that's okay. Maybe, I'll be uncomfortable with it in the beginning, but I'll deal. If you want to date, you should."

Naina sharply inhaled and held in the bubble of air as she closed her eyes and turned her head sideways.

Then she interlaced her fingers with Amaya's. "I love you, my darling."

"I love you too. Seriously, it's okay if you want to date. I'll deal with it and Karan will have to learn to deal too. It will be much harder for him, of course . . . but he's a grown guy. He'll come around."

How easily her daughter could speak to her in that oh-so-insightful, cool, emotionally competent psychotherapist tone. So easily.

"My darling, Amaya. You are a very sweet, considerate, and thoughtful daughter. Thank you very much, but I . . . I don't want to go out with anyone . . . or date or whatever. Please don't presume anything about me. Also, by the way, I think I should thank you for the permission to go on a date if I ever wanted to. Perhaps I should call you Mom too?" Naina laughed thinly.

Amaya furrowed her brow. She swung her head from side to side. "Gosh, you're so all over the place. Please don't be offended, but I really, really think you need a therapist. To help you with your transition into this new life."

"So now I'm crazy too? Is that what you think of me? A crazy woman who wants to start dating in her fifties?"

"Oh, stop it. Just stop it."

CHAPTER TWELVE

NAINA PACED AROUND the empty gallery, her high heels clicking against the wooden floor. She was sipping a glass of red wine, her heart filled with the rising and accelerating music of anticipation. Jai was coming to the gallery in a short while to see the Anat Hawass paintings. They were meeting alone for the first time in the New Year, for the first time since she had acknowledged her feelings for him and turned herself upside down.

She put her wrists next to her nose to check her new perfume, but she barely caught a whiff of the luscious scent of tropical flowers with a spicy, citrusy edge. She rushed toward the office area, took the perfume from her bag, and added a little more Ferragamo's Signorina Ribelle to her wrists and neck. She sat down and looked out of the small window; the night was dark and cloudless, and a full moon beamed in all its glory. She knew the connection between a full moon and madness, held true for centuries, was a myth, but coincidence or not, she was certainly feeling a lot loonier these days.

Naina checked her watch. Fifteen minutes until Jai was due to arrive. Fifteen long minutes. She checked her email. She saw a curatorial proposal from a woman called Mailey, who had been referred by one of Susan's contacts. Mailey. That was the same name as Amaya's friend whose cousin had asked Amaya out. Naina glanced at the proposal, something unoriginal about the depiction of women's bodies in advertisements, and stared at the moon again.

She imagined Amaya holding hands and giggling with a fresh-faced boy with short, cropped hair; she pictured her fixing the tie of a serious investment-banker type in a suit; she envisaged her with a messy-haired, torn-jeans-wearing startup millionaire, clinking champagne glasses in their first-class cabin on a flight to Turks and Caicos.

Such visions had become commonplace, triggered by Amaya's mentioning of her friend Mailey's cousin's interest in her, and multiplied when Amaya described the wonderful qualities of a new male colleague. Since then, her imagination had taken flight, conjuring up all sorts of romantic scenarios for Amaya. Always with someone younger and richer than Jai. The future seemed ripe with male prospects for her daughter.

Naina walked back toward the main gallery space, the lyrical beauty of the paintings around her affecting her almost every time. She stood in front of her favorite: turquoise-and-orange leaves wafting upward, as if they were on their way to a mystical communion with the universe.

Once more, as she had been doing during the preceding few weeks, Naina told herself Jai was not right for Amaya. Jai was too passionate, too capricious, too unconventional, and her daughter was too earnest, too grounded, too lacking in fire. It could never work. It would never work.

She moved away from the paintings and darted around the gallery, sipping her wine.

Jai needed to be with someone like her, she thought, feeling that deliciously sweet certitude that Jai belonged to her—she belonged to Jai. They were soul mates; they were kindred spirits; they were made for each other, the conviction of it hardening inside her like a clay bowl in a kiln.

So what if he was twelve years younger than she? So what? They never felt the age difference when they were together. And didn't men marry women twenty years younger than themselves . . . and sometimes even younger than that? She had finally found the one, the one who was even more marvelous than the ones in her dreams, the one whose colors only she could match. *How* could she let that go?

She walked back to the crepuscular office area. She left the light off. Again, she stared at the moon. Of course, there was Amaya. She enshrouded her face in the obliterating darkness of her hands. She could not hurt her daughter.

Haltingly, Naina lifted her head and fixed her eyes on the moon. She thought of Selene, the spectacular Greek goddess of the moon, who drove a silver chariot pulled by two winged horses across the night sky. It was Selene who possessed the power to illuminate the sky after sundown, dispelling the darkness and offering the gift of light to the world so people could still see.

Once more, Naina concluded that it wasn't going to work out between Amaya and Jai anyway. Her daughter would be hurt, of course; she believed she was in love with Jai, believed that they were right for each other, and seeing her mother with that man would be hard. Initially at least. But Amaya was smart; she was strong; she would see that she and Jai weren't right for each other and eventually get over it. She was a psychologist after all—she would be able to see things clearly and deal with things sensibly. Sacrifices had to be made.

Naina gulped the last sip of her wine. And Amaya was young and she would find someone else, her own soul mate. She had already had so many suitors. So many prospects. Unlike her mother.

The bell rang. Naina jumped and hid her empty wine glass behind some books. On her desk were two glasses filled with one of Jai's favorite Malbecs and a plate of Gorgonzola cheese.

She rushed to the front of the gallery and opened the door. Jai was standing there, wearing olive-green corduroy pants and a chocolate brown trench coat that matched his eyes. He looked academic, fuddy-duddy, and hip at the same time. A lovely, quirky mélange. His eyes lit up like rich amber gems. She wanted to hold those eyes in her hands, roll them around on her open palms.

"Hello, Madam Butterfly," Jai said in that low, slow voice he used whenever they were alone together. That voice, the hue of blushing burgundy, that feel of raw silk. Gosh, how she had missed him. But Madam Butterfly, she just registered. What did he mean by that?

Now, unabashedly, he ran his eyes over her fitted black top and full chiffon skirt with butterfly-like forms all around the hem. As goose bumps speckled her skin, a warmth coated her face and she understood what he had meant. She laughed, louder than usual, but this time she didn't care.

"Butterflies suit you. I think they represent color and joy, just like you."

"Thank you," Naina said, meeting his eyes. "That's a lovely compliment."

He looked at her as if he were taking in every detail of her face, just as she was taking in every detail of his face. The jagged scars, the long eyelashes, the thin, wide lips. They held each other's gaze. In Naina's imagination, the wood burned and the fire crackled and the smoke seared every sensible thought in her head. All cares vanished into the smoky air. She pictured herself clasping those hands, those fingers like a violin's strings, and those palms barely touched by the lines of fate.

But she too stood there, tracing the outlines of her pendant.

Jai's eyes went to the pendant in the middle of the deep V of her blouse, just above her cleavage.

"Ah, it's that Wiccan spider pendant," he noted, his eyes still on her chest. "So, who are you looking to ensnare in your web, Madam Butterfly?"

Naina laughed and tilted her head. "Oh, some poor, unsuspecting person . . . Just a second, please."

She went to her office and returned with a tray with the Gorgonzola cheese and the wine. She offered a glass to Jai. With the glass in hand, Jai stared at the paintings, his expression serious and cryptic, seemingly blocking out everyone and everything from his thoughts.

Naina was especially uncomfortable in moments like this, like a random tourist trying to get access to a citadel. "What do you think of the work?"

"I'm not sure." His expression was still impenetrable.

She waited impatiently as he examined the other work. She was so keen for Jai to appreciate these paintings, the first works that had earned the gallery praise in the art world, thanks to her efforts. She was so excited to show him the reviews.

"Actually," Jai said, after he finished his tour of the show, his face opening up, "I think these paintings are growing on me." A smile touched his lips. "I think I like them."

"I'm so glad," Naina said, smiling broadly.

"You know, when you told me about the show, I didn't think I would like the work because I wasn't sure how I would feel about Arabic calligraphy-inspired paintings."

"Then why did you want to come and see them?" Naina tossed her head back and put one hand on her hip.

"Because I was intrigued." He cocked his head, his voice sounding like the bass notes of a jazz guitar and as tactile as fabric. "Because I sensed they were interesting. And when I first glanced at them I still wasn't sure how I felt . . . But now that I've spent some time with them, I've decided that I like them . . . In life, and this might be clichéd but still deserves to be said, one has to have an open mind . . . you think you will like something and then you don't. And you don't think you will like something and then you do. Life is filled with all sorts of surprises, isn't it?"

Naina tightly and carefully held on to every word, as if they were precious rubies in danger of slipping away. She continued looking at Jai expectantly, certain he was only pausing and going to say more. Surely, he was talking about more than just the art. Right now, he was going to say something that was going to change everything. Excitement shot up in her like a bird taking flight.

Instead, he turned toward one of the paintings, the one that looked like a beehive. "I really like this one. The colors are so radiant and it's just so idiosyncratic."

Naina dropped her head and crossed her hands against her chest.

"Hey, what's the matter with you?" Jai said, his voice twirling slightly with levity. "Am I going to get the see those wonderful reviews I've heard about or not?"

"I'm . . . I'm fine." Naina silently commanded herself to smile. "Of course, of course, I'll get them right now . . . Can I refill your glass?"

Naina was glad to be back in her office for a few minutes to collect herself. Just because he hadn't said anything at that moment didn't mean he wasn't going to. It was a complicated situation and probably needed some time to work itself out. Every signal he was giving her was positive; every signal he gave her suggested he felt the same way as she did.

Naina stepped out into the gallery, smiling daintily at Jai as she handed him the reviews. Then, she went to get a couple of chairs from the office.

Soon, they were sitting adjacent to each other, leaning forward in their chairs, their knees pointed toward each other, her legs neatly crossed, his spread slightly apart. Their feet just inches apart.

Sitting so close to Jai, Naina could again take in his distinct scent. The smell of the hills of Shimla. Of pristine, nippy air invigorating the senses.

"I like the descriptor 'fanciful' that this reviewer mentions. But I think the work is more whimsical than fanciful." Jai placed a closed hand on one side of his face and looked directly at Naina, his lips impishly curling. "The work is more like a whimsical fantasy, I think, sort of like its champion, the lovely Madam Butterfly."

Naina felt her cheeks burn and she giggled. She twirled some strands of her hair. "So is that what you think of me, a whimsical fantasy?" The real world was quickly receding and she was entering something out of one of Anat Hawass's paintings—a universe with an indecipherable script that adhered to no rules or regulations, not even gravity, she was flying away to meet the radiant, floating clouds in the sky.

"Maybe. Perhaps . . ." Jai leaned forward and spread his legs further apart. "Isn't fantasy a wonderful thing? It allows you copious, uncensored pleasures in the mind, made all the more delicious by the fact that they can never materialize. Do you know what Dr. Seuss once said? 'Fantasy is a necessary ingredient in living, it's a way of looking at life through the wrong end of a telescope.'"

Naina's hands were loosely on her knees as were Jai's on his. So close to each other. She could almost feel the smooth, hairless skin on the back of his hands. It was just the two of them in this universe with the flying indecipherable script.

She was going to do it. She was going to touch him. She was going to breezily stroke his fingers and knuckles. She stretched out her hand and placed it above his.

But it would not move. It remained in mid-air, limp yet frozen.

"Is this some kind of yoga pose, Madam Butterfly?"

She abruptly stepped out of the world of flying cryptic script. Back into the gallery with the old steam pipe in the corner, with the giggling voices in the hallway . . . and with her daughter's boyfriend.

"Oh, don't be ridiculous." Naina playfully tapped him and drew back her hand. "I was just stretching, that's all."

If Jai didn't believe her, he didn't let it show. He didn't bring it up again and they continued bantering and talking for about a half hour, then Jai got up and said he had a dinner and needed to leave.

"ARE *YOU* PLANNING to make yarn?" Jai asked, arching his thin eyebrows as he watched Naina roll her newly bought wooden spindles in her hand. "I could be wrong, but you don't seem like the yarn-making type."

Naina laughed. "You're right. I'm not."

It was an unusually warm day in February, and Jai was sitting as close to Naina on a bench in Washington Square Park without actually touching her body; he moved his face closer to hers. "Then why did you buy the spindles? And pay sixty-eight dollars for something that doesn't look worth even thirty dollars to me. Are you collecting spindles?"

Naina could feel his warm breath from his nostrils, going in and out, in and out. The force of life repeating itself, over and over again. The force of Jai's life. She could barely breathe.

"No, I'm not collecting spindles." She stared at the small wooden spindles with totem-like birds painted on them. They had looked beautiful just a few minutes earlier, but now she wasn't so sure. "Actually, I don't know why I bought them . . . And you're probably right, I paid way too much." She looked at Jai, pulled down the edge of her short dress, which had ridden up dangerously close to her thighs, and smiled. "I'm horrible at bargaining, but what's done is done . . ." She gazed up at the sky, a sweet blue, the color of a baby boy onesie and pint-sized pajamas and socks. "Ah, this breeze is so beautiful, who would think we are in the dead of winter?"

The temperature had soared above seventy-five degrees—a fifty-year record high for the month of February—and the entire city was in a good mood, as if it were the season of lights and gifts and new beginnings again. An assortment of people were hanging out in shorts and T-shirts, sweat dribbling down their bodies. On the southwest corner of the park, all the chess tables were taken and there were lines of people waiting for their turn to play against one of the expert amateurs who made their living playing chess in the Park. Faint sounds of jazz were coming from the nearby fountain and some bodies were sprawled on the dry grass.

Somehow, the day was further confirmation of what Naina had come to believe—things did not always happen on a linear prescribed path. There could be summer in winter, winter in summer, fall in summer. Anything could happen. At any time.

"Do you know lapses of reason are quite common in this weather?"

Jai faced her. "In this weather?"

"Yes," she said, fluttering her eyelids and dramatically moving her hands. "Pleasant weather can be quite detrimental to a person's judgement. I read an article in the *New Yorker* by some researcher . . . I can't remember his name now . . . but he did a study that showed that good weather led to a 'disconcerting lapse in thoughtfulness.'" She shrugged.

Jai laughed, a richer, riper, grainier laugh than usual. His head was tilted back just a little, and his mouth was open, revealing those perfectly set white teeth. It sounded like something rippling from deep in his chest, not just from his throat, as it normally did.

The laugh entered Naina's body through pores that expectantly opened and enlarged when she was around Jai, and lodged itself in her body—obliterating fear, submerging guilt, washing out shame.

Naina laughed too, just like him.

"I've never heard of that before," Jai said. "How do you come up with all this zany stuff?"

"I don't know," Naina said in a girlish voice. "I just do . . . You probably think I'm completely crazy, don't you?"

"Think?" Jai uttered the word in one upward stroke, his eyes wide and chocolatey, and flickering with amusement. "I know you are, Madam Butterfly." He placed his hand on her forearm and squeezed it ever so slightly.

Her skin jumped, spun, and did the triple-step as if it were swing dancing. It was the most physical contact they had ever had with each other. The other times had just been brief handshakes and the one time she had playfully slapped his hand. But this time felt like a real touch, a touch of intimacy, a touch of wanting greater intimacy. His hand was finally where it belonged—on her skin. Again he was propelling her toward him, inviting her into his orbit. More directly than he had ever done before. Her skin did another vigorous swing dance-like turn and then drew itself inward, creating a hollow bowl waiting to be filled with a banquet of amorous delights.

His hand was still on her forearm and his eyes were still twinkling with amusement. How long had it been?

Suddenly, quickly, Naina moved her face closer to his, reaching for his lips.

Jai stopped her and shook her by the shoulders. "What do you think you are doing? Are you crazy? Are you totally out of your mind? Don't you realize I'm your daughter's boyfriend?"

His hands were rough and menacing like those of a nun when you did something wrong. His words were slaps on her face.

She was rapidly sinking and shrinking, sinking and shrinking, sinking and shrinking, sinking and shrinking, until she was an infinitesimal insect on the ground and Jai was this large, powerful human looking down at her disgusting insignificance. She wished the ground would just open and swallow her up the way it had swallowed Sita in the epic *Ramayana*.

She sat there with her shaking arms crossed protectively against her bosom, her face burning and downcast, unable to say a word.

"I can't believe you would do this, Naina." Jai stood up and towered over her like a police dog. "I just can't. Hit on your daughter's boyfriend? What the fuck? What kind of person are you anyway? And, what kind of person do you think I am? Some asshole who wants a woman and her mother at the same time?"

Naina buried her face in her hands, unable to bear the humiliation tearing her apart like a mob of greedy moths ripping wool sweaters. Stripping the wool of mad dreams, foolish hopes, and deluded self-worth. She wept, despite her best efforts not to, and she sank her face deeper into her palms to muffle its graceless sound.

"I'm sorry, I'm so sorry, I thought, I thought . . ." Naina whispered, softly and meekly.

"Thought what?" Jai thrust his face toward her. "That I might be interested in having an affair with my girlfriend's mother?"

Each word was hard, staccato, and stinging. Like her mother's slaps. One, two, three, four, five, six.

Naina hadn't been able to look at him, but then something stirred in her, something solid, something deeply embedded and impervious to all the ups and downs of circumstances and emotions, pushing her forward, compelling her to stand up for herself, to speak up.

"But I didn't . . . I didn't . . . make the whole thing up," Naina said, her voice wavering. "You . . . You . . . did lead me to think you felt the same way . . ."

"I led you to think I felt the same way? I did? Me?" Jai thrust his face closer to hers in the manner of a bully.

She couldn't help but raise her head and glance at him. His eyes were no longer delicious balls of chocolate, but angry puddles of dirt in a Delhi slum during the monsoon. His fingers were no longer strings of a violin; instead they were thin rods meant to discipline errant students in Catholic Schools. His chin, which she had never really paid attention to, jutted out in an unsightly, pointy shape, like that of her grandmother who tut-tutted at every little thing.

"How? How? How did I lead you on? By treating you as a friend?"

Naina continued to sink and shrink, sink and shrink, sink and shrink. She felt as if she had no center of gravity and could topple anytime. Ordinary objects took on bizarre shapes and proportions and evoked strange emotions.

So that's all she was to him. A friend. Merely a friend. And what was she really? A witch, a bitch, a madwoman with a harlot's itch. A sinful, wanton *mother* who shamelessly trespassed all boundaries of decency and propriety, chasing not true love, but a depraved, self-indulgent delusion.

She could feel the tears forming once more and reached again for the blanket of her hands.

"Please leave," Naina said in between sobs. "Please leave . . . I'm so sorry."

"Hang on," Jai said, his voice as sharp as knife. "I hope you're not going to tell Amaya any of this. I'm not going to let you ruin my relationship. I couldn't stand to think of Amaya knowing that her mother is—"

"Amaya won't know anything." Naina saw an image of her bad, evil self, resembling that of the wicked stepmother in *Snow White* fastening her daughter's laces with extraordinary severity to asphyxiate her. It seared her. "And, Jai, please, please, please don't tell her anything."

"*Goodbye*," Jai said, his rapid footfalls disappearing on the busy sidewalk as Naina continued to cry alone in Washington Park on the most beautiful day of that winter.

CHAPTER THIRTEEN

WHEN HARISH HAD died, Naina's anguish was black, like the sudden onset of night when you can't see anything and you're terrified that you've lost your way. But after Jai spurned her, it was bloody, bright red, and bursting with an agony that was as spirited and vibrant as the fervency of first love. She cried and cried and cried—at home, on the street, in the subway, in public restrooms, at the grocery store. Anywhere except the gallery, which she returned to about ten days after that terrible February day.

The world inside and outside her was spinning and spinning so fast that everything felt like a haze, a daze, ablaze with chaos. And, at other times, everything moved so slowly that it seemed like a sluggish, melancholy drizzle where she could feel every raindrop collapsing in her hand, exhausted from its long journey from the sky, woeful about its separation from the clouds.

She must have been hallucinating to even entertain the idea that Jai felt the same way as she did. His words on that sunny February day felt like welts that would not go away. Jai had never loved her, she would constantly tell herself, forcing herself to accept that, to stop herself from hoping against hope. And then she would remember his gleaming eyes swallowing every feature on her face, that bantering hint of a smile, his hand squeezing her forearm like it wanted to travel further, and his voice the color of whispery wine when they were together. And that velvety feeling of love would find its way into her again, making her tense body soft and pliable. And make her doubt what she had told herself. He had to feel the same way about her. Their connection was extraordinary and exceptional. They were indeed made of the same material—that rich terracotta clay. They were kindred spirits.

And logically, everything didn't add up. Why would a man want to spend so much time with his girlfriend's mother if he weren't interested in her? And, yes, her mind was prone to flights of fancy, but she had not completely made up the fact that he had flirted with her. Why had he done that? Why? Why? She would spend hours working over these questions as if they were complex calculus problems . . . and yet, the answer was always the same. No answer. Just as there was no answer to so many important questions in her life. She was at the same mortifying, frightening place she had arrived at after Harish's death. It was the unfortunate fate of human beings to be able to imagine spaces filled with neat, clear answers, and yet have to confront gaping voids so many times. Just as they could visualize a future and have it still remain a blank hole. She could feel herself crumbling into tiny, slippery bits like the pieces of Gorgonzola cheese Jai had dropped on the floor at the gallery a few weeks before. Again, she started to weep.

Those days, her body felt heavy, her footsteps sluggish, her face hard—all in all, she felt the weight of her years bearing down on her like never before. She was fifty-four years old now, the number taking on a new, ominous meaning after Jai's rejection. Men wanted to be with younger women. That was just a fact of life.

She was in bed, half-asleep, when she heard the ringing of a bell, heavy and forbidding, like the bells in school. Science class was going to start in two minutes and she was sprinting. Up two flights of stairs. But two teachers were walking down the stairs. She had to stop. Running was not allowed in school. Good girls did not run around like hooligans. The bell was ringing even louder now. She walked up the stairs as fast as she could. She better make it or Mrs. Deshpande would have her stand outside the class. Twenty more seconds. Her heart was racing.

Naina reached for her pillow and hugged it. As the sound continued, she became more awake and realized it was just her phone ringing—the pleasant melody of a Mozart Sonata. She picked up her phone. It was Amaya, again. She let it go to voicemail, again.

She went to the bathroom mirror and stared at the crow's feet around her eyes. They looked as if they were carved into her skin. Hideous. She stepped out of the bathroom, but she was back soon. Several times a day now, she would stand in front of the mirror, fixate on all her imperfections: the crow's feet, the dark circles under her eyes, the lines in her forehead. They all seemed deeper, darker, bigger, and uglier, the more she looked at them. And reeking of the numerous years she had spent on earth. Sometimes, she couldn't bear to look at herself. Yet, she couldn't stop.

Naina also ended up doing some strange things, or at least things that were odd for her. One night, she got very drunk at an Irish pub near her apartment. When she was on her fourth or fifth drink, she couldn't immediately get the bartender's attention. She started yelling and slapping the bar countertop, oblivious to everyone staring at her, until the manager threatened to throw her out. Another time, she went to a free lecture on plastic surgery in her neighborhood, something she had always turned her nose down at, associating it with foolish, frivolous celebrities with fat, frozen lips. She even booked a liposuction procedure for her stomach and hips, paying the $500 deposit. But when she went home and read some horror stories about women who had been scarred and bruised after the procedure, she changed her mind and asked for her money back. The clinic, however, would not return her money, citing the clause in the contract—which she had blearily signed—stating the money was non-refundable.

When Naina returned home from the clinic, Amaya called again, and this time Naina picked up the phone, her voice cracking.

"What's the matter?" Amaya asked. "Are you okay? I'm never able to get a hold of you. I've been worried sick about you."

"I'm . . . I'm fine . . . there's just been so much work . . . piles of it, in fact . . . there's nothing to worry about."

"But you don't sound okay. What's the matter, Mom?"

"Amaya, I'm . . . just under a lot of stress right now . . . That's all. That's all. Nothing . . . Nothing to worry about."

"What kind of stress? How can I help?"

"You can't." Naina stopped, realizing her words had come out too harsh. "I just need some time alone, to myself, please. Can you understand that? Can you, please?"

NAINA WENT FOR many long, brisk walks. One lambent Sunday afternoon, she was walking in Central Park and saw a group of elderly people beating their chests and stomping their feet. When they took a break, she asked the stocky man in a red beret leading the crowd what they were doing and he told her they were having a weekly class called "Expression Through Motion." It was held in different places in the city and the aim was to release grief. People could scream, curse, cry—do whatever they needed to do to release it from their bodies into the limitless universe. If Naina wanted to try it, she was welcome to join for the remainder of the class. Naina first hesitated and then decided to give it a shot. The stocky man in the red beret asked another stocky man to play the drums, and by the end of the class, Naina was softly murmuring, "fuck you, fuck you, fuck you," to the bare branches, the first time in her life that she had uttered the expletive. It felt good to say the word, cathartic and liberating. It made her feel as if she belonged to the present moment, a *contemporary* woman. Still, she never signed up or returned to the class. But she continued to say the word *fuck* occasionally when she was alone, the taste of forbidden pleasure undeniably delectable.

Naina barely slept during those days, finding herself restive and exhausted as thoughts and emotions hurtled around inside her. She also worked very hard, a near desperation motivating her. Many days, she was at the gallery until almost eight o'clock, working on—besides her usual tasks—preparatory curatorial details for a summer show on young women and eating disorders. And for the very first time, she started courting new donors for the gallery. Even her boss, Susan, who never thought any amount of work was too much, told Naina she was overdoing it and kept cautioning her that she would fall sick if she continued at that pace.

Susan turned out to be right. Naina did fall sick. She got a terrible case of the flu and had to stay in bed for a week.

EVENTUALLY, AMAYA PERSUADED her mother to meet her. Naina decided to take her daughter to *Chicago,* the Broadway musical, the kind of enthusiastic performance that filled her with ennui, but the sort of thing Amaya loved. And going somewhere like that would give them little opportunity to sit and exchange intimacies. Or so she hoped.

When Naina saw Amaya walking into the theater, looking sophisticated and stylish in a fitted white blazer and black pants, her hair falling loosely yet neatly over her shoulders, her little bow-shaped lips—lips she used to continuously kiss when Amaya was a child—covered in sandstone-colored lipstick, Naina quickly moved away, to the left, behind a cluster of people near the box office so Amaya wouldn't see her.

She couldn't bear it. All these days she had immersed her entire self in the bile of her torment so that there had been no room for remorse. But now, one glance at her daughter, and her head poked out of the acrid liquid, and she was enveloped by blood-colored guilt. She wanted to hide like a tortoise in its shell or run. Fast. Away. From everyone, including herself. Turn herself into a weightless shaft of light.

"Hi, Mom," Amaya said, coming up behind her.

Naina could feel her daughter giving her one long, slow look. She kept her head down, but she knew Amaya's eyes were blinking and her lips were fluttering.

"What's the matter? What's going on?" She held Naina by her hunched shoulders. "You look unwell. How much weight have you lost? What's going on with you?"

"I'm okay," Naina said finally, forcing a smile, lifting up her head a little but still unable to meet her daughter's eyes. "You know I had the flu."

Uttering even a single coherent word was an effort. The words sounded incongruous and strange.

"Oh, Mom," Amaya said, holding Naina's hand.

Naina wanted to pull it away, yet she also wished Amaya would keep holding on to it.

"Let's go sit down."

"But the show's about to start."

"The show is not going to start for another twenty minutes." Amaya led Naina to a plush maroon bench. "So are you going to tell me what's the matter?" she asked in that psychotherapist voice of hers, gentle and soothing, yet probing and persuasive. "I can tell something is really bothering you. And I really want to help."

For a brief moment, Naina wished Amaya was an anonymous psychotherapist, and she could unload all the weight pressing down on her, this enormous cargo that did not even allow her to breathe or eat in peace. But Amaya wasn't a stranger. She was her daughter. A daughter whose boyfriend she had tried to steal. She felt a painful stab. The blood-colored, sharp-edged guilt continued to zigzag all around her.

She held her breath, hunting for something to say, something that didn't sound foolish, something that Amaya would find believable. Again, Amaya's eyes, with those expanding pupils, looked sinisterly piercing, causing Naina to wince. She instinctively knew Jai hadn't said anything to her and felt grateful to him for that. But there was something about Amaya's expression that said she meant business. Something that said she would dig deeper and deeper until she discovered the devastating truth.

"Amaya, remember . . . I . . . I . . . said I was under a lot of stress." Naina clasped her hands between her chest and her abdomen and crossed and uncrossed her thumbs.

"Of course, I remember." Amaya intently gazed at her mother, steepling her hands in her lap.

"I've . . . I've just been feeling so . . . so . . . old lately." Naina looked up toward the ceiling chandelier, which had a gaudy golden glare. Too bright for her right now. "I came to New York so filled with high hopes and now it just seems . . . just seems . . ."

"Go on," Amaya said, squeezing her hand. Her daughter's hand felt so good, so comforting.

She rubbed her neck. Ah, the struggle to be cogent. And pirouette around the truth.

"It just seems . . . just seems . . . I'm too old for this life. Everyone is so young, toned, and gorgeous around me. What if Susan wants to replace me with someone younger, more vibrant and just way hotter? What kind of career can I hope to have when I'm fifty-five or fifty-six when there are so many young girls always around? Will the people I know still want to know me as I get more wrinkled and slow?" Naina slumped a little against the bench's cushions and stared at the scarlet carpet smeared with dull coffee stains or some kind of pattern. She couldn't tell what it was. But those messy smudges seemed to be permeating her mind. No, she told herself. She had to sit straight and sound intelligible. "I'm just too bloody old for everything here, every damn thing . . . I can't . . . I can't . . . compete with all these young girls." The words came out raw and intense, like a piece of rare meat. Just as she had felt them.

"Oh, Mom." Amaya gently hugged her. "Everything will be okay. I promise you."

"No, nothing will be okay, nothing will be okay . . . ever again." Naina pulled away from her daughter.

"You seem like you're in a lot of pain. Can you please tell me what's brought this on?"

"Nothing . . . Nothing, in particular."

"Well, something must have happened to cause you to feel this way. Did something happen at the gallery? Or somewhere else?" Amaya gazed at her with such focus she looked like a detective ready to swoop at any sound, gesture, or word that might reveal something.

Naina folded her arms and hid her clenched fists under them. Her heart was sprinting. She looked to her left, at a young girl in a short dress laughing throatily.

"No, no, no. Nothing specific happened. Why do you always assume something has to happen for people to feel a certain way?" Naina raised her voice. "Are human emotions so simple? A teacher shouts at you and you feel bad? Do such basic rules of cause and effect always apply to the human heart and mind?"

"Oh, poor mom." Amaya's voice was soft and smooth like fine muslin cloth. "I'm so sorry you're going through this."

"I don't need pity, thank you very much."

"No, you're right. You don't need pity." Amaya turned her face sideways and rubbed the end of her own sleeve. "What you need is . . . what you need is . . ."

"Oh I know what you're going to say," shot back Naina. "That I need some bloody therapist. Somebody to dig into my head and tell me how crazy I really am."

Amaya shook her head and bit her lip. She did not say a word. The silence between them loomed larger and larger and Naina felt smaller and smaller. She saw Amaya's oval face with those chubby cheeks creased with worry and confusion, making her look older than her years.

"Oh, Amaya, I'm so sorry," Naina said, in a high-pitched voice, hugging her daughter who responded with a bewildered expression and a tentative embrace. "I really didn't mean to be so horrible. Gosh, I didn't mean it . . . I love you so much . . . so much. I just don't know what's got into me . . . I just don't know." She looked at Amaya with moist eyes, feeling like a regretful, pleading child who has done something wrong. "Please forgive me . . . please forgive me . . . please forgive me . . ."

"Forgive you for what?"

Again that deplorable feeling slashed into Naina. "For my crazy behavior today, for ignoring you these last few weeks . . . For . . . I'm so so sorry."

Amaya lightly squeezed Naina's hand. "It's okay. You're clearly in a lot of pain and it saddens me to see that."

"Oh baby, don't be sad or worried about me," Naina said softly, stroking her daughter's face. "I'll be just fine. Everybody goes through stuff like this." She tried to put on her brightest smile. "I'll be just fine. You don't need to worry about your mother. You don't need to worry about anything."

Amaya arched her eyebrows and rolled her eyes in that condescending way that Naina generally hated—as if her mother was a trifling child unaware of the ways of the world. "If you say so."

"Listen," Amaya said, cradling Naina's hands in her own and looking at her in a way that caused Naina to avert her eyes. "I've been noticing now for a quite a while that there's something going on with you inside, and you need to take control of it before it takes control of you. I know you are in not favor of going to a therapist but there's no shame in going. Many, many people go to therapists. Even Indians. Not just Americans. Promise me you'll think about it." She squeezed Naina's hands tighter. "Or about other constructive ways to get yourself out of this funk."

Naina's body stiffened and she suspended her breath, then quietly released the trapped air. "Oh, my darling Amaya," she said, clasping her daughter, taking in the faint yet refreshing scent of her child's lime-scented body cream, something she had used since her teen years. "Yes, I promise, my darling. I will think about it. I will. I really will. You're the best daughter in the world and I love you so much."

"I love you too, Mom."

"Oh, you're fabulous, you're so fabulous, so amazing" Naina said, her voice suddenly high with extreme gaiety. She stood up and smoothed her skirt. "Now, let's go and enjoy the show."

CHAPTER FOURTEEN

ON A SLOW afternoon at the gallery one Wednesday when Susan was out, Naina got up from her desk to divert her thoughts from her work. She walked over to the window to watch the sun, which had made a sudden, short-lived appearance in the afternoon. Even though it was spring now, the past couple of days had been cool and cloudy and Naina was once again craving the sun to give her energy and lift her mood.

As she stood by the window with her palms outstretched so she could get as many rays as possible on her hands, her eyes wandered to a group of young women who looked like they were in their early twenties. Most were dressed in short skirts and sitting at a newly opened cafe opposite the gallery. Their tanned faces were fresh and glowing, and their bodies were slender and toned. They were chomping down mouthfuls of pasta, without guilt or hesitation.

It was past four o' clock and they were eating their lunch now. So late. My goodness. Why in the world did that surprise her? The order of time had such little meaning in New York. One could eat brunch at three o' clock, dinner at one a.m., buy groceries at five a.m., have babies at forty-six, and have visited every corner of the Met and Guggenheim before the age of three.

Still, even New York couldn't change some things—that people's bodies inevitably aged as they got older and that men still preferred younger women. That larger-than-life specter of Jai's rebuff still hung over her, albeit smaller and less robust than before.

Every day, she still thought of Jai. She pictured him walking into the subway, eating a bagel, reading a book, his tapered fingers carefully turning the pages, his cacao eyes deep in concentration. Leading his life. A life that would never include her.

If only the longing wouldn't pinch. If only the pain would stop. If only the guilt would end.

Naina's face drooped to one side and she stroked her cheek. Her leg felt extremely sore from her overly vigorous workout yesterday.

A part of her continued to look out at the girls, and another looked inside herself, both gazes misty, as if her eyes were peering through a veil of chiffon. One of the girls dressed in tight Lycra pants suddenly got up from her chair and did a quick handstand while her friends clapped and hooted.

These girls—they looked so unencumbered. They made her think of air, like a breeze circling the bougainvillea hedges in Delhi. She placed her palms—

which felt as limp as overcooked asparagus—against the window. She imagined dividing life into voluminous phases based on the elements. Life started with air and ended with earth. Fire was most likely to heat up things during the air and water phases. Early childhood's abandon was akin to air while adolescence's recklessness was like fire-inflamed air, perfect for setting off blazing, bounding, bonfires.

As people got older, jobs and marriages came into the picture, and a heaviness permeated the air and turned it into water. Still, at this stage, there were enough remnants of fire left to make things exhilarating and enticing. Scientifically impossible, of course, since water extinguished fire, but not metaphorically.

Then people had children. And the years dragged on. Age made regular visits like a loud, uninvited guest. The water coagulated and turned into earth. Became something solid and heavy. Firmly anchored to the ground. Without the sinuousness of air and water. Unfortunately, she was in the earth stage, feeling the weight of her tired body and the strong pull of gravity beneath her. Yet she had behaved heedlessly as if she possessed the dynamic motion of air and fire. She was so foolish. Out of sync with the elements. When it was her time to be reckless, she had behaved prudently, like most good Indian girls she knew.

Naina's head slumped forward as she now watched the young women lapping up large helpings of chocolate cake or something chocolatey with likely more calories than the young women could count. They were probably single and probably never had to think of anyone but themselves.

A white-over-red Mark Rothko painting came to Naina's mind, its edges blurry, paint from one color field seeping into the other, creating a mélange of shapes and colors. That's what boundaries should look like. Permeable. Mingling. Spilling.

The air in the gallery was getting staler and drier. Naina opened the window a crack and immediately closed it because it was too cold. A man came to join the dessert-eating women and the way he moved his tattooed arms while talking, reminded her of Rob, her tabla player friend. She felt more wistful now.

Her legs ached more and her interest in the café women waned. She returned to her desk and leaned back in her chair. "Make Me a Channel of Your Peace . . . Where there's despair in life, let me bring hope," she hummed under her breath with her eyes closed. It was the song from her Catholic School prayer book that used to iron out the wrinkles of trepidations in her mind every school morning. Recently, after so many years, it had reappeared in her head, and she found that the tune still had the same effect.

Naina thought about Rob who had left New York now, saddening her. He had to move to Santa Fe because he had lost his job as the manager of a bookstore. Though they had not seen each other that often, she had been fond of him, and found that they had more in common than she had initially expected. His spirit was like buoyant air—around him she could feel big bubbles and balloons floating upward.

Massaging her temples, she remembered him laughing wickedly as he told her about his Jerry Falwell-worshipping family. In that way, he was a little bit like Alannah, but in his passion for anything new-agey, he was more like Mara. And, he was a self-described David Bowie-style metrosexual, making Naina feel very contemporary to have him as a friend.

And, Rob, like her, had gone to a strict Catholic School. However, he was always spewing vitriol when it came to Catholic School, something she could relate to—although only partially. Of course, she had hated some things about her schooling, but there were aspects, glorious aspects, that had made her feel whole, hopeful, peaceful, and grateful. Like the hymns—soft, gentle, and comforting, the purest of silks that wrapped her soul every school morning. Songs whose sublime messages about gratitude, kindness, love, and peace transcended religious boundaries. When she sang those hymns, her spirit leapt high into the air like a ballerina doing a grand jeté.

And then there was the sense that all answers were waiting for you if you just had faith in God. Answers—solid, monochromatic, immutable truths—that would hold you close and reassure you, like the kind and loving Virgin Mary, anytime doubt or distress assailed you.

How bizarre that answers would abandon her so completely later in life. Did they actually abandon her or reveal themselves to be shifty, fickle, motley motes of slivered dust? She emitted a throaty, staccato sound, a lamentation of a loss of innocence. And then the absurdity of it struck her. To think about losing one's innocence at her age. Like a fifty-something-year old losing her virginity.

Naina stretched her legs, moved her hips closer to the edge of the chair, and rested her head against the vinyl top, coming as close as she could come to laying down at work. She felt drowsy and looked up at the ceiling, her eyelids drooping. Soon, she became fixated on a cluster of tiny cracks, forming an arc. She found them strangely beautiful.

"Bye, Nains," Rob had said as they exchanged a long farewell hug outside an Indian restaurant along the Hudson River. "And don't be too good. Life's too short for that. Fuck all that Catholic School bullshit."

"I'm not too good. Far from it."

At that moment, as they stood under the moonless, starless night and the Hudson River whooshed and swooshed in the furious wind, Naina had a sudden urge, urgently urging her. To tell Rob about Jai. To tell another living soul the ugly truth about herself. If she released it now, into the wind, what if it became small and insignificant? Just another particle getting tossed around in the universe. And Rob was a *man*, someone with a bad relationship with his mother, someone who would soon be gone thousands of miles away.

"In fact, Rob, there's something . . . something that I did that would shatter your good Catholic-school-girl image of me," Naina said, fingering the zipper of her purse, her eyes on the restive water.

"Oh really. I'm all ears."

"Well, there was this attractive man I met, very attractive in fact, and we met alone and and . . ."

"Don't tell me. You had a one-night stand. Woo-hoo. Way to go, Nains!" He raised his arms above his head in a cheering gesture.

"A one-night stand? Me? What?" Somehow the idea of her having sex with a complete stranger, an encounter that involved nothing except for lust, shocked, even outraged her. "No, that's never going to happen."

"Oh, aren't you such a good little Catholic School girl. Never say never. So what did you do with this attractive man? It better be good. I'm dying to have my image of good little Nains broken into little pieces."

But the words remained inside her, bound up tightly in a sack, pushing against the seams, unable to escape.

"Well, we had coffee and held hands," Naina said in mock seriousness. "And then we read books. Lots of books." She cocked her head. "And more books."

Rob laughed. "Well, you had me there for a second. I should have known better, Miss Goody Two Shoes."

JUST BEFORE SHE closed the gallery for the day, Naina heard a loud swoosh of the door and a short, flamboyantly dressed man with huge dark circles under his gray eyes—an unusual sort of gray, the kind of heavy, menacing color that envelops the sky before a thunderstorm—walked into the gallery. She smiled, but he took no notice of her, and quickly strode toward the paintings.

He stared at one wall, dramatically exhaled fistfuls of air, and turned toward Naina. "It's amazing how you guys put this crap up. I mean, come on, isn't it so obvious the artist is trying to copy Brice Marden?"

"Sorry, copy who?" she said, before thinking.

"Brice Marden, sweetheart. Brice Marden. Go, do yourself a favor and buy a book on him. You might actually learn something."

Even after the man left, Naina could feel the blistering air of his sigh in the gallery, whipping her for her enormous inadequacies. She could not bear to be in the gallery anymore. She quickly closed it and walked out.

Chelsea was bustling. There were several openings that night, and there were at least ten in her building. The elevator, the only one for the eight-floor building with twenty galleries, took fifteen minutes to come, and then she was squished in among a group of twenty-something European hipsters who were talking about how "American," "superficial," and "like Mickey Mouse" contemporary artist Tony Oursler—an artist she thankfully knew a bit about—was. Every sound poked at her nerves. She couldn't wait to leave Chelsea, but as she approached Ninth Avenue, she ran into a curator, a friend of Susan's she had met a few times, who wanted to talk about Red Circle's latest show. After a few minutes, Naina excused herself, apologizing and smiling profusely, her lips feeling all wobbly, saying she had to meet a friend for a drink.

She skipped going to the gym and went home instead. She sat in her apartment and stared at her walls, gradually soothed by their enveloping whiteness as she so often was. Like air, white was light and ethereal. And probably why she had found the hue so peaceful to be around after Harish's death. And after Jai broke her heart. Colors, sensual and inviting as they were, could also be oppressive, like a life with cares. Color was pleasure; color was life; color was love; but color was also stain; color was also taint; color was also pain. The empty mind must be white. Like a traditional Hindu widow's attire.

That night, Naina decided to forgo both wine and mint tea, preferring to sip water instead. After heating a frozen pasta dinner, she planned on reading some more poetry by Ryokan, a Japanese Zen monk whose poems she had started to read a few days earlier. She wasn't in a mood to read any of the long discourses in the Buddhism books she had recently embarked upon. It was all so mind-boggling and never gave her exactly what she wanted. Every time, she would pick up one of those books, a sense of possibility would well up in her, like that of a woman wondering if her blind date might turn out to be her soul mate. She would wonder whether those pages might offer her the missing pieces of the jigsaw puzzle she was fervently looking for, pieces that would allow her to see a vision-like picture of life completely and clearly. Or reveal an illuminated portrait that would unveil wisdom and knowledge, or an extraordinary scroll linking disparate forms that would banish all the chinks of uncertainty in her head. But that had not quite happened yet.

She flipped the pages to find a Ryokan poem she had not read before.

The night is fresh and cool
Staff in hand I walk through the gate.
Wisteria and ivy grow together along the winding mountain path.
Birds sing quietly in their nest and a monkey howls nearby.

As she pored over the words for the second time, Naina felt a yearning. For her garden in the suburbs, the long, curving petals of plum-colored irises, the sight of Harish in his cricket cap nimbly trimming flower stems with his oversized shears, the hypnotic hum of crickets at night. Often, during the summer, if she woke in the middle of the night, she would go out and sit in the garden and listen to the crickets. But there were no crickets or irises in her life anymore. Now there was only the thick smell of humanity and asphalt, the roaring sounds of cars and construction, the smells and sounds of man's triumph over nature, the gurgling sounds of her addled pain.

"Make Me a Channel of Your Peace . . . Where there's despair in life, let me bring hope," she hummed to herself again and again.

NAINA MET AMAYA two or three times a month, more than Naina would have wanted, but she knew she had to do it. Who knew what Amaya might think if it were any fewer than that? She had to be careful. But meeting her daughter was not easy. It always left her flustered and sharpened the arrows of her guilt. Fortunately, she didn't have to contend yet with Jai since he was in South America for another long work-related trip.

She chose to do only activities Amaya liked. They went to Broadway musicals, shopped for things for her apartment and scented bath and body products, listened to gospel music in Harlem, got hot stone massages in Connecticut—the kind of massage Naina herself hated. After a while, to Amaya's delight, Naina also started cooking again, and on certain Sundays, even prepared a feast. She cooked all of Amaya's favorite dishes, foods her daughter complained that were never as good in restaurants as they had been at home. Naina made South Indian style chicken curry with cardamom, sautéed okra with onions and cumin, penne and sausage in a spicy tomato sauce, grilled lamb chops with mint sauce, and Burmese khao soi with lots of nuts. All dishes required a great deal of work and regardless of whether she was tired or not, she would immerse herself in cooking to the point that her spirit would leave her body and sputter and splatter with the frying onions and cumin.

When the two of them met, Naina was initially like someone singing falsetto. She made a great deal of effort to be in high spirits, laughing a lot and gushing with enthusiasm. But it didn't work. Amaya soon recognized it as a pretense and started to worry and question her mother further. Naina toned it down, but made sure there was always at least a hint of a smile on her face, even if she had to consciously stretch her agitated lips to do so. Still, there were moments when she let her guard down. Only later would she'd realize, pinching herself, her daughter had probably seen her face wither, watched her mother's eyes darting in different angles, seen her mother's head dropping forward. But Naina ensured she was never as volatile as she was the first time she saw Amaya after Jai's rejection when they had gone to see *Chicago*. Nevertheless, Amaya continued to question her, and each time, Naina repeated with the same answers and conundrums. It was aging. It kept distressing her. How could she stand a chance when she was surrounded by so many freshly blossoming women? Had moving to the city been a blunder?

Despite all this, she was feeling much better, she would tell Amaya, something that contained some grains of truth. She'd say she was no longer as agitated and despondent and rarely, very rarely now, did that wretched melancholy came back, she'd say. Something that was not exactly true because the cold, dry, black bile would spurt out from time to time, though not with same chilling crush as earlier. And not for the same befogged, unknowable stretches warped by time.

Of course, Amaya would say all the right things. *Age was just a number. Live your life and forget your age.* Regardless of the wisdom or lack thereof, such phrases from her daughter's lips tasted vapid, like thin, insipid wafers without any chocolate.

And then Amaya would bring up the therapist issue again and again. And Naina would just respond with a sweet smile and say she was looking into it, while trying to stop her lips from twitching. At one point, Naina said her friend Mara had a great therapist, but she wasn't taking on any new patients for the next few months since she just had a baby after a challenging delivery. Maybe the doctor would be willing to take her on in a few months.

Well, what about another therapist, Amaya would ask, intently gazing at her mother. She could give her plenty of recommendations.

Oh no, there was no need for that, but thank you for the offer, Naina would quickly reply, averting her eyes yet another time. Mara's therapist was supposedly fabulous. Good things come to those who wait, don't they? Again, Naina would muster a smile, consciously stretching her lips, and keeping her voice cheerful— but not excessively so. And then as she'd watch Amaya's face tighten, Naina could feel her body hunch over, her heart pulsate, and hear herself saying what she knew her daughter wanted to hear. She might be open to another therapist. She just needed some time to think about it.

"Amaya, darling, guess what?" Naina said brightly one evening when they met after a gap of nearly three weeks since her daughter had gone to Costa Rica on a holiday with Jai before he returned to the U.S. "I think you're going to be proud of me. I've started reading a bit about Buddhism. It's very intriguing . . . It doesn't give me all the answers, but it does bring me peace. Some peace. Sometimes."

Amaya's face lit up. "Really?"

"Yes, really. I think it's making a pretty big difference." Naina knew she was flexing the truth here, but it seemed worth it to make her daughter happy. "And I found this Japanese poet called Ryokan . . . he was also a Zen Buddhist monk . . . he's marvelous. Darling, every time I read him, I feel like I'm lying on the warm earth, smelling the sweet flowers with the sun's warmth on my body and the butterflies buzzing away. It's such a delicious feeling."

"That's awesome! I'm *so* glad. I'm *so* happy you've found something. And it's great that it's giving you peace. That's just what you need. Tell me more. I can't wait to hear about it. . ."

They were sitting in a new pan-Asian restaurant decorated with long hanging Chinese lanterns, which by some miracle of technology swayed constantly, making its patrons feel as if they were floating in a trance. Naina watched Amaya, delicately illuminated by the lantern lights. Her pretty face looked so tender, and she was smiling like she hadn't smiled around her mother in a long time. Amaya's slightly chubby cheeks were bunched up, the corners of her eyes were puckered, and her almond-colored eyes emitted little wisps of light, like the swaying lanterns above her.

Naina was reminded of Amaya as a five-year-old, dressed in frilly lavender dresses, laughing away on a swing, begging her mother to push it higher and higher. The swing was Amaya's favorite thing on the playground, and even though she was otherwise a cautious child, she was fearless on the swing. Going higher and higher, her laughter like wind chimes.

Naina got up from her chair and tightly hugged her surprised daughter and stroked her hair. "I love you, my darling girl. I love you so much . . . You're my tenderest, kindest, and most beloved girl . . . You were made perfectly to be loved . . ."

"Mom, we're in a restaurant. People can hear us," Amaya whispered as a lotus pink hue wafted over her cheeks and a smile hovered at the edges of her lips. "Thanks, Mom, for those . . . florid . . . I mean lovely lines . . . but aren't they from some of your Madam Bovaryish novels?"

"Yes, of course, my darling. At my age, what else do you expect? Some of the words are from the English poet Elizabeth Barrett Browning's letters."

"Elizabeth Barrett Browning? I've heard of her. Do you remember Karen's sister, Anna? She's not yet twenty-four, but she's fallen for a string of guys, and she writes about *all* of them in her diary, always starting with "How I do love thee? Let me count the ways.""

"What? A girl in this day and age does that? No way!" Naina erupted into bubbles of giggles.

IN SPITE OF the warmth they displayed toward each other, there remained a wild, restless elephant in the fragile bloom between them, the animal with its ears vigilantly spread out, ready to trample the small, delicate blossoms of the Virgin's Bower flowers twining around them as it exuded a frothy, sweet vanilla scent. But, to Naina, it seemed like only she could clearly see, feel, and identify the gigantic, trunked creature. The most monstrous sin committed by a mother.

Jai, luckily, it seemed, still had not told Amaya anything, and as far as Naina could gauge, her daughter suspected nothing. At least nothing she let on. Naina had avoided seeing Jai since that awful day in February, yet Amaya didn't press her about it—probably given her perturbed state and the fact that he had been away for a while, Naina suspected. Not at first in any case. Naina imagined Amaya was probably worried her mother would suddenly start behaving bizarrely around Jai and embarrass her. If only her daughter knew how big a fool her mother had already made of herself.

Amaya continued to talk about Jai, describing the panoramic views of Manhattan from the cruise he had taken her on for her birthday, how they stayed up at a jazz club until the sun peeked out, the adventures of their vacation in the tropical jungles of Costa Rica and how it was so funny to see Jai scream and run whenever he saw a spider, even though their guide had told them those spiders were harmless and never attacked humans.

Every time Naina heard Amaya talk about him, she winced, as if someone were peeling off a layer of her skin. Like when her leg hair was ripped off with honey-coated swatches of cloth at the beauty salon and she would suppress her screams to avoid embarrassing herself.

"So, when we were in Costa Rica, Jai said something very strange when I asked him why he was so afraid of the spiders," Amaya said one day as they sat in Bryant Park after watching a matinee production of *The Phantom of the Opera*. "It was very late at night, and we had had a couple of drinks. Out of the blue, he said it's probably because of his complicated relationship with women."

"*What?*"

"That was my reaction too."

"Did he say anything more?"

"Although he had had just a couple of drinks, he seemed quite drunk and was talking in a tone I'm not sure I'd quite heard before. There were other people he knew at the bar in Manuel Antonio Beach and he was sort of joking . . . maybe? In some Neanderthal way?"

"But what did he say?"

Amaya rolled her eyes and let out a long puff of air. "I'm embarrassed to repeat such prejudiced nonsense. But anyway, he said, 'Spiders, those damn spiders, are always female. Look at any culture. In ancient Egypt, there was Neith, the spider goddess of war and weaving and there's some Spider Grandmother in Native American mythology. I mean, isn't that enough to scare a poor man off spiders?' And everyone around us laughed, though I didn't quite see the humor. Jai's far from sexist . . . no, he's a feminist and proudly proclaims as much, and this is the only such remark he's ever made. Since others were there, I couldn't get him to explain more that night. And when I asked him about it the next day, he just laughed it off, saying he was just talking nonsense after having a couple of drinks. It meant nothing."

Amaya's narrowing eyes had that knowing look. "But I don't know if I believe him. There was something lingering there when he said that, something in his face changed, some memory was triggered, some issue beneath the surface lying unresolved."

"Or maybe he just wanted to spin his own myth."

"What?" Amaya swerved her head to peer at Naina through squinted eyes.

Naina bit her lip after she realized how acerbic her words had sounded. Every part of her was still stinging from Jai's shocking words about spiders and women. Still, she had to swallow the tartness in her voice—even if it made her intestines roil.

"I was just joking . . . Bad joke, obviously . . . very bad . . . not funny, not even a smidgen . . . What do you think it might be?"

Amaya looked up, her thumb and index finger pressing the edges of her jawline.

"I don't know . . . My friend Erica thinks it's just plain sexism and misogyny. But not me since this was a drunken one-off and I know him . . . but there's something else, something ambiguous I can't put my finger on . . . Do you have any idea what it could be? You know him pretty well."

"Me?" Naina said, jerking her neck back sharply and opening her eyes wide. "How should I know?"

Amaya emphatically shook her head, her voice hard and admonishing. "Mom, I don't know what's gotten into you. Every time I bring up Jai, you show no interest. You don't seem to want to meet him anymore. What's the matter? Did he say something to offend you? Or do you just disapprove of him? You know, he always asks about you."

"He does?" Naina was genuinely surprised even as she heard a faint, melodic buzz of crickets rise from within herself. The bastard. The abominable male chauvinist pig who used his charm to lure women into his spider web. His male spider web.

Naina sat up straight and cleared her throat. She clasped her hands on her lap, her fingers tightly interwoven. Her heart lurched like a shaking ship gulping vodka, but she had to steady her body. She had to stop anything that made the elephant raise its trunk, lift its tusks, and trample their little, precious bloom. She took a quick, large sip of water.

"Amaya, darling, it's nothing personal. Really. He did nothing, really nothing to offend me. As you know, I've been preoccupied lately. With myself. You know how self-centered I've been." Naina heard a low, hollow laugh emanating from her.

"That part is true." Then Amaya paused. "But lately you've also been very giving. The wonderful dinners, the hot stone massages, the musicals. In fact, you've been very, very generous and I want you to know I really appreciate that. Especially given that you've been going through a hard time psychologically."

Naina knew Amaya meant what she said. But she could also see her eyes did not soften. They were studying her, questioning, and demanding an answer.

Naina took in a long breath of air and held on to it. "You know I'm very fond of Jai, don't you?" she said, incredulous she could get those words out without stammering. "He's been like a friend to me."

"Well, then why don't you want to see him?"

"Of course, I want to see him, of course, I want to see him, of course, I want to see him. Very soon, very soon, we should all get together, don't you think?"

"Okay then. Tell me when. What about next week?"

"Oh, I'd love to, really love to, but next week is way too busy at the gallery with all these meetings Susan has set up and so many openings. Another time. For sure. For sure."

"Mom, I can't help but feel you're avoiding him." Amaya's gaze practically pierced Naina's skull.

Naina's insides felt like the all-too-familiar fluttering wings of a frightened bird in a cage. She frantically sought to form a coherent, plausible sentence.

"You're not entirely wrong, Amaya. I've been too embarrassed to see him. My emotional state has been . . . well, you know already . . . fraught . . . and I didn't want my daughter's boyfriend to see that."

"Hmm . . . I see." Amaya tapped her lips with her forefinger.

What was her daughter thinking?

"Well, uh, you know the whole Indian way of thinking . . . never let yourself look bad in front of your son-in-law," Naina said in a rapid and animated voice. "You know whenever your dad stayed at nana and nani's house in Delhi, he used to be treated like a king. New pillows and towels would be bought, the best tablecloths and blankets would come out, his favorite food would be prepared, and there were always two desserts after lunch and dinner. Two desserts. Almost no other time in my life, unless there was some big party or celebration, would there be two desserts."

"Wow, how wonderful that married men are treated like kings in India," Amaya said, rolling her eyes. "And since when did Jai become your son-in-law? And since when did you start subscribing to these old-fashioned beliefs?"

Naina slowly let out a stream of air. She looked down at the damp, shining green grass of Bryant Park and wished she could just burrow her face in it and forget about everything.

She reached over and squeezed Amaya's hand. "Amaya, my darling. I'm sorry for the way I've behaved . . . I really am. I love you very much and your happiness means the world to me. Could we just let bygones be bygones? I hadn't been myself for a while and I wasn't thinking straight and didn't want to embarrass myself. You can understand that, can't you?"

Amaya looked toward the tall trees.

"Can't you? Can't you?" Naina realized she was sounding almost hysterical and shut up.

"Yes, I can," Amaya said slowly nodding, her expression still inscrutable. "But you do understand that Jai is a very special man in my life and it means so much to me, so much to me, that you guys get along and you are supportive of this relationship. Even if Jai and I have some ups and downs. Everybody does. And you know that this is not the first time I've said this." The muscles in Amaya's face relaxed and her eyes softened. "Dad is not around and even if he was I'm not sure he'd support this relationship. And Karan, he's definitely not supportive, but you know that already." Her eyes turned from a radiant almond to a sad brown. They seemed to be looking out at nothing in particular. "So that leaves just you, just you, Mom."

Naina's heart swelled with a gust of love. Suddenly, all she wanted was to see her daughter's cute, plump cheeks scrunched up, the corners of her eyes crinkled, and hear her chiming laughter, as she went higher and higher on the swing.

"Darling," Naina said, squeezing both Amaya's hands even as she could still feel, tucked under layers, the sting of her and Jai's last meeting at Washington Square Park and that terrible spider story. "I'll meet Jai whenever you want. Whenever. And I mean it."

CHAPTER FIFTEEN

UNEXPECTEDLY, KARAN CAME to New York on business for a couple of days, and Naina invited him over for a Mughlai feast she had prepared. Amaya was supposed to have joined them, but she had non-refundable tickets to a Broadway musical.

That Sunday night, Karan dropped a bombshell. Things between him and Arti, the girl he had been seeing for the past six months, had been getting really serious and they were likely to get engaged soon. Arti, a dentist, had grown up in a conservative Gujarati family in Fremont, a section in the San Francisco Bay Area with lots of Indians. Naina had met her briefly during one of her trips to California and distinctly remembered not liking her. Arti was one of those girls who behaved like she owned the world, someone who seemed like she had never been dented by anything and never expected to be dented by anything. Short and stocky, Arti had been wearing a red designer dress that was clearly too short for her chubby legs.

"Mom, aren't you happy for me?" Karan demanded when Naina was silent.

"Of course I am, beta," Naina replied. "I'm thrilled for you. Of course. What a question! If Arti's the one you think you can build a life of love and joy with, then I couldn't be more delighted . . . But I am still your mother, your Indian mother to boot, so naturally I'm protective. I want to ensure you're making the best possible choice. Marriage is one of the biggest and most important decisions of your life. And you haven't known Arti for that long . . . Marriage is not easy, you know . . . Are you absolutely sure?"

"Have you ever known me to make a decision if I'm not one hundred percent sure and haven't thought it through?" He shot a look at her, his eyes flashing. "Oh, now I know what your problem is. You don't like Arti because she's not an intellectual like Amaya's boyfriend. Because she's not a professor and hasn't lived in Paris and traveled all over South America."

"Don't be ridiculous," Naina said, fighting a strong urge to smack him. "Jai has nothing to do with this. Nothing at all. I've nothing against Arti . . . I hardly know her. And anyway, you're the one marrying her. Not *me* . . . Beta, I'm still your mother and I'm here for you if you'd like to run anything by me or . . . I just want to see to it that whatever step you take makes you happy in the long run."

"And since when do you care so much about my happiness?" Karan said, slapping his knife down on the plate.

The sound of metal striking china boomed in Naina's head, like an admonishment for all the ways she had failed her son—by selling their home in New Jersey, distancing herself from the Indian families he had grown up around, and taking up a bottom-rung job he regarded with disdain.

She looked down at the chicken swimming in the curry. Neither said a word for a minute or two.

"Trust me, I know I'm far from perfect, darling . . . But your well-being means the world to me . . . you and Amaya are my pride and joy . . . I understand you may not approve of some things I've—beta, I'm truly sorry . . . I didn't mean to hurt you . . . Reasons for things are often complicated."

"Complicated? I hate that damn word. It's just a fancy term for irresponsible, confused thinking and behavior."

He shoved his empty, dirty plate to the side.

The clank agitated Naina. She got up from the table, leaving her half-eaten meal, and went to the bathroom where she turned the tap on full force and rinsed her hands and face several times, engulfed by the whooshing of the water.

ON AN EARLY autumn afternoon, Naina lay on her couch listening to music. Her back was arched against its right arm, her head tilted slightly backward, and her hair unruly because of the early afternoon wind. She was on her second glass of wine, a new Italian from the Puglia region in the south of the country, her nerves tattered like moth-eaten wool. On the coffee table lay an unopened book of Buddhist quotations.

Today was going to be a big day. She was going to meet Jai for the first time since that sunny February day. All three of them were going to a concert in the evening.

Through Naina's compact, silver-colored CD player, the Cape Verdean singer Cesária Évora's songs of longing and melancholy flowed languorously and viscously through the living room like honey. Whenever she listened to Évora, she imagined fancy Parisian bars (though she had never been to Paris), countless clouds of smoke creating a blinding haze, smooth red wine being poured from lovely carafes, inebriated people swaying as if in a trance, tragic souls dressed in silk and chenille, and everyone perched on this fine string where beauty and sorrow came together.

Today, she pictured Jai standing straight and tall, not leaning on anything, wearing a cobalt blue scarf looped around his neck like a European, drinking a glass of dry Bordeaux. Through the smoke, his chocolate-colored eyes lightened and floated away as his scars flickered, chiffony specks moving in and out of sight.

Naina wrapped her arms around herself as sorrow flowed out of her and into Évora's bluesy "morna" ballads sung in Kriolu, a mix of Portuguese and West African dialects.

How was she going to get through this? How was she going to see the only man, the only man she had ever passionately loved in her fifty-plus years, the man who had so cruelly spurned her? How was she going to see the man who had made such a deep incision in her heart that she dreaded bearing a scar for life? How was she going to see Jai holding Amaya's hand, putting his arm around her shoulders, whispering in her ear? How was she going to hold all her emotions inside and present a cheery picture of composure like that Monet painting of his first wife with their child in their flower-filled garden? Was her body large enough to contain all these emotions? Or would they, without her consent, spill out, like an ugly, messy, smelly gush of vomit? Would she topple over? Would she dissolve into a freakish flood of misshapen, gaudy tears? And disgrace herself and shame her poor daughter?

Why had she agreed to see him? Why had she let Amaya talk her into this? Why? Why?

She pounded her thighs with her fists as "Mar Azul," Évora's soulful ballad pleading with the sea swelled in the room like an ocean of tear-salted port wine.

Oh Sea
Please calm your waves and let me go
Please let me go see my land once more
Please let me save my Mother, Oh Sea

Finally, Naina dragged herself from her couch and turned off the music. She paced around her living room. The Chinese dry cleaner and his wife were arguing anew in Mandarin below her. A car was honking on the street so loudly and relentlessly that it sounded like a supremely spoiled brat throwing a tantrum. Her neighbor Laura was screaming on her cellphone in her brassy, insolent voice.

And then, either from outside or inside her head, or both, she heard the leaves rustling, whispering secrets to the wind and echoes of the word *sodade*, longing, from Évora's eponymous song.

Naina put her feet on her bamboo floor. She had to keep them there. She could not escape reality and waft into Cesária Évora's world. She had to meet the charming cad, the chocolate-eyed delight who dared to compare women to those creepy, cunning spiders. She remembered the gleam in Jai's eyes whenever she wore her Wiccan spider pendant—probably misogynistic revulsion that she mistook as interest. But was *she* really in a position to castigate Jai?

She sat down again on her couch, drawing comfort from the whiteness of her ceiling she could not take her eyes away from. "Make Me a Channel of Your Peace . . ." she hummed again and again and again.

NAINA STEPPED OUT of the subway on 96th Street at about seven-fifteen. The sky was bluish-black and a pale sliver of moon, veiled by big, burly clouds, struggled to make an appearance. She stood on the corner of Broadway and 96th Street, not wanting to move. She wished she could stare at the sky forever. Without paying much attention to it.

She was wearing a grass-green cotton kurti, decorated with blue embroidery inspired by the intricate lattice screens in Mughal architecture, with a pair of jeans. She wore subtle beige-toned make-up, and the only touch of glamor was a pair of high-heeled blue shoes. It was the look she had strived to create. Neither striking nor unimpressive, neither formal nor casual, neither too auntyish nor too girlish. She was headed to Symphony Space to listen to a famous Algerian musician called Cheb Mami who performed Rai, a high-octane form of music with Bedouin roots and a feel of the expansive, empty, enchanting desert. Typically, she loved Rai music, but not today, not today. To put off seeing Jai a little longer, Naina went into the first store she could see, a place that sold an array of cushions. She went to the corner of the store and, as her thoughts raced, glanced at the heavily embroidered silk cushions she knew had to be from India. There was no way she could have got out of tonight, she thought, as anxiety constantly bit her like a relentless mosquito.

The man in the store stared at Naina and she quickly moved to the section with mid-century modern cushions, pretending to look at the bold, geometric-patterned cushions in red and white.

When she reached Symphony Space, she just stood on the corner of the street, blinking at the illuminated letters of the place's name. Somehow, she managed to propel herself forward, feeling as if she were tiptoeing on shards of shattered emeralds, hearing her blue heels make a clicking sound despite her sluggish, stuttering gait . . . and stopped. She spotted a head of wavy black hair glinting with strands of steel gray. Ribbons of excitement spiraled through her, filling her with color. Another part of her stiffened, appalled and chastened.

He was wearing the same thing he had on when they had first met. A black V-neck sweater, a burgundy shirt, and light-colored jeans. He was holding hands with Amaya. The ribbons tore. The colors faded.

"Hi, Naina," Jai said. "Long time no see. Where have you been hiding?"

Naina was flummoxed. Her lips trembled and her heart lurched. He greeted her so easily, as if they were casual friends who hadn't seen each other in a while. As if nothing untoward had happened between them. As if he hadn't crushed her heart into throbbing scraps of blood-weeping pus. As if he hadn't utterly humiliated her. Either he was a great actor or had no feelings.

"Hi . . . Jai," Naina said, her voice wavering. With effort, she smiled, but could not bring herself to look at him. She kept toying with the zipper of her purse. "It's . . . nice to see you . . . I know . . . it's been a while . . . I've just been so . . . so caught up with work."

Naina heard her own voice, drifting away like a lost postcard in the wind, and felt her body droop like a bent old woman who had once gone to a Convent School. She could feel Amaya's gaze, sharp and pointy like a needle, taking in everything.

Slowly, Naina straightened her back and lifted her head. From the corner of her eye, she noticed Jai's eyes, still the hue of chocolate, but now they looked like the most bitter of dark chocolates, like something that had a hundred percent cacao and not a grain of sugar.

"Did I tell you that another one of the shows Mom curated with her boss got a great review in one of the art magazines?" Amaya said, tightly interlacing her hands with Jai's. "What was the name of the magazine again?"

"*The Pacific Monthly.*" Naina was glad she could get those words out without stumbling and tripping over them.

"Really, that's excellent," Jai said in that singular voice of his. It was brushing her ears, stroking the back of her hands, and tickling the skin beneath her collarbones. "What's the show about?"

Jai was standing tall, with his shoulders back, his legs slightly apart. She remembered her first impression of him—a man who emitted an air of easy confidence, as if doubts were strangers to him. She felt the nerve endings of her skin rise and arch their backs in delight.

She ran a hand through her hair. "It's a show of self-portraits of the . . . of the . . . artist as Hindu goddesses . . . different Hindu goddesses, you know, a variety of them, there are more than a thousand . . . maybe even hundred thousand . . . in contemporary settings, like driving sleek Japanese cars on highways and . . . working out on treadmills."

Normally, when Naina talked about the show, she could hear a flourish in her voice and feel her face brighten. But this time, she heard herself discussing it in a dry, concise way—the way a stuffy teacher would talk about some dull topic in a forgotten history book.

"That sounds very fascinating and rather amusing," Jai said. The corners of his mouth turned upward into his trademark half-smile. Before, she would have found such an expression playful, and it would have immediately put her at ease. But now, it seemed contrived and askew, as if he were holding something back. Was he mocking her? She felt her stomach clench at the thought and turned her face away.

"Maybe you would like to see the show," Amaya chimed in.

"Maybe. Maybe. Though to be honest, I can't say Hindu goddesses running around on treadmills is quite my thing."

Thank goodness. Naina tried to stifle a sigh of relief.

"Oh, give it a chance, Jai," Amaya said, looking up toward him with that adoring expression in her eyes. Naina pinched her lips together, swallowing her feelings.

"Unfortunately, the show is closing in a couple of days," Naina said.

"Sorry, darling, there's no chance I'll be able to make it by then," Jai said, eyeing Amaya with an equally doting expression.

Since when had he started calling her darling?

Naina squeezed her lips together even tighter, trying to gulp so many feelings at once that they would not go down easily and left a smarting sourness in her mouth. A sensation reminding her of the bitter hue of Jai's eyes.

"Amaya, that's a gorgeous dress," Naina said. She actually looked kind of sexy in the fitted purple dress with a slit at the back and the color complimented her dusky skin. Around her daughter, Naina probably looked like a middle-aged aunty.

"She looks beautiful, doesn't she?" Jai said, possessively putting his arm around Amaya.

"Absolutely beautiful," Naina said, trying to hold on to some form of composure, which felt like fleeing brushstrokes in that Monet painting of his wife and child in their flower-filled garden. "Absolutely gorgeous." Somehow, she had to get through this evening, somehow she just had to.

DURING THE CONCERT, Naina kept fidgeting the whole time—with her hair, with the gold chain around her neck, with the loose threads of her kurti. She glanced at Jai and saw the crescent moon-shaped birthmark near his nape, and, of course, those fingers she had missed so much. But most importantly, she could smell him, fully, completely—that familiar smell of the mountains. She felt herself fleeing to Shimla where she and Jai would be holding hands, watching the sun set behind the mountains and tripping over pine cones.

Someone coughed. Naina was back with a thud at Symphony Space in New York, sitting next to Amaya holding hands with Jai. Both guilt and yearning clawed at her, so tangled with each other that she couldn't separate them.

At intermission, Amaya needed to use the restroom, leaving Naina and Jai alone. Naina started to read the brochure again.

"It would help if you didn't act so odd," Jai said, his voice slicing into her like a sliver of ice.

She flinched.

"C'mon, Naina. I don't care if you're nice to me or not, but I care deeply about Amaya. If you behave oddly around me, she might suspect something. And I would hate for her to be hurt in any way. And as *her mother* I imagine you feel the same."

Naina still stared blearily at the brochure, trying desperately to stop her body from twitching.

"Or maybe you don't. Because you are one unusual kind of mother."

Naina felt as if he had struck her. *An unusual kind of mother.* He might have just said *terrible* mother. He might have just called her Medea.

"We have to learn to be civil to each other. And maybe we can become friends again too. Because it's possible we might be linked for a long time."

Linked to each other for a long time? What did he mean by that? Was he planning to marry Amaya? Was she going to be his *mother-in-law*? She felt herself sinking down and down, to the bottom of the seabed where myriad psychedelic creatures could attack her.

Naina draped her left leg over her right and sharply inhaled. "I know it might not appear to you that way. But I do love Amaya very, very much."

Jai threw his head back and sniggered. "Ya right, Naina . . . My mother also used to do the same thing when . . . never mind . . ."

Naina swiveled her head to look at him. What did he mean? Was there another side to Meena, his bold, trailblazing mother who came alone to the US in the sixties to study and ended up marrying an American man? Were there splotchy, sinister feelings lurking beneath the glow of a son's admiration of his mother and the shadow of her loss? Were these the spiders he so feared and despised? What could have possibly possessed this peculiar man to speak about his mother in a tone spewing such bitterness? One that perfectly matched those bitter chocolate eyes.

She noticed the condescending expression made Jai look jaded and ugly, like a man who had been imprinted by all the scars on his face. Scars that suddenly looked spiky, sharp, and curved, like the legs of a scorpion, those creepy crawly, stinging, sometimes more dangerous cousins of spiders. With his chin jutting out, his extravagant eye roll, his tight, twisted smile, he also exuded the air of a scorpion-like predator with a monstrous appetite. Someone who wanted to feast on a mother, a daughter, and God-knows-who-else. Jai had never seemed as malevolent and remote as he did at that moment.

Naina slowly sat up straight and held her clenched fists against her upper arms. She could feel her nails making indentations in her palms. She didn't want to ask any questions.

"And because I love Amaya so much, I think she can do better than you," Naina said, her voice crackling. "I made a mistake, a terrible mistake, but you did too. There's no reason for you to act all holier than thou. Don't pretend you didn't lead me on and deceive Amaya."

Naina couldn't believe she had been able to get all those words out coherently. Jai laughed, a grating, sarcastic laugh.

"Naina, you're nuts and that's what I like about you. You live in an alternate universe, which can be charming for those of us who don't. But when you're so far from . . ."

"Amaya's coming," Naina said.

"All right, immediate change of tone," Jai said. "And don't you dare screw this up. I love Amaya very much."

Naina closed her eyes, feeling fury and misery bubbling into blubbering, bloated blots. She wept inwardly until Amaya took her seat and then she strong-armed herself to look at her daughter and smile.

AMAYA ASKED NAINA to join her and Jai again a few weeks later at a Peruvian restaurant and she couldn't say no. It was a quiet, intimate restaurant in the West Village, the kind that people went to for leisurely dinners and hours of conversation. For Naina, there couldn't have been a worse choice of restaurant. Now she had to sit opposite Jai as he was being his warm, chatty self, acting as if there was no tension smoldering between them.

For most of that evening, Naina said little and answered questions in a matter-of-fact manner when asked. She also drank lots of wine. Something she generally avoided doing around Amaya.

Jai told a lot of stories: one about being solicited for plastic surgery in Brazil, another about an African-American student of his who had become a devout Hindu, and another about a chance meeting with Sting that led to an interesting conversation. Again, Naina felt herself pulled by Jai's storytelling voice whose textured timbre alternated from something weighty like deep indigo to something airy resembling the indistinct blue of a cloudy sky. It lulled her into a rhythm that gradually pushed everything else out.

But she could not allow herself to get swept away to rhapsodic, rapturous realms by these feelings. The fantasy was over, she reminded herself again and again, the thought of it slashing her every time. Jai did not love her. She was not his kindred spirit. In a symbolic gesture, she made sure both her feet were touching the floor during the whole evening.

"Amaya was always a sensible girl, even when she was little," Naina said, when Jai asked about Amaya's childhood. "I never had to worry about her."

"And where did she get that from?"

"Not from me, that's for sure . . . From her father."

Toward the end of the evening, Amaya stepped out of the restaurant to respond to an urgent text because the cellphone reception inside was terrible.

Jai intently gazed at Naina, his large pupils looking like they were swimming in cocoa. She sensed the palpable pressure of his stare pressing into her collarbones partially peering from underneath her plum-colored round-necked dress, which showed very little skin. She felt his eyes move upward to her lips, also covered in deep plum. Soon, her body was stirring, the fibers inside gleefully scurrying about. She hoped he couldn't see her hardened nipples beneath her sweater dress. She jerkily played with her hair and took a big gulp of wine.

"You look resplendent in purple," Jai said, his voice once again lower and slower. The voice he used when the two of them were alone together. "Like an orchid."

A spasm of anger shot through her, making all her chest muscles tighten. She folded her arms and jammed her hands into fists. She sat up straight, wanting to sear him with a glare. But she couldn't. So she gazed at the wall above, feeling her eyes blaze. Tersely, she said thank you and Jai shrank back in his chair.

CHAPTER SIXTEEN

NAINA WAS EXHAUSTED. Leaving the gallery early, she dragged her body into the old-fashioned cage elevator. She shuttered her eyes and leaned against the metal back as the elevator crept down five floors. Fortunately she did not know the elevator operator and did not feel obligated to make conversation.

The day had been unusually busy, filled with continuous movement, mostly of the mind. It had been like a one long paragraph without commas, semicolons, or periods. Just an endless rambling of thoughts, most of which were pragmatic and dull. Susan was on vacation, so Naina had been running the gallery by herself with a little help from an intern. Oddly, the most challenging part of the day had been writing a grant proposal to get funding for some future projects. She had been working on it for a couple of weeks, without much difficulty as long as she concentrated. Today, however, the sentences would not flow. Like water from a tap on an unfortunate Delhi day, words just sputtered and stopped. Sputtered and stopped. Sputtered and stopped.

And then there were all these arguments with Red Circle's new treasurer, Melinda, an impeccably dressed, hard-nosed businesswoman who always thought she was right. No, Naina's budget for the grant was too extravagant. No, they did not need any money for most of the items Naina had listed. No, they did not need to print higher quality brochures. No, they did not need more brochures. No, they did not need more guest curators.

The conversation with Melinda sounded like a never-ending page of No's without any punctuation. Without any pause to show she was actually thinking before refusing. Melinda, who still retained a Southern accent even after living in New York for almost thirty years, would speak to Naina in a chiding maternal tone, especially elongating her vowels as if she were speaking to a baby whenever she said "No" and "Honey." She spoke to Naina in the same way she spoke to the twenty-something gallery intern, who in Melinda's eyes, knew nothing about money except how to spend it. Today, Naina got so furious that she told Melinda her real age and that she had run a household on a fairly tight budget when first moved to America, a foreign country to her at the time.

Eventually, Naina phoned Susan in Italy—even though it was late there and she hated calling—and asked her boss to support her suggestions. Susan sent Melinda an email, and they finally agreed on a number in-between for the grant proposal.

The day was now over, thank goodness, and Naina was able to leave early because of the intern. Naina ambled down the sidewalk, her body feeling heavy and slow, her eyes glazing over. Suddenly, the heel of her sandal got caught in a crack of the pavement, and her body pitched forward.

Her fear almost came true. But she wasn't even rushing—yet it didn't stop her from almost falling. She must definitely be getting old. The life of the working woman was so far from her idealized version of it. On days like today, it was just endless, thankless, listless drudgery. A foggy melancholy, echoing a Cesária Évoria song, slowly draped her bulky, flaccid body.

"Weeping Coconuts. That's it. Weeping Coconuts." Naina turned to her right, roused by the sound of the words, the title of a powerful Frida Kahlo still life in which the round, tropical fruits are imbued with human-like features and emotions.

On the opposite side of the street was a group of young female gallery assistants dressed in effortlessly chic, severely minimalist designer outfits in all the possible variants of black. One of them must have talking about Kahlo. On their feet were dramatic animal print high heels, accentuating the masterful femininity of their gait. These women were sometimes called gallerinas, a suitable term considering their overarching, levitating youthfulness, sylphlike bodies, and touch-me-not aura of culture and sophistication. Technically, Naina thought she could also be a gallerina, but no one would ever think of using that descriptor for her. She was just a gallery assistant at a small nonprofit gallery. Nothing more.

Her legs ached. She longed to sit down. There was a café down the street. Maybe she could go there and get a cup of coffee.

Naina walked slowly, her eyes on the sidewalk, and heard the insistent click of high heels. She looked up and recognized one of the gallerinas moving toward her. This statuesque young woman in her various hippie-dippie stilettos worked at a medium-sized gallery in her building. Although they had been in the elevator together many times, they had never spoken to each other. Maybe they had exchanged smiles—if one could call the faintest stretching of lips a smile.

"Hi," the young woman said, smiling brightly and extending her beautifully manicured hand. "My name is Lisa. I work at Myrna Weber's. You work at Red Circle, right?"

"Yes," Naina said, hesitating. What could this beautifully dressed, extraordinarily poised young woman possibly want from her?

"I saw your show with the Hindu goddesses and really loved it. It was really amazing. You were one of the curators, right?"

"Yes, the executive director and I worked on it together," Naina said, brightening up.

"I have a huge interest in Hinduism, particularly as it relates to women. I want to do some research on it for an essay I'm writing and I'm hoping you could suggest some books I might read."

"Sure," Naina said, smiling. "Would you like to get a cup of coffee down the street and talk? I really need to sit down."

Lisa turned out to be very nice and had a genuine interest in Hinduism. And surprisingly, she was very respectful to her, like a pupil might be to a teacher. Now, Naina felt important, valuable, and knowledgeable, her age briefly feeling like an asset.

"So do you want to return to the art world after you finish graduate school?"

"I'm not sure," Lisa answered, looking much younger with her long, straight hair tied in a high ponytail. "Maybe the art world, maybe academia. Or maybe something else. But I'm not thinking about that yet. I haven't even started graduate school. I've got plenty of time to figure it out."

Of course she did. Lisa had plenty of time. Plenty of time. Soaring mountains and endless rivers of time. If only everyone was so fortunate.

THE COFFEE MADE Naina restless, so instead of going straight home, as she had originally planned, she decided to take a short walk. It was a nice quiet day in Chelsea.

She passed by James Cohan Gallery and through the lofty glass doors saw a headless sculpture dressed in a jacket made of brightly patterned, exotic-looking fabric. She felt pleased she could identify the artist. The headless piece was made by Yinka Shonibare, a British-Nigerian artist who made theatrical works commenting on colonialism and post-colonialism. He must have a new show up. Naina wrote a reminder in her taupe-colored notebook to go and see it. She had to keep current.

She kept walking, writing a couple of more reminders in her notebook, until she reached Metro Pictures Gallery where she knew a big show by the famous photographer Cindy Sherman had just opened. Peeping through the glazed façade, she saw large photographs of well-dressed women in elegant settings. She had read a book on Sherman the year before and recognized the trademark theatrical quality of the artist, known for photographing herself in various female guises. Something about Sherman's work reminded her of Frida Kahlo, something she couldn't put her finger on. There was also something different about these Sherman photographs from those she had seen earlier.

Naina said a quick hello to a woman she had once met with Susan at an after-party following an opening as she stepped into Metro Pictures, one of the largest and most prestigious galleries in Chelsea. She fixated on the photographs. The women in these works seemed older than the others, seeping with a quiet desperation, like blood that keeps trickling, drop by drop, drop by drop, drop by drop, from a dirty maroon wound that refuses to heal. She took in the photographs, one by one, until the distance between her and those women dissolved.

Naina's heart beat faster as she stood rooted in front of a photograph of a woman in a red dress. She held a chunk of her hair below her left ear. Did she look like one of these women, only less elegant and less affluent? Is that how Jai saw her? Did Jai see her like the woman in the red dress, the creases in her face popping out despite all the makeup, the fan in her hand ridiculous as if she were living in a bygone era?

The lady in the photograph was so ugly. She had these hideous brownish-black blemishes on her right forearm. Her dress needed to be fully long-sleeved so that those blotches could be disguised. They were too obvious. And her stare. Her stare was so pointed it was almost rude. No, not almost rude. It was rude. Absolutely rude.

Naina wanted to move away but couldn't. She twisted the chunk of hair between her fingers.

The upturned eyes of the woman in the red dress were brown and crystallized like topaz, but there seemed to be a tiny glimmer of molten dreams and desires from a long time ago trapped inside the frozen, stony eyes.

Perhaps that's how Amaya saw her too. Naina felt even more tremulous. She twisted the hair in her fingers faster and faster, again and again. A small, invisible space grew between her and the woman in the red dress.

Things had not been going so smoothly between her and Amaya lately. Though she had made a great effort to maintain her composure around Jai, even going as far as being so friendly with him that it made bile rise to her chest, Amaya remained suspicious, with her penetrating gaze as she repeatedly asked questions. Someday, sometime soon, Naina knew she would be found out. Amaya would know what a debauched mother she really had.

Did Naina really look like that woman in the picture? Like someone with a sad, mysterious past, something so deeply embedded in her being, that she couldn't hide it despite that nice red dress, red lipstick, and seeming sangfroid? She bit down hard on her lip until she could feel her teeth marks on it.

Had her broken heart so altered her that the color of her soul was now the greenish-brown of a withering plant? An ugly, dismal hue that seeped into her body, muddying her almond-colored eyes, discoloring her olive-colored skin, and stealing the shine from her black hair? Is that what Amaya saw? Is that what Amaya meant when she said something *fundamental* had changed about her?

Amaya had been haranguing her with the same never-ending questions. Mom, why are you behaving so oddly around Jai? Why do you seem uneasy? Why do you seem aloof and—almost—surly around him? Oh no, no, no, Naina kept insisting at first. None of this was true. She felt fine around Jai. Amaya was just imagining things. Except, maybe, like Naina had told Amaya before, she was worried about embarrassing her daughter by seeming distressed and not together in front of her daughter's boyfriend. After all, no man wants to see his girlfriend's mother as being crazy, Naina had said, hearing herself titter, and how ridiculous that sounded.

Jai was a wonderful man and she, as her mother, was glad he made her happy, she assured Amaya, feeling a spasm in her ribs.

Still, Amaya didn't look convinced.

Her daughter never brought up the spider comment again. How unusual for someone like Amaya. Maybe even being a psychologist did not make you immune to focusing on what you wanted to believe and ignoring the rest.

Naina was alone in the main exhibition area of Metro Pictures. So much space. Just for her and these photographs of women who looked as real as she.

When was something real and when was it not? Did one ever know for sure? Did anyone know anything for sure? Did these women with their vacant, searching eyes also once believe, like she did, that they had all the answers?

Naina tightly entwined a large chunk of her hair on top of her head and continued to study the woman in the red dress. The woman wore dangling earrings that looked as if they never dangled. The woman had a hand fan that looked as if it never moved.

After a while, Naina revisited an old concern of hers with Amaya. While Naina said she obviously thought highly of Jai, she was slightly worried Amaya might be acting too hasty. Maybe that's what her daughter was noticing. At Amaya's age, it was crucial to keep all her options open. Sometimes, the ideal partner may not be who you believe it is, so it was important to keep exploring. When she had said that, Amaya looked at her incredulously for a minute and then laughed, a hard, sardonic, humorless laugh.

The red-dressed woman's mouth was tightly set. She seemed like she hadn't laughed in years.

And then, in a fit of desperation, Naina had brought up their age difference. Jai was eleven years older than Amaya. That was a lot. She just didn't want her daughter—if she were to marry Jai—to become a young widow like herself. Or be stuck with an aging, ailing man while she was still in her prime.

"Really, Mom?" Amaya said, widening her eyes and laughing that harsh laugh again. "You can't be serious. You've known how old he is for a long time, but it's never been a problem for you before. Now suddenly you expect me to believe it's a problem?"

One time, when the two of them were sitting in a quiet section of a household goods store swathed by comforters and pillows, Naina blurted out, "Remember what you told me about Jai's fear of spiders and how he spoke disparagingly about women, linking them with spiders . . . that's kind of . . ."

Amaya jerked her body back, almost imperceptibly, against a pink, puffy down comforter, and her upper lip clamped down on her lower lip. "No, I haven't forgotten . . . I don't need to be reminded. It was egregious, but he just said it once, and many people say awful things occasionally. He truly is very much a feminist and I appreciate that." Amaya let out a stream of air. "Still . . . maybe there's something gnarled beneath those words of Jai's, there might be. Human beings are complex creatures. Not just black-and-white. It's foolish to kneel at the altar of the ideal. But I think you already know that . . ."

Naina turned her face away, not wanting her daughter to know how many rings of truth her words contained, each gripping her mother in firm, pinching circles.

Naina swept her gaze across Sherman's not-black-and-white photos of women seemingly kneeling, as Amaya had put it, at the altar of the ideal as they haughtily posed in various positions. She wondered what they really thought of perfection . . .

"I think I have an inkling about what the problem might be," Amaya had said on a recent autumnal evening when the scarlet moon hung low to the ground, ballooning away like an unmarried woman brazenly walking the earth with a baby in her belly. Her eyes were intent and sharp, her fingers touching in a reverse steeple on her lap. "But please, seriously, please . . . don't be offended or . . . embarrassed."

Naina felt a chill of nervousness go through her and bent her head. "Amaya, for God's sake . . ."

Her daughter deliberately inhaled a spate of air. "I think you might be heartbroken, I think you fell in love with someone, and, for whatever reason, it didn't work out. Maybe he hurt you. Maybe Jai reminds you of him. Maybe seeing me and Jai together reminds you of something you've lost."

Amaya had spoken in that low, self-assured voice that suggested she already knew the answer. The all-knowing voice of a therapist or parent. Naina was dumbfounded. How close Amaya was coming to the truth. Yet so far.

Even amid the silent sobs from the pictures enveloping the gallery, Naina could hear Amaya's voice ringing in her head. The kind of omniscience Naina could not envision herself—or any of the older women in the photographs—possessing, regardless of any glossy veneer.

But then, all of a sudden, in that madly bright night, Amaya's voice softened and became pliable, like cotton balls. "Did he hurt you a lot, Ma?"

Ma? Amaya almost never called her Ma. Only in exceptionally intimate moments. Fleetingly, Naina had felt overcome by a surge of emotions that she wanted to tell her daughter everything. About how she had fallen in love with Jai, how he had led her on, and how she had tried to kiss him. An urge greater than herself pushed her to confess and beg for forgiveness. And she couldn't let her daughter be hurt by this duplicitous man. After everything, it was her duty to rescue her. After all, she was her mother.

But she hadn't been able to summon up the courage. She didn't know if she could bear it. She could lose her daughter forever. Never hear her tinkling laughter again. That tinkling laughter, like the sound of wind chimes, as she went higher and higher on the swing. Never hear anyone call her Ma again. Never squeeze her soft hands again. The thought itself sent her into a bout of panic. She didn't know if she could ever confess.

So she had remained frozen, like the woman in the red dress in front of her. She had vehemently denied being in love with anyone and said Amaya was just dreaming. Being a therapist might make her inclined to constructing creative narratives. No, there had been no man in her life. No man had hurt her. And no man was going to hurt Amaya either. Ever.

And then, all of a sudden, big, blubbery tears rained down her face. Amaya reached over and hugged her, and Naina kept saying, "I love you, I love you, I love you" like a fervent prayer.

"All right, you don't have to tell me, Ma," Amaya said as she gently rocked her.

"SO DID YOU like *Eat Pray Love*?" Mara asked as they walked toward the yoga studio.

"No, I can't say I did. I thought Liz was whiny and irritating."

Mara looked surprised. "Really? I thought you would love it considering you seem to be starting some kind of spiritual journey."

"I didn't feel much of a connection to her," Naina said, the thought of her starting some kind of spiritual journey sounding odd. "Liz's tone was so glib. The book felt a bit light and superficial even though it's supposedly about a deep topic . . . finding of the self. C'mon, who wakes up one day and thinks about telling God 'I'm a big fan of your work'?"

Mara vehemently disagreed, saying the book had touched her soul in a way few books had.

"I want to go to India one day too," Mara said, adjusting her bindi, a miniscule version of the Hindu God Shiva, on her forehead. "I can't wait to feel the power of its spirituality."

Naina smiled, not wanting to tell Mara, yet again, that she had never felt this mysterious spirituality in India that Westerners went on about. To her, it was a country with an ancient civilization, a colonial past, and a tumultuous present. And of course, the place where she had grown up, the place that was now both home and not home.

"Don't you want to feel the spirituality of the Sistine Chapel?" Naina had always longed to go to Rome. She remembered Sister Maria, a gentle four-feet-five-inch nun from Kerala, going into paroxysms of ecstasy every time she spoke about the Sistine Chapel at her school in Delhi. Of course, Sister Maria had never been outside of India, but she had a book about the chapel she excitedly shared with all her students.

"No, it's not the same," Mara insisted. "Christianity just doesn't have the soul of Eastern religions. It's all about sin, rules, and commandments."

"But Hinduism isn't just mysticism you know," Naina said. "It has all kinds of rules and rituals too. You have to fast during certain days of the Navratras, wear red sindoor in your hair if you're a married woman, wipe it off if you're a widow etc., etc. Not that I'm a very good Hindu just like you're not exactly Mother Mary."

As they walked, Naina and Mara continued debating Hinduism versus Christianity. Recently, Naina had been spending much more time with Mara, often discussing the larger questions of life. Mara's take was, in Naina's opinion, informed by a feel-good, new-agey spirituality where every problem could be solved, every dream achieved, every doubt annihilated. Somehow, everything could be all good and the divine was just waiting for you if you were willing to reach out to it. It was a vision Naina could not quite buy, but she did like hearing about it. A vision of unfailing optimism. A balm she desperately craved. A uniquely American salve.

Sometimes Naina would wonder what Alannah, the eternal skeptic, might say, but they hardly saw Alannah these days. She had fallen head over heels in love with a man called Damien, a British journalist who worked for the *The London Times* in New York. They had met online, on Alannah's tenth blind date. When Naina had met Damien, she was taken aback. She hadn't expected to see a lanky, highly refined gentleman—almost like a character from a Merchant Ivory period film—doting on her straight-shooting, Italian-American friend. And equally interesting was the change in Alannah. Her face was now flushed with a radiant glow and she behaved in coquettish and feminine ways—ways Naina had never imagined her friend capable of. She had also never seen Alannah so happy, evoking in her a potent wistfulness. A feeling that tasted like those small, bitter, mouth-burning gin and tonics that her friend Reena's father used to sometimes sneak to them. "Cheers, girls," he would say in his perfect English, enunciated even more perfectly. "Here's to some poor colonial chap stuck in some tiny flat in cold, dreary Manchester, dreaming of the days when there was sun, the Gymkhana Club, and the swagger of the Raj."

IT WAS MARA who insisted that Naina try kundalini yoga, a type of yoga Naina had never heard of. Mara said it cleared psychological and artistic blocks and made a person very creative. Apparently, it was practiced in India by a small, select group of people, and therefore was not well-known in India. But Yogi Bhajan, a Sikh who became a master of the science (Mara constantly referred to it as a science) at the age of sixteen, moved to the US in 1969 and openly taught its closely guarded secrets. The kundalini energy, imagined as a coiled and dormant serpent at the base of the spine, was awakened by a series of exercises, breathing techniques and chanting.

"It's not about explanations," Mara said in her melodious, sing-songy voice that sounded like relaxing bedtime music as the two of them approached the yoga studio on a Sunday morning. "It's about the experience. You'll see when you try it."

Naina could see a glass door with the word Shakti in big gold letters arranged in a circle, glittering in the sun. She started to feel nervous. She had not done yoga since eighth grade and had not liked it at all then.

"Mara, I'm middle-aged and haven't done yoga in over thirty-five years. I will make a complete fool of myself. People will laugh at the Indian woman who can't do yoga."

"Naina, honey, this is yoga, it's not about judging," Mara said, tying her long, blonde hair into a loose knot with a tie-dye scrunchie. "Yoga will meet you where you are. Everybody can do yoga, just differently. Promise me you won't compare yourself to anyone else?"

The interior of Shakti was an enticing combination of serenity and sumptuousness. Two walls were decorated with thangkas, colorful and intricate paintings depicting Buddha and his entourage on silky fabrics, and on the floor were two mattresses covered in a gleaming orange fabric. And there were turquoise-colored cushions with lots of paisleys. A young clean-shaven man, dressed in khaki shorts and a white shirt proclaiming, "I AM," lay sprawled on a mattress, reading a book.

On one wall was a shelf with books on Hinduism, Sufism, and yoga, and another shelf contained books with names like *Be, The Spiritual Way of Letting Go of Anxiety*, and *Invite Your Inner Bliss*. On the bottom shelf, tucked between a book of poems by Rumi and *Introduction to Kundalini Yoga*, was Mara's book *The Creative Goddess Within* protruding outward. At the front desk, dressed in a peach-colored kurti and loose white pants, was an oval-faced, blonde-haired woman who called herself Sat Kaur.

Naina had brought black sweatpants she normally used at the gym and a pink T-shirt from Banana Republic to change into and didn't know what to make of any of this. Even though there were sandalwood incense sticks, books on Hinduism, and several of Zakir Hussain's CDs, the place didn't quite feel Indian, yet she couldn't exactly say why. Even Sat Kaur did not quite seem Indian. But where she was from, Naina couldn't figure out either. (Only later did she find out she was previously known as Jean Holbourn and had traveled extensively in India, including to the Sikhs' holiest site in Amritsar—where Naina had never been.)

She overheard a couple of people praising the benefits of yoga and thought of Harish, religiously going for his jog in an oversized polo shirt three times a week.

He had little regard for yoga, describing it as quackery. "I don't understand these Americans sometimes," he said to her one time. "They have the best, most advanced modern medicine in the world, and they want to practice all this bogus yoga and ayurveda. They are so gullible, you know. Some sadhus, corrupt people that they are, tell them some rubbish and they believe it."

"We have to be quiet here," Mara whispered in her ear. "We're early so I'm going to browse the books. Do you want to?"

Naina shook her head, standing in a quiet corner, her eyes vaguely on the luminous turquoise cushions with paisleys.

As for herself, Naina didn't know what to believe. All she knew was that she was stooping under a mound of mostly invisible troubles and needed some peace. And some answers, if possible. She remembered the woman in the red dress in Cindy Sherman's photograph. Frozen. Unmoving. Standing under bricks from a long-gone past. What should Naina do? Stand still or move? If she moved, how to move? In which direction?

She looked around her, hearing Jai's voice in her head, compressed like a tight fist, condemning all yoga in America as "shameless highway robbery." He said Americans had stolen yoga from Indians and then "crushed it into palatable glitter" to do what Americans liked to do best—make money. "In *every* single place in the US, it's completely commodified now. *Everyone* is in it just for the money. That's it."

His words had fallen like hot bricks. One thudding after the next. No pauses for queries or dilemmas. No lulls for nuances or distinctions.

Yes, Naina had once loved Jai's air of confidence—as if few uncertainties ever touched him—but now she wasn't so sure. Didn't wise people question, doubt, differentiate, regret, and even change their mind?

"You can buy yoga tank tops, yoga botanics, yoga ropes, yoga toe stretchers, and get a yoga butt," she could hear him saying. "*All of them* sell *all of this* junk and much more rubbish. It's ridiculous. Fake hippies."

Jai hated all kinds of hippies as well. So many of his views were so hard and intransigent. In this way, they were different from each other. How could she not have seen that before? He thought Florida was just one ugly Disneyland; vegetarianism was against the inherent carnivorous nature of human beings; and Ecuador was indisputably the most beautiful country in the world.

"Look at you, Naina." She imagined Jai teasing her, his voice pleasurably tickling as if it were a thread of raw silk. "You're reading about Buddhism and God knows what else, and you're about to do yoga for the first time since eighth grade. What are you, the Indian answer to Jack Kerouac and Allen Ginsberg forty years later?"

As she heard Jai's fictitious words in her head, Naina silently laughed as Mara picked up a book titled *The Real Me*. She began to see herself as comical, as one of those fifties or sixties seekers who traveled to places like India or China to find themselves, or to find answers or whatever else they were looking for—one of those many troubled or curious souls who turned to the East to learn about concepts like impermanence and inner peace, concepts she had never been taught. But she was an Indian in New York, in the twenty-first century, looking toward the East for answers by reading books on Buddhism by white people and going to learn yoga from a white person. "That is totally, utterly absurd," she could hear Jai saying in a voice as hard as concrete. Maybe it was funny and absurd, but it wasn't completely senseless. Surely, people from the East weren't the only ones who had the authority to teach yoga and Buddhism—as long as Westerners did it respectfully and Asians had equal opportunities to teach these practices?

"From now on, you know what I'm going to call you . . . an Indian flower child," she pictured Jai saying. And then, his voice, which still had the power to make her organs do a haphazard tango, would become harsher as his disdain toward anything associated with hippies would gush forth, like dirty, muddy water from a pipe in a slum.

The yoga studio itself was minimal with unadorned white walls and blonde-wood floors. Green-and-blue mats, neatly rolled-up, and folded Mexican blankets lay at one end of the room. A large round metal object—a musical instrument, she later learned, called a gong and used for deep relaxation—stood next to the platform in front, framed by a thangka painting. The studio emanated a greater calm than Naina had expected and she slowly took in the big empty space, yet unoccupied except for the two of them. Mara quickly got into a cross-legged pose and shut her eyes, while Naina's gaze soon became fixed on the thangka painting hanging on the wall.

The elaborately patterned Tibetan Buddhist painting, meant to represent a mandala, was deep red with a trademark circle. Naina loved circles. They had no beginnings and no ends. No birth and no death. No sides. Both whole and a hole. Full and empty simultaneously. Like the Earth and the shape of its annual orbit around the sun. All curves like a voluptuous woman.

Naina lowered her gaze slightly to Buddha sitting on his throne, meditating peacefully as the hustle-bustle of design and pattern in the thangka continued around him. Her eyes kept moving until they finally rested for a few seconds on the dot on Buddha's forehead, and her head felt quieter than usual, like a momentary pause at a dinner party when someone says something unexpectedly profound or unexpectedly stupid.

Soon, a tall man with a symmetrical Nordic-looking face, as if all his features had been carefully sculpted, entered the studio. He was dressed in a kurta pajama—the kind that Harish would wear to bed, in his early years in America, before switching to shorts and a T-shirt. Naina's heart tightened. Harish might not have been the most open-minded man around, but there had never been any sharpness about him. His edges were soft if not pliable.

The man, whose name was Nick, sat cross-legged on the platform in the front, fiddling with a music system. Three more people walked into the studio: a studious-looking boy with a goatee and wearing a T-shirt with an image of Jim Morrison; an older woman with big hoop earrings and bright red lipstick, who had the air of someone quick to explode; and an exceptionally short woman with a soft, angelic face, who seemed as if she had just returned from the Peace Corps or some other do-good mission.

As everyone confidently sat on their mats and placed Mexican blankets next to them, Naina started to feel awkward, like an interloper among people who were well versed in a game she didn't quite know how to play.

"This is one of my favorite sets because it not only cleans out the toxins in our body that we get from so much of the bad food in this country, but also the mind, things that we can't see, that are buried in our subconscious," Nick said in a voice that burst with sweetness, like too much sugar in tea. "That horrible thing that your Aunt Ethel said to you when you were five, that bad grade that made your poppa wanna kill you, and that terrible prom date. Remember that? Or have you forgotten? Nothing is ever forgotten, guys, nothing. Just as your body needs to digest the food you eat, so does your mind need to digest and process your thoughts. So, are we ready to rock n roll?"

"Yes," the class said enthusiastically. Naina was quiet.

The set was not easy. They had to squat on their toes in frog pose, raise their buttocks with their hands and feet on the floor in downward dog, and lift their upper bodies as they lay on their stomachs in cobra pose. Naina could barely concentrate as the postures felt weird, their silly-sounding American names felt weird, and Nick's slangy accent and analogies felt weird. And the fact that everyone else so gracefully did the asanas, particularly someone called Dana who made downward dog look like some sort of cool contemporary dance posture, made Naina even more self-conscious about her fumbling attempt at yoga. What would everyone think? And then there loomed the specter of Jai laughing at her in her head, a harsh, grating laugh that resounded in her ears.

She felt a yearning outstretch its palms inside her heart. The yoga class felt so unfamiliar, yet somewhat familiar. She wished she had someone with whom she could relate, someone who could help her make sense of the experience, someone with whom she could laugh about the whole thing, someone reasonably close to her age, someone who had grown up around kurta pajamas, someone who instinctively knew how to pronounce words like Shakti and Sat Nam, someone who would crack up at Nick's pronunciation of Shiva, someone who had had a yoga teacher like Mrs. Chandrashekhar growing up, someone who would automatically know lotus pose's Sanskrit name was padmasana. Obviously, such a person would have to be an Indian who grew up in India, and the fact that she no longer had any Indian friends suddenly bothered her.

Lightheaded from the almost seventy-five minutes of yoga she had done, Naina quickly lay on her mat and closed her eyes when the time came for deep relaxation. She heard the rippling sounds of the gong, and briefly opened her eyes to see Nick striking the instrument. The sounds of the gong swelled and swelled and swelled until they sounded like operatic thunderstorms. Gradually, her mind slowed down until she heard nothing but soft murmurs in her head.

And when she finally opened her eyes, she heard a whisper from the ocean floor of her mind. Do it. Tell Amaya the truth. Regardless of the cost. Because it's the right thing to do.

She quickly tucked the thought in the back of a mental drawer and slowly got up and rolled her mat.

CHAPTER SEVENTEEN

IT WAS NOW the middle of September, but the temperatures were still in the mid-eighties, making it feel like a delightfully long summer. Despite the temperatures, the New York art world was in full back-to-work mode. For Naina, though, there had been little indolence. As part of a small, emerging nonprofit gallery, there was always work to be done—maintaining and upgrading the space, dealing with finances, reviewing artist submissions, writing grants, etc. etc., regardless of the season. But she didn't mind. Work was good. It kept her focused and productive.

Susan said she hoped to promote Naina within the next few months to gallery manager. Naina could hardly believe it. In her mid-fifties, she was moving up the ladder of the New York art world.

It was three p.m. on a Thursday and in a few hours Red Circle would be hosting an opening for a new show, the first one of the season. Naina had been working since seven in the morning. She desperately needed a cup of coffee. Desperately.

As she stepped out of the gallery, she realized that in the bedlam of the preceding hours, Jai had not crossed her mind even once. She felt pleased with herself. The warm breeze outside was refreshing after being cooped up in a frosty air-conditioned space for seven hours. She hated air conditioning—she always had, and it had been something she and Harish used to argue about quite often. He liked the temperature to be around sixty-eight degrees as did Karan. When Naina was in air-conditioning, her body shivered and cringed like a bird whose feathers were being pulled out. Also, it made her feel like some sort of perishable food put in a fridge to be protected from natural decay—except that air-conditioning did not prevent the decay of humans.

The week had been a complete roller-coaster; everything that could have gone wrong, had. Samantha Ali, the artist whose work was being exhibited, had promised to ship all twelve paintings for the show five days earlier, but ended up shipping only eight. Susan, who always became fierce and intense when she was stressed, kept telling Naina to get the artist on the phone, but Samantha could not be reached on her land line or mobile phone. It was only this morning that Samantha had showed up from upstate New York, with the four paintings in tow. But then, the art installer could not be tracked down for several hours. And the computer, which had been throwing petulant fits in the past few weeks, suddenly crashed in the midst of sending important emails.

But now Naina sighed with relief as she determined that the only things left to be done were to print more copies of the artist's statement and get ready for the opening.

She had just wanted to get a quick coffee, but when she saw the café's chairs on the sidewalk, under the rays of the sun, she couldn't resist the temptation to sit down. As her body sank into the spongy plastic chair, she realized how tired she was; once again she was taunted by fact that she was no longer young. To hell with everything. She was going to sit down for a bit. The gallery could wait. The opening could wait. She felt surprised by her own reaction.

Her phone beeped. It was a text from Amaya, saying she was sorry she couldn't make it tonight. Unexpectedly, she had to work late. And what was the name of that kathi roll joint in the forties that Naina had been talking about the other day? Maybe she and her colleagues would go there for a quick bite after work.

As Naina typed the name of the place, she thought about the bizarre things Amaya had told her a few weeks earlier when she came over for dinner. Things that had flabbergasted her. She was still in shock.

Jai had been behaving oddly since Amaya had started her new job at a different substance abuse center. Yes, the hours were more erratic, including working Sundays, but she liked it a lot more. She also got along much better with her colleagues in this job and, in fact, one of her colleagues, Ryan, was someone she had gone to college with, but only now had they got to know each other properly and discovered how well they got on.

Naina had perked up when Amaya spoke of Ryan. Should she or shouldn't she? Should she ask if Amaya was interested in Ryan? Amaya had not been bothering her recently with questions regarding Jai, so was it worthwhile to risk this welcome calm? And anyway, it was a long shot for Amaya to be interested in anyone but Jai.

But, in the end, Naina hadn't been able to resist. She just had to know. So she did it as gingerly as she could. Is Ryan just a good friend or is there something—? She stopped, waiting for her daughter's reaction. Amaya flashed her eyes with a fierce *don't you dare* look and Naina dropped it.

But then Amaya suddenly said that Jai had asked her something similar, which made her mad. As Naina heaped her daughter's dinner plate with her homemade chicken biryani, Amaya said Jai didn't like her going out with her colleagues, which she did now more than before because of the erratic hours and the fact that they got along so well. Often, he would get suspicious and interrogate her about it. Even though she had invited him plenty of times to join them whenever possible, he would rarely come and when he did, he would make little attempt to be friendly. Instead, he would just sit and sulk. And now, almost every time she came home after eleven, regardless of where she went, she had to let him know beforehand. And Sundays, forget about

Sundays. Whenever she couldn't spend Sundays with him, he either pouted or threw a tantrum or both.

Naina's jaw dropped, and she just sat there opposite Amaya with her plate still full, trying to digest this information. She couldn't understand this. She couldn't picture it. Who was she talking about? Professor Jai Silverstein, who embodied the very essence of self-assurance, whose very posture gave off a leather-and-musk scent of authority? That Jai Silverstein was a peevish child sitting in company, with his arms crossed, nose wrinkled, and squeezed lips pushed out? That Jai Silverstein was like a jealous first child acting out because he feared his parents loved their new baby more? How could this be? How could he even imagine that someone as loyal and steadfast as Amaya would deceive him or neglect their relationship?

Naina heard footsteps to her left. She hoped it wasn't anyone she knew. "Hi, Naina, how are you?" Anna said, a curator she had met a couple of times. "Taking a break before the opening?"

"Yes. But I need to get back." She hoped Anna wouldn't sit down. For just a little while longer, she wanted to be alone, not obligated to carry on a conversation.

Then realizing she might have sounded curt, Naina said, "I hope you'll be coming to the opening."

"Definitely. But I've got to run now because I have a couple of errands to do. See you later."

Naina sipped her cappuccino as the sun warmed her back. She still shuddered with shock every time she thought of all she had learned that evening with Amaya. Even now, it sat like undigested red meat in her stomach.

When Naina had asked Amaya why she thought Jai was behaving like a needy and jealous child, Amaya said, "It probably has something to do with his childhood issues with women." Amaya wrinkled her forehead and rested her chin firmly on her knuckles. She looked like such a therapist. Their biryani, which Naina had spent a great deal of time preparing, sat mostly untouched.

"What do you mean?"

"I should have probably thought more about Jai's strange dread of harmless spiders . . . it's probably the transference of fear from unsafe early relationships with women . . . Okay, maybe you were right, and I should have given it more thought. I did sense there might be something beneath the surface, but I didn't quite think it had that much intensity or would have manifested like this . . ."

Any reminder of those words equating women to those execrable, eight-legged, eight-eyed creatures had scorched Naina. What a bloody bastard. What a low-class, woman-bashing scoundrel despite all that education and professorship at Columbia. To hell with all those polite and overly compassionate therapeutic niceties like "unsafe early relationships with women" defending abominable words and actions. They were inexcusable and unforgivable, regardless of whatever childhood issues he might have had or not had.

Naina's eyes had turned toward her daughter as she tried to quell the fire burning within. What was Amaya feeling? Were there shadows behind those rigorously cogitating eyes? Was there an invisible quiver in the mouth that spoke so articulately? Or was she imagining things?

She squeezed Amaya's hand. "Are you okay?"

"I'm fine." She flashed another *don't you dare* look. "Everybody has issues. Every person, every relationship has issues. It's okay . . . And don't start telling me again that I need to keep exploring. I have no desire and no need to do that."

Again, that evening, that whisper rose from the ocean floor of Naina's mind. Louder than before. Confess. Do the right thing. Stop your daughter from getting hurt.

Her heart pounded. "Amaya," Naina said slowly. "There's something—" And then her insides screamed like a woman in labor pain, a baby who was terrified his mother might never come back, a woman who had just been told that her beloved husband had been cheating on her. She couldn't do it. She just couldn't.

Naina went to the bathroom and covered her face with her hands. She was such a coward.

She was so selfish. She had to save her daughter from Jai. It was her duty. And then her insides howled again.

And then, amid all that cacophony in her head, she heard the muffled, sweet song of the koel bird flitting through her mind. The song that, while she was still in her bed during Delhi mornings, she would eagerly wait for. Right then, the koel seemed to be singing the sweetest of songs. Possibly, very possibly, Jai would reveal himself to Amaya to be horrible and duplicitous, and they would break up on their own. And there would be no need for Naina to wreck her relationship with her daughter. The koel continued to melodically coo. Naina smiled to herself.

"You know, Jai's relationship with his mother was very conflicted," Amaya said, her voice low and guarded as she stared at an empty space on Naina's white wall.

Naina recalled how startled she had been when they were at the Cheb Mami concert and Jai had mentioned Meena—his bold and brilliant mother whom he had always spoken of as if she were this incandescent inspiration—in a tone oozing with the sourness of raw lemons. She leaned closer to Amaya, feeling herself tingle with expectancy as she waited to hear more about Meena. But below that tingling, she had also felt indignation, hot and pregnant, ready to flare as she had anticipated hearing some pathetic reason to absolve Jai of his behavior. Her own gash also started to throb, and she exhaled to cool herself— very consciously since she had learned from the kundalini yoga teacher that it was a technique to calm oneself.

What could poor Meena have done to her son to cause him to hold grudges against the dead woman decades later and portray his relationship as conflicted? Not drive him to some silly sports practice? Push away girls before he could seduce them? Or dress up as Neith, the Egyptian spider goddess, on Halloween?

Amaya had not said anything more. Her favorite biryani was getting cold.

"Darling, tell me why his relationship was conflicted."

Her daughter continued to stare at nothing, her hands cradling opposite elbows, her mouth sewn together.

"I don't know if I should . . ."

"What? What are you talking about? Of course, you should tell me. Of course, you should. I need to know . . . I'm your mother, after all. You're the one that says it's so important to talk about things. C'mon, tell me, darling. I want to be there for you."

"I don't want you to judge him harshly . . ."

"Judge him harshly?" Somehow, the idea of Naina sternly judging anyone struck her as ironic at that moment.

"Of course not. Why would I want to do that? I just want to learn more so I can understand and help you . . . Please tell me . . . I don't want you to get hurt . . . And please, please, let me support you."

Amaya gave her one of her looks.

"Only if you need the support, of course . . . I know you're a grown woman, but we all need to share don't we? . . . C'mon, Amaya . . ."

"All right, all right." Amaya threw up her hands and then interlaced them in a fig leaf shape near her thighs. Her vacant eyes gazed downward.

"I don't know everything, but recently he's told me a lot more. Until his teenage years, his mother had been great, taking him to museums, giving him books to read, encouraging his talents, but then she met another man whom she fell madly in love with. She suddenly left him and his father. He says they remained connected, but he won't tell me how much. Or how he felt about her leaving. But I suspect he was very hurt. I know her death really devastated him."

"What?" Naina said, her head reeling. "What?"

Amaya gulped down some water. "I think I need some wine. Do you have some?" She shook her head. "Of course, you always have some."

"And then his ex-girlfriend . . . Amanda . . . also behaved unpredictably, always kept him on edge . . . although I don't exactly know how . . . she started drifting away from him, and Jai felt powerless . . . to do anything about it. In reality, she was doing drugs and never told him . . . and . . . and ended up disappearing in the most final way possible . . . she died from a drug overdose."

Amaya sighed deeply and took small sips of one of Naina's special California Merlots.

Naina's head spun, still fixed on the mother. Who was this dissolute, conscienceless Meena? What kind of woman would just forsake her son and husband? And then didn't engorge herself with the milk of contrition every single day like Naina did? Did Meena find her inspiration in Lady Macbeth? Or the demoness Putana in Indian mythology, who tried to kill Baby Krishna by making him suck milk from poisoned breasts? A rivulet of tenderness for Jai washed over her.

"It's a lot. I know. But we'll get through it. I think he's insecure and afraid of being abandoned. That's why he's acting the way he is. At least that's what I think." Amaya smiled feebly. "But I really care about him. I really do. Deep down, he's probably hurting a lot . . . We'll get through this."

Naina thought she could hear the inaudible tremors in her daughter's voice and see the tiny, invisible pores of anxiety in her clear complexion. Her sympathy for Jai instantly dried up. A rush of fury mingled with other indistinct emotions. *He better not hurt my daughter. He better not hurt my daughter.* If he did, she would make him pay for it. Really, truly, pay for it. Though she hadn't exactly known how she would do this.

Back in Chelsea, Naina had very little time to spare before the opening and downed the last few sips of her cappuccino as she mindlessly studied the gigantic painting of a solitary, storm-whipped, *Wuthering-Heights*-like manor in the gallery opposite the café. Who was Jai? Who was he anyway? There was her original picture of him, her changing picture of him, and now this new picture of him, all bleeding into each other, pouring onto each other, washing out each other, distorting each other, until he had turned into a kinetic mist in her mind. How could she have ever imagined that they were soul mates and kindred spirits?

Just like that Heathcliff, whom Naina now found despicable, Jai was not grand, brooding, and mysterious but childish, wicked, and egotistical. Yet, and it was baffling to her and she hated to admit it, she still had feelings for him, albeit much more muted feelings.

As for Meena, Naina found herself wondering what could have driven a woman, a mother at that, an Indian mother at that, irrespective of how bold and modern she was, to openly commit adultery, and then discard her husband and young son for another man—especially since she had a Mills & Boon type of romance most women could only dream of, a Chantilly lace sari of courtship and marriage, delicate, silky, and ultimately extravagant.

Time was ticking away, but Naina refused to look at her watch and ordered a small latte, her thoughts of Meena's story still twisting and turning. Did Jacob have an affair? Did he turn into a violent alcoholic? Did he become mentally ill? Or was it her? Was it her mind that was held by the vice-like grip of a tormentor spawned from within? Stirring her latte so it would cool faster, she thought about how even the finest of Chantilly laces could rot and rip into rancid shreds. Or somehow turn into a terrifyingly exquisite labyrinth that suffocated a person.

Amaya had met Jacob, who now lived in Florida, and she said that he seemed nice, kind, and generally jovial. Except when the topic of Meena came up. Then he would wax eloquently about all her phenomenal qualities or fall silent with his head drooping forward.

No, the driving force behind Meena's abandonment probably emanated from within her, powerful and restless like an electromagnetic charge. Naina took a long sip of her latte as she felt convinced of this. She remembered Jai once saying his mother liked to veer off to the extreme. Meena probably—no, not probably—most likely—got bored as the sheen of life with Jacob wore off and went in search of a newer, glossier gem. She was a greedy and selfish woman. Just like her son.

Naina felt a painful stab of hypocrisy in her criticizing Meena when her own past actions were well . . . she didn't want to think of the words. She inhaled and clung on to the air inside her body.

But, if she were to analyze it objectively, as bad as her own behavior was, it was nowhere as egregious as Meena's. After all, her illicit feelings didn't actually lead to anything, there was no real impact on anyone, except herself. And her behavior was fleeting, but her regret was endless. Unlike Meena's actions which damaged a child, Naina's behavior only had the potential to affect an adult woman. Not a child. That was a big and significant difference.

Naina felt her feathers fluff up and unfurl, like a peacock, spurred on by her pride in her relative virtue.

"IT'S FOUR-FORTY, you idiot," a male voice barked from somewhere behind her into a cellphone.

Naina jerked away from her thoughts, realizing she was more than twenty minutes late. The upcoming opening immediately pushed everything else to the back of her mind. After paying the check, she grabbed her stuff and walked as fast as she could while eyeing the cracks in the sidewalk.

Susan, who had been in a foul mood all week, pounced on Naina as soon as she walked through the door. Naina had taken too long of a break and not left the catalogs for the show on the second shelf of the office as Susan had asked her to. An important critic had come by, and she had no catalog to hand him. Naina had to do everything to keep silent. She had worked so hard for the last couple of weeks and things had finally fallen into place, yet Susan was picking on her and speaking to her as if she were some twenty-year-old girl who had sneaked off from work to chat with her boyfriend. Her apology sounded insincere even as she said it. After, she told Susan she needed to get ready before Rob, the college student who was going to be serving drinks, arrived. Grabbing her makeup bag, she dashed to the bathroom at the end of the long hallway.

In the spartan public bathroom, there was no room to put her large bag of cosmetics, so she just placed it on the edge of the sink, hoping it wouldn't topple over.

Her phone beeped. It was another text from Amaya. *Jai wants to go out on Thursday night, but I can't because I'm working late. He wanted to know if Ryan was working late too, and I said yes. He got annoyed and said he was busy the whole weekend. OMG. He needs a therapist but refuses to go. I certainly have my hands full. No need to comment, just venting. Have a great opening.*

Naina gritted her teeth, but then slackened her jaw and curled her lips into a tiny smile. The red-eyed, glossy bluish-black koel sitting on the branch of a tall eucalyptus tree was singing her joyful song once more inside her head. The possibility of the two of them breaking up on their own, without Naina needing to risk losing her daughter, was becoming more real.

She looked at the time. She needed to rush. After quickly cleaning her face, she applied an age-defying moisturizer. Then she dabbed on lots of line-smoothing concealer under her eyes and around her lips, spread some powder over her face, and highlighted her eyes with mascara. She stepped a few inches away from the cracked mirror and considered herself. She was looking rather nice, she thought, pleasantly surprised. During these last busy weeks, she hadn't spent much time in front of the mirror. Her eyes, those almond-colored, almond-shaped eyes, looked so lustrous despite everything. But she needed to better accentuate her eyes. She applied more mascara and then batted her eyes, giggling to herself in the mirror.

Naina ran back to the galley and went straight to the office to change. She closed the blinds and pulled out the dress she had bought from Bloomingdale's on an impulse a couple of days earlier— a white A-line cotton dress with spaghetti straps, a scalloped neckline, and a thin belt that tied at the waist, the simple beauty of the design enhanced by intricate cutwork and detailed embroidery at the bottom. She had made the right decision. The freshness of the outfit appealed to her all over again, and she carefully put it on to avoid leaving any makeup stains. She slipped her feet into white slip-on sandals, sprayed some grassy-smelling perfume, and then decided to wear her flying hawk pendant choker, instead of the pearls she had planned, to add some verve to her outfit.

When Naina stepped out into the main gallery space, she noticed that Rob had set the table nicely with a white tablecloth; the plastic cups were neatly arranged in stacks and the two big bottles of *Yellow Tail* Shiraz and Chardonnay were alongside each other. Naina did a quick check to make sure that all the paintings were labeled correctly, copies of the press releases were at the front desk, and when she was satisfied that all was well, she sat down for a few minutes.

The space did really look beautiful. Again, she beheld Samantha's yellow-gold drawings gleaming against the white walls and the empty space. Initially, she hadn't particularly liked the ballpoint pen creations, which had seemed somewhat like doodles, but the thick tangle of swirls and lines had lured her in. Now, she gazed at her favorite drawing to the far left, a piece packed with so many coils that it reminded her of a woman's tousled hair or whirling cosmic energy. Every time she saw this drawing, she felt sensuous stirrings spinning and swimming in her. Every time she saw this drawing, she was reminded that she was alive. And still a woman with desires.

She asked Rob to pour her half a cup of red wine. As she quickly sipped it, the delicious berry and pepper flavors unfurling in her mouth, she promised herself she would enjoy tonight. She had worked too hard on this show not to. Tonight, she was going to put all her worries aside.

By six-thirty, the gallery filled up with all sorts of people: hipsters wanting to be cool in every which way; artsy youngsters with worn-looking bags slung across their shoulders; corporate types aspiring for an artsy look with bohemian-inspired designer wear; older, pearl-adorned women attired in expensive clothing; earnest-looking artists, academics, and critics who seemed like they didn't give a damn about what they wore; professional sorts in stylish business attire; and eccentrics of all ages flashing their personality with idiosyncratic pieces of clothing or accessories.

And which category did she fit into? None of the above.

Openings always perplexed Naina. As was typical, a few people went around the gallery and seemed to look at the art, some cursorily glanced at it, and others barely paused. Naina watched the crowd chatting away or bumping into one another as they rushed to say hello to someone they wanted to meet, or getting a glass of wine before it ran out, or racing to the exit to catch another opening. She wondered, yet again, how anyone could even look at art in such an atmosphere. The world of contemporary art, which was often so abstract and oblique, demanded an almost meditation-like concentration to gain even the slightest insight into the concoction of forms and images that frequently did not correspond to anything easily recognizable. In contrast, her other love—the universe of books—had a known vocabulary where each word had a meaning that everybody understood. That made the world of the written word so much easier to penetrate. Maybe that was why many more people read books than looked at contemporary art. But the universe of art also seemed so much more vast and liberated than literature, broadly speaking, since people could invent their own lexicon and were not limited by conventions such as grammar and syntax. Today, when it came to the visual arts, there were no set rules governing how forms, images, or materials should mingle. Contemporary artists were freer than ever before to be creative in any way they liked.

Naina just wished she could comprehend more of their world. And be as unrestrained and ingenious as they were. And if she could somehow manage it, even be a little hip. Society at large had too many rules everywhere, stifling as antiquated corsets, preventing the life force (a term she had learned from her kundalini yoga class) from blossoming.

"There's someone I'd like you to help me out with," Susan whispered from behind. "Isidora Friedman. She's totally batty, fancies herself as some sort of Peggy Guggenheim, can barely hear, but she has deep pockets."

Naina followed Susan, who was her usual no-nonsense self in a beige summer suit, across the room toward an elderly woman wearing a black velvet dress, a red hat with purple feathers, and a huge pearl-and-diamond necklace. She appeared to be about a hundred years old. Her face was a labyrinth of creases, lines, and hollows, but her bright green eyes sparkled inside their sunken sockets.

"I bet you're wondering why I'm wearing this dress in this blasted heat," Isidora Friedman said, soon after they were introduced.

"No, no, not at all. It's a beautiful dress."

"Well, let me tell you something, young lady."

Naina felt her mouth widen into a big smile, the kind that made her eyes squint with amusement and brought out the shallow dimples in her face. It had been a long time since anyone had referred to her as a "young lady."

"When you get to my age . . . I'm ninety-four, you know . . . you start feeling really chilly and then they turn up the air conditioning to make it seem like damn winter when it's eighty degrees out. So, that's why I'm wearing what I'm wearing."

"It's really a beautiful dress, Mrs. Friedman—"

"Mrs. Friedman, sheesh, young lady, please. Jack's been dead for forty years. And thank God for that." She cackled, making the sort of strident sound Naina imagined a hen might make if a predator came after her recently laid eggs. "Sorry, did I shock you? Let me tell you somethin', the older you get, the more you tell the truth. Because you know you won't live long enough to suffer the consequences, so why the hell not?" Once again, she cackled. "Call me Isidora, honey."

"All right, as you wish . . . so have you known Susan for a long time, Isidora?"

"I've known everybody for a long time. Hah. I knew Mr. Go Go Gagosian before he had all these fancy galleries and I knew Franz Kline when he was a nobody. Jackson Pollock, that useless artist, even came to dine with me and Peggy one time. He could barely stand straight. I've no idea what Peggy saw in him."

Soon, Isidora's eyes got this faraway look as she drifted into another world— looking like a plumed gargoyle—telling gossipy stories about famous artists in her husky, cackling voice. She talked about how Barnett Newman slept with a waiter in Chicago, the bewildered expression on Andy Warhol's face when she offered him foie gras, the intimations of suicide that Mark Rothko had given his close friends. Naina suspected these stories had been told a million times before and was careful to pay attention and not look skeptical, but a few minutes later when Isidora seemed to show no signs of letting up, her eyes wandered. And she started to crave another glass of wine.

From the corner of her eye, she noticed a tall man with the sort of chiseled face she imagined a mixture of good English and French blood would produce. He had a patrician nose, his lips curved to form a medium-sized bow, and he had an angular jaw that was masculine but not overwhelmingly so. He had brown eyes, like Jai's, except lighter, and narrow cheekbones. His neck was long and robust like a horse's, and he was even taller than Jai, who had towered over her at six feet. In jeans and a well-cut black jacket, he looked rather poised and self-assured. He was listening intently to a loquacious art student-looking type in cargo pants and an oversized T-shirt. All of a sudden, her heart started to beat faster, and tiny tremors of excitement scuttled through her like mischievous children.

"So then, Donald Judd came over with this lovely lady called Beatrice, but she turned out to be far from beatific," Isidora continued. "He was yet another player, dear. They were all players. That idiot Pollock killed himself and that poor Edith playing . . . honey, are you ok? I hope I'm not boring you, am I?"

"Oh, no, no, not at all. Your stories are fascinating . . . absolutely fascinating . . . would you mind excusing me for a minute? I think I just spotted a friend who's probably looking for me."

"Sure, dear. I think Susan did well in hiring you. You might be older, but you're not like these brittle girls I see in the galleries these days, who think they know it all. You know the old saying, don't you? The more you know, the more you realize how little you know. It may be a damn cliché but it's damn true . . ." Isidora ran out of breath from speaking so fast and took a small sip from the glass of water in her hand. "All right, Isidora, shut up, don't hog a young lady's attention like that."

Naina walked as far away as she could from Isidora and wondered if she looked okay. Maybe her lipstick was slightly smudged or her under-eye makeup had faded. What was she thinking? It wasn't as if such a good-looking man would look at her. He looked younger, maybe in his late thirties or early forties. She had already had her experience with a younger man rejecting her, feeling the pain, emerge from the shadows, red and raw, once more. She was not going to go to the bathroom to check on herself.

Naina saw him glance in her direction and she looked the other way. Had he seen her looking at him? She was being silly now. She headed to the bar, suddenly conscious of the way her hips swayed when she wore high heels. She waited in line for Rob to fill her cup.

"Naina, what I can get for you?" Rob asked.

"White, please."

"Sounds like white's the way to go in this weather," a polished voice said from behind.

Yes, it had to be him. The voice matched his appearance. She tried her best to control herself from blushing. Should she respond to his comment? What should she say?

"Yes, white is cooling." She immediately felt stupid. Couldn't she have come up with something less banal to say?

"I've just gotten into the habit of always drinking red, but there's no reason one can't break a habit, is there?"

He stood to her left and she noticed that his eyes were dazzling. Hazel-colored cat eyes. Much lighter, both literally and figuratively, than Jai's intense eyes.

She averted her gaze. "No, there isn't, I guess, no, there isn't a reason . . ."

"Are you a wine lover?" he said.

Naina hurriedly straightened her too tight hawk pendant. "Ummm, yes, I do like wine . . . and you?"

"Me? I love wine. Too much, most people would say. I'm embarrassed to admit that I try to make every tasting in my neighborhood wine store."

"Umm . . . Sounds nice . . . So you must be a wine connoisseur then?"

"Oh no, just a dabbler. In wine, in art, and some of my friends accuse me of just dabbling in life."

She brushed a few strands of her hair back and smiled.

"That means you must have many interests," she said.

He looked pleased at her interpretation of dabbler. She felt a small drip of confidence enter her veins.

"What can I say? I try. So, I noticed you were talking or maybe I should say listening to great grandma over there for a long time. You were very patient. I was impressed."

So he had been looking at her. She lit up from the inside.

"Oh, she was very entertaining," Naina said, her voice steadier. "Had these crazy stories about famous artists in the fifties and sixties."

"Did she know any of them?"

"I'm not sure, to be honest. She says she's ninety-four. I suspect the boundaries between fiction and reality become quite fuzzy at that point." She emitted a soft, brief laugh.

"Hey, I just realized we've been talking, and we don't even know each other's names," he said with a broad smile, revealing a wide gap between his front teeth that seemed at odds with the rest of his sophisticated persona. "I'm John Winters." He reached out his hand and she noticed his fingers were slender, but neither long nor short. And his palms, unlike Jai's, were broad. More manly and less artistic. And he was not wearing a ring. And neither was she, at least not on her left hand. A year after Harish had died, she had taken off both the diamond ring he had given her at their engagement ceremony and the antique emerald-and-gold ring her mother-in-law had given her when Amaya was born. The only ring she now wore, on her right hand, was a paisley-shaped ruby-and-sapphire ring she had custom made in Delhi fifteen or sixteen years before.

Naina introduced herself and was flattered when he asked her if she was an artist. He told her he ran a hedge fund, something she didn't quite understand but did not question further, and that he had been interested in art for a long time. Yes, he was also somewhat of a collector. He often went to Larry Weinstein's, the gallery where Susan had worked for two decades.

"So, what do you like about them?" John asked when Naina said she liked Samantha Ali's drawings.

She wasn't sure how to respond. He sounded like he had been around the art world for a long time, and she didn't want to come across like a fool—compared with the other people he must be used to meeting.

He continued to study her, clearly waiting for an answer.

"Well, they're sort of like a maze you can just get lost in . . . Do you know what I mean?"

He seemed to like the term "maze" and said he thought he could see what she meant, telling her how he loved maze puzzles as a child. Though now, he said, he never got lost in anything and could be considered a prime candidate for ADHD.

A while later, as a couple of people came to say goodbye to her, Naina noticed that the gallery was almost empty. She discreetly glanced at her watch and realized that it was a couple of minutes past eight.

"Do you need to go?" John asked.

"Yes . . . The opening's ended, and there are a few things I have to do."

"Oh, that's too bad. I was hoping you could tell me more about Samantha Ali's work. Have you eaten yet?"

He sounded so confident, so sure of his place in the world as he effortlessly talked to her, a stranger. Like Jai, but there was a difference. Was his confidence more arrogant? Or less? Harder? Softer? She couldn't say. Oh yes, that was it. John's self-assurance seemed inborn while Jai's seemed acquired. How she wished she had that same assurance of her place in the world.

"No . . . I haven't had a minute."

"Neither have I. Would you like to have dinner at this new place called Manzana on 25th and Ninth? I've heard great things about it and I'd love to learn about what's going on in the art world since I've kinda been out of the loop recently and it would great to talk to someone like yourself."

She fluffed up like poori submerged in hot oil. Why did someone like him want to go out for dinner with her? What could he possibly want from her? These young men in New York—they were tricky, and she didn't want to fall in their trap again. Again, she fiddled with her hawk pendant, which was hurting her neck.

"Thank you, John, that sounds nice, but I don't think so."

"Why not?" He sounded surprised by her response.

"I . . . I have to finish up some stuff here . . . There's a lot to do."

"That's fine. I'll go check out this other opening at Augustin Vaughn's on the next block, which is on until nine. I could just meet you there and we could go for dinner."

NAINA LEFT THE gallery a half hour after John left, after paying Rob and counting the remaining catalogs, feeling a need to double and triple check her numbers. She almost left without storing the remaining wine bottles, but thankfully turned back in time.

When she was sure she had done everything she was supposed to, she took her time walking to the next block, feeling as if she were in a trance as sensations of exhilaration and anxiety billowed with every unsteady step. What in the world was she doing? Had she lost her mind again? Hadn't she behaved badly enough already? Maybe she was imagining things. He probably did want someone to help him get up to speed with the art world. But why choose her? It wasn't like he didn't know what she did. She hadn't wanted to tell him her exact role in the gallery, but his questions had been so pointed that she couldn't help telling the truth.

The pedestrian signal changed to "Don't Walk" as she reached the middle of the road. A car screeched next to her, the driver yelling something that sounded like obscenities in an unidentifiable language. She scurried to the sidewalk.

When she was a few yards away from Augustin Vaughn's Gallery, she spotted John, half his body in front of the polished glass of the gallery, the other half in front of the jagged wall next to it, littered with squished coke cans, smashed beer bottles, and a bunch of empty cigarette boxes. He was alone, smoking a cigarette, looking up at the sky, cutting a James Dean-like loner figure. In the dark, he looked even more attractive with an air of brooding that added more soul to his persona. She came to a stop a few feet away from him, while he, seemingly unaware of her presence, continued to look at the sky and smoke.

"Hi," he said, looking sideways. He smiled broadly, showing off the cute gap in his teeth. "So you made it."

She inched her way toward him, and they lingered for too long of an awkward silence.

"Hey, aren't those clouds gorgeous?" John said, looking up again. "I love clouds. What about you?"

"Me? Ummm . . . I like clouds sometimes. But, mostly, I prefer clear blue skies." She shrugged. "Conventional tastes, I guess." She let out a slight laugh.

"Conventional tastes? Oh, I don't believe that for a second . . ." He leaned in closer, scanning her face in a way no one had ever done before. Not even Jai. "There's just something about you, Naina. There just is . . . I can't put my finger on it, but there is . . ."

She stared at the cracks in the sidewalk, not knowing where else to look. His directness was so foreign, so casual, yet so overwhelming, that she wanted to curl up in a shell and jump out of it at the same time.

"By the way, I love your dress. I love white on women. My mom used to wear white a lot when she was younger. I don't understand this obsession with black . . ."

"So, are you saying I look old-fashioned then?" She raised her head, feeling offended.

"Of course not, don't be silly. You look beautiful. White is a timeless color. Plus, it reminds me of clouds . . . so I'm definitely biased."

Naina became chattier on the walk over to the restaurant, realizing that she felt slightly less nervous when she was talking. Even though neither of them had been to Manzana, she knew more about the restaurant than he did. She told him that Manzana, which meant apple in Spanish, was supposed to mimic an art gallery. It was the brainchild of Jason Brown, a little-known British sculptor who, after meager success with his geometric welded metal sculptures in the sixties and seventies, ended up sinking into a life of drugs and alcohol for numerous years. But once he emerged from it, he decided to reinvent himself as a restaurateur cum artist, which ended up making him much more famous than being an artist did.

"Aaah, that's too bad, isn't it?" John said, as they walked up the brick steps that led to the restaurant. "Good food can always get you places, but not necessarily good art."

Manzana had unadorned white walls, small ceiling lamps that cast a soft glow, and straight-backed metal chairs. Brown's new bronze sculptures that fused geometric and fruit-inspired shapes lined the walls, giving the minimalist space an understated materiality, while the sounds of Wynton Marsalis wafted through the room and a white candle atop every table added a touch of romance. Naina thought the place was beautiful but a tad pretentious.

As they waited by the door to be seated, John said, yes, yes, he could definitely see what Naina meant and see something of the likes of Anthony Caro and David Smith in Brown's works. By the way, what did she think of Smith's work? She replied she had recently gone to his retrospective at the Whitney, but wasn't quite sure how she felt about it yet. But the scale, yes, the scale of Smith's welded metal sculptures was definitely awe-inspiring.

Thank goodness she had kept up with her reading about art and gone to major museum shows. She couldn't bear to think how foolish she might have sounded otherwise.

Once they sat down, they steadily drank wine, and the conversation became less and less as glances that suggested desire, cryptic half-smiles between sips of red wine, and the brushing of legs under the table took the place of words. The chemistry between them felt palpable.

John, by most standards, was a much more handsome man than Jai. His face was not broad like Jai's but elliptical and chiseled. His nose was straight, slender, and turned upward, in symmetry with the rest of his face as opposed to Jai's dominating nose. And his brown-black hair didn't have the touches of gray that Jai's had, which made John look younger.

Energy, marinated in pleasure, pirouetted in her like a ballet dancer, spinning and spinning on one leg. She tried to contain herself. She remembered that civilized behavior demanded conversation when two people were sitting opposite each other and sharing a meal. So when John seemed to happily lapse into a wordless state, Naina tried to slow down the kinetic speed and perforate the silence.

She asked polite questions and John slowly obliged. She learned that he had grown up in Westchester and his father had been a doctor but was now a full-time leisure golfer in West Palm Beach. His mother, a housewife who loved music, had passed away a couple of years earlier. He had worked as an equity research analyst—something Naina didn't understand but did not inquire about—for several years before starting a hedge fund five years ago. He loved minimalism—Frank Stella, Ad Reinhart, and Agnes Martin were his favorite artists. New York had been his home for the last ten years and couldn't imagine being anywhere else. What he did not reveal was whether he was married or had ever been married, whether he was in a relationship or had just got out of one.

John was not an engaging narrator like Jai, and Naina suddenly missed the cadences of Jai's storytelling voice, curving like a semicolon, rolling into a dot, pausing like a hyphen, swooping down like a question mark. When Jai looked into eyes, he used to hold her gaze for long periods of time—how long she couldn't say—and she would feel as if she were falling into magic pools of chocolate. And Jai's gaze was mysterious, immobile, hardly ever calling for action.

But John's gaze was quick, casual, and its message was unambiguous. His dazzling hazel eyes lingered over her bare arms and shoulders and rested on her ample breasts made more pert by her push-up bra. She had never felt a man look at her with such naked desire. Tiny sparks raced up and down her body and then crackled between her legs, like fireworks going off on Diwali, the Hindu festival of lights.

Embarrassment dappled her. She looked around, fidgeted with her pendant, and played with her hair. She crossed and uncrossed her legs even as she felt frozen. She was an older woman, a middle-aged widow, she reminded herself.

And then those kinetic and carnal sensations enlarged and expanded, enlarged and expanded, enlarged and expanded, until they were like balloons with lights inside them, gigantic, bright and boogying, obliterating the presence of everything else.

The waiter came by and asked if they wanted more drinks, and Naina sat up straight and declined, knowing that whatever semblance of decorum she had left would be gone if she drank another glass.

Then John, as if suddenly remembering his manners, asked his round of polite questions. She kept the story of her life short, somehow sensing he really wasn't that interested. She told him that she grew up in India, had a younger brother who was still in New Delhi and that both her parents had died. Then she veered the conversation toward her growing interest in video art and newer jazz musicians. Somewhere in there she casually tucked in a husband who had died and living in the New York area prior to moving into Manhattan. About children, he didn't ask and she said nothing.

Everything about John seemed light—the color of his eyes, its tissues, the manner in which he conversed. It seemed fitting that clouds were his favorite thing in the world.

Naina couldn't take her eyes off his lips. They had just enough flesh on them to make them lush but not excessively so, and they curved so nicely to form a bow. Jai's lips were lean and wide, never lush. But John's—they looked so edible. She suddenly wanted to kiss him.

Again, she scolded herself. Again, it had little effect. Then, she pursed her lips, asked something banal about hedge funds and looked down to study the dessert menu.

After she ordered a tiramisu, Naina went to the restroom, strutting more than usual. As she refreshed the area under her eyes with line-smoothing concealer and reapplied her mauve-colored lipstick, which she noticed again went very nicely with her silver eye shadow, she smiled at herself in the mirror. Right after she returned to the table, she placed her hands on her legs and John reached under the table and took her hands into his own. Her body jumped. She pulled her hands away.

"Do you have to go to work tomorrow?" John asked.

She didn't answer. He reached for her hands again. She pulled them away, more slowly this time.

"Do you have to go to work tomorrow?" he asked in a softer, more urgent voice.

"No . . . no . . . I don't."

He took her hands again and this time, Naina did not pull them away. His hands felt good, so good. So this was what holding hands under a table felt like. His hands were not as soft as Jai's, remembering her two brief encounters with Jai's hands with a momentary stab of nostalgia. John tightened his grip. The nerves in her arms hopped and skipped. In retrospect, she had touched Jai's hands so fleetingly that it was more like a tease, like having a hasty sip of wine that gave no more than a hint of its flavor, leaving the drinker guessing and wanting. But this, this intertwining of fingers, this warm pressure against her palms, this stroking on the top of her palms, was like actually tasting something. Like letting something linger in the mouth and go down the throat so one could sense the flavor and be at least a little satiated.

"Great, so you can have another drink then," John said in his matter-of-fact tone, as if the matter had already been decided.

"I . . . I don't . . . think so." She was already feeling tipsy from the three—or was it four?—glasses of wine she had had.

As he caressed her hand, John described "this wonderful 1991 Rioja" he had back at his apartment. It was better than anything they could get at Manzana or at any nearby bar. If she liked Rioja, she just had to try this one.

JOHN LIVED IN a new building in the East sixties, a soaring skyscraper that towered over all the other buildings in the neighborhood. As Naina stepped inside the building after the courteous Hispanic-looking doorman opened the glass door, discreetly examining her, she felt the jitters, and wondered whether John had felt them or whether it was a just a coincidence that he clutched her hand tighter at that instant. She glanced around at the spacious lobby and saw two stylish aubergine-colored sofas that looked like half moons and realized she was around not just money, but a lot of it.

She had an impulse to flee. Quickly. Through the side door a few feet to her left.

Before Naina knew it, the elevator doors opened, and she was zoomed up to the thirtieth floor. When she entered the gigantic penthouse apartment, which looked like a contemporary design museum and offered one of the best panoramic views of the city she had ever seen, she felt as if she had entered another realm. The Manhattan skyline seemed so close, and even the sky, bloated with huge clouds didn't seem that far away. The duplex apartment, whose first level must have been at least two-thousand square feet, was also unearthly with its immaculate minimalism. Decorated in black and white, she felt its strong masculine energy with the angular lines, geometric forms, and materials like metal and leather. She noticed, on one wall, a powerful Agnes Martin painting composed of fine white lines etched on black, and opposite it was a feathery and fiery ink-and-brush painting by a famous Chinese artist whose show Naina had attended a few months earlier, but whose name she couldn't remember. She particularly liked the ceiling lighting; an aluminum lamp from which sprung thirty or forty twisted arms that provided accent lights in different colors. It made her think of a crab's legs and the multiple-armed Kali, the Hindu Mother Goddess of destruction. Naina could barely feel the ground beneath her feet.

John offered her the 1991 Rioja he had promised and after they had a few sips, he touched the edges of Naina's lips with his fingers, slow, circular motions that drove her wild. Then he quickly kissed her, his lips and tongue enveloping her mouth. She broke away from the kiss and got up, tottering both in body and mind. She had to stop this. What was she doing? She was losing her mind. She had to run out of here now.

John gently tugged at the tips of her fingers and rubbed the inside of her wrist. Naina found herself sinking into the sofa. But soon she teetered up again. John got up and kissed her as he held on to her. He tasted of expensive red wine and smelled slightly smoky. Naina felt heady and breathless. All thoughts melted. There was no more conflict between mind and body.

After a brief break from all the kissing, Naina took the initiative and kissed John. Soon, he was alternating between nibbles and kisses on her neck while resting his left hand on her breast. The thrilling, trilling sensation between her legs was throbbing. Then he slowly moved his hands along her legs, lingering on the back of her knees before moving up her thighs and caressing her just a few inches away from her white lacy panties. It was only when he touched her moist panties that she briefly regained some awareness.

"I'm . . . I'm not sure I'll be comfortable with that," she said weakly, uttering the first words since they had started kissing.

"Why not?" he said, stroking the back of her knees again. "You're enjoying it and I'm enjoying it. We're both adults."

"But . . .

"No buts," he said, kissing her again. Those lips, those lush lips felt so good. And that taste of red wine and smoke. She felt like she could kiss him forever.

Soon, he guided Naina to the bedroom on the mezzanine level where he quickly took off her clothes. As she lay naked on his crisp ivory linens, he stepped off the bed and quickly undressed as she watched. She enjoyed seeing him unzip his jeans and watching his erect penis pointing at her. Once he was naked, he swooped down, opened Naina's thighs and licked her between her legs. First, he started with soft, teasing flicks, and then increased the pressure with up and down motions around her clitoris and then sucked on it. Her body breathlessly did the jitterbug, taking her to a new plateau of pleasure. She moaned in a low voice, opened her legs further to give him greater access, and, when she climaxed, a huge shudder shot through her body. That moment, so sensual and so sublime, drew her so inside herself, that she involuntarily shut her eyes, completely relaxed.

"You're fucking hot," John said. "I've never seen a woman come like that."

Naina opened her eyes, and it was as if she were looking at him through a misty lens; he seemed like someone else in another era and another country. And she felt like Mona Lisa with a cryptic hint of a smile.

"You taste great too," he said, just before he got on top of her and kissed her, his penis rubbing against her thigh. As he was kissing her, she felt a salty, very bodily taste on his mouth, and wondered what it was. When she realized it was her own fluids from him licking her between her legs, she was curious and aghast.

"Will you go down on me?" John asked, standing on his knees.

Naina was taken aback, not expecting such a request. She had never done something like that before.

"Are you uncomfortable with the idea?" John when she didn't answer.

"No, no, not at all," she lied.

"Awesome!"

And then, desperately trying to remember everything about sex she had ever read, she sucked his penis, feeling weird as she realized she had a male organ in her mouth. And one that was, in fact, circumcised. She sucked his whole shaft vigorously until John said, "Hey, could you concentrate on the head? It's the most sensitive part. And a little easy on the teeth."

"I want to fuck you," he said as she came up for air in between her diligent sucking.

And then he grabbed a condom from his nightstand, put it on, spread her legs apart, and entered her. His thrusting was forceful and hurled her into another wild ride of sensations. She didn't climax, but the feel of him moving inside her was so exquisite that she didn't need to go any higher. Her eyes remained closed most of the time, but on the rare moments she did open them, she watched the frenzied expression contorting his civilized features. She felt as if they were two creatures in the wilderness, far away from everything and everyone else, and that deepened her sense of abandon. Then she noticed his thrusting becoming more urgent, the guttural sounds becoming louder, and, all of a sudden, he was as still as a sleeping child as he lay on top of her. A couple of minutes later, he rolled over, tossed the condom on the floor, and started snoring. She covered his naked body with a sheet and then covered her own before turning on her right side and falling asleep.

CHAPTER EIGHTEEN

IT WAS JUST after six in the morning when Naina woke up, freezing from the chilly temperature in the room. She wrapped the sheet around her body as she dreamily looked around, finding it odd to be able to see so clearly; through the tall glass windows near her, the sun was peeping out of a cloudy sky. Turning to the left, she saw skyscrapers looking small and unimpressive reflected in the red-edged mirror placed high on a wall, and, as she turned her eyes farther to the left, she was struck by a hallucinogenic burst of colors from what looked to be a photograph by Jeremy Blake. Where was she? The objects continued to look foreign: pictures of a gray-haired white couple in golf gear on a frosted glass shelf, the ebony-colored platform bed she was lying on, and books on hedge funds and Ayn Rand's *Fountainhead* stacked against the wall, in mid-air, without any seeming support.

It was only when she saw her dress littered across the black floor, covering one cup of her bra, that, like sand moving grain by grain in an hourglass, awareness of where she was came to her. She saw John, asleep on his back, with fine dark hair curling on his exposed chest, a slight stubble starting under his chin, and his bow-shaped mouth slightly open, making him appear somewhat childlike. The memory of what had happened the previous night ran through her mind as if they were frames from a surreal footage.

Naina remained motionless for a while, cradling her head in her arms as the images kept repeating themselves in her head, faster and faster, becoming less and less surreal. When the image of her taking his penis in her mouth flashed in her mind, she jumped out of the bed, seized by shock and disbelief. This was the *only* other man she had slept with besides Harish. Oh my God. With her eyes bulging, she stared down at her body, buck naked and alien, as if it belonged to someone else. She patted it in in several places just to make sure she wasn't out of her mind or dreaming. Then she picked up her clothes from the floor and hurriedly dressed herself.

John stirred, stretched his arms above him, and looked at her, his eyes half open. He seemed nothing more than a stranger. Speaking to her from the faraway country he belonged to. "Hey Nona, what's the matter?"

She didn't answer, desperately trying to contain her emotions from spilling over. Nona, he had called her. *Nona*. She was outraged. Did he sleep with so many women that he couldn't even get their names right? Was she just another body amid the thousands in New York? She yanked the clasp of her choker into the loop.

"Is everything ok?" John asked, now yawning. "I thought we could go grab breakfast. You must be hungry."

"No," she heard herself snap. "I . . . I have to go."

"What? Now? Why? Is everything okay?"

NAINA RUSHED OUT of John's apartment, slamming the door behind her. A strong odor of Mexican food emanated from the elevator; the doorman smiled as she exited the building; the cab driver cursed on the phone in Hindi as he was driving; an old lady almost got hit by a bicyclist in front of her—but she hardly registered any of this. She entered her apartment after frantically searching for her keys and sat down on her sofa. Then she opened her bag and started to dump out its contents, the sounds of clanking, cracking, shattering, and rolling taking over the room.

Blisters of feelings she could not quite pinpoint swelled in her like a chicken pox rash, bright-red and unrelentingly itchy. *What in the world had she done? What in the world had she done?*

Naina harshly pulled her hair and gritted her teeth until her jaw hurt. It was incredible. She, Naina Mehta, had got drunk and had sex with some strange man. What would Amaya or Alannah call it? A *one-night stand*, a *hookup*. The association of those words in relation to herself almost made her quake. Had she again forgotten that she was a middle-aged widow with grown children? How could she? How dare she?

Naina could feel her mother emerge, so hot that she was boiling over, and strike her hard with her hands, as if she were trying to disfigure her daughter. Her mother was foaming at the mouth, her saliva writhing with unspeakable disgust.

She heard ambulance sirens wail outside and rushed to shut the window. She sat back down on her couch and hurled her empty bag on the floor. Then she leapt to shut the drapes and the blinds and sat down again with her face deeply entombed in her hands.

In the darkness of her living room, her mind drifted to 1969. Naina had only been thirteen years old at the time, unaware of the massive social and cultural upheaval in the West, but she knew about the big scandal brewing in her neighborhood. Mrs. Asha Kapur, an average-looking woman with typical Punjabi sharp features, had left her husband—a successful businessman at that—for a singer ten years younger than she. The forty-five-year-old housewife moved in with her lover, Rajesh, and would stroll with him in the neighborhood in her bright-colored, well-starched saris, her back long and erect in those sleeveless sari blouses, while everyone else would stare from their gardens, kitchens, verandas—wherever they could get the best view. Naina recalled straining her own head in various directions through the pink bougainvillea hedge so she, too, could get a glimpse of this illicit affair; meanwhile her mother and a posse of neighborhood friends would sit back in their blue-and-white garden chairs, sipping tea and passing endless comments.

"Shameless woman, Asha is just a shameless woman," her mother would declare in her booming voice, looking a bit ridiculous as her chubby face became all pinched. "What kind of woman does that? Leaving Mahinder . . . such a good man . . . for some singer type. And the two children? Leaving them too? For some strange man! Chi!! Chi!!"

"Filthy, dirty woman," Chanda, another lady from the neighborhood, would chime in, in Hindi. "At this age to follow *those* desires? With grown children? I tell you, I can see some wrinkles on her face already . . . indulging in the ooof . . . how do I even bring myself to say it . . . like that? What kind of example is she setting for our children?"

"A bad one, a terrible one," her mother would say. "Naina, what are you doing looking like that? Go inside. You're not supposed to listen to grown-ups talking. I don't even want that Asha's shadow falling on you."

"Yes, Ma," Naina would say, moving away from her perch for a few minutes and then run back to get another look at Mrs. Kapur as her mother became absorbed in her own diatribe.

Had she been alive, what would her mother have said about what her daughter had just done? She couldn't bear to think about it. After her father had died, she never ever saw her mother again in colors like red or pink, or caught her dyeing her hair.

Shifting her crossed ankles to her right, Naina recalled how she used to be amazed at the way Mrs. Kapur had remained so calm, her face generally expressionless in the midst of such fevered scrutiny. She must have known how people thought, felt their stinging hatred of her, yet she never left the neighborhood or bothered explaining herself to anybody. In fact, Naina could not ever remember hearing her speak. Not even to Rajesh. Mrs. Kapur's thin red lips were always pursed; her eyes were always looking forward; her long feet, in kolhapuri chappals, were always moving steadily along as she continued going on her walks.

Naina closed her eyes and then suddenly opened them, feeling an ache hammering in her head. She wobbled her tired, gnarled body toward the medicine cabinet. As she swallowed three aspirins, she smelled the stale odor of her mouth and realized she hadn't brushed her teeth since yesterday.

The bathroom's bright light was making her feel uneasy as she vigorously brushed her teeth—and brushed them again. When she looked at herself in the mirror, she could see her lips were still swollen from the night's encounter and big smudges of mascara under her eyes; she gazed at the image she presented in befuddlement, like a voyeur staring at a freakish face of a tramp. She scrubbed and scrubbed and scrubbed her skin.

Not only had she fallen in in love with her daughter's boyfriend and pursued him, but she had also slept with a stranger. She. Her. Naina Mehta. A woman of easy virtue. Or more like no virtue. Again, her mother jumped out and struck her. Without wiping her damp face, she ran back to her couch.

She imagined the letters of her name unhinging themselves from the distinct shape and form they made when yoked together. And then each letter shattering into gasps of mutilated, meaningless glass that slipped through her fingers in derelict streams. Feeling herself sink into this cutting stream, Naina pulled her hair again and kicked the couch so hard with the back of her legs that pain shot through her calves.

Even though it was probably afternoon, her apartment was pitch-dark since her blinds were closed. She liked it this way. She didn't need any damn light. She preferred to be swallowed by the darkness.

At some point unmarked by time, her thoughts, cleaning themselves a bit, wandered to Harish, gingerly and carefully so they wouldn't startle him. She remembered the two of them eating doughnuts, drinking his delicious Turkish coffee, his inevitable offering of aid to fasten a necklace or bracelet, his patience in teaching her how to drive, and the laughter on his face when he, during the first month of their marriage, came home to find her helplessly pressing buttons on the laundry machine.

Naina shut her eyes and let out a huge, heavy heap of air, feeling the urge to cry, but unable to do so. Although Harish was dead, had she betrayed him by sleeping with John? Had she? Had she? That damning thought made her nerves painfully twist and turn, twist and turn, twist and turn, rapidly creating more knots in her already knotted and throbbing body.

She was so mad, so bad, so sad. She was a rudderless woman tossing about in the sea; a strumpet without a moral compass, heeding to nothing but the whims of her wants; a wanton woman on a train to nowhere with gray hair flying all over her face, dimly able to perceive the world, so clouded was she by her own wants. Adrift, disintegrating, and betraying all those to closest to her.

For hours, Naina's self-flagellation continued to bite her, one thought feeding off the other; one feeling feeding off the other. By the end, she was lying on her bed, feeling raw and withered, her body like a void spilling lament.

When Naina woke up, she was surrounded by darkness and wracked by pangs of hunger. She reached over to her nightstand to check the time on her alarm clock—ten p.m. There was something about knowing the time that made her feel bound to her earthly existence. It was sort of grounding. She craved Mexican food, but she remembered none was in the fridge. She could order it in, but the thought of seeing anyone—even an unknown delivery man—

seemed more than she could handle. She slowly got up and switched on the light. It seemed so bright, too bright.

She went to the kitchen and heated a frozen chicken pad thai dinner and ate it, without appetite, standing against the kitchen counter. Then, she changed into a pair of old sky-blue pajamas, a pair she often wore right after Harish's death, and sat up on her bed, her stomach too full to lie down. Soon, images of the previous night haunted her again, each one taking its time to form like a Polaroid picture, crystal clear once materialized, each one making her wince. But despite all this clarity, the whole incident still seemed remote, afar, foreign, as if that wasn't really her and there had been some gigantic confusion.

Naina staggered toward her long bamboo wood bookshelf in the living room, looking for a novel called *The Book of Shadows* by Namita Gokhale, a brilliant and macabre tale of a woman seeking refuge in a crumbling house in the Himalayas after her face had been unrecognizably disfigured by an acid attack. After a great deal of searching, she spotted it on the right-hand corner, tucked between Claire Messud's *The Emperor's Children* and Anais Nin's *The Spy In The House Of Love.*

She read the first page, fixating on the fourth paragraph:

> Who am I? This essentially philosophical question has suddenly assumed a tangible immediacy. We define ourselves by the people that we know, by the face that we see in the mirror. In my case all the parameters have changed. I can feel the doors to self-knowledge banging shut upon me. Even the face I meet in the mirror is no longer mine. Although it is to an extent familiar, it is mostly strange.

Reading this, Naina felt a special bond with Rachita, the story's narrator and protagonist, greater than the connection she had felt with her own reflection in the mirror. As she read that passage over and over again, Rachita felt like a friend, her despair leaping off the page, fully formed, giving utterance to Naina's amorphous feelings.

Naina took the book with her back to the couch, laid it half-open on her belly, and started to cry—her cries turning into wails as she felt sorrow lashing inside her like the convulsing sea in a Mumbai monsoon. She surrendered to the onslaught, deriving some solace as the tears rinsed her from the inside.

OVER THE NEXT few days, Naina felt numb and stayed in bed for most of each day, not wanting to meet anyone. But eventually, she couldn't stand the darkness in her room any longer and opened the blinds, letting some of the weak light outside percolate through the thin drapes. She remembered a line she had once heard or read somewhere, a line that kept repeating itself like a chant in her head: What if evil is something dreamed up by man, and there is nothing to struggle against except our own limitations?

And she couldn't eat any more frozen food, the only thing in her fridge. One night, she finally ordered a gyro platter and even exchanged some pleasantries with the delivery man who happened to be Indian.

Several days later, Naina ended up telling Alannah and Mara about what had happened with John, unable to keep it inside her.

"So you're finally letting go," Mara said, smiling that extra-sweet smile. "And getting in touch with your sexuality. How wonderful."

"Gosh, Mara, why do you always sound like you're giving some new age speech?" Alannah said in her gravelly voice. "Naina, I'm so glad you got laid. You needed it, honeybun. You really did."

Naina was not surprised by their reactions, but it was still strange and discomfiting to hear something so grave and novel for her to be spoken of like some frisky, frothy frolic. Yet, it was also comforting. The magnifying capacities of the lens through which she viewed her own actions shrank even more. She realized her feelings about her transgression were much stronger than her actual belief in her wrongdoing, but her feelings and beliefs were so tangled together it was too difficult to separate the two.

"Did you like it? Was it fun? Was he good?" Alannah always got straight to the point.

Naina felt herself blush and looked down at the cubes of ice melting into the water in her glass. "I did. And that's all I'm going to say."

"Woo-hoo, you go girl," Alannah said, clapping her hands with delight. And then she took a big gulp of her iced coffee, holding her glass almost upside down. "Wait, didn't you say some nonsense earlier about cheating on Harish? Harish has been dead for how many years now? Now, let me tell you something. This may or may not be news to you, but you can't cheat on dead people. You just can't."

Naina started to crack up, the first time she had laughed since her encounter with John.

AS THE FLIMSY clouds were playing hide-and-seek with the earth on a breezy October day, Naina headed to Alannah's opening at a gallery on the Lower East Side. Naina had decided earlier to work only a half day, a rarity for her, and return to Shakti for another yoga class. Now, as she walked on Stanton, then Orchard Street, she could feel her legs aching from all those downward dogs and the squatting. Even her arms hurt. Her mind had been quiet for less than a minute, and the teacher had been too sugary and upbeat for her liking. She still didn't know what to make of yoga, but something in her—nebulous yet compelling—had urged her to go.

Rising above the rowdy Lower East Side chatter were the sounds of a waltz by Chopin, gliding into a sky filled with gilded drawing rooms and long silk gowns. The music seemed to match the mirthful surroundings so well she didn't notice anything unusual about it. But the sound continued, isolating itself, demanding attention. It was Naina's phone with its new ringtone.

Amaya. She quickly answered it. Her daughter was in Whole Foods and wanted to know the name of the nutrition bar she had at her mother's house a few weeks before.

"I'm sorry, Mom, I haven't been able to see you lately. Things have just been really busy."

"No problem. No problem at all . . . I've been busy too . . . you don't have to worry about me . . . how is everything?"

"Not bad, not bad. Jai's been behaving a little better. He's come out with us a couple of times. Although he didn't really say anything, he wasn't as pouty. He still barely talks to Ryan though. He's suspicious I know, but no longer interrogates me . . . I'm sure we'll work it out."

How I hope not, Naina thought, feeling that familiar panicky sensation roiling in the pit of her stomach. If things improved between Jai and Amaya, she would have no choice but to reveal everything. To save her daughter from an unsavory man. And it would be the only right, moral thing Naina had done in a long time. But hopefully it wouldn't come to that. Jai was perfectly capable of engineering the destruction of his own relationship.

She glanced at a sandy, peeling image of the fiery multi-armed Hindu goddess Kali, her body jet black and her tongue protruding hotly, adorning a street wall she was passing; it was one of the few traces of grittiness on the glossifying Lower East Side.

The opening was packed. Alannah looked glowing in a red-and-black mod dress; Damien, her dapper-suited British boyfriend, was by her side. Naina got herself a glass of wine and then went to look at Alannah's work, elaborately staged videos that tracked the surreal journeys of animated everyday objects in settings ranging from suburban houses to the streets of Harlem to a woman's body. It was the first time she was seeing this work, and it turned her mind topsy-turvy and cockeyed while scattering and condensing it at the same time.

Each inanimate object suddenly took on a life of its own, secretly, mysteriously; there were never any people in the videos except for a lone naked woman in one of the pieces. The objects went on fantastical adventures: a matchstick enlarged itself and wildly danced on an expensive-looking patterned sofa, then it shrank and started a fire under the bathroom sink after the bathroom cabinet slowly, ever so slowly, opened by itself; a tiny pen furiously wrote gigantic letters on the streets that never seemed to coalesce into any known words, all the way from the Apollo Theater to Lincoln Center; and a spoon traversed a woman's naked body, languorously traveling up and down, then picking up the pace, circled her neck and shoulders and feverishly danced on her thighs, and then the spoon turned itself upside down and the woman alternated between screaming in pain and moaning in pleasure. Everything was set at night, heightening the videos' haunting quality.

Naina felt herself drowning, diving, plunging, plummeting into the works. She was pulling the knob on a bathroom cabinet and setting towels on fire. She was vigorously writing letters on nameless Manhattan streets, no not EAMNTU and LVUTG, like in the video, but her own STLVY, LRUQP, and PROLXV. Hers was the body on which the spoon traveled up and down, and hers were the thighs that the spoon danced on. And then the spoon turned upside down and morphed into John's fingers, stroking her palms, circling her lips, teasing her thighs, and swirling between her legs.

The memories of that night with John kept repeating themselves in her mind, until she felt herself careening with pleasure. When she went to the restroom, she smiled in front of the mirror. A handsome forty-something man had desired her. Kissed her like he couldn't get enough of her. Touched her like she had the most inviting skin on earth. She cocked her head up, pursed her lips, and then giggled as she looked at her reflection. To hell with Jai. There were other men who wanted her. More handsome men. Younger men. For a brief moment, she felt proud of herself for having the audacity to sleep with John. But soon enough, grayish-black mortification, like the hue of thunder, appeared, attempting to drown out her purple gratification, flamboyant and regal like an empress's orchid.

CHAPTER NINETEEN

AT WHOLE FOODS, a throng of people were clustered around a tall, burly man in a chef's hat showing people how to make some kind of super-nutritious smoothie (enough to give you energy for weeks and weeks, he claimed in his New England accent) with weird ingredients like camu and moringa, names Naina had never heard of.

All Naina wanted was a shopping cart. But all the enthusiastic, earnest people in her way were too engrossed in Chef Marco and his special smoothie. Could the smoothie be frozen? Did it have any historical origin? Could you substitute raspberry with strawberry? And what about the child who was allergic to camu? Nobody seemed to realize that they were blocking the carts. Or they knew and just didn't care. Naina first said excuse me, softly, politely, as she usually did, but when the person ignored her and shouted to Chef Marco if cacao could also be included without giving the smoothie any stimulant properties, she raised her voice further. And finally, after being ignored for several more minutes she got so exasperated that she squeezed herself through a tiny space between two people and went and grabbed a cart. An interloper in the smoothie-worshipping crowd. People turned and glared at her.

Naina quickly pushed her cart away only to see that there were a whole bunch of carts just a few feet to the left that she had missed. She shouldn't have charged in like that. What was the matter with her? Why hadn't she stopped and looked around properly?

But it didn't matter now. The smoothie worshippers had already forgotten her; it was late, she was tired and there was so much to buy for this big meal she had planned for Amaya. A big elaborate meal that would be so delicious, so succulent, so flavorful, that not only would her daughter's mouth melt, but her heart too, like chocolate ice cream softening into rivulets of forgiving, sticky sweetness everywhere.

She could hear Chef Marco's blender whirring, an angry, noisy sound. She hated smoothies, those sloppy, gloppy, slimy, clumpy, watery things. And Jai, that giant scorpion of a man, loved those damn smoothies. He would make his own, filled with kale, blueberry, strawberry, and some other ingredients that sounded as dubious as he was. What was it—mango spleen? Baga, raga, caga? Every time he had spoken about them, she had felt dizzy with nausea.

She ventured toward the produce section, in front of the various varieties of organic onions: white, red, shallots, scallions, and leeks. The memory of the potato leek soup, heavy, garnished with rosemary, she had that night with John at Manzana, came to her, bringing with it creamy, delicious sensations. Harish's shadow appeared, tall and lanky, and she readied herself to be scolded. But it was a silent shadow that minded its own business. It cast a bit of darkness and then went to sit at the dining table to read the newspaper.

She looked at her list. She needed to buy three white onions and two red onions. And scallions? The scallions looked so beautiful with those long, green stems—couldn't she add some to the vegetable korma? No, she decided. It could ruin the dish. She couldn't take a chance. What she was planning to do was risky enough.

Things had improved between Jai and Amaya, her daughter had told her last week. He was less jealous and much more affectionate. He had said he recognized he had issues he needed to resolve and had promised to go to a therapist. But he wouldn't say when. And at the end of the month, he was taking Amaya on a weekend trip to New Hope, Pennsylvania, where he was going to surprise her.

When Amaya had told her that on the telephone, Naina felt her skin turning as white as the onions now in front of her, and the blood in her body rushing like a frenzied river. What did he mean by a surprise? Was he going to propose to her?

Her resolve had coagulated and solidified, like wet clay turning into an immobile fork, spoon, or bowl. She was going to do the right, moral thing. Tell Amaya the truth. She had to protect her daughter from harm.

Again, Naina's organs had screamed, shrieked, and wailed. And even now, five days later, those primal sounds still reverberated in her, stopping her, startling her, unsettling her.

Naina picked up some onions and examined them with unusually meticulous care. No, this one had too many soft spots. No, this one was not firm enough. Everything had to be just right. It was then that was she was going to tell Amaya the truth about Jai.

How was she going to do it? How would she start? How would she portray Jai's role? Would she be able to go through with it?

Two onions dropped from her hand with a thud to the floor. Another glare from a stranger.

Of course, she knew the chances of Amaya forgiving her for what she had done were slim, but there was always a chance, she thought, picking up the onions from the floor. There was always a chance. Hoping against hope. Dreaming when there's no good reason to dream. This was what she had learned in her years in America, the only place she associated with a dream. As a psychotherapist, Amaya worked with people who had done horrible things and she had found a way to empathize with them. Perhaps she might be able to empathize with her mother as well.

Perhaps Amaya would understand that her mother started with a small hole in her soul that over the years grew and grew and grew, becoming vast, deep, and dark, like a well. So much bigger than she was. And so much more powerful. Pulling her into its cavernous depths where she fell headfirst, disabling her eyes and head.

Or perhaps Amaya would understand that her mother too was a flawed human being like everyone else and then—who knows—she might forgive her.

Naina picked up the bright orange sweet peppers. Were they organic? How could such large and vibrant peppers be organic—they never looked like that in India, not that she cared about organic stuff that much. But Amaya did care, which was why she was shopping at Whole Foods. One pepper's stem curled like a finger pointing at her. She put it back down.

Naina moved her cart to the adjoining herbs section. There she saw mint, both her and Amaya's favorite herb. She held some tiny mint leaves in her hand, inhaling their cool, calming scent. Of course, all this was superstition, and she didn't really believe it, but her grandmother used to tell her that, according to Hindu sacred texts, when you cook, all your emotions seep into your food. If you cook with anger, the person eating the food will be able to taste its hot rancor, whether they realize it or not. Her grandmother's aunt was an excellent cook, but a very sad woman, and even her sweetest gulab jamuns and ladoos had a tartness, an absence of something. Therefore, her grandmother's aunt was forbidden from cooking at weddings.

Now examining the waif-like coriander leaves, Naina said to herself that she would cook this meal with all the love she had in her heart for her daughter. That probably wouldn't make a difference, but she was going to try anyway. If it didn't help, it certainly couldn't hurt.

After spending more than an hour shopping, Naina walked toward the checkout counter, passing by boxes of blueberries, deep indigo and plump— they too had a big sign announcing "organic," but once more she had to wonder how anything organic could become so big. She pictured Amaya and Harish sitting at their mahogany Queen Anne dining table, gobbling blueberries, always two at a time. Blueberries were their favorite fruit, their little squishy balls of bonding. Something Naina herself was indifferent to. Staring at the blueberries, Naina sighed and rubbed her forehead—Amaya and Karan would never see their father again. Death was so ruthlessly final.

Was she doing the right thing in telling Amaya about herself and Jai? Was it really the correct, ethical thing to do? Was it really the best thing for Amaya? Why were these blueberries with the tiniest, barely noticeable seeds planting seeds of doubt in her?

She walked away and lined up at the checkout counter. No, she was not going to second guess herself. To the best of her judgement, this was the honorable thing to do.

SOUNDS OF THE toy piano and clock chimes bounced, clinked, and dangled off the walls of Naina's apartment. Sometimes, they wildly swung across the space. She was listening to a work called the "Mundane Intricacies of Flight" by the Contemporary World Group. This piece had now become one of her favorite pieces of music. It was a special kind of piece—it had the sweetness of a child's make-believe world and the haunting knowledge of an adult's world. The music became more frenzied. Naina's mind whirled.

Flames roared around the one-legged tin soldier who was still standing at attention, melting him, while the paper ballerina flew off the table with her tinsel rose. The ballerina was quickly fluttering into the fire and, along with her love, the tin soldier, was burned to nothing at all.

It was Hans Christian Anderson, the master of fairy tales, who had first taught her about tragedy, irreversible, heartbreaking tragedy, as a young child. Naina had read Hans Christian Anderson when she was just five or six years old. But she had not given those stories to Amaya until she was eight or nine years old, wanting to protect her from the dark side of life for as long as she could. And now she was about to expose her to the darkest darkness. Her hands trembled, and her heart tumbled into the infernal pit of her stomach. She got up from her dining table where she had been eating a simple lunch of arugula and pear salad and paced around the room.

The music ended. Naina sat back down. She wanted silence.

Sometime later, she finished up the last few pieces of pear and wanted music again. But this time, something more familiar, more conventionally melodic. Something calming. Or pleasantly distracting. She put in a CD of the bossa nova king Antonio Carlos Jobim, and his music transformed her apartment into a moody, atmospheric space where the warm sea languidly swished, carrying away secrets of the heart.

The buzzer rang. Naina did not register it. She was floating away, weightless, on a melancholy ocean, somewhere far away. Dusk was turning into nightfall, the clouds were getting heavy and dark, and land was nowhere in sight. All she could see was water, the sustainer of life, the substance of tears. The buzzer rang again, more insistently. It registered somewhat on Naina's brain, but she ignored it. She was not expecting anybody and had no desire to see anybody. It must be for another apartment. But the buzzer rang again, for a long time, wailing like an infant crying for food.

Naina was back on land, on her bamboo floor in New York, and there was no water in sight. She was annoyed. She got up from the dining table.

From the video intercom system, she saw a black-and-white image of a disproportionately long face of Amaya and bare shoulders. Naina was surprised. Her brain became more alert.

"Let me in," Amaya shouted.

Why was she shouting? What happened?

"Is everything okay?"

"Just let me in. Right now."

"Of course."

As soon as she saw Amaya, Naina knew something was very wrong. Her daughter looked much older, as if she had learned something terrible about the world, like a child suddenly grows up after reading Hans Christian Anderson. What happened? Had Jai done something?

Amaya slammed the door behind her. She roughly shook Naina by the shoulders, looking at her directly with eyes that were spewing fire.

"How dare you? How could you?" she screamed.

Naina's heart sank down to her ankles. "What . . . what are you talking about?"

"Oh, don't you play innocent with me. Don't you dare. I know something happened between you and Jai. Something that you both kept a secret from me. You make me sick."

Naina's head slumped and she covered her forehead with her hand. She could no longer hear the sounds of Jobim that were still wafting like silk across the room. All she could hear were babies shrieking, the moon howling, and trees falling. Each word that Amaya uttered felt like rocks hurled at her.

"Jai was out today, and I went into his computer to get some pictures of our Costa Rica vacation. I was scrolling through the pictures and what do I see in a folder named "Cinema." A murky silhouette of the back of a woman's body . . . she's dressed in a tunic-like top with some sort of abstract design . . . the kind that you would wear . . . shoulder-length, layered hair, and your short, thin neck. And the tiny curl of a birthmark on the right shoulder. Though I could not clearly see the face, I knew it was you. It all makes sense now, it all makes sense. I don't know how I could I have been such a fool. Your wanting to buy him that silly bug tie, your encouraging me to go out with other men, your so-called stress, both yours and his discomfort around each other. My gut told me something was off, it told me so many times, but never, never in my life could I have imagined such a thing . . . my own mother and my boyfriend. You make me sick."

Again, Amaya shook Naina by the shoulders, and she could feel the rage and sorrow, electric rivers of blood and fire, convulsing her daughter's body. Amaya looked as fierce as Goddess Kali.

"What kind of mother are you? What kind of woman are you? How could you? How could you?"

Naina continued to stand motionless and silent, her head slumped forward. Earlier, guilt had stabbed her, pinched her, and shaken her, but now it had a different power. Now there was no skin to protect her; she was just a skeleton.

It punched her in the stomach, kicked her in the ribs, bludgeoned the chambers of her heart. She felt as if she were going to crumble. She deserved to crumble. She deserved to be kicked. Somewhere out there, Sister Rosemary, the Goan nun with the bushy unibrow at St. Therese's Convent School, was declaring in her hoarse voice, "Girls, sin is an offense against God. Against God. Do you understand me? Like the first sin, it is disobedience, a revolt against God through the will to become like Gods. And you are not Gods. Just mere mortals. Mere mortals. Is that clear?"

Naina could no longer stand. She sat down on the floor, a couple of feet away from Amaya's feet. She broke down into tears.

"I'm sorry, I'm sorry, I'm sorry," she said while hearing how feeble and foolish those words sounded. "Forgive me, forgive me, please forgive me my child, please forgive me."

"Were you ever planning to tell me or just keep this a little secret between the two of you?" Amaya said, thrusting her face in Naina's direction without bending an inch.

"I was . . . I was going to tell you . . . in two days . . . I was going to prepare this big meal and then . . . then . . . tell you everything." Naina could hear her voice cracking; it was becoming harder and harder to combine syllables to form words.

Amaya snarled. "You liar, you witch."

Naina closed her eyes. The babies shrieked with more agitation, the moon howled more savagely, and the trees fell with bigger, noisier thuds.

"All I want from you now is to tell me everything. Everything that happened between both of you. Say something, dammit. Don't just sit there, deaf and dumb."

"I'll . . . tell you . . . everything. Everything."

"And dammit, I want the truth." Now Amaya's voice had heightened into a lancing scream. "You owe that to me, dammit. You owe that to me."

Naina could feel the searing hurt in her daughter's voice. On the fine hairs on her skin. On her skin itself. In her bones. In her blood.

"Why don't . . . why don't we sit down?"

AND THEN NAINA told Amaya. Sitting on the couch, staring at the window. In a quivering, strained, halting voice. She told her that Jai was the kind of man she had always fantasized about, and when she met him, she tripped and fell. For the longest time, she never even realized she had fallen for him. She just thought they were kindred spirits and that she enjoyed spending time with him. Yes, she had been selfish. An awful mother. The worst kind. The thought gnawed at her every day. But it—whatever it was—had ended a while ago. Still not a day passed when her transgression didn't eat her up.

As for Jai, yes, some of it could have been her own imagination, but not all of it, not all of it, for sure. Jai did lead her on and gave her the impression that he was interested in her.

"Did you sleep with him?" Amaya asked, her lips and hands shaking.

"No. There was nothing physical between us. Ever." Naina left out the part about her trying to kiss Jai. She told herself that was irrelevant and there was nothing to be gained from telling her daughter about it.

Amaya looked relieved. "Well, thank God for small mercies."

And then there was a silence. A charged, potent silence. Naina could feel her daughter's entire body throbbing. She shrouded her face with her hands.

"You did remind Jai of both his mother and his ex . . . wild and unpredictable . . . that's how he described you—" Amaya suddenly stood up. "What did I ever do to you to deserve this?" she shrieked, flinging the empty salad container across the room. "What did I ever do to you? What? What?"

"Nothing, my darling . . . nothing . . . It was all my fault . . . my fault . . . my fault . . . and Jai's. You, sweetheart, you did nothing wrong . . . nothing at all . . . nothing."

"Don't you dare *darling* and *sweetheart* me, you witch."

Witch. Witch. Naina hung her head down before digging it into her hands again. Another silence.

A little while later, Naina slowly uncovered her face and clasped her twitching hands tightly in her lap. "Amaya, I know there's no good reason to . . . I know it's all my . . . I know I did something terrible, too terrible, but I do love you very, very much . . ."

Amaya laughed, a dark, hollow laugh, and headed toward the door.

"Will you please, please, please, at least consider forgiving me? I'm begging you . . ."

"You witch. You disgrace of a human being. How dare you even ask?" Amaya snarled before slamming the door.

PART TWO

CHAPTER TWENTY

NAINA WAS SITTING by the sea in the late afternoon, enjoying the sound of the lapping waves and the sensation of the sea breeze cooling her skin. It was lovely how the sun could warm your body until you felt like you could just melt into a liquid pool on the powdery white sand, but then the breeze roused you, preventing you from falling into any such state. Forcing you to stay solid. The elements of nature working in conjunction with one another. Or against? She wasn't sure.

It was July 4th weekend, and Naina had gone by herself by to Tulum, a Mexican town on the southern tip of the Mayan Riviera next to a sapphire blue ocean. Tulum also had spectacular Mayan ruins sitting atop a cliff facing the sea, and the whole town had a distinctly new agey vibe. It was the first time in her life she had taken a trip alone.

Naina had been desperate to leave New York. That summer, about eighteen months after she had last seen Amaya, everything about the city was just irritating her. The endless sea of buildings, the cramped spaces where she could feel everyone else's breath heavy on her skin, and the never-ending assault of sounds—all of it just annoyed her.

In Tulum, Naina stayed in one of a cluster of seaside cottages that had thatched roofs, old-world fans, and stone steps along with modern conveniences, such as hair dryers, twenty-four-hour hot water, and ergonomic pillows. Some of the other tourists—mostly American, Canadian, and European—were seeking an alternative from the rattle, ruckus, and restrictions of civilization (nudity was permitted on some beaches and the minimal electricity used in hotels was turned off by ten p.m.); some had spiritually grander ambitions; and some were simply backpackers who wanted to be next to a beach in a distinctive town with plentiful accommodation in Mexico.

Initially, Naina had been somewhat concerned about traveling by herself, but after she got there, she felt more at ease. There were several women, anywhere from thirty to sixty years of age, who were obviously by themselves as well. But most of them didn't seem to want company, she surmised; they seemed wrapped up in their own worlds as they leisurely ate organic enchiladas, quietly read books, and softly booked massage appointments. Naina would surreptitiously observe the women and wonder: Had the beautiful, ageless-looking woman with a straw hat and big Jackie-O glasses reading a book called *Buried Emotions* come to Tulum to recover from some great tragedy? Had the young woman with deathly pale skin, thin lips and a shaven head reached some kind of enlightenment as she sat motionless on the beach, with her eyes closed for hours in the afternoon heat?

Naina looked up toward the sky. It was big, blue, and cloudless, and the sun was beaming through it. She rarely felt the expanse of the sky in New York, and her heart lifted at the sight. It was boundless and eternal.

Here, Naina felt small and infinitesimal. A little like the grains of sand on the beach, a little like the small apartments in Manhattan, a little like the mosquitoes buzzing around her all the time. As she gazed at the waves caressing the beach and then swimming away from the shore, this eternal rhythm of life repeating itself over and over again, with no beginning and no end, like a circle, she felt a stirring rise within her. She found herself thinking about the ever-changing nature of all things that she had read so much about in her Buddhist books. She was not the same person that she had been five years before, seven years before, ten years before . . . or ten months before. Neither was the coconut tree, neither was the patch of land her villa was on, and neither was Helena, the British woman she had met at the beach, recovering after being abandoned by her American boyfriend. The ocean intuitively seemed to understand that concept, manifesting it so effortlessly in the physical world.

Somewhere, deep within herself, Naina no longer felt sure that there was one grand answer, one magical key to open the gate of wisdom and knowledge, one fantastic image that would dispel all doubt. This notion unsettled her. But, if her hunch was right and she was not going to find a grand answer, she hoped that, at least, she could gain a couple of glimpses into the mysterious unknown and catch some scraps of wisdom before she died.

For dinner, Naina ate cochinita pibil, a slow-roasted pork marinated in juices. Native to Mexico's Yucatan region, it was one of Amaya's favorite dishes and she would look for it at every Mexican restaurant. Naina missed her daughter terribly. From the toes on her feet, to the curving intestines in her abdomen, to the muscles in her heart pumping blood, to her restless eyes—every part of Naina yearned for her daughter.

Naina remembered the thrill of the first kick when she was pregnant with Amaya, her smacking her lips when she sucked on her breasts, her face smeared with lipstick when she was six or seven years old, the excitement on her face when she got a 4.0 GPA in tenth grade, the confidence radiating from her when she left home for college. But most of all, Naina remembered how persistently Amaya had persuaded her to move to New York after Harish had died. Instead of being grateful, Naina had behaved ungratefully.

She shut her eyes and rubbed the side of her neck, the smell of the bitter oranges of the cochinita pibil evoking a tart despondency.

Naina had not heard from or seen Amaya since their contentious encounter. She had tried to call her several times, but her daughter refused to pick up the phone. Meanwhile, Karan told his mother Amaya had not said a word to him about what had happened, except to say it was something terrible and they were no longer speaking to each other. Naina suspected Amaya would not have divulged anything to Karan in order to protect him, knowing that he would have been irreparably shaken if he knew the truth. He had already lost a father, and, to him, his mother was already a morass of self-indulgence and carelessness. Her daughter always thought of other people's feelings. Unlike her mother.

Still, whatever Amaya did say to Karan had caused a further dent in the already-fragile relationship between mother and son. Karan kept asking Naina what had happened; she could tell he presumed it must have been her fault. When she went to San Francisco six months earlier, soon after his dentist girlfriend Arti dumped him and got engaged to a man her parents had chosen, she felt a glare constantly following her around, hot and accusatory. She tried to bring him closer to her, tried to talk to him, even stayed in San Francisco for two weeks, but her son still seemed distant, in a far-off place where her flailing, stretching arms could not reach him.

For months, Naina was haunted by a desolation that felt like a large wasteland where there was not a soul in sight and a twilight that seemed perpetually on the verge of turning into an ominous night. There was just old, dank dust for miles and miles. Dust that would erupt into a storm, dust that would lay still for hours like a dead body, dust that would blind her with its swirls. She had lost her husband and her daughter, and her relationship with her son was strained. Essentially, she had no family left. When she had first moved to New York, she had liked that she had broken away from a bigger superstructure and become a charged, untethered fragment, like the millions in the city. But now, she felt trapped in her unbinding—a mere fragment spinning alone like a madwoman. And she would be haunted by that same old image. A wanton gray-haired woman, disintegrating and adrift, alone on a train to nowhere, her hair flying all over her face, dimly able to perceive the world, so befogged was she by her own desires. Naina was free, so free, freer than she had ever been. But freedom not only came with weightlessness and buoyancy, it also came with the burden of weight. The weight of loneliness, the weight of severance, the weight of the lack of weight.

As Naina's guilt had taken on demonic proportions after the last time she saw Amaya, she developed all kinds of bizarre fears: the sound of ambulance sirens sent frightening shivers up her spine; the brawny new neighbor, who had a big and straggly beard like the roots of a banyan tree, petrified her; and the terrifying idea her apartment could catch fire compelled her to unplug all the electrical appliances before she went out. She also became afraid of walking in the dark although she was now walking along the beach under a pallid moonlight, glad no one was around.

She noticed the palm trees dancing to the whoosh of the breeze and the ripe coconuts heavy and full, like breasts filled with milk. Her mood began to lift. The splendors of nature were limitless, to be slowly savored.

Naina had eventually told Mara and Alannah about what happened with Jai and her encounter with Amaya. As she had expected, they were horrified—nothing shocked people, any kind of people, more than the wickedness of a mother. But, being good friends, they did help her navigate through troubled waters. They uplifted her, reassured her, made her laugh. And even during the worst of times, Naina rarely neglected work—it had been about nine months since she had received the promotion to gallery manager.

A month or so after Amaya had stormed out of her apartment, Naina returned to reading about Buddhism. She read conscientiously, underlining passages that initially confused her and then returned to them again and again until they made some modicum of sense. Which they sometimes did and sometimes did not. She even started going to kundalini yoga classes, though not at the yoga studio Mara had taken her to, but at another place called Surya where she found a down-to-earth teacher called Carolyn about her own age.

Naina let the anguish and guilt pummel her voluptuous body like a furious animal; she let herself writhe in pain like a cockroach smacked by a stiletto heel; she permitted all her emotions to spill out of her like sweat on a sweltering day.

After a long while, she slowly learned to stop constantly beating herself up and the purple bruises faded, though they never completely disappeared. She learned that battering oneself with shame was pointless and, according to one Buddhist article she read, might even be a "tricky form of self-centeredness." She had to move. Onward. Not keep circling around in a grinder. If only it were that easy. Yet, she had to try. It was the only choice that seemed at least halfway decent.

When she did yoga, Naina began to feel her body in ways that she, so busy bustling around her head, had not experienced before. She noticed the coils of discomfort that had gathered at the base of her spine from sitting for so many hours a day, the constriction in her shoulders and back when she was stressed, the sense of expansiveness in her body when she breathed deeply for a long time. Naina had never played sports in her childhood or in her adult life, and she began to enjoy the sensation of her body in motion; circling her hips as if they were pepper mills grinding peppercorns, jumping up and down with crossed legs like a gleeful child who has just got an unexpected chocolate treat, standing gracefully with her legs wide apart and pretending to hold a bow and arrow as if she was an archer like Lord Ram. Her mind, though generally calmer when she was doing yoga than at any other time, was much harder to subdue, and she would often be restless during those periods of long meditation, furtively looking around the room and seeing most of the others with serious faces eyes shut, backs erect, and hands in gyan mudra.

The sea breeze in Tulum had become fairly cool and Naina was glad she had brought along a wrap. It was a long piece of cotton with a colorful geometric pattern. Carolyn, her yoga teacher, often wore wraps like this. She smiled as an image of Carolyn and her big bottom raised upward, her white kameez climbing halfway up the mound of flesh, came to her. It was Carolyn's favorite yoga pose, this downward dog, where you had to raise your buttocks while placing your hands and feet on the floor. Although Carolyn waxed eloquently about the benefits of downward dog, Naina hated the pose. It made her head spin and her hands hurt. The truth was, though Naina liked doing yoga, there was a still a part of her that was not fully comfortable with it. The slangy names for asanas (downward dog, cat cow, frog, fish, baby) sounded silly, students wearing T-shirts with images of very blue Lord Krishnas or Shivas seemed farcical, and even Carolyn's pronunciation of the words "kundalini" and "chakra" sounded funny. Naina still wasn't quite sure what to make of all the white women—the majority—who regularly came to class: some in designer jeans and tight tops and even sexier yoga gear; some dowdy and weary-looking, seeming like they needed something, anything, to uplift them from what she presumed was an abysmal void in their lives. But the most inscrutable of them all were the Sat Kaurs of the world, those Americans with Indian names in teacher training, smiling beatifically, so maddeningly sincere in their commitment to yoga, so unflappable, so comfortable around everything Eastern as they chanted in Gurmukhi, sauntered around in white kurtas, and talked about these places in India they had visited during their numerous trips there. She couldn't help but continue to wonder where she, an Indian woman who grew up in India and a novice to yoga, fit into this whole scene. Yet, she didn't feel a great need to fit in either. That was American-style individualism merging with American yoga, and she liked that fusion.

Naina came to realize that every tradition, every species, every person, everything in the world evolved and changed with time and place. Buddhism, which originated in India, morphed when it traveled to Tibet, China, and Japan, adapting to the various cultures; as a result Indian Buddhism ended up being very different from Japanese Buddhism.

She did not believe any tradition had to adhere to its roots, but believed it shouldn't be totally distorted either. Only what was the boundary between regular adaptation and destructive distortion, and who decided that? Another question with no clear-cut answers.

Even her relationship with Buddhism was not simple. Many of the ideas, in which Naina heard echoes of Hinduism, appealed to her. Yet, she could not bring herself to fully embrace Buddhism. The prospect of distancing herself from the world she perceived, illusion or no illusion, seemed too dismal; the notion of giving up the self, too destabilizing; and the idea of rejecting one's desires and attachments, too impossible.

The breeze had become stronger and Naina's wrap was now flapping like a bird's wings. She gazed at the sea, spread like a satiny, eternal sari on the planet, and thought about how much Amaya would like it here. Someday, hopefully someday soon, she would get to see her daughter. And get a chance to bring her to this magical place called Tulum.

CHAPTER TWENTY-ONE

NAINA WAS WALKING slowly, the dull pain in her left hip not easing up. Placing her hand on her hip, she worried if she was limping. She shouldn't have been so keen to try that particular exercise—what was it called again—pigeon pose, and not listened to Carolyn go on about all that "finding the zone between comfort and discomfort" stuff. The pain shot through her like a bolt of lightning, and she stopped on the street. After it passed, she took small hesitant steps toward a deli and bought a bottle of Advil.

As Naina quickly swallowed four tablets with a Diet Pepsi, her thoughts drifted to Mridula, one of the women who used to come to the health education workshops at the South Asian nonprofit in New Jersey, and her mortal fear of Advil. She was convinced that her teenage son's bad grades were because he regularly took ibuprofen for his migraines, and so she banned it from the house.

Now, all of it seemed so far, yet not quite murky. Every impression, every memory, was indelibly marked in Naina's mind, determined to stay. And reappear more frequently. So many layers, the disjointed pieces of a lived life, on top of each other, parallel to each other, never obliterating each other.

Naina was on her way to an opening of Zarina Sultan's work at the newly opened Lalit Kumar Gallery for Indian contemporary art; the artist was a well-known Indian painter who made vivid and poetic art about women and the conflict in Kashmir. And Naina was also excited to be seeing the gallery for the first time.

Lalit Kumar Gallery was a large space on the ground level of 29th Street, and through the tall glass doors, Naina could see a large number of Indians—the largest gathering of Indians she had seen since leaving New Jersey. The ornate patterns of Indian fabrics glinted at her, sumptuous and resplendent, at odds with the damp bleakness of the New York evening. She saw intricately patterned jamevar shawls flitting and fluttering, long kundan earrings dangling and dancing, silk kurtas with zardozi embroidery flowing and flaring. And then there were the few white people in their nicely fitted black dresses and brown jackets. Naina refreshed her lipstick, feeling discomfited. These were well-to-do Indians her own age and older, and she was dressed in just black slacks, a maroon silk top, and a tie-dye scarf. Luckily, she was wearing ruby-and-gold earrings. She lingered at the steps, the pain in her hip pushed to the back of her mind. Everybody inside looked like the married type. This wasn't like the other openings of Indian artists she had gone to. They had generally been smaller affairs in intimate, less grand galleries, where the crowds consisted of hip second-generation Indians in their twenties and thirties wearing jeans with a hint of the "exotic"—chunky Indian jewelry, nose rings, Mexican-craft-designed footwear, African print clothing—and telling her how they wished their mothers were like her.

Naina was right—most of the attendees were married, but, near the bar, she met Vipasha, a breezy and friendly single woman, an investment analyst who was originally from Ranchi and now lived in a Tribeca loft with the array of paintings she had collected over the years. She said, flinging her dyed bronze hair to one side, she was still looking for the right man and until then had no choice except to be satisfied with the art in her apartment. Vipasha seemed to know everybody at the opening, particularly the single women. Vipasha introduced her to Bandhini, a lively grandmother from Calcutta who had divorced her British husband and now lived on the Upper East Side. She claimed to be the executive director of the Indian Society for the Arts—an organization Naina had never heard of—and spoke of singledom as a real boon for older women.

"Oh come on, who wants to be cooking and cleaning for an old man at this age," she said in an Indian accent with British overtones, wrapping her orange and green jamevar shawl around her stout, salwar kameez-clad frame, looking like a big mother hen painted orange and green. "When the time was right, kids were needed, they were important. But now, I like doing what I like. And the silence. And all old men do is complain, chutter putter . . . they are like babies who always have some ache or pain and expect you to act like Florence Nightingale and take care of them. Bas, *bas*, enough is enough, raising two children was enough. Who wants a third?"

And then there was Aparna, a political correspondent for *Time* magazine, in a beige kurta with kantha embroidery from her native Madhya Pradesh and jeans. She had a big shock of white hair, untidy black eyebrows, and an attitude.

"There's no need to beat around the bush like that," she snapped when another woman, with a sparkling diamond on her left hand, asked her if she had any family in the U.S. "I know what you're asking, am I married? Why didn't you simply say that? And to answer your question, I'm not and I like it that way . . . jeez, it's the twenty-first century and all people care about is bloody marriage."

Naina's favorite person was Soma Iyer, a divorcee from Bombay, who seemed to be about her own age. Soma was tall, willowy, and had straight long black hair, the kind Naina used to have before she chopped it off in the interest of efficiency and convenience. She emitted a firecracker-like air of self-confident glamor and feline sexiness. The world did not turn around Soma, she turned the world around with her pert charm. They got along instantly and soon they were talking and laughing about their first impressions of America when they had arrived more than thirty years earlier.

"I used to love going to the supermarket because the lady at the checkout counter, well to be quite honest she was no lady, would start telling me all about her terrible boyfriend, using all kinds of colorful language the minute I put the milk down at the counter," Soma said in a voice that suggested she was beyond caring what people thought of her. "Me, a sweet newly married woman, had never heard talk like that in my life, but I have to say I was quite keen to learn."

"I used to get so spooked by answering machines, my goodness, the sound of people's voices, no complete sentences actually, coming out of thin air," Naina said. She laughed and sipped some red wine. "That was just too strange."

The whiff had now become stronger. What perfume was that? Michael Kors, Naina guessed. Soma seemed like the kind of woman who would never be without perfume.

Soma, too, had moved to America in her early twenties because of her husband. He came to New York University as a law student. But unlike Naina, Soma had a love marriage with Ram, a man she had met in college in India. Her parents were dead set against marriage because she was Maharashtrian and he was Tamilian, but they went ahead and got married in a small temple outside of Bombay. The early years of marriage were great, Soma said. They lived in a tiny apartment near Washington Square Park, went to free concerts, ate different types of cheap international food, bought furniture from flea markets, and reveled in the bohemian free-spiritedness of the time.

But Ram changed after he graduated. He ended up becoming one of the leading immigration attorneys in New York and the airy bohemian hardened into an inflexible, proud bourgeois.

"All of a sudden, he wanted to live in Westchester, drive a fancy car, wear stuff from Brooks Brothers, and go out golfing all the time," Soma said. "I mean, when we had no paisa, we would talk about going to places like Thailand and Africa and Brazil, but when he made some paisa, he wanted to stay far away from the Third World, except India of course, and only go to London, Paris, and Rome." She made a sneering sound. "Bloody upstart."

"Did you ever think of getting married again?" Naina asked, feeling such an affinity to Soma that she was able to pose such a bold question to a virtual stranger.

"I did . . . I dated a little . . . but it was hard with a young *bachcha* at home, but once Araan was at college I did go out with some people," Soma replied. "Then I had a couple relationships that didn't work out and now there's someone I've been with for a few years."

Naina looked at Soma, sipping a glass of red wine, tucking loose strands of hair behind her ears, and speaking with unflappable candor about her marriage, divorce, and, most importantly, post-divorce dating. She was surprised. She had rarely met Indian women of their age, who spoke so openly about things like that . . . and to another Indian woman they hardly knew. If it were an American or European woman discussing such things, Naina wouldn't have batted an eye. In fact, even if it were an Indian woman talking to an American or European woman, it wouldn't have been that surprising because Indians assumed Americans and Europeans whirled in and out of different beds their whole lives. That they were like ships who quickly changed direction with the slightest shift in the wind, which was why they always seemed to be at sea.

But there was an unwritten rule that governed communication between Indians in America; show your best side, talk about your accomplishments, and avoid mentioning anything irregular or controversial. And the best thing to do if you had so-called embarrassing problems such as marriage troubles, mental health matters, or financial woes that you absolutely had to share, was to talk them over with an American. They would not judge you.

Even Naina, come to think of it, had exposed herself in the most intimate way to her American friends, Alannah and Mara. Suddenly aware that her twenty or thirty seconds of silence after Soma had finished talking about her boyfriend Deepak might be interpreted as some sort of disapproval, Naina took a sip of wine, adjusted her scarf, and said, "Deepak sounds really wonderful. I'd love to meet him sometime."

"So what about you?" Soma asked. "Have you thought of getting married again? Or maybe you're already in a relationship?"

Naina fiddled with her scarf again, not sure how to answer that question. She hardly knew this woman. "Uh, well, you know, I've never given it much thought." She laughed nervously.

"Not yet that is."

Naina fingered the straps of her handbag. "Yes . . . So how did you and Deepak meet?" She was bursting with curiosity—how did older Indians date?

"No one believes me, but we actually met at Barnes and Noble. I was looking for Pankaj Mishra's *The Romantics* and so was he. There was only one copy left at the time and we started arguing about it."

"I see," Naina said, disappointed. How incredibly ordinary.

Naina noticed the lights were dimming, people were starting to leave, and she had yet to see Zarina Sultan's paintings. Oh well. She would have to come back to see them another day.

About twenty minutes later, Naina was alone and her hip started to ache again. She carefully swallowed an Advil without water. She watched the light rain come down in a hush from her taxi. If it weren't that cool, she would have opened the window and put her hand outside and cupped the rainwater. It had felt so good to speak Hindi again after such a long time and slip into the familiar sing-songy rhythms of the language. The sing-songiness that extended to the way Indians spoke English as well. The rhythms of most of her life. The rising and falling inflections embossed on her brain. The words, rounded and always laced with some drama—unlike the slender, efficient, crisp, and staccato utterances that came out of the mouths of the British upper classes—had been aching to get out of her head and come out of her mouth.

A FEW DAYS later, Naina and Soma met at a dingy Indian restaurant on 28th Street. Once more, they spoke in Hinglish without conscious thought, seamlessly moving from one language to another.

"Soma, when my son Karan goes to India, he is constantly irritated . . . too much garmi (heat), too much mitti (dust), the ACs aren't powerful enough or keep tootoing (breaking), servants always bhagoing (running) around you." Naina took a bite of her samosa, feeling her taste buds lurch toward the sweet and tart flavor of the tamarind chutney she hadn't had in the longest time. "You know, that sort of thing."

"And when was the last time you went to India?" Soma asked.

"Five or six years ago. The year before Harish died . . . It had changed so much, I barely recognized it. I'm pucca going to back at some point soon. But this time, I want to travel. I actually want to see India. I want to go to Mysore, Kerala, Mahabalipuram, and Pondicherry. Not always be stuck in Delhi."

"I really want to see the Northeast," Soma said. "Sikkim, Arunachal Pradesh, and Mizoram, and vo sab. Shayad we can all go together?"

The two of them continued talking about travel in India as they moved from samosas to pakoras, chastising themselves for eating such heavy food, like gluttons. Still, they moved on to mutton biryani—grains of saffron rice and chunks of meat beaten into submission by pools of oil. Once again, they started recounting their childhood days in India.

"My dad used to love sitting alone by the radio on the veranda, smoking, drinking cups of chai, and listening to nostalgic Hindi music," Naina said. "Remember that song 'Gaata rahe mera dil'? That was his favorite . . . he would keep humming it all the time."

"That sounds like a Bengali neighbor of ours," Soma said. "Mr. Chakraborty. He would be sitting in a dhoti, smoking a pipe, and listening to Rabindra Sangeet while his biwi would keep bringing him roshogollas, one after another."

Soma leaned back in the greasy plastic chairs even though there was not much space to lean back. "Ah, those were the days . . . long afternoons spent doing nothing. No groceries, no bills to pay, servants asking you how much cheeni (sugar) you wanted in your milk, hot samosas in the evening . . . Deepak and I often talk about how our children will never know anything about that life . . ."

Naina nodded in agreement as her mind drifted to those long summer days where every afternoon, from the age of eight to eleven, she would read and reread Enid Blyton's stories in a quiet corner in the back of the house, imagining she was stranded alone on some island close to England, away from the dust, din, and constant congestion of relatives and family friends in India.

"Did you ever read Enid Blyton as a kid?" Naina asked.

"Of course." Soma's eyes shone at the memory. "What kind of question is that? Everyone did. All the bloody time. Remember Malory Towers? I used to keep hoping I could go to a boarding school in England and have friends called Darrell, Sally, and Gwendoline."

Soon, Naina and Soma were going back and forth on whether they wanted dessert, but quickly succumbed. They decided on gulab jamuns, round brown balls of pure sugar, pure ghee, and pure delight.

"So tell me more about your daughter, Naina," said Soma after biting into a syrupy chunk of her gulab jamun. "I wish I had a daughter . . . the things you can share with a daughter . . . they're just different from a son." And then Soma laughed, her sparkling laughter as joyful and carefree as a girl's.

Naina stopped. Stopped eating her gulab jamuns, stopped talking, stopped feeling the warm air of familiarity between her and Soma. She tightly crossed her arms and looked down at her half-eaten gulab jamun. She felt as if her eyes had turned in their sockets and she was looking with the backs of her eyes instead, squinting at the gnawed dark balls. Her sense of sight was now in the opposite direction, peering at the sun-and-moon-bereft moors within.

"What's the matter?"

Naina did not answer.

"Arree, kya hua? (What happened?)?"

"Actually, Soma." Naina could hear her voice strained and thin, like severely skimmed milk. "Amaya . . . that's my daughter . . . and I have . . . well, we've kind of a had a . . . a . . . falling out."

"A falling out?" Soma said, her round black eyes narrowing into sharp ovals. "What kind of falling out? Why?"

Pain pierced Naina, a fleshy, pink pain. Suddenly awake and crying like a baby. She held her arms more tautly and pressed her lips together.

"Well," Naina said. " Well . . . the kind of falling out that two grown-ups can have."

"What does that mean?"

Gosh, this woman was so nosy. Just like an Indian. What does that mean? What did anything mean? Naina wanted to close her eyes but didn't. She exhaled deeply, as quietly and discreetly as she could.

"A relationship with an adult child is very different from that when they are children," she finally said, slightly raising her head. "As I'm sure you know . . . So sometimes things can happen . . . I'm hoping it will be resolved soon." She stroked the side of her neck. "If you don't mind, I . . . I really don't want to talk about it anymore."

"No problem. No problem at all, Naina. Sorry if I was being intrusive. I guess all of us have a nosy Indian aunty in us, don't we?" And then she skittishly tittered in her girlish way again.

CHAPTER TWENTY-TWO

"SO, I'M COMING out of Dunkin' Donuts in some hick town near Dallas . . . really *gora*, shithole town, where they've got big cutouts of that idiot Bush all over the place and everyone's as big as an elephant, and I see a bunch of *desi* guys hanging out and smoking," Deepak said, his left arm draped around Soma and right hand alternating between lifting his glass to drink big gulps of whiskey and making dramatic gestures. "Young guys, college students, straight from some bloody small town in India, talking in Hindi about how none of them could get bloody laid. I felt damn bad for them and wanted to give them a few tips . . . hey, don't want all that expertise to go waste, man . . . but then a chick walked by . . . really hot, yaar, really hot . . . and the guys started to talk about her in crude ways in Hindi that I won't repeat and embarrass you proper ladies. So these guys had a bet that whoever had the balls to approach her would get fifty dollars. This big, tall, macho guy with a leather jacket, looked like a bloody dada, goes up to her, sounding really confident, and says, 'Hi, Miss, you are very beautiful. My name is Mohan. Can I take you out for a beer or a Coca Cola sometime?'

"The girl looked at him, smiled, fluttered her eyelids like all you chicks know how to do and then all the bloody guys start whistling desi style, like they're in a cinema hall watching Karishma Kapoor singing 'Sarkai Lo Khatiya' in Haryana, and Mohan had that expression on his face like he's just scored big time. And then that girl says sweetly, 'Sure, I'd love to go out with you, but unfortunately you're not my type.'

"'Oh miss, you don't know what you haven't tried yet,' that Mohan said, puffing up his chest and all. 'You will be bowled over, madam . . .'

"'I doubt it,' that hot chick said, still smiling so sweetly and batting her eyelashes. 'I prefer nice breasts . . . I like women, you see.'

"Oh my God. Uski to phat gaiye. You should have seen that poor guy's face. Oh man, it was bloody hilarious. He became a little mouse, bloody chuha, got scared and just ran way. Bhaag gaya bitchara."

"I like the girl's attitude, but Mohan must have been so embarrassed, na?" Naina said as she and Soma roared with laughter.

"Ladies, it was the funniest thing that I saw in that boring Texas in three bloody months."

"So you didn't manage to give your tips on . . . on getting chicks, then?" Naina asked.

"No, all the guys ran away. So sad, all this great wisdom's going to waste." Deepak's elbows were on the table and his hands and forearms were theatrically moving back and forth. "I only have daughters and Araan seems to be doing great with the ladies without my help, and even those poor bastards in Texas, who desperately needed my wisdom didn't get it. So sad, so sad."

"Aw, so sad indeed," Soma said. "Think of all the great treasures that the world's young men are missing out on."

Deepak laughed. He wrapped his arm around Soma's shoulder, casually, squeezing her upper arm as he often did—but that would be the extent of the physical contact between them. At least from what Naina had seen. And Deepak, even though she was quite certain he was joking about all his so-called expertise with women, had he slept with many women? Of course, she supposed Soma and Deepak had sex, but somehow she couldn't picture it. There were all these jokes and allusions about sex, but never any reference to the actual act that must regularly occur between them.

It's a grand tragedy, ladies," Deepak responded, his expression of mock sadness even more exaggerated on his meaty hale-and-hearty face. "Of Shakespearean size."

Soma gave him one of her irritated looks. "It's proportions, Deepak. How many times do I have to tell you?"

"Ok, Soma darling, sorry I keep forgetting. My English is not perfect like you convent-educated ladies . . . Yes, ma'am. No, ma'am. God save the pretty little queen, ma'am."

Naina burst into laughter again.

INITIALLY, WHEN NAINA met Deepak after he had returned from Texas, she was taken aback by Soma's taste—Deepak was loud, crude, drank too much, and could be a complete devil. He was also utterly and unapologetically ignorant about anything cultural or intellectual. Unlike her and Soma who had gone to convent schools and grew up speaking English like good daughters of upper-middle class families, Deepak came from a solidly middle-class home. His father knew only broken English and mother knew very little, and they conversed with their five children exclusively in Punjabi and Hindi, and sent them to second-rate private schools where even the teachers could not speak proper English. Deepak had a thick, typical Indian accent where the t's, d's, and r's were emphasized and it grated on Naina's ears in the beginning, as did his loud guffawing in public.

But he was tall and robust, containing so much life force that it constantly bounced around his broad shoulders and his muscular chest. And he made Naina laugh with his endless funny stories and comments that he always relayed with a grandmother's sense of hyperbole, a tabloid writer's penchant for wicked drama, and his natural comic ability to mimic other people's accents. He loved mocking all forms of New York pretensions and attitudes, and one evening, in between big bites of seekh kebabs at an Indian restaurant near Port Authority, he decided to target art openings.

"Arre, you think those stuffed up tadpoles in suits sipping wine and all know anything at all about those messed-up canvases?" Deepak said. "Arre, they're not there to see those ugly paintings in those Chelsea galleries you ladies go to, but the hot chicks. And some of them are pretty damn hot. But they've all got a bloody stick stuck up their skinny assess . . . I don't know why these good-looking white chicks have no bloody flesh these days . . . arre, in India everybody would die for the voluptuous bodies of Hema Malini and Sridevi and Madhuri Dixit . . . wah, wow, those chicks were hot, man, bloody hot. Even though they're old now, they're still bloody hot."

"At least those stuffed up tadpoles go and see art unlike you," Soma retorted. "Now, can you please pass me some daal?"

"The daal is useless, janeman. No butter at all. Tastes like diet food. Have some of the chicken korma. It's rich and juicy and will make you even more juicy."

"Aah, men, I tell you, Naina," Soma said with exaggerated mock exasperation. "You're lucky to be without one."

"You think so?"

"Without a doubt."

NAINA, WHO HAD started hanging out with Deepak and Soma, always feeling welcome and always enjoying their company, was intrigued by this relationship, the first Indians she knew who had found and pursued love later in life, well after the designated rites of passage of marriage, child-rearing, and the pursuit of financial security. She noticed they never used Western jargon like "boyfriend" or "girlfriend" or "partner" to describe each other, sticking to the neutral "friend."

"We are not boyfriend and girlfriend because we are not boys and girls," Soma would say. "And man friend and woman friend just sound too strange."

In private or around close friends, they often used a combination of English and Hindi endearments, though Deepak tended to use them more often than Soma: darling, sweety, janeman, janoo, babyjaan. They rarely touched each other in public, and when they were around Indians they didn't know well, they never made it obvious that they were a couple. But they never tried to hide the fact either. Except when they visited his cousin or closest friend Rita in Connecticut, they never went together to see Deepak's other cousins in Western Jersey and Northern Virginia or Soma's nephews and their families in Pennsylvania. Around their children, though, they were fairly open about their relationship; Soma's son, Araan, and Deepak sometimes played tennis or went out for a beer, and Soma bonded with his daughters by taking them to bargain boutique shops when they came to New York. None of the children ever referred to their parents' partners by their first names, always using the traditional all-purpose monikers "uncle" and "aunty."

Despite his swaggering air of machismo and coarse talk of booze and women, Naina was surprised to find that Deepak was far from chauvinistic in many ways and was unfailingly loyal to Soma. He was the one who encouraged Soma, the more cautious one in the relationship, to take bigger risks in life, and it was thanks to his persistent encouragement that her company's line of sculptural aromatic candles had made it to high-end resorts in the Caribbean and the Southwest. Even though he constantly teased Soma about her "artsy fartsy" ways, he clearly admired her, and whenever he lost an argument to her, he would farcically slap his forehead with his hand and say something like, "Arre, I've lost once again, yaar. Thank God, I'm now with a lady with brains rather than that dimwit my parents got me married to, but please God, just for my ego's sake, please let me win an argument just once at least so my ego doesn't die and go underground like a dead dog."

Soma did not try to persuade Deepak to engage in the cultural activities she so enjoyed; instead she nourished that part of herself with her friends. Just like most Indians, she compartmentalized her life and did not expect Deepak to fulfill all her needs. And, most of the time, Soma seemed unperturbed by his boorishness, easily laughing it off.

Naina would watch with keen curiosity how the relationship between the two of them worked smoothly despite such notable differences in personality. She envisioned it as a large collage where different colors and patterns remained separate yet overlapped, rather than as an intricate tapestry where multifarious designs and hues wove into each other and became a third blended entity.

It seemed like a good way to have a relationship.

NAINA WALKED DOWN Fifth Avenue, along the east side of Central Park, on a crisp early fall Sunday where, under the beaming sun, red, orange, and gold leaves were gleaming like Indian bridal jewelry. She had just had a drink with Alannah—whom she was happy to finally see without Damien—preceded by tea and samosas with Soma with Deepak. Entranced, she gazed up at the jewel-dripping trees. Short, snappy barks penetrated her reverie.

A small apricot-colored poodle, wagging its tail, looked at her with big bright eyes.

"Stop disturbing the lady, Medusa," a man said. He had a small, angular face, and eyes as big and bright as his dog's, except that his were a kindly gray as opposed to the dark brown of his pet.

"I'm sorry," he said. "She normally doesn't go around barking at people. Normally she doesn't even go near strangers . . . unless she thinks they're interesting."

His smile was teasing and Naina felt a certain awareness come over her. An awareness she hadn't felt in a long time. She flicked her hair to the left.

"It's all right," she said. "Medusa . . . that's kind of an odd name for such a cute dog?"

He laughed. "At least you know who Medusa is. That's a good sign. I like unusual juxtapositions."

"Hey, Josh," a distant voice said from behind her. "Hurry up."

"Oh, that's my friend," the man said. "He's waiting for me . . . have a nice day."

"You too." And the man rushed off, falling out of her mind, leaving just a lingering trace of an awareness of their encounter in her.

Naina continued walking, past the Cooper Hewitt, past the swirls of the Guggenheim, and, entering the park, past the Jacqueline Kennedy Onassis Reservoir, and then she stopped. She spotted a ruby-throated hummingbird flapping its wings so rapidly that they disappeared into tiny missiles of light as it adroitly darted from one peach-colored hibiscus to another. As usual, it was making its jerky twittering sound. Naina wrapped her shawl tighter around her because of the wind. Hummingbirds, these tiny, haughty, fearless, astonishingly graceful birds, the stuff of fairy tales really, were one of her favorite birds.

Now, the hummingbird was perched on a curving branch, its eyes bright and sharp, its neck adorned, it seemed, in a fantastical piece of ruby-colored jewelry. And then it flapped its wings again.

But Naina couldn't keep track of the bird. A large group of people, who appeared to be tourists, emerged to her right, loudly speaking in French, blocking her view, and drowning out the little bird's song with charged-sounding words, loud exclamations, and peals of boisterous laughter. On top of that was the sound of a bus coming to a screeching halt and the high voices of children arguing about who could run the fastest.

It was all too much, this jolt of unnecessary sensory information shattering her moment of peace. She felt her nerves ripping into shreds.

Naina moved away from the tourists, but then encountered another group of tourists, followed by a large gathering of people listening to drums, and a group of families playing ball.

Finally, behind the madness of the Great Lawn, she found a hilly spot below a tall tree shedding its leaves, where no one was within three feet of her. There was still some noise, but it was muted, and she tried to block it out.

Her heart crumpled with longing. She remembered those ruby-throated hummingbirds, shimmering like evanescent gems as they flapped their wings, she had learned, as often as seventy times per second, in the open blue skies of the New Jersey Botanical Gardens, looking like creatures that belonged to the suspended state of midair, to both the earth and sky. Or to neither.

At the New Jersey Botanical Gardens, where she used to go with Harish and the kids, she could observe, without disturbance, the movements of the ruby-throated hummingbird, a solitary creature except during the brief courtship phase, as it captured an insect mid-air, uttered quick, squeaky chirps, pugnaciously confronted the much-larger hawk when it came too close to its nest, poised itself before the large, lush, trumpet-shaped petals of a hibiscus flower or flew backward to find a coral honeysuckle.

The last time she had been at the Botanical Gardens was the summer before Harish died. Amaya had wanted to see the white lilacs, her favorite flowers. While Harish examined the soil, Naina watched a ruby-throated hummingbird as it flew forward and then backward—the only bird that could do so—and sat in space, rotating each of its wings in a circle like a helicopter. The tiny bird was the ultimate symbol of flexibility and adaptability, and Naina had said to Harish that immigrants should adopt the hummingbird as their icon.

It was there, at the gardens in New Jersey, that she experienced what was as close as she would come to communion with nature. Uninterrupted, undivided moments of peace. God, how she missed that. Something needed to change.

CHAPTER TWENTY-THREE

BY THE TIME Naina reached home, with the sounds of the hummingbird still in her head, she realized she was ravenous and quickly ate the sushi she had just purchased; she ruminated about what Carolyn, her kundalini yoga teacher, had told the class about hummingbirds. In the Andes Mountains, hummingbirds were regarded as symbols of resurrection because they appeared to die on cold nights and then come back to life again when the sun rose. Though Naina had not known that before, somehow it had not surprised her. There was something about those feisty, magical birds that weaved their way through the world, that moved their wings in a circle, that instinctively told her that they could renew, regenerate, revitalize. Defy all traditional rules of death. Perhaps, she had always known that.

A little while later, before she poured herself a glass of wine, a slightly sweet Chardonnay Alannah had introduced her to, her buzzer rang. She put the opened but yet-to-be-poured bottle of wine down with a thud on the kitchen counter. Who could it be? Really, there was no peace in New York. She went and looked at the monitor and could not believe her eyes.

It was Amaya, her beloved daughter, at the door. After almost two years.

"Amaya, is it you?" Naina screamed, vertiginous first with surprise, and then with elation, the two emotions ferociously zigzagging through her. "Is it really you?"

"Yes, it is," Amaya said flatly.

"Oh my goodness. How I have waited for this day . . . don't leave, don't leave, please don't leave."

Naina rushed into the hallway and repeatedly pressed the down button on her elevator. The elevator was not coming. The elevator was not coming. Each second lengthened itself into a minute, a potentially dangerous amount of time. Amaya might leave.

Naina ran down all five floors, barefoot, in a loose, slightly transparent caftan, the kind she wore alone at home, and opened the double doors to find Amaya standing there.

Breathless, she felt the skies opening, dead cells springing back to life, coagulated blood turning into bright, life-giving red fluid and flowing through her veins again.

She rushed to hug and kiss daughter, touching her thin, sloping shoulders, her stem-like long neck, and inhaling that scent of aloe vera and seaweed of her shampoo—quickly as if to reassure herself that Amaya was really there. Amaya did not hug her back, but Naina did not care. Amaya's body stiffened as her mother hugged her even tighter, but Naina did not care,

"Please stop this." Amaya said slowly, softly, and deliberately. Naina, too, busy listening to her daughter's heartbeat, barely heard the words.

Amaya jerked her body away from Naina's. "Please stop this right now. You're making a spectacle of yourself. You look like a lunatic standing out here in your caftan . . . I want to talk to you . . . can I came up?"

"What, my darling?" Naina asked, feeling like her mind was a jumping jumble. She couldn't focus on anything; all she felt was a primal urge, urging her to touch her daughter again to make sure that what she had imagined for so long was really real, and not just another heartbreaking chimera.

"I said I want to talk to you. Can I come up?" Amaya's voice was hard.

Naina's heart tightened with worry. "Is everything okay? Is your health okay? Is Karan okay? Are you all right?"

"Just fine. Let's go up."

"Come sit, darling, come sit," Naina said once they were in her apartment. "What can I get you to eat? There's some aloo samosa, some hummus and pita, some nachos and salsa, and if you want I can make you some chicken curry or khao suey. Tell me, beta, what do you want?"

"Chill out. It's still afternoon and I've already had my lunch. Why don't you come and sit down?"

"I will, I will. But something to drink, then? Diet coke, orange juice, or some wine?"

Amaya rolled her eyes. "Just water will do. Thank you."

"All right then, darling," Naina said, unable to keep her eyes off her daughter. "It's so fabulous to see you after so long, it's so fabulous, you have no idea."

Choking up, Naina held herself back. She wanted to feel Amaya, the physical body affirming her child's existence, but by then she realized it might not be a good idea. "You look so gorgeous."

And the truth was, Amaya was looking very attractive. Her hair had grown longer, and it sleekly framed her face with razor-like bangs, a bluish-black eyeliner added a slight touch of drama to her almond eyes, and her slim-fitting jeans that accentuated her full hips had an unstudied sexiness about them. But there was something in her face that made her look much older than thirty-one, as if a lot more than two years had elapsed since Naina had last seen her, wrenching at her soul. Amaya's skin, though still soft and smooth at first glance, had, on closer examination, a hardness borne out of the experience of something terrible, and her eyes, though always sharp, had an uncharacteristic, razor-sharpness to them, like her bangs. As if, burned by the worst of betrayals, her eyes always had to be open, even in her sleep, lest someone stabbed her in the back.

"Please sit down," Amaya said, her voice filled with a new authority.

Naina found herself intimidated. She sat down on the couch, diagonally opposite Amaya. Neither of them said a word. An awkwardness loomed over them, loud like a squawking parrot.

"So like I said, there's something I wanted to talk to you about," Amaya said finally, steepling her hands on her knees and lightly tapping her left heel on the floor. "I recently worked with a patient, an Asian dentist who cheated on his wife." Amaya paused, her lips pursed. She shook her head. "I'm not sure why I'm here. Why I'm telling you all of this."

"Tell me, darling, tell me, tell me," Naina said, hearing herself almost plead. This was her child, borne by her, made by her, a part of her, and yet entirely separate. An entity of its own. How had it come to pass that Amaya, once safely ensconced in her womb, the two of them one unit, seemed continents away even though she was sitting just a few feet away from her?

"Stop staring at me," Amaya chided.

"I'm sorry . . . you have no idea how happy I am to see you . . . just how happy."

"All right then."

"Please tell me what you were going to tell me. Please."

"All right." Amaya uncrossed her legs and loosely put one hand over the other. She gazed straight in front of her, at the black-and-white abstract landscape painting by a Chinese artist.

"So there was this Chinese dentist, let's just call him Clifford, and he had been married for ten years and had a son," Amaya said, an indecipherable expression on her face. "His wife, whom he claimed he was completely in love with, worked very hard and his son was busy with school. Clifford had made some money and was feeling really confident about himself. He used to take his son to violin lessons and then he became very close to the violin teacher. The violin teacher, like him, was Chinese American and offered to teach him the violin as well, and he agreed . . . I suppose you can guess what happened next. He had an affair with the violin teacher and both his wife and son found out. His wife kicked him out of the house and his son wanted nothing to do with him. That's when he started doing drugs, serious drugs. A relative put him in touch with our center and that's when I met him."

Naina was speechless. Why was Amaya telling her this? Was Amaya dating a married drug addict? The idea sent tremors of anxiety through her body. But she didn't say anything.

"I know what you're thinking," said Amaya, looking at her mother. "That I had an affair with Clifford."

Naina looked down and gazed at the flower-filled lines and circles of her caftan.

"I'm not such a fool. I was made a fool of once by a man and my mother. I'm not about to do anything foolish again."

Naina winced. Guilt again reappeared from behind the curtains, pummeling her. It was like a chronic disease, it never went away. It lay subdued, under the folds of the skin, for periods at a time, and then suddenly flared up again. And again. And again. "I'm so sorry, Amaya," said Naina with her head hanging down. "I really, truly regret what I did . . . You have no idea how terrible I've felt . . . everything I've put you through . . ." Her eyes were getting moist, but she had to stop herself. She had to. "I know what I did was unconscionable . . . I know . . . and I've . . ."

"I think I know," Amaya said, her voice softer now. "That's why I'm here."

"Really?"

"No, I didn't have an affair with Clifford . . . But Clifford more than any other person I've worked with . . . and I've worked with many people who've done bad things and felt terrible . . . showed me the depths of shame a human being can feel . . . and how terrible it can be . . ."

Amaya paused and closed her eyes. Then she opened them and gazed at the Chinese abstract landscape painting again. "I really ended up feeling for Clifford . . . his guilt seemed so vivid, so all-encompassing like a chain he couldn't shake off, it was like a cancer growing inside him," Amaya said, her voice low and concentrated with emotion so dense, so contained, that it was almost palpable. "I really ended up feeling sorry for him and thought that was no way for a human, even a human who had committed a wrongdoing, to live, especially since he so clearly realized his folly and so deeply regretted it . . . and I would talk to him about forgiving himself and redemption and second chances and you would keep appearing in my mind, alone in the apartment, wracked by guilt, screaming to the walls . . ."

Amaya stared at the white ceiling, a faraway look in her eyes.

"I just couldn't get that image out of my head . . . I just couldn't, you alone, screaming, tossing, and turning with guilt like Clifford . . . and then I would feel a burning anger toward you and toss that image out of my head . . . But again, you would come back in my head, tormenting yourself, numbing yourself with wine and then I thought . . . then I thought . . ."

"Go on, darling . . . Please go on . . ."

Amaya kept her eyes on the ceiling and toyed with the edge of her fitted black top. "I then thought if I'm talking to Clifford about forgiveness perhaps, perhaps, I should see if I could bring myself to . . . mend things with you . . ." Her voice was lower, more tender, almost confessional.

Naina closed her eyes, feeling an indescribable, infinite, incandescent joy flowing through her. Her soul knelt in gratitude. "My baby." She hugged Amaya and stroked her hair. "Thank you. Thank you. Thank you."

Amaya pulled away. "I'm not a baby. Stop talking to me like I'm a child."

"Oh," said Naina said, scooting away. "You're right. I'm sorry. You're not a baby. You're a strong woman who clearly knows her mind. Much smarter than I was at your age."

"Look," Amaya said. "I don't want you think I've showed up here, everything is fine, and we should all just sing kumbaya. I'm still working on this, I don't know how it's going to end up, but until then, I really don't want you touching me, please."

"Ok . . . all right . . . If that's what you want."

And then came the question that had been on perched on Naina's mind like a crow, crowing away for an answer. "Do you think you might be able to forgive me?"

Amaya frowned. "I'm not sure yet. But I'm willing to give our relationship a shot. Let's just see what happens."

NAINA HAD TO wait ten days before she got to see her daughter again. When Amaya had left her apartment, Naina had asked her when she could see her again and Amaya had said she would call her. Which meant don't call me. But Naina hadn't been able to resist, calling her two days later and then regretting it. It took about a week for Amaya to call her back and they decided to meet for a movie. Amaya still had an air of reserve about her, the kind that seemed to say she was willing to shake hands but not hug, and Naina did not aim to pierce it. Whenever Amaya was ready.

After the film, they went for a Thai meal where they mostly talked about what they had just seen. Amaya did not mention Jai or Naina's transgression, and Naina did not bring it up. Outwardly, it was all very civil with pleases and thank yous and talk about innocuous topics like the weather apart from the movie. Naina imagined if someone did not see the imperceptible long python stretched out to its full length at almost thirty feet and weighing almost four hundred pounds between them, they might think they were acquaintances getting to know each other.

They met again two weeks later to see *Mary Poppins*, a new Broadway musical, and Amaya still did not talk about Jai. Naina was awfully curious to know if they had broken up, and if so, how Amaya had dealt with it, what had happened in Amaya's life during the past two years, but Amaya revealed nothing. And Naina asked no questions. Things between them were tenuous, like a rickety cart overflowing with lemons. She didn't want to topple the cart.

Over a glass of wine, they disparaged *Mary Poppins*, agreeing that it was too sweet, too full of ridiculousness, and too Disneyfied.

"Do you remember how annoyed Karan used to get when we used to keep watching that song "Sister Suffragette" when you guys were young?" Naina said. "How that line about adoring men individually but agreeing they were stupid as a group that would drive him crazy . . .

"Yes, yes," Amaya said, smiling. "He used to go around singing that men as a group were supercalifragilisticexpialidocious *even though* he couldn't even get out the word supercalifragilisticexpialidocious without stumbling on it."

And then Amaya laughed, her jingling laughter, like wind chimes, as she went higher and higher on the swing. The first time Naina had heard Amaya laugh since they had reconciled and it suffused her heart with a warm flicker of light.

One time, Amaya came to visit the gallery and Naina could tell her daughter was impressed by her mother's increased confidence in her new role as gallery manager as she saw Naina give directions to the intern, answer questions with authority, and speak to Susan with markedly less deference than before. Naina showed Amaya a show she and Susan had curated—an exhibition of mixed media paintings inspired by Buddhist iconography, dealing with themes like cultural hybridity as well as fragmentation and wholeness.

"Wow, Mom, I'm so proud of you," Amaya said once they were outside. "You've done really well for yourself. That's a great show."

Naina beamed. This was the first time, since their reconciliation, that Amaya had called her "Mom."

Later when they were eating dinner at an Italian restaurant, Naina asked Amaya if she wanted to get together on Sunday.

"No, no, Sunday's not possible," Amaya said. "I have a date in the afternoon."

"All right then."

Amaya cocked her head and took a sip of wine. "You did do me one huge favor, Mom. I mean, if you hadn't decided to have an affair with Jai, maybe I would have never found out what an asshole he really is." She raised her glass in a mock toast. "So, for that, dear mother, I thank you."

Naina bent her head and bit her lower lip until she could feel her teeth bruising its sensitive skin. There was nothing to say.

NAINA AND AMAYA continued to meet off and on after that, sometimes going out and sometimes staying in at Naina's apartment where she would prepare Amaya's favorite dishes. One night, as Amaya was drinking her second glass of white wine after claiming she had eaten too much of the delicious khao suey Naina had prepared, she said, "You know Jai was furious when I confronted him."

Naina spun around from the kitchen sink where she had been loading the dishwasher.

"It's true," Amaya said, tapping her heel on the floor, her hands loosely intertwined on her lap. "I told him I had seen the photograph, met you, and he said I was crazily making up stuff in order to forsake him . . . That there had never been anything between the two of you and the picture was of you, but it suggested nothing. His denial of the truth was etched all over his face. Suddenly, I felt like I could see everything clearly and I hated everybody and everything."

Naina closed her eyes. *What* had she put her daughter through?

"He flew into a fury, accusing me of leading him on, nurturing his hopes of marriage and children only to cruelly snatch them from him on a flimsy excuse . . . You know, there was something almost infantile about his anger, as if he were acting out his abandonment issues."

The pain and betrayal in Amaya's voice made it seem harder and softer simultaneously, rising in anger, dipping in pain.

"Is that new?" Amaya abruptly asked. She pointed to the abstract Chinese painting.

"What? . . . I . . . I . . . bought it about a year ago."

"I like it. It's very peaceful and mysterious."

"Uhumm . . . I'm glad."

"I've spoken to you about his abandonment issues." Amaya turned toward Naina. "I told you how his mother left his father for another man, how his girlfriend committed suicide."

"Yes . . . you . . . you have." The transference of "unsafe past relationships with women." How could she ever forget? The couple of women who had allegedly mistreated him. The maltreatment for which he had decided to punish every woman out there. The reason he had reduced all women to spiders.

"I'm surprised you're not asking more questions. It's not like you to not be inquisitive."

"Darling, I just don't want to make you uncomfortable. You tell me as much as you want when you want."

"Impressive," Amaya said, nodding approvingly.

She turned to the Chinese landscape painting again. "I wouldn't buy any of his cover-ups and he realized that I knew. That I could see right through him. More clearly than I had or had been willing to admit to myself. That I could see through his layers of veils, that I knew that behind them was a vacuum of desperate brokenness and vulnerability. A horde of defense mechanisms protecting an empty, crumbling, fairytale fort."

Amaya inhaled and exhaled deliberately, looking like a picture of both authority and vulnerability as she knifed Jai's psyche with analysis, yet also seeming like she had been cut herself.

"And then Jai had tears in his eyes and got all choked up . . . even his voice became baby-like as he begged me not to leave him. He insisted I was the best, most stable thing that had ever happened to him. He said he couldn't live without me and needed me for him to keep sane in an insane world."

"What?" Naina exclaimed, unable to contain her astonishment. Little about Jai Silverstein now surprised her, but she just couldn't picture him crying and begging like a baby.

"It's true," Amaya said. "Hard to believe, but true."

Somehow, despite everything, Naina felt a wave of sympathy and tenderness for Jai as she pictured him, bereft, his mouth stuffed with books and tennis balls when his mother left, his heart severing itself from his body and turning into a loose, flimsy organ, at the mercy of every vicissitude of life.

"There was the gaslighting, the rage, and the tears of collapse. Classic . . . in my mind, he had shrunk into something as small as a speck of dirt. For so long, I had really cared for him and even though I was angry and sad, I hated seeing him in that pitiable state. But even when he was crying, it was all about him . . ." Amaya forked her hands through her hair a few times. She kept hitting her heel on the bamboo wood floor, the jerky rhythms, like an afflicted heartbeat, the only sound between them.

"He finally admitted he was attracted to you," Amaya said. She stared intently at the Chinese landscape painting, now silent.

Naina bit her lip. It would have almost been better if Jai hadn't admitted that. That way, Amaya wouldn't have had to feel in competition with her mother.

"He said you were like a fantasy to him. More like a dreamlike phantom figure than someone he wanted a real relationship with. Sort of like the photograph . . . a murky, fantastical silhouette. Something you enjoy from a distance, but don't touch . . ."

Naina's heart caved as she looked down, clenching her hands and biting down even harder on her lip.

So that's all she was to Jai? A flight-of-fancy, a murky silhouette like an outline of a tourist destination? That's it? Their relationship, which had once meant the world to her, reduced to one hazy photograph?

Then she remembered how she had tried to kiss Jai, the memory heating her blood with humiliation and worry. And that omnipresent, inflammable chronic disease called guilt appeared from the shadows once again.

"Did he say . . . say anything else?"

"He swore you guys had never had a physical relationship and kept begging."

Naina exhaled a sigh of relief. At least he hadn't told her that. Thank goodness.

"But he was playing the victim, as if he were the one wronged by my leaving him for very legitimate reasons, when I was the one who had been hurt . . . such blame-shifting. While he never admitted it, I bet he led you on because he's a narcissist . . . or at least has lots of narcissistic traits and that's what narcissists do. He was the grand victim and I was merely in a supporting role for him." Amaya's lips curled into a sneer. "Do you have any idea how many times I'd tried to help him through his issues and encourage him to go to talk to a therapist? But no, he was perfectly fine, he would say . . ."

Naina just sat there listening, all her senses open and alert. She couldn't swallow all of it at once, and so much remained stuck in her throat, refusing to go down.

"Of course, I wanted nothing to do with him after that," Amaya said. "Nothing. That was the last time I saw him even though he kept calling for months, imploring and telling me how much he loved me. Need masquerading as love." Her daughter scoffed. "As if he's capable of love . . . no, I'm wrong . . . he's capable of great, everlasting love for one person . . . *himself.*"

"Did you ever consider forgiving Jai?" Naina said.

"No. Never."

"Well . . . well . . . my . . . behavior was imperfect too . . . to put it mildly so . . . how come you considered forgiving me and not him?" Naina felt spasms of anxiety—what if Amaya decided to shut her out of her life again?

"There's a world of difference between the two of you," Amaya said. "You recognized what you did wrong and admitted it to me fairly honestly. Or at least that's what I think. And you felt guilty, healthy guilt, at what you had done. Like Clifford. But not Jai. The only thing he felt bad about was losing me because of his own desperate need . . . his behavior suggested to me that he was not only a narcissist, but would likely continue to be one . . ."

Amaya paused and looked up. "Look, I'm a psychotherapist and do sympathize with his abandonment issues and his mother wound. But I also believe that while trauma isn't a person's fault, healing that wound is definitely an adult's responsibility . . . and he was not ready for that."

Naina felt her entire self humming with a chorus of emotions. Her daughter was so smart, so wise, so insightful, and so kind. And she could set her own boundaries so well.

Amaya was now quiet. A pensive, faraway expression came over her face as she turned to the window.

The silence tensed the room, making the lazy threads in the couch stretch, the backs of chairs more erect, and the cushions sit up straight.

"Do you . . . do you . . . want so more wine?" Naina said a few minutes later. "Or maybe some tea?"

"No." A loud, resounding no.

More silence.

"I didn't like the way I found out about the two of you," Amaya said, her eyes flashing.

Naina averted her gaze.

Amaya got up. "I need to leave now."

"What? Why?" Then Naina stopped herself. "Are you sure?"

"Completely sure. I need to get out of here."

Amaya took long strides toward the door and started putting on her shoes.

"When will I see you again?" Naina asked, hearing the pleading in her voice.

"I don't know . . . But don't call me . . . I'll call you when I'm ready . . . If I'm ready."

After Amaya left, Naina's head spun and she felt unsteady on her feet. She went and sat down on her couch, and sought refuge, once again, in burrowing her face in her palms.

When she got up, there was only one thing she wanted to do. Turn on her computer and find a hummingbird. She scrolled through the videos on YouTube until she found one that said *hummingbird taking a bath*. She clicked on it and saw a bouquet-feathered, keen-eyed bird bathing in the rain, skipping from leaf to leaf to leaf in a circle, its wings flapping hypnotically. The image of the hummingbird cleansing itself somehow, mysteriously, seemed to have a cathartic effect on her. Then the jeweled creature softly twittered, as if it were telling her something then flew backward and then the video ended. Maybe it was going to find food, a mate, go back to the past, or resurrect itself? She would never know. But its twittering would stay within her as she felt the fibers in the corner of her mind trying to decode the bird's message.

CHAPTER TWENTY-FOUR

NAINA WALKED ALONG the pathway of the Georgian-style house slowly and carefully, trying to hold up both her sari and her umbrella. Though there were lights along the walkway, there was an engulfing, womb-like darkness in the suburbs, the kind one never experienced in New York. She stood by the door, waiting to ring the buzzer. Her nervousness escalated like a lightning bolt, leaving her body and reaching upward to meet the lightning bolt in the sky. Two lightning bolts coming together. One the result of divine power, the other borne of human weakness.

She could hear the high-spirited voices of people inside the house. There seemed to be a lot of people. But then today was Holi, the Hindu festival of color heralding the arrival of spring, and Rachita and Sushil, being the generous hosts that they were, would have invited the whole Indian crew from Montcrest and surrounding towns.

This was Naina's second time to New Jersey in recent years. The previous time, just a couple of weeks earlier, was for Aditi and Samesh's thirtieth wedding anniversary party, a lavish affair but with no more than ten or eleven couples. They had been inviting her to parties for years, but she had always made up some excuse. Still, that had not deterred them from calling her every single time. And it was a thirtieth wedding anniversary, a big deal, and they were good people, and they had been good friends. She had found herself wanting—no, it was more like needing—to go.

Judging by the number of cars parked and the numerous streams of voices she could hear inside, this party definitely seemed bigger, which meant she would encounter people she hadn't seen last time. She raised her trembling hand to ring the doorbell, but it stayed up, inches away from the bell.

So far, Naina had been pleasantly surprised by how her worst fears had not come true. She had brushed the New Jersey people off for the past few years, yet when she showed up, she had been received with much more warmth than she had expected. Friends like Aditi and Samesh, Rachita and Sushil, Richa and Naveen, and Lata and Abhijeet, whom she had always liked more than the others, seemed genuinely happy and admiring of the fact that she had found a job and created a satisfying life for herself in New York. And to her surprise, they had not probed, as Indians were prone to doing, about her abrupt disappearance from their lives or her unexpected reappearance except to say things like, "Naina, hey, you forgot about us. We just weren't cool enough for you, na."

And then embarrassment would course through her like a cowering flower skulking away as she would attempt to offer some sort of explanation that was always more long-winded and feeble than she had intended. But even before she could finish her story, waves of hands and voices would interrupt her. "Let bygones be bygones, Naina. We understand how painful Harish's passing must have been for you and you didn't want to be reminded of anything to do with him. We understand. Don't worry. You don't have to explain anything, Naina. We've known each other too long. Come, come, have something to eat. We have garam samosas."

This was, for Naina, a blessing. To be thought of as the poor wife who couldn't bear the thought of coming to New Jersey because it reminded her of her beloved husband.

She planned to do nothing to correct that image.

Of course, not everyone had such a benevolent perspective and a couple of women had openly given her the cold shoulder, saying nothing except a couple of pleasantries and offering fake smiles. But at least no one had said anything unpleasant or hostile at Aditi and Samesh's anniversary party. She could not count on that happening again at this party.

Naina opened her mirror and looked at herself under the porch light. She adjusted her filigreed gold pendant, added some eyeshadow, and brushed her hair one last time. She hadn't worn a sari in a long time and hoped she had done the pleats right so the whole thing wouldn't unravel in front of everyone.

Finally, she plucked up the courage to ring the doorbell, and it unleashed fast-paced, rhythmic, lark-like sounds. She jumped. This was new. And so incongruous with the soporific feel of the place.

"Happy Holi, Naina. Happy Holi," Sushil said, the host, hugging her. "Welcome, welcome. So good to see you. So glad you could make it. Come, let me take your coat."

The minute Naina walked into the house, she could feel all eyes in the living room turn toward her, some discreetly, some unabashedly. Numerous dark-colored irises enclosing her in their orbit. Leaving her flailing like an animal in a zoo. Some people smiled, some even waved. She collected herself and nervously smiled back.

Rachita, Sushil's wife and the hostess, rushed toward Naina, gushing Happy Holi and bringing her a plate of gujiyas, a sweet traditionally served at Holi. "Okay, Naina madam, can you eat this or is that too bad for your lovely New York figure?" Rachita said, looking plump as usual in her red salwar kameez with Swarovski crystal beads.

"Of course I can," Naina said, trying to stop her voice from wavering. "I love gujiyas. Thank you."

And then Sushil arrived with two glasses of wine, one white, one red.

"Okay, so this is a Chilean red and this is an Italian Pinot Grigio," Sushil said. "Which one would you like? Hopefully, at least one is adequate for a real New Yorker."

"Oh, Sushil, you will never change," Naina said, feeling genuinely touched. "You've always been the best host in the world."

"And what about me?" his wife Rachita said, her hands on her hips.

"All right, both of you are the best hosts in the world. Happy? Khush?"

As Naina made her way into the living room, checking to see if her sari was still neatly tucked in at her waist, she was, not surprisingly, first greeted by her favorite people, all those who had been warm to her at Aditi and Samesh's wedding anniversary party. Followed by the women who exchanged pleasantries and offered her their phony smiles. Though they feigned no interest in her, Naina could feel their eyes on her back, monitoring her movements, assessing her figure, her sari, her heels, her jewelry, and her hairstyle.

And then, as she stood to one side, picking up a seekh kabab from one of the server's trays, the barbs started.

"What, madam went to New York and became too big for her old Jersey pals," the caustic yet helpful Ranjana said—who had not been at Aditi and Samesh's party—coming up from behind her. Ranjana was a pear-shaped woman with a pear-shaped face, uncommonly thin lips, and a big red bindi on her forehead. She was gesturing with one hand and sipping a Coke as usual with the other. Never Diet. Always regular, sugar-filled coke.

Naina wasn't certain how to respond, but she didn't have to worry. Ranjana wasn't done.

"What, we weren't glamorous enough, cool enough, smart enough for you after thirty years? Think you are too special? Let me tell you, we are very cool and smart too. Don't ever forget that. Just because we don't go hopping from one bed to another like those goras (white people) and keep sleeping next to our husbands, whose snoring, by the way, gets louder and louder every year, doesn't mean we are no good."

Why couldn't this woman just shut up? Shut the hell up. Just leave me alone and stop staring, Naina wanted to shout. This woman had the worst stare—a stare that felt as if it were dismembering her.

"Let me tell you one more thing, Naina," Ranjana said, placing her now-empty glass of Coke on a table so she could gesture with both her hands. "Though I don't hold any grudges against you, as you know, I am a very frank person. You reap what you sow in life. You give up on people and they give up on you."

"I know that, Ranjana," Naina said, finally. "And New York hasn't been just glamorous and fun. I . . . I . . . have reaped what I've sown . . . And it's not always been easy."

"What do you mean by that?" Ranjana's eyes were wide and greedy. She wasn't one for missing an opportunity to snatch gossip.

"Nothing. Just that you're right. Everyone reaps what they sow."

"You haven't changed a bit, Naina. Still so secretive."

"Neither have you, Ranjana. Still so nosy. Excuse me." Naina started to walk away to find better company when she was accosted by a stick-like, gold ring-encased finger pointing at her.

"So, Naina, forgetting all your friends, forgetting their birthdays, forgetting their anniversaries when you were just a few miles away," Sheela said in her raspy voice, a tall, rail-thin woman known for her generosity, and whose son Karan was very close to. "Very bad, Naina. Very bad. You were just in New York, across the bridge, not in Siberia, you know. When you needed us, we were always there for you."

Naina lowered her gaze, not knowing what to say. Sheela was right. All she could finally say was, "Sorry. That's all I can say."

"Okay, okay, at least you're back now," Sheela said, smiling weakly.

"Yes, I am . . . I am."

Other acquaintances who appeared as awkward around Naina as she imagined she appeared around them stood near the mahogany-framed French doors overlooking a huge garden. They exchanged clumsy pleasantries, their eyes shooting darts of unasked questions. Two of these people, Nilanjana and Kanchan, were the women who had commented on her going to Rutgers at an advanced age. Now, both plumper and both in fuchsia-colored salwar kameezes, they spoke to her in markedly uncomfortable voices, saying things like, "So all is well?" "New York must be so different from here, no?" "Is Amaya still living in New York?"

About half-an-hour or so later, Naina needed a break. She went to the bathroom where she stayed for a few minutes, leaning against a wall with her eyes closed, inhaling the jasmine-scented candle on top of the toilet. The questions kept swiveling in her head. Why was she here? Why hadn't she come back sooner? Why did this place seem just the same? Why did this place seem different from what she had remembered? Why did it discomfit her? Why did it make her feel at home? She looked out into the garden through the window, barely able to make out the sounds of the crickets, and saw a red feeder in the dark. Rachita loved hummingbirds just like she did and probably got to see them regularly. The thought made her wistful and evoked images of Amaya. If only Amaya would call her back—Naina hadn't heard from her in two weeks, their meetups were now sporadic at best—they could go to the New Jersey Botanical Gardens together. Though Amaya's uncertain behavior made her terribly anxious, she had, grudgingly, learned to live with it, accepting it as the price to be paid for her terrible mistake.

Naina came out of the bathroom, and Sushil offered her another glass of wine, which she gladly accepted, but resolved to not drink more than two glasses. People would talk, plus she had to drive her rental car back to the city.

She stood near the dark wood bar, away from the crowd, looking at the living room, which she hadn't seen for about five years. There was the same tawny-colored sofa with curved arms and carved wood, matching chairs, the big Victorian-style table made of glass and wood with carved, scalloped edges jutting out, and the intricately patterned light mustard and orange Kashmiri carpet. The chandelier, with dripping crystals, still presided over the room like Queen Victoria presiding over her Empire. There was the familiar collection of Mughal miniatures above the sofa, vibrant paintings depicting royal portraits, court scenes, hunting life, and battles. One new addition Naina was both surprised and pleased to see was a print by the well-known Indian artist S.H. Raza, known for his abstract, colorful paintings exploring themes of Indian spirituality. The print had a big black dot in the center and colored V-shaped bands above and below it. It looked like a cosmic diagram, and made her think of her kundalini yoga classes. The flow of the bands, akin to energy moving; and the dot, akin to concentrated meditation. Something she hadn't quite yet mastered.

Naina tried to recall the many times she had spent in this living room. The birthdays, the anniversaries, the dinners, the Christmases, the Diwalis, and the Holis. She especially remembered the Diwali card parties—sitting on that tawny-colored sofa and participating in light gambling, a customary activity among North Indians before the Hindu festival of lights. Everyone would gamble without restraint in the jocular, high-spirited atmosphere of the festival season. Rachita, meanwhile, would keep the samosas and chaat coming into the wee hours of the night. For some reason, Naina always seemed to win the most money in this living room; she could never forget those feelings of exhilaration whenever she got three aces or three kings or three queens in her hands. It had been so long since she had played cards.

During Diwali, this house always glowed with flickering clay diyas, and all the guests would invariably trot down to the basement where there would be a big altar with over-painted idols of Lakshmi, the goddess of prosperity. And then, in front of the huge altar, they would all sing "Om Jai Jagdish Hare," the devotional Hindu hymn she had always sung on Diwali ever since she could remember, fumbling over the words.

Naina could still picture Harish standing next to those French doors and drinking whiskey, him falling asleep on the sofa after one of the dinners and spilling the reddish-brown tamarind sauce from Rachita's chaat on the Kashmiri carpet during a late-night Diwali card party. Both Harish and she had jumped up, quickly got towels from the kitchen, and tried to wipe out the stubborn stain. Poor Harish, he had been so embarrassed, his thin face looking even thinner, almost like a scarecrow. And his stammer, which only came out when he was nervous, quivered as he profusely apologized. Naina felt warm knots of tenderness gathering in her chest, the memory of him coagulating in her.

Everyone today, except for her, was still a couple. Everyone had a warm body to sleep next to while she slept in a double bed next to a lifeless mass of pillows; everyone had someone to fasten a stubborn necklace while she spent forever, contorting herself in the mirror to get it right; everyone had someone to always go to dinner with while she, if she couldn't find anyone, sat opposite an empty chair. Even Karan and Amaya were in relationships now, though she suspected neither was going to last.

"What are you doing here all by yourself?" Samesh asked, walking up to Naina in his cream-colored kurta pajama, still looking thin as a rail. "Come, come, join us." And she joined a group, consisting mostly of her favorite people, clustered near the S.H. Raza print.

"So, Naina, where do you keep your car in Manhattan?" Abhijeet said.

"I don't have a car. Cars are more of a liability in New York, and if I need to go out of the city, like this evening, then I just rent one. But really, in the city, you don't need one with all the taxis, buses, and subways."

"Really?" the group said in a chorus.

"But aren't the subways dirty and dangerous?" Lata said, Abjijeet's wife.

Naina smiled. Ah, the suburban stereotypes of the city. "Well, I wouldn't call them clean. But they are not dangerous. Very, very convenient. You avoid all the crazy Manhattan traffic."

Lata blinked her tiny kohl-lined eyes in surprise and wrinkled her already-wrinkled forehead.

"So, how large is your apartment?" Samesh asked.

"About eight hundred square feet."

Again, everyone's faces contorted with astonishment, and Naina had to suppress the urge to laugh.

"Eight hundred square feet?" Lata said, blinking again. "Your old living room was bigger than that."

And the questions continued—about New York, about her work, about Amaya, about Karan, whether either of them had any "good news," meaning a wedding in the near future. But the topic of any romantic interest in connection with Naina never came up. She intuitively suspected some might speculate that a romantic interest might explain her long absence from Jersey, but no one said anything. Such things were not supposed to be spoken about—at least not loudly. Like when Sita, Samesh's cousin, got divorced after twenty-five years of marriage and married an American man, she was always seen alone at the few Indian parties she attended, and most people never mentioned her divorce or her new husband. Only a couple of people would awkwardly ask a few perfunctory questions about Howard, her new husband.

Rachita announced that dinner was served. Starving, Naina rushed toward the Queen Anne dining table where the feast was laid out, buffet-style. There was chicken curry, lamb biryani, fried okra, spinach with cottage cheese, black dal, yellow dal, chapatis, naans, parathas, and her favorite—cucumber and mint raita, a thinner form of yogurt. It was white and creamy, and bits of cucumbers peeped out from it, like little green girls clad in white veils. As Naina was pouring raita on her biryani, Usha, a relative of Sheela's whom Naina had sporadically met over the years, came up to her.

"So, Naina, looking all slim trim, glam sham. Looks like New York is really suiting you."

Usha's voice was sugary like Coke, but Naina could sense it was not real Coke, but Diet Coke, fizzing with artificial sweetener. She tentatively smiled, saying an even more tentative thank you. She went and sat next to Aditi on the tawny-colored sofa. Aditi, a scholarly-looking radiologist with her thick wavy hair neatly tied back in a ponytail, was, as usual, wearing a traditional sari. A purple South Indian silk sari bordered by pyramidal patterns inspired by South Indian temples woven in gold. Naina's sari was much more modern, something that she had bought just a year before Harish died—six yards of rust-colored silk with an embroidered border made with gold thread, beads, and semi-precious stones. Now, sitting next to Aditi, Naina wondered if she looked too show-offy.

"Your anniversary party was really terrific," Naina said. "The music, the food, the flowers . . . everything. Thanks for inviting me."

"Arre? What's wrong with you?" Aditi said. "Why have you turned so formal shormal? How could we not invite you? How long have we known each other for?" She shook her head. "We will always invite you. Now, it's up to you whether you come or not."

Naina lowered her gaze.

"Okay, baba, sorry, sorry, sorry. I understand. Of course, I understand." Aditi smiled broadly at Naina. "Samesh and I were so happy you came. It's so good to see you."

Rachita announced that dessert was served. There was a big bowl of rasmalais, gooey cottage cheese balls in sweet milk. Naveen, a balding man with a belly to rival that of a pregnant woman, was the first to help himself, heaping his plate with four or five rasmalais.

"Naveen, what are you doing?" Richa, his wife, rebuked.

"I'm just enjoying Rachita's food." Naveen shrugged.

"But so many rasmalais . . ."

"Oh, janeman, don't worry about my figure. It's too late in life for me to start dieting." Naveen turned to Naina. "Not all of us can have a Bollywood star figure like Naina."

Naina grinned. She had forgotten just how funny Naveen could sound. And what a different world she was in. One where people were unabashedly heavy and readily joked about weight and age—in contrast with New York where most were slim and trim and would consider it offensive to mock anyone for their flab or advanced years, even as they themselves tirelessly strived for the toned youthfulness the city epitomized.

"Look, it's still bloody raining outside," Naveen said later, after taking a bite of his third rasmalai. He shook his head and made a clucking sound with his mouth. "You know Holi is just not the same in America. Look at us. We are celebrating at night when we are supposed to be drunk and asleep at this time from too much color and too much bhang (an Indian liquor) during the day. But who's going to give us a holiday for Holi here? Who?" He took a swig from his beer mug. "Last year, I was in India for Holi and, man, it was so much fun. Arre, not only was there the usual color and water stuff, but my nephew brought a whole boatload of eggs. Nothing could beat that, let me tell you. Eggs cracking on people's behinds."

Everybody burst into laughter.

"That's disgusting, Naveen," Aditi said.

"Sorry doc, but it was a lot of fun."

And then Naveen recounted more tales about his Holi experience in India and Aditi continued to look disapprovingly.

By this point in the evening, Naina had started enjoying herself. Here she was listening to the sorts of stories that, besides Soma and Deepak, nobody else could tell her, listening to animated crosscurrents of Hinglish conversations that felt so comfortingly familiar, hearing the cascades of intonations and expressions that were deeply embossed in the fabric of her consciousness.

"Hey, does anyone remember 1987?" Sushil said. "The weather was in the eighties in late March, and we all played Holi at Harish and Naina's place. Naina, you were completely wicked- I remember that. Sneaking up on everyone and throwing buckets of water. And that color in the water . . . it didn't go for days, and I had to explain to the Americans that I looked like a multi-colored joker because of some Hindu festival. Though my boss never said it, I could tell that Jack thought I came from a jackass of a country . . . And my behind is still sore from the water balloon you aimed at me."

"You probably deserved to have that water balloon thrown at you," Naina retorted as images from that day swirled joyfully in her head.

Once again, everyone burst into laughter, their voices rippling like firecrackers in the living room.

Naina left at almost one in the morning. Several people invited her to spend the night at their houses, expressing concerns about her safety, but she declined. Instead, she got back into her rental car and was struck by the fact that she was the only one going home by herself with only her own company to look forward to. As she drove on the deathly quiet, winding streets of New Jersey, she couldn't help but wonder if it would always be like that. Or if there was a way for her to change it.

CHAPTER TWENTY-FIVE

THINGS HAD BECOME more stable with Amaya, and they regularly met at least two or three times a month. Gradually, Amaya let Naina massage her hair the way she did when she was a child, though not with the coconut oil of the past. Now, she only wanted a dry massage. Still, Naina behaved cautiously and tentatively around Amaya, like someone treading new waters. Always upright and keeping her head above the water. Anything could change. At any time. At a moment's notice. If there was a moment's notice.

Amaya was pleased Naina was renewing her relationships with her old friends, describing it as a "mature move." Karan, as to be expected, was thrilled as well, and the edges in his voice smoothed out, the bewilderment mitigated, and some affection started to trickle out of him again. Naina surmised that he probably saw her return to New Jersey as a return to sanity, as the restoration of the natural order of things.

Also, Soma and Amaya became close with Soma assuming the ostensible role of an aunt. Soma did not resist being called "aunty" and Amaya treated her with the kind of deference that one would accord someone older and more experienced. A mutual recognition of boundaries not to be crossed. The bond between two people who are friendly but not friends. An unspoken agreement about who had greater authority. With Soma eliciting the sort of respect from Amaya that Naina no longer did. Amaya and Soma both shared an interest in Broadway musicals, hot stone massages, and were especially passionate about Ethiopian food, and made it a point to explore Ethiopian restaurants together, with or without Naina.

Amaya was still dating Nevin, a Chinese-American man who designed interiors for restaurants, but there was never enough enthusiasm when she spoke about him. Amaya had asked Naina to meet Nevin numerous times, but Naina kept emphatically refusing.

"Why won't you meet Nevin?" Amaya had demanded one time after they were driving back after a leisurely afternoon at the New Jersey Botanical Gardens, her tone fierce. "What are you afraid of?"

Naina had not responded, looking down, as guilt, that chronic disease, had appeared again. Chewing into her like an army of ants ripping into a piece of bread.

"What? What?" Amaya said, thrusting her face closer to Naina's as they stalled in traffic near a toll booth.

You know the reason why, Naina had wanted to say. You know. Then why do you keep asking me? But instead she replied, "I just want to hold off until you're really serious about him. I mean . . . I mean . . . there's really no reason for me to meet him right now."

"I don't know that I can trust anyone again," Amaya said slowly and softly, cupping her forehead with her right hand.

Naina gingerly held Amaya's hand, a touch her daughter did not resist. "You will, Amaya. You will."

Amaya seemed impressed when Naina told her she was practicing yoga and reading more about Buddhism. "So do you believe the Buddhist idea that there is no self at all?" Amaya asked one day as they were having a drink at a wine bar.

"I've thought about it and don't think I can really believe that," Naina said. "I prefer the Hindu idea of the atman, the eternal soul. Somehow, the idea of no self sounds too nihilistic to me. Maybe I'm too Western in my way of thinking. I just can't negate the self."

"Neither can I," Amaya said. "I think therefore I am, then?"

"I am, therefore, I am, is what I prefer."

"Oh, that's a good one."

And then they softly laughed, holding onto their respective selves, as an old ceiling fan noisily creaked overhead. Each of its blades moving slowly and deliberately. Never whirring like one of those speedy, modern fans where the blades disappeared into one giant kinetic blur.

AT THE END of summer, Naina and Amaya went to Oaxaca, a colonial Mexican town nestled in a valley and renowned for its arts and crafts. It was lush, bohemian, and a tad bit eccentric. Naina loved it. Amaya did too, but not with the same fawning passion as Naina. Beautiful colonial homes and small hotels and bed and breakfasts, owned mainly by foreigners, dotted the cobblestone streets of the city, as did several baroque cathedrals and small first-rate museums and galleries.

Everywhere there was a profusion of color—vivid pinks of the bougainvillea flower sang songs of joy; rich blues like peacock feathers sat in the cradle of ornate beeswax candles; bright oranges like the rays of the sun exhorted Naina to forget her troubles; and the maroon color of the houses was so resplendent that they looked as if they had been painted with sindoor, the powder worn in the parting of the hair by married Hindu women.

Naina and Amaya stayed at a charming bed and breakfast owned by a Mexican woman and her American husband. Rosa had long black hair that swung down to her hips, and an intense, piercing face with too much makeup; she was a lover of the folksy and sorcerous, particularly the wood carvings of fantastical creatures called Alebrijes. All over the bed and breakfast were brightly colored, bizarrely shaped dragons, peacocks, porcupines, and a mélange of hybrid animal figures. In their room was the sky-blue partial body of a bird with a gigantic parrot-green beak. The beak was wide open and it looked like it could swallow an entire animal.

Flowers bloomed everywhere in the hundred-year-old home. In the mornings, after a leisurely breakfast of tamales, Naina and Amaya would sit on the terrace and read. Naina was reading a romance set in seventeenth-century Mexico, and Amaya a book on Buddhist psychology. During this time, they were typically quiet with Naina drawing comfort from Amaya's presence. And then they would venture out during lunchtime, toward the zocalo, the town square, and indulge in the flavorful cuisine of the region. Oaxaca was known for its seven moles or sauces, and Amaya and Naina had distinct preferences. Amaya liked mole negro, a brown sauce with chocolate, cinnamon, chilies, and other spices while Naina liked mole verde, a green sauce with vegetables, pumpkin, sesame seeds, and herbs. There was no overlap in their tastes and, as a result, no sharing of food.

With all its color and arts and crafts, Oaxaca, for Naina, felt a bit like India and was a heady affirmation of life itself. Somewhere deep in her body, she felt intensely that color was pleasure, color was life, color was love. She couldn't get enough of it.

One evening in a nearby village, she saw a woman weaving a rug, her hands shrunken yet nimble, and Naina was struck by her resemblance to her grandmother. Except that her grandmother would have been dressed in a white sari, lots and lots of neat folds of white without any adornment—the archetypal Hindu widow. As the Oaxacan clouds gathered above Naina, she pictured her grandmother by her two most distinctive traits: an absence of color, and sharp, birdlike eyes—like those of the weaver in front of her. And every memory of her grandmother came with, attached like a permanent tag, her didactic words about how people should live their lives in accordance with their age, repeated again and again. Naina felt a surge of fury go through her.

Even after they left the village, the image of her grandmother continued to follow Naina around like a spirit, a hot and haughty moral superiority shooting out of her straight back, her tiny, sharp eyes inspecting her granddaughter. That night, Naina dreamed of her grandmother and, in that dream, everything about her grandmother was white. She looked like a ghost and Naina woke up in the middle of the night with a scream. Amaya quickly jumped up from her bed and held Naina, stroking her hair in the way that Naina used to stroke Amaya's.

"What's the matter, Mom?" Amaya asked softly as Naina rested her head on her chest.

"I . . . don't know," she said, straining to breathe, the darkness in the room contrasting sharply with the white in her head.

"Did you have a bad dream?"

"I . . . I . . . dreamed of my dadi . . . she was all white . . . all white . . . like a ghost."

"Don't worry, don't worry, she's not here to judge you," Amaya said, her voice both assured and soothing. "You've just had a bad dream. It's okay, it's okay . . . You can wear whatever color you want."

Naina clutched Amaya tighter, her chest pounding. Amaya was still stroking her hair.

"She's dead . . . why is she in Mexico?" Naina said, almost hysterical. She was frightened by her own voice. "Why? Why?"

"She's in your head. Shh . . . go to sleep, Mom. Shh . . . It's just a bad dream."

"It is?"

"Just a bad dream. That's it. All right, Mom?"

Naina kept holding on to Amaya, inhaling the smell of her aloe vera and seaweed-scented hair until they fell asleep, their bodies intertwined.

THEY WERE EATING lunch one afternoon at an open-air restaurant near the zocalo, and a woman, who could not have been more than twenty-two or twenty-three years old, walked into the restaurant, trying to pacify a crying child.

"Pollo en mole negro, por favor, pollo en mole negro rapido," the harried mother said to the waiter, adding that it would be the only thing that would mollify the child.

"He's just like me," Amaya said, who was watching the child with great interest. "A lover of mole negro."

"She looks so young," Amaya said later, referring to the mother. "Maybe I would have had an arranged marriage and been a mother by now if you had stayed in India."

Naina said nothing as she tried to digest Amaya's words. "And you think you would have liked that?"

"Who knows?" Amaya said, her face resting on one hand. "Maybe. I wouldn't have had to go through all this hassle of dating then . . . I think you already know that things aren't probably going to go anywhere between Nevin and me."

Naina nodded and then squeezed her eyes shut in bewilderment. "Do you really find dating a hassle?"

Amaya laughed. "I know, it's hard for you to believe, right? But it can be draining and exhausting, the constant testing, the constant uncertainty, the limited pool of people who are interested in you that you are interested in."

"I see, I see," Naina said even though she really couldn't see. "You know Alannah went online and met someone wonderful. She says there's a whole pool of people out there you can meet."

"Oh no," Amaya said in that inflexible, too-sure voice of hers that Naina hated. A stone-solid voice that rebuffed so many new possibilities. So much like her father. "Too many psychos online. So many people I know have wasted their time on pointless emails only to discover that the other person was nothing like what they imagined. I'll try and meet people the old-fashioned way."

Amaya was still staring at the child who looked satisfied now that he had got his mole negro. A rush of tenderness made its way into Naina. Her daughter wanted to be a mother.

"But if you're not happy with the pool of men you're meeting, maybe going online might not be such a bad idea," Naina said. Even in Oaxaca City, a city where ancient Zapotec and Mixtec cultures mingled with those of colonial Spain and contemporary Mexico, a city where the recent past, distant past, and the present become like one long, vast present (in that way it was also like India), she heard people would go online to find love.

"Maybe, but it's not for me," Amaya said, tying her hair up tightly into a high ponytail. "So what about you?" She looked at Naina. "Have you thought about seeing someone? Soma Aunty has someone."

Naina was taken aback. She had not expected this question. She gazed at the embroidered flower-patterned tablecloth as she fiddled with the stem of her wine glass. "No I have not thought about it. It's not . . . not important to me . . . the most important thing is for you and Karan to be well-settled."

"Oh, come on," Amaya said. "You try to steal my boyfriend from beneath my feet and now you pretend you don't need a man."

Without saying a word, Naina immediately got up and went to the bathroom where she sat burrowing her face in her hands as sounds of hand washing, flushing, and chatter raced against the thoughts in her head.

AT BREAKFAST, TWO days later, a young man appeared at their table. Aviv was from Israel and though he said he was twenty-seven, he didn't look more than twenty-one or twenty-two. He had a boyish face, puppy-dog eyes, and a smile that seemed to say that his soul contained only pure, unadulterated spring water.

"Your eyes shine like black fish in the water," Aviv said to Amaya in his Israeli accent as he sat opposite her at the big breakfast table. "I've seen black fish in Indonesia. Have you ever been to Indonesia?"

"No," Amaya said, laughing and playing with her bangs. "But I'd like to."

"I can show you my photographs of Indonesia if you like after breakfast," Aviv said. "And I have many of the black fish that look like your eyes."

And, as soon as breakfast was over, the two of them bounded off to the computer area where Naina could hear peals of laughter from her balcony.

The following day, Naina and Amaya decided to go to Monte Alban, one of the first cities in Mesoamerica built in pre-Columbian times, and Aviv asked if he could join them. It was a day of thick, low-lying clouds spread like clumps of cream across the sky and they took a bus up to the mountain-top ruins of Monte Alban. Through the uphill drive, you could see panoramic views of the Oaxaca valley, all the more captivating because of the clouds that kept appearing and disappearing, as if the heavens were playing peekaboo. Naina had not slept well the previous night and would have liked some quiet, but Aviv and Amaya kept talking throughout the drive. Naina wished Aviv had not joined them, however it was clear that Amaya liked having him around. Around Aviv, Amaya took on some of his youthful buoyancy. She walked in a looser, more carefree manner, her womanly hips blithely swaying, her laughter easier and more girlish, her irises floating in her eyes instead of being firmly fixed in the center.

Founded around 500 B.C., Monte Alban was the social, political, and economic capital of the Zapotec people and, unlike Oaxaca City and its neighboring craft villages, these ruins had tall, imposing stone structures, an unrelenting geometric quality, a dearth of color and a powerful sense of order and symmetry. There were no signs of the swell and swirl of curves—the stark structures seemed inexorably male to Naina. Reminding humans of their smallness. In an odd way, like New York City.

Amaya and Aviv ran up the countless stairs leading up to the South Platform, asking Naina, who did not have enough energy to join them in their climb, to take pictures of them. It was odd watching the two of them together. Aviv, who looked so young, and Amaya, who looked younger than usual, but still a grown woman. So this was what an older woman and a younger man looked like, she thought, wondering if she and Jai had looked incongruous like that. And then she corrected herself for thinking in such a sexist way . . . and for thinking of Jai.

As Naina saw the two of them laughing on the South Platform, almost thirteen hundred feet above her, she suddenly felt a stab of loneliness. Whether it was Aviv, Nevin, or someone else, Amaya would eventually find someone to love. It might take a while; she might have to overcome issues regarding trust, but she would. It was clear that that was what she wanted, and when Amaya put her mind to something, she eventually got it. And though Amaya was thirty-one, she was hardly old by New York standards and men seemed to be attracted to her. Not only was she attractive and intelligent, she was capable. Someone who could—what was the phrase?—*keep it together.* Yes, *keep it together.* Keep a man afloat if he were in danger of sinking. Sort of like a life jacket. Or a mother. Perhaps men liked that quality in women. What was it that Alannah had said again? *Men, even the most neurotic, never want to marry neurotic chicks because they are afraid the women will make the men drown with them. Damn hypocritical cowards.*

And as for Karan, well that was a foregone conclusion. It was a truth universally acknowledged that a single Indian man from a good family with the right credentials and a decent job would find plenty of women to marry.

Which left her alone, at the bottom of the stairs, talking to the air and the clouds, scrambling to find the Ben Gay in her bag as she hurt her ankle.

Amaya and Aviv ran down the stairs with remarkable speed and Naina remembered that at Amaya's age, she had patiently led her daughter down the long stairwell to the One Thousand Steps Beach in California on a vacation.

"Wow, Naina, we look like small specks on top of the steps," Aviv said when he saw the pictures Naina had taken. Then he covered his mouth with his hand. "Oh my God, I'm supposed to call you aunty, aren't I? I've known so many Indians and yet I forgot. I'm sorry."

Aunty. Meaning the kind of woman who was never admired; meaning someone who only spoke of pleasures in the past tense. Naina stiffened. That dreaded word from her past had appeared again, all of a sudden, like an artifact coming to life in the ruins of Mexico.

"It's okay, Aviv. Feel free to call me Naina."

"That's the way my mother likes it," Amaya said. "Aunty is not her style. She likes to feel young and youthful."

Naina cringed at the barely perceptible bite to Amaya's words.

Later, they went to the cafe, and when Aviv went to the bathroom, Naina asked, "So do you like him?"

"Oh God, no," Amaya said, interrupting her reapplication of lipstick. "Aviv's just a kid. But a delightful kid. He's filled with endless optimism and quite uncomplicated after New York. He's fun to be around, but, no, I'm not interested. Are you? I mean, you do like younger men."

White-hot feelings rumbled inside Naina. She stood up and raised her voice. "Amaya, that was uncalled for. I know what I did was awful and we both know I feel terrible about it." She let out a fistful of air as Amaya jerkily moved backward in her chair. "I . . . I . . . refuse to let you taunt me for the rest of my life about what I did . . . I refuse. There is nothing to be gained from such barbs. Enough is enough." She was surprised that she had been able to utter what she so deeply felt.

Amaya was quiet, her face pale. Finally, squeezing her hair between her fingers, she said, "You're right, Mom. I shouldn't have done that. It was unnecessary. Uncalled for, as you said . . . I don't know what got into me . . . what keeps getting into me . . ."

"It's okay," Naina said, her voice softer. "Let's not talk about it anymore."

Amaya looked out at a distant mountain through the vast open space of the valley. "You know there are times, really there are times, when I imagine that you are not my mother and I try to look at the situation objectively and . . . and

. . . I can see your point of view, even feel sympathy for you . . . and then there are other times that I remember you're my mom and I feel . . ."

"Enough," Naina said, extending her hand, upturned palm flashing. "Enough . . . I don't need to know any more. I don't want to know any more. I can understand that you need to talk about it, but I'm not the right person." She lowered her hand. "There are plenty of outlets for you to talk about this. But then I don't need to tell you that. Can you understand that?"

BACK IN NEW York, Alannah announced that her British boyfriend, Damien, had proposed to her. She was over the moon. Damien had proposed to Alannah, getting down on one knee, of course, as they had gazed at the clay Florentine rooftops from the sixteenth century Boboli Gardens while the sun bade a spectacular marigold-hued farewell to the day.

"It was so incredibly romantic," Alannah said breathlessly, flashing her art deco style engagement ring at Naina and Mara. "I just know he's the guy. I can't believe I'm going to be a married woman in less than a year."

While Naina was happy for Alannah, the truth was she found it hard to picture her as a married woman. She had always been such a free spirit and protective about her space, though that part of her had receded as the coupling glow of a woman in love had pushed into the foreground. But now Alannah would have a man next to her every night.

Naina also noticed something was off about Mara's tone as she congratulated Alannah. Mara's enthusiasm seemed forced, as if her heart were in some other place. Mara had been behaving odd lately.

For the reception, Alannah said she wanted to wear an Indian outfit, gushing about how regal and luscious they were. "I want to look memorable. Like a queen. And red is such a sexy color. Let's plan a trip to Jackson Heights to see some of those lovely red-and-gold clothes, okay?"

"Sure," Naina said while Mara, whose eyes darted about like restless birds, said nothing.

Later that afternoon, Naina and Alannah headed to Alannah's studio where she promised to show Naina her new paintings. This was a big deal. After years of being a contemporary video artist, Alannah had started painting again. It was a risk for someone known for her video work and sort of like going back in time, Alannah had said. Naina had smiled, the image of the hummingbird flying backward reappearing in her mind.

Naina entered Alannah's Lower East Side studio and was mesmerized. There were large canvases leaning against the paint-splattered walls, like proud, gargantuan creatures from a fantastical otherworld.

"Oh my God . . . wow," she said.

Drunk with colors like fleshy pinks, bloody reds, brilliant sunset oranges, and intense cobalt blues, the abstract works flirted with figuration, glinting with a physicality that was raw, ecstatic, and sinister. When she looked closely, she saw intestines curling like ringlets, fragmented body-like forms copulating, piles of tongues with blood oozing from them, macabre cat faces ready to pounce, streaks of white daisies, all whirling and twirling together in raucous, frenzied motion. From the paintings, Naina could hear battle cries for carnival, chest-thumping invitations to a grand feast, and thunderous drumbeats urging everyone to dance. They were crazy, fearless, bacchanalian, and exuberant. And less dark than Alannah's videos.

But above all, these were *knowing* paintings, thought Naina, still feeling as if they were speaking directly to her. They knew about all the dark side, knew it was a part of the messy, mixed-up business of life. Still, they refused to give darkness the starring role in the grand show called life.

CHAPTER TWENTY-SIX

THE LIGHTS WERE dim and two long lavender-scented candles glowed on the coffee table, casting trembling shadows against the bamboo wood floor. The dreamy, honeyed music of Miles Davis came from her new sleek speakers and a bottle of California Zinfandel stood on the corner of her desk, like a sentinel ready to be summoned. It was a pitch-dark October night and early snow was falling in continuous wisps from the sky, a perfect shade of pure white, like a benediction from the heavens. Naina sat in front of her computer in pajamas, gazing out at the snow as she labored to compose the right opening lines.

I am well-read, interested in culture and love everything that New York has to offer—museums, plays, walks in Central Park. She read it and deleted all of it, thinking it sounded dull, clichéd, and pompous. The next attempt, she decided, would be more adventurous.

I am a work in progress and I suppose, like many of us, am a contradiction, a sphinx, and, often, a mystery to myself. But in recent times, I've tried to accept these discordant parts of myself.

She read these lines aloud to herself and deleted them, turned off by how pretentious and self-indulgent they sounded.

Her third attempt began, *Honestly, I can't believe I'm actually writing this. I don't even know how or where to begin.*

She screwed up her nose and shook her head as it sounded immature and silly.

After her fifth failed attempt, Naina poured herself another glass of Zinfandel and stood in front of her windows where she watched the gusty winds making the snow jiggle before it came to rest on the ground like a dead bird. Why was writing about oneself so hard? Why was it so hard to strike the right note? Why was it so hard to come up with even two basic lines when she had been a good writer, deftly crafting letters to her sister-in-law and her cousins in Delhi during her early years in America?

Naina still couldn't get over the fact that she was actually doing this, and the thought sent choppy shivers of apprehension through her body. She was not going to put a proper picture of herself up. The image was going to be vague and no one would be able to identify her. Of course, she knew that the chances of meeting someone at her age were slim, but what was the harm in trying? And it seemed like so many people met online these days. It was discreet and potentially offered an entire constellation of unknown men. She was too old to try it the old-fashioned way, the Amaya way. And it was time to try something new.

Naina changed the music from Miles Davis to the psychedelic electric violin of Michael Vaughn, a little-known indie musician, to recharge her. It was late and her body tired easily. She looked toward the painting in the middle of her living room, a kind of living being whose colors threatened to jump out of the canvas. It was one of Alannah's new paintings, something she had paid a small fortune for despite a hefty discount, but she had loved it. Her apartment had desperately needed color—it was the harbinger of pleasure, love, and life. The painting was a deep turquoise that gave it a shimmering underwater feel. Amid the strokes, whirls, and twirls moving, always moving in riotous motion, she saw a multitude of things. Hands clasped together as they were dancing or copulating or bidding each other a final farewell, a stream of red ovals that looked like they could be tears of blood or decorative bindis, a black-winged shape dappled with purple that seemed to be a forbidding bat or an exquisite eccentric robe from another era. The painting was almost cosmic in its encompassing nature, but it never, ever, let the aphotic forces reign. Her eyes then turned to the two hummingbird sculptures she had bought from Oaxaca flanked on both sides of the painting—deep aubergine with rainbow feathers, their irises a fiery, mischievous orange, urging, urging, urging.

Naina forced her eyes back to the computer, determined to write something. But the next two attempts were also unsatisfactory. By now, it was past midnight and she was still staring at a blank screen. She decided she would give it another hour and then, well, then she would decide what to do.

This is not the kind of thing I ever expected to do and I never thought writing this would be so hard (hopefully you can relate), she finally wrote. *How are we supposed to introduce ourselves in this context? What is the right tone? How do we balance sincerity with humor, reveal enough details about oneself without sounding like an advertisement, give a sense of ourselves but preserve enough mystery to allure? I don't claim to know the answer to any of these questions, but as you can probably tell, I think too much.:} My yoga teacher says excessive thinking is an excess just like any other and I, unfortunately, am guilty of it. Maybe you are too. But I'm digressing (as, to be honest, is my tendency) and not giving you any facts.*

Naina had typed these words fast, without stopping after every few words. It was almost one-thirty in the morning and the snow had turned into a dawdling drip, the flame on one of the lavender-scented candles had died, and Vaughn's hallucinogenic sound had given away to complete silence. Yawning, Naina read what she had written a couple of times, only somewhat satisfied. The rest she would write tomorrow, she decided, before brushing her teeth and going to bed.

TWO HOURS AFTER Naina had posted her profile on mysoulmate.com on a Sunday, she received her first three responses. Nearly quivering, she opened the first one. It was from someone called hotbod777. Naina recoiled. What kind of screen name was hotbod777?

> Hi Whisperinthewind, You sound cool, hotbod777 had written. Way cool . . . I LOVE OLDAR WOMEN! Know what they want, none of this—lets get married and make babies shit . . . just FUN all the time! I'm 28, healthy (check out that great bod in the pics), ready to rock 'n' roll. Sure youre real hot but you gotta better pic? Cant see your gorgeous bod in this one . . . waitin to hear from ya . . . Jake . . .

Naina read the response again, horrified. What in the world was that? What kind of freaks were trolling the Internet? She should take her profile off right now. She could be putting herself in danger. Maybe this man was a murderer or a rapist. Who knew? This was certainly no arranged marriage where the backgrounds of men were carefully scrutinized.

She needed to get up. Make herself a cup of coffee. Strong coffee. She searched through her coffee jars, but she had run out of her strong Arabica blend. Damn. That Jake, she imagined, must use the word Fuck a lot. Fuck this, fuck that, fuck you, fuck everything. Twenty-eight years old. A mere child, a boy the same age as her son, writing to her. Insane. She shook her head. It was really shocking.

The next email, fortunately, was not disturbing, though Naina thought the man looked and sounded very dull.

> Hi, I'm a 50-year-old Latino man who works for a nonprofit, NiceGuy had written. I'm not rich, but I'm a real nice guy. Kind to women and always willing to open the door. I'm smart too. I don't know much about art but I can talk politics and social issues. I'll listen when you talk and won't bore you when I talk. Please write soon. Btw, I don't use any four-letter words in public or private.

NiceGuy hadn't signed off with his real name. Maybe he was as scared as she was. Naina heard a door banging shut, the sort of deafening noise that only her neighbor Laura was capable of. It always took her a minute or two to reclaim her nerves after Laura's signature slam. They still had never had a proper conversation. She massaged her temples and sighed. In New Jersey, at least you never had to hear your neighbors flushing their toilets or slamming their doors.

Naina opened the third email. It was from someone called PlatosCave.

Dear Whisperinthewind (what a lovely name you have chosen), PlatosCave had written. Fate has a strange way of conspiring in favor of us human beings. Here I am, a never-married highly educated man who has just turned 60 with no one cerebral and sophisticated enough to match me and there you are a presumably beautiful (love the hazy picture, but would still like greater clarity) and highly intelligent and articulate woman who is looking for a mature relationship with an intelligent man. (Let me tell you lady, I'm not just intelligent, but blindingly brilliant). I am not given to superstition, but I really think that Cupid's arrow will strike us immediately in the center of our hearts when we lay our eyes on each other. We are truly lucky to have found each other. Since I am a lawyer and used to presenting cases, I am going to take it upon myself to make a case for myself.

1. Brilliant. I went to Yale Law School and work at a top-notch corporate law firm.

2. Highly interesting. I like reading serious literature by writers like Kafka, William Thackeray, and Philip Roth. I like listening to both jazz and classical music and frequent Lincoln Center. My favorite museum is the Met (of course you know where that is) and I love Michelangelo.

3. Gorgeous. I look just like Clark Gable as you can see in the picture.

4. Rich. I don't want to disclose my exact net worth, but I'm worth several millions.

My dear whisperinthewind — pray do tell your real name? Also, let me know which night this week you're free to meet at Daniel's for dinner. Wednesday or Thursday at 8 works for me. Let us let destiny chart its course this week. Seriously, I think this is a once in a lifetime opportunity and let's seize it. Cheers, John."

Naina laughed so hard she had tears rolling down her cheeks. He looked funny as well. He had a serious face with line-thin lips, a bushy mustache, closely set eyes, and a pointy nose. He was wearing a dark-colored bow tie with polka dots and the picture was in black and white. He looked like a bad version of Charlie Chaplin. Now, she was feeling wicked. She had to write back to him.

My dear PlatosCave. Your brilliance stuns me. I agree with you — it's blinding. I'm sure Plato's cave is blazing with light when you are present. Thank you for your email, but, unfortunately, I don't think I am good enough for you. My intelligence is blunt like the edge of an old knife and the hazy picture is really to disguise the scars that Botox left me with. Cheers, whisperinthewind.

Over the next few days, an avalanche of messages from a variety of men flooded Naina's inbox and she took to checking her email whenever possible. There was the fierce-faced, muscular man from Kiev asking her, in broken English, if she was a US citizen who would agree to a Green Card marriage in exchange for great massages since he could not offer her money. She wrote back saying it was oddly coincidental that he was looking for a Green Card marriage because she was looking for the same thing. There was a fifty-five-year-old New Jersey-based Indian restaurant owner who asked her if she wanted to have a discreet affair. He was happily married, he said, but his wife had lost interest in sex. Now he wanted to have "adventure" with a "modern Indian lady" and described, in great length, the lingerie he wanted to buy her. *Flesh-colored seamless thongs, red lace v-string panties, green-and-blue lace trim Brazilian panties, leopard print satin push-up bra and fuchsia pink lace baby-doll nightie with ruffles at bottom,* he wrote. She shot back a rejoinder saying he should look for a hooker and not a "modern Indian lady."

Then there was the self-described hippie called Darshan, with streaming white hair from Queens, who said India and not this materialistic hell called America, was his real home and he wanted to be with an Indian woman so she could take him home.

And then there were the more conventional emails from single, divorced, and widowed men in their fifties and sixties, all claiming to be young at heart and open-minded, looking for companionship, good conversation, and long walks on the beach. They wanted partners to share long-cherished desires like a month-long vacation to Greece, an art class in the city, a ski trip to the Alps, a cozy second home in the Hudson Valley. More often than not, these sorts of men tended to be white and Jewish, though there were some Indians as well. Yet despite smatterings of wit and culture thrown in, they all seemed frightfully dull and conventional to Naina, who, buoyed by the sheer number of men writing to her, felt free to dismiss anyone who did not sound quite perfect. These days, the possibilities of men seemed to have quickly inflated from the size of a grape to a big jackfruit swinging from a tree. She felt herself (a much swollen version of herself), floating high into the clouds, lithe as a hummingbird, youthful as during those days when her face was unblemished and marriage proposals would regularly pay their visits to her parents.

NAINA HAD ONLY told Alannah and Mara about what she was doing. Of course, Alannah heartily approved, but she did not know what Mara thought. It was so hard to tell with Mara these days. There was that shift in her that was so hard to pinpoint. The slow erosion of that sanguine manner, the feeling that she was curling inward like a leaf. And when Naina asked her what was wrong, she brushed it off in her typical airy way.

And Soma, she wanted to tell her about it, but couldn't bring herself to do it. After all, even though Soma was liberal and an older woman with a boyfriend, she was still Indian. What if she found online dating for a fifty-plus Indian woman ridiculous? Indians could be so odd sometimes—very open-minded in one way and then unexpectedly judgmental in another. Spending their life's savings sending their daughters to medical school on one hand, yet pressuring them to get married to a suitable boy before they turned thirty on the other. And Soma was also quite close to Amaya, whom she had no intention of telling about her online venture, unless and until something became quite serious. Which was unlikely. Although Amaya had said she did not mind her dating, who knew how she would really feel if she found out? And then Naina needed to reclaim her standing as Amaya's mother. Which meant not trading dating stories. A daughter did not need to know about her mother's dating life. Just like parents did not need to about their adult child's sex life. Some boundaries must be preserved.

ON A RAINY Friday evening, almost time for the gallery to close, a journalist—a garrulous man with an untidy mop of salt-and-pepper hair—had been picking her brain for more than two hours and would just not stop. Susan was out of town and Naina was handling the gallery by herself, which meant she was the one fielding all the questions about their new show, a series of photographs featuring eunuchs in India. He came from an esteemed publication, so she was obliged to be nice to him. *What exactly was a eunuch? Why did they dress in female attire? What legal rights did they have? Where did they live? Why did they attend weddings and births? Why did people give them money?*

Fortunately, Naina knew the answers to most of the questions, but there were some that she, to the condescending surprise of the journalist, did not know. His unusually large, sagging green eyes hung over his face like overripe avocados, and seemed to say, *You're Indian. How could you not know everything about this topic?*

When he finally left—well after the gallery's closing time and after the intern had gone—Naina was wiped out and angry he had expected her to be the spokesperson for everything Indian. What bloody arrogance and ignorance. Would that disheveled fool have known every fact about Kansas or Hawaii? He probably wouldn't even know something as basic as the population of the states of *his own country.* He was the kind of well-educated man she wouldn't touch with a barge pole.

Naina felt too charged to sit at her desk and put her head down for a few minutes, as she sometimes did. Instead, she rushed to check her email. She had just checked it a couple hours before the rotting avocado-eyed journalist showed up for what seemed like an eternity.

The pace of emails, though still brisk, had, to her disappointment, slowed down since her profile first went up two weeks earlier. So more than likely, no one new had emailed, but there was no harm in checking.

She opened her inbox and found only one new email. At least there was one. She eagerly clicked on it.

> Whisperinthewind,
>   Let me get straight to the point. I'm a nasty motherfucker, not one of those castrated assholes begging for pussy with flowers and chocolates. I've eaten pussy of every nationality in the world — Russian, African, Brazilian, Jamaican, Chinese, Japanese. But, I've never done Indian. Nope, nothin yet from the land of the Kamasutra. So, if it isn't clear by now. I wanna eat you. I wanna lick you. I wanna bite you. I wanna try those exotic positions in the Kamasutra, like that Cat One where you lay on your stomach when I'm inside you and I hold on to both your ankles with one hand and lift them high. Oh yeah, baby. Those Indians knew how to get down and dirty and have some fun. I want to take you from behind and rock your ass . . . give me some baby. This Rocky will rock your world . . . bet you never thought you could do that :} Write back and lemme know when you will bring your hot Indian ass to my place in Queens . . . Rocky

Naina was flabbergasted. This did not feel like a slap; it felt like a kick. A sharp, swift kick. She was not some exotic whore, she thought, hiding her face in the crook of her elbow. Or one of those unfortunate eunuchs in India, stripped of all dignity by society, and forced to disrobe or prostitute themselves for money. A bolt of rage shot through her, making her body convulse. How dare this man write to her like this? How dare he?

She couldn't continue with this online thing. She couldn't continue with this. Amaya was right. There were too many psychos online. She lifted her head up and planned to delete her profile.

CHAPTER TWENTY-SEVEN

NAINA TOOK SMALL, careful strides as she walked back home after her yoga class as a mild pain darted across the back of her legs. Today, she had been clumsy in class. Was she getting too old for this? When Carolyn, her yoga teacher, asked the students to put their legs up in half plough pose, Naina could barely get her legs all the way up, and when she did, they soon dropped to the floor, like heavy, listless objects. To her embarrassment. But no one seemed to care. Everyone appeared too preoccupied with themselves. Of course, almost everyone in the class had their legs straight up, feet flexed, for the full three minutes, their firm legs like judicious watchmen on duty.

Reaching her block, Naina saw a woman whom she had seen many times before. Somehow, they often seemed to be on the block at the same times. The woman—always beautifully dressed in furry coats and stylish hats with a melancholy look in her tiny eyes that seemed to say she had nothing to look forward to—was, as usual, walking her bulldog. She always walked back and forth, back and forth, back and forth, on the block for long periods of time, even after the dog had done what it needed to do. Always alone. They had never spoken to each other, and Naina suspected they never would. Now however, they did exchange smiles. Carolyn had said something so true today recalled Naina, entering her building. "Extreme self-denial can lead to extreme self-indulgence," she had said, sitting on the platform in front of the class, dressed in a white salwar kameez, her dirty blonde hair tied up in a loose bun, her mid-section slightly bulging. "And extreme self-denial can also become a form of extreme self-indulgence."

As Naina took a leisurely hot shower, she mulled over Carolyn's words and wanted to read something philosophical. But as soon as she finished dressing, all thoughts of philosophy were pushed aside as she headed to her computer. Could anyone have emailed her in the last four hours?

She was back online. That rainy Friday evening after reading Rocky's crude comments, she ended up not deleting her profile, choosing instead to hide it, which meant she could reactivate it easily. And it had remained hidden for days until she showed the email to Alannah who broke into a fit of laughter when she read it.

"This, this . . . is the funniest piece of garbage . . . I've read in a long time . . . This made you hide your profile? Oh come on . . ."

"It's insulting, humiliating . . . and so . . . so . . . unbelievably obscene."

"Oh my little Catholic School virgin . . . This is the real world . . . not the four walls of a convent or a sweet mansion in New Jersey . . . do you have any idea how many nasty emails I've got?"

"No, I don't," Naina said, genuinely surprised. When it came to dating, she clearly had no experience. She was like a virgin to this territory. "Were they this crude?"

"Sure," Alannah said, laughing. "Many of them. You've got to go through the chaff to get to the wheat."

Naina looked at Alannah—her wild chestnut mane of hair; her heart-shaped face always full, so full; her green, mischievous eyes so clear, seeing everything— and thought it was apropos that Alannah was the creator of those magnificent, knowing paintings. She knew all about the unpleasant side of life but refused to be deterred by it.

"C'mon," Alannah urged. "This guy's probably not even a real person . . . Let me read it aloud to you so you can hear how funny it really is."

And as Alannah read the email in an exaggerated, dramatic manner, Naina, despite herself, laughed softly.

Now, as Naina sat in front of her computer, enjoying the scent of tangerines emanating from her skin thanks to a new body wash, she saw that there was one new email. From someone called TechnicolorDreams.

> Dear Whisperinthewind,
>   It's an odd thing to say this to someone you've never met, but after reading your profile, I feel like I just know you. Not very articulate am I?:}. Like you, I too feel that words can sometimes be so inadequate. Maybe you think I'm some kind of crazy kook trying to say nutty things like I know you, but I have a feeling you are too intelligent and perceptive for such dismissal. This, too, is the first time I have ever done anything like this and I also grappled with some of the same questions as you did when I was writing my profile. And as for thinking too much, I can totally relate:}
>   Now for the basic facts about me. I am a 51-year-old white male (British mother, American father) architect who has never been married before. (No, I'm not one of those New York commitment phobes that everyone talks about—I just never met anyone I wanted to marry.) I grew up in upstate New York, but have lived in Manhattan for the past 15 years, and, like you, like to take advantage of all the great cultural opportunities this city has to offer. I am a complete travel junkie and have to say that of all the places I have visited in the world, I found India the most amazing (once again words are inadequate). In the early 90s, I traveled in India for about six months and fell in love with Jaisalmer with its honey-colored sandstone fort majestically

rising from the yellow-gold sand. It was a complete delight. I stayed in a cheap hotel in the fort for about three weeks, feeling like a raja, marveling at all the grandeur (remember, I grew up in a small, dull town upstate:}) reading Agatha Christie and P.G. Wodehouse, walking through the bustling medieval lanes, drinking beer during the marvelous sunsets on top of the fort, and practicing my Hindi. During the six months I spent in India, I did pick up some Hindi (kya haal hai? aajao, chalo, chup) which Indians would tell me I didn't seem to speak with that horrible, stilted accent that most foreigners have when they attempt to speak in Hindi. But I'll let you be judge of whether they were right or just saying it to make me feel good:}

I'm not big on emailing back and forth only to find out two people don't connect in real life. I'd love to take you to dinner if you're still interested after reading this email and my profile. And then, maybe we can go listen to some live music after that . . . I'm probably getting too ahead of myself:} Look forward to hearing from you soon.

Cheers,

Marcus

P.S. I don't typically write such long emails, but after reading your profile, I couldn't help myself . . .

Naina's heart was aflutter. She was too nervous to open his profile and see his picture, lest he turned out to be physically repulsive. So, smiling to herself, she re-read his email a couple of times, the music in her heart swelling, swirling, and swooning. Then she made herself a cup of peppermint tea and sat in front of her computer again and clicked on the link to the profile, then peered at his photograph.

She breathed a sigh of relief. He wasn't gorgeous, but he was not bad. He had short ringlets of salt and pepper hair, a roundish but not plump face, sparkling blue eyes, and full, pink lips. He had a cute, teddy-bearish quality to him and she felt a wave of warmth toward this stranger who didn't quite seem like a stranger. Then she read his profile, and her heart crooned to the music of ambrosial possibilities. It was a delightful profile, better than any she had read before.

I am not fond of marketing or clichés so I apologize if this does not come off like the advertisement that typically passes for a profile. Like most people, I have flaws, doubts and bad hair days. But, despite my flaws (of which they are plenty, let me warn you, but will reveal more when I get to know you), I try to have an optimistic, cheerful approach to life. My favorite book is Chinese writer Lin Yutang's Importance of Living, which is the most uplifting, practical, and intelligent treatise on living I have ever read. My ideal life would be to live like Yutang's ideal philosopher which I am going to quote for you (it's brief, don't worry) for fear that I might not do it justice if I paraphrase it.

"For the ideal philosopher is one who understands the charm of women without being coarse, who loves life heartily but loves it with restraint, and who sees the unreality of the successes and failures of the world, and stands somewhat aloof and detached, without being hostile to it."

So, now that you've read this, either you think I am pretentious for quoting my favorite philosopher or the words resonate somewhat with you and you understand why I might have decided to include them in my profile. In all honesty, at this point in my life, I'm looking for something serious and long-term, and want to make sure we are on the same page and don't waste each other's time. So, if you think you might be up for talking about everything and nothing on a Sunday afternoon, drinking cappuccinos (tea is fine too:}) in a cozy café in the West Village with your iPhone switched off and reading the unwieldy New York Times with no care for what time it is, I'd like to know you.

LATER THAT WEEK, Naina stood in front of her apartment, looking for her keys in her bag. She remembered how baffled Harish used to be by such behavior. He always kept his keys in the left front pocket of his pants, his wallet in the right back pocket, and loose change in the right front pocket. She ended up finding her keys in the right pocket of her pants and entered her apartment. On a side table in her short foyer, she spotted a brown package. She rushed toward it, anticipation rising in her. After ripping the brown packaging apart, Naina found the book inside in particularly bad shape: its spine was held together by scotch tape; it had a funky odor that made her think of garbage; the edges of the pages were yellowed and tattered; and it was covered with thick stains. This copy of *The Importance of Living* was clearly used, the only type that Amazon had available. Yet, it contained important words, words Naina had been waiting for, words that might light up a new path. She put it down and washed her hands.

After dinner, standing as far away from the book as possible, Naina cleaned it with a rag, sprayed some Lysol on it, and showered it with some strong rose-scented perfume. Then she put some Ravi Shankar on, placed the book on a newspaper and began reading it in bed, the iridescent light from her bronze night lamp shining on it, exacerbating all its ugliness.

Naina finished the book at three in the morning, now barely noticing its hideousness, still-lingering foul smell, and the partially faded words. She had fallen in love with this quirky, breezy, and profound 1938 book with its stories and anecdotes of ancient Chinese poets, philosophers, and epicures, humorous takes on Western culture, and delightful sections extolling loafing, lying in bed, and smoking. Pleasure was good, valuable, and appropriate, both the road and the end of the road, according to the book.

Why had she never come across this sage hedonist or heard of him before? Marcus had great taste, she thought as a frisson of excitement tingled through her. She yawned but was determined to stay awake a little longer. Changing the music from Indian classical to more vivacious Brazilian jazz, she wrote down her favorite passages in her taupe-colored notebook, starting with the one she liked the most. The whole time, she was smiling to herself.

> I rather think that philosophers that start out to solve the problem of the purpose of life beg the question by assuming that life must have a purpose. This question, so much pushed to the fore by Western thinkers, is undoubtedly given that importance through the influence of theology. I think we assume too much design and purpose altogether. And the very fact that people try to answer this question and quarrel over it and are puzzled by it serves to show it up as quite vain and uncalled for. Had there been a purpose or design in life, it should not have been so puzzling and vague to find out.

> What strikes me most is that the Greeks made their gods like men, while the Christians desired to make men like the gods. That Olympian company is certainly a jovial, amorous, loving, lying, quarrelling, and vow-breaking, petulant lot; hunt-loving, chariot-riding and javelin-throwing like the Greeks themselves—a marrying lot, too, and having unbelievably many illegitimate children . . . The Greek men were not divine, but the Greek gods were human. How different from the perfect Christian God!

THE NEXT EVENING, as Naina returned home from work, tired and bleary-eyed from staying up so late the previous night, she found an email from Marcus saying he did not have to leave town that weekend. If she was still available, he would like to take her out for dinner on Friday to an Indian restaurant called Registhan, which he had never been to, but had heard good things about. If it was okay with her, they could meet at the bar at eight.

This was the missive she had been waiting for, the one she imagined would oust the touch of doubt in her mind that despite how wonderful Marcus sounded, he wasn't just an Internet pipe dream, a bored conman peddling fantasies to vulnerable women. He wanted to meet on a designated date, at a designated place, at a designated time. She had expected to be elated, to feel the music in her heart rise to a new crescendo when the possibility became real, rooted in certainties like time and place. To turn what had essentially been a wonderful, airy conversation between two formless entities into the distinct possibility of a flesh-and-blood encounter. Yet, as she read those words again—*Registhan, 108 East 20th Street, Friday at eight*—she felt arrows of nervous panic darting within her.

She got up from her desk and paced around the apartment. She poured herself a glass of Riesling, craving sweet wine. She had never been on a real or semi-real date before. Ever. Not even with Harish. The closest thing she had had to a date was the evening with John. If one called that a date. Alannah had once called it a warm-up for a hookup, appalling Naina. As for those encounters with Jai, they certainly could not be called "dates." There was no right word to describe them.

How was she to behave on a date? How was she to talk? How was she to flirt? How was she to dress? She had watched a program a few days before on *Lifetime* where a group of middle-aged divorced American women complained about how the dating rules had changed since they were last in the game and they no longer knew what to do. But, at least, those women had been in the game at some point in their lives. What if Marcus didn't like her in person? What if he thought she was unattractive? What if he stood her up or walked out on her? What if he thought she looked too *old*? After all, the picture he had seen of her was hazy, and, as for age, all she had said was fifties—which could mean fifty-one or fifty-nine. She did have some crow's feet and dark circles that showed even when she applied heavy concealer, she conceded sadly, touching the area under her eyes. And he, who had given his exact age on his profile, was a few years younger than she was. At her age, wasn't she just too *old* to go on a date?

Maybe this whole dating enterprise would expose itself to be what it was— ill-advised and ridiculous. She accelerated her pacing, walking repeatedly from the dining area to the living area and then back to the dining area. A few minutes later, she sat down on her couch exhausted and slightly nauseous from the sickly sweet wine. Maybe she should listen to that chubby, curly-haired blond woman on *Lifetime* and enjoy the protection and discretion of a purely online relationship and let the imagination fill in the blanks. After all, as the woman had said and Naina very well knew, imagination was always better than reality.

CHAPTER TWENTY-EIGHT

NAINA REACHED REGISTHAN ten minutes late, attempting to look cheerful and confident while trying to steady the restiveness inside her. She was wearing a knee-length, empire waist black woolen dress with tan suede boots, both items she had rushed to buy the previous evening from a designer she liked in Soho—after having rummaged through her closet and deciding she had nothing appropriate to wear. She dressed it up with a mustard-gold silk wrap, a garnet-and-emerald paisley-shaped pendant her mother had given her when she got married, and simple gold earrings. She had left work early in the afternoon and gone to a yoga class. She was as prepared as she was ever going to be for the "date," she told herself. Yet, like a pack of blood-sucking mosquitoes, the anxiety refused to go away.

Registhan was large and striking with a narrow passageway lined with rose and marigold petals. A woman in a sari greeted customers with folded hands and said Namaste with a perpetual smile. The walls were honey-gold and textured to look like waves of sand and draped with a few vermilion tie-dye cotton dupattas so firmly glued on they barely resembled the fluttering, falling wraps that Naina had worn with white salwar kameezes in college. Hypnotic fusion music, which she instantly recognized was played by Zakir Hussain, thrummed in the background, adding to the "ethnic enchantment" of the place.

Before going to the bar area in the center of the restaurant, Naina discreetly glanced around to see if anyone resembled that picture of a man with salt-and-pepper hair and bright blue eyes. No, there were only five people at the bar, and no one looked even close to that image. She felt her heart racing. She had an impulse to run out of the restaurant. He was not going to come. Maybe he was really a seventy-year-old man in Dubai? She started to fiddle with the straps of her handbag.

No, no, she commanded herself, she was not going to run away. She was not a child. She raised her chin and pressed her lips together. She would sit at the bar and wait for Marcus. He might be running late too. And if he didn't show up, well, she would deal with that then.

A short while later, Naina snapped out of staring at her half-consumed glass of wine at the sound of her name coming from a high-pitched voice that sounded like it emanated from Jason, her acquaintance Shona's hyper-friendly friend. The voice uttered her name perfectly.

Marcus was walking toward her. He looked like the photograph, yet nothing like it. His hair was curly and salt-and-pepper, but it looked so coarse and messy that it reminded her of the unwashed hair of the poor, half-naked children begging at intersections in Delhi. His face was so perfectly round and without definition that it looked like a pink ball, and his chunky, shapeless body made her think of a whale flopping around. The sparkle in his kind eyes was the only thing that was as nice in real life as in the photograph. She felt herself suddenly dip, like the temperature rapidly plunging in a desert when the sun goes down. The portrait of Marcus, which she had stitched together and embroidered so thoroughly in the last few days, was floating away from her, and she did not know what to do.

"I hope I haven't kept you waiting too long," Marcus said, looking genuinely contrite. "The subway was stuck for about twenty minutes somewhere between 14th and 23rd Street."

"Umm . . . no . . . I . . . just got here a few minutes ago." She hoped her horror was not too evident. She attempted a smile.

"I hope you like this place."

"Yes, yes, yes, . . . it's really beautiful."

"Sort of makes me think of Rajasthan, you know . . . so, I see you already started on the wine. I like that. Are you ready to order your second?"

Naina jerkily touched the stem of her wine glass.

"Are you okay?" Marcus asked.

"Yes, yes, I'm fine," Naina said quickly as she felt a flush spread across her cheeks. "No, thank you, I think I'll finish this first."

Marcus turned around and ordered a beer from the turbaned bartender, mixing in some Hindi words. He wasn't joking. His Hindi accent was quite good.

He sat down with his beer and moved closer to her, but still at a respectable distance, and asked—his shrill voice much lower, "Is this your first time?"

Naina leaned back, nonplussed "First time . . . for?"

"Meeting someone you met online."

"Umm . . . yes."

"Figures. The first time is always the most awkward."

Naina tried to smile as she looked down and toyed with the ends of her mustard silk scarf. She couldn't think of how to respond. She could feel the awkward silence between them, a pause stretching longer and longer. "What about you?"

"I've met a few people before . . . nothing worked out though." He shrugged and Naina noticed how blubbery his shoulders looked, and then scolded herself for having such mean, superficial thoughts about a man who seemed so nice. "It's New York. People are strange about relationships in this city."

Marcus lifted his glass and clinked it with hers. "Cheers. Here's to finally meeting you and to not-so-strange relationships."

"Cheers . . . It's nice to meet you."

Marcus again leaned closer to Naina, his kind blue eyes sparkling, and said slowly, the volume of his voice barely a decibel above a whisper, "Naina, you're much more beautiful in real life than in that hazy picture. In fact, I think you're very beautiful."

"Thank you," Naina said, feeling herself turn bright red like a silly tomato, conscious that she shouldn't abruptly back away from him again. He sounded *so* sincere. She felt bad . . . for herself, for him. "You're . . . you're a very good writer . . . Did you ever study writing?"

Marcus laughed, a high-pitched laugh like his high-pitched voice. It grated on her ears.

"Thanks . . . No, I've never studied writing and I was a terrible writer until I was in high school. But my mom could be a real ball buster, and made me write essays at home on top of the essays at school. Hated it then, but I guess it wasn't so bad at the end of the day."

As the evening progressed, Naina tried to tuck away her disappointment and attempted to put on a good front. Marcus seemed like a good human being, and she wanted to be as dignified as she could be. The conversation between them was never smooth, but it definitely improved after the first half hour where it was like a sluggish Ambassador car constantly stumbling into speed breakers in Delhi. They talked about the Chinese philosopher Lin Yutang for a long time, and when that topic was exhausted, they talked about India, and then their favorite places in the West Village. When Marcus attempted to get more personal and ask about her marriage, Naina responded pithily and steered the conversation toward *The New York Times*, Agatha Christie, and P.G. Wodehouse. She passed on dessert, hoping to end the evening, and Marcus, whom she sensed wanted dessert, followed her cue and declined as well. The check arrived at ten-thirty, and Naina insisted on paying her share, but Marcus refused to let her.

"It was very nice to meet you, Marcus," Naina said, extending her hand when they were standing on the sidewalk in their hats and coats as the cold wind struck them. "Thank you for dinner."

"My pleasure, Naina. It was splendid . . . that is for me at least." He smiled wryly and gazed at the sidewalk. His body looked so much more serious in a black trench coat in the dark. Then, he slowly looked up. "Naina, if I had my way, I would love to see you again. But I've been at this game a long time and know when someone isn't into me."

"Well, that, that . . ." Naina mumbled as she felt the color in her face vanishing and her eyes and mouth falling open.

"It's okay, you don't need to be embarrassed," Marcus said, that nice kind smile on his face. "And please don't apologize . . . life is like that and we're both grown-ups." He laughed wryly again. "I just wanted to be honest with you, that's all. You're a great lady and I know you'll find someone very soon."

Naina stood quietly in front of Marcus, not knowing where to look, her nerves standing up on end.

"I . . . I . . . had a great time tonight," she said, unable to stop her voice from careening like a car with a drunk driver. "I . . . I really did . . ."

"It's okay, Naina. You don't have to say or explain anything. I didn't mean to put you on the spot like that."

"I'm really . . . sorry . . . if you misunderstood me . . . it's not that I don't like you. I don't want you to think that . . . I just . . ."

"It's okay. It really is. I know you like me, just not in that way. Listen, if you'd like to be friends, drop me a line. I'm going to go now and not put you through any more embarrassment. He quickly kissed her on the cheek, said goodnight and started to walk away as she mustered up a faint goodnight.

On that sub-freezing, starless night, Naina went for a walk alone as gusty winds howled and thunder growled in the sky. She passed the Calvary Episcopal Church on Park Avenue and 21st Street and stood by the grim Gothic Revival structure. She saw barren trees in the city resembling ghostly skeletons as they got flogged by the wind on the unusually deserted Manhattan streets. She watched spindly branches drooping like withered, defeated souls; she watched them make ominous shapes like witches' claws and broken limbs; she watched how they formed cupped hands supplicating to the heavens. The thunder and wind continued, yet Naina walked all the way to the East River where she sat down on a cold bench, reluctant to part ways with that November night.

CHAPTER TWENTY-NINE

WORK, MEANWHILE, HAD been going exceedingly well for Naina. She had been advocating the work of Sahiba Habib, a Syrian-American video artist, and Susan, who did not love the work at first but now trusted Naina's judgement, promised to seriously consider it and eventually gave Habib a show. The video artist made dreamscape-like videos of traditional black chadors and fancy red lingerie floating in turquoise-green waters, creating hypnotic, erotic, dancing, and haunting shapes where both the absence and presence of the body were equally felt. At least that was the way it was described in the esteemed *Art Today* magazine—the review thrilling Susan, and, of course, Naina. Even *New York Contemporary Art* magazine, another acclaimed publication, positively reviewed the show, saying that "the show urges the West yet again to move beyond the simplistic equation of the chador with female oppression."

Around the same time as the Sahiba Habib show, there were two other shows at well-known Chelsea galleries dealing with the female body in Islamic culture, and Naina suggested they have a panel discussion on the topic at their gallery. Susan concurred and the two of them put together a discussion entitled, "The intersection of gender and Islam in contemporary art." They got an art historian from Columbia University, a Pakistani curator, and a freelance art critic. The panel discussion was a success and was attended by almost a hundred people. After that, even more new faces trickled into the gallery, including well-known critics and curators. Following the discussion, Naina also started the first of the gallery's monthly tastings of different types of teas for donors and potential donors.

Since the fiasco with Marcus, Naina had been on five or six more dates. The first, more than three weeks after Marcus, was with Karim, a forty-seven-year-old Lebanese American divorcee who had received a Ph.D. in mechanical engineering and ran a private equity firm. Her heart skipped a beat when she spotted him, muscular and tanned like he had just spent a week working out at a gym and sunning himself in the Caribbean at the same time. He was leaning against the dimly lit glass bar in a fitted black shirt and stylish black pants with his face looking up toward the ceiling, and one set of fingers restlessly tapping his leg. He looked like a Lebanese version of Marlon Brando, she thought, struck by his strong jaw and conspicuous air of animal magnetism. Slowly and nervously, she had gone up to him and introduced herself, feeling old and underdressed, scared he might just take one look at her and say he had to leave. But that didn't happen. He did look at her, a sweeping but thorough appraisal that made her blush, and then he nonchalantly turned to his drink. Her heart sank to her knees, craving some cover. She knew he was not interested in her.

After that, Naina met Bob, a fifty-seven-year-old graphic designer who was into Buddhism, at a tranquil tea shop on the Lower East Side. Their forty-five-minute-long awkward tea ended uneventfully as did her next drink date at a pub a few days later with Steven, a divorced fifty-two-year-old Irish journalist who wrote about local politics for *The New York Daily News*. Then she met Raj, a fifty-five-year-old half-Trinidadian, half-British anthropologist at Sheep's Meadow in Central Park and though there was nothing instant between them, she felt they had a lot in common. He had serious eyes but a laughing smile and was very easy to talk to. Even though she wasn't an expert at this, she sensed he liked her too. After an afternoon at Central Park, he asked her out for dinner where they ended up spending three or four hours. She felt quite certain he might call her or email her, but he never did. Naina was mystified by the whole incident. She felt that by signing up on mysoulmate.com she had stepped into a universe that had its own secret code, as cryptic as hieroglyphics to everyone else except the initiated. And the initiated did not include her.

After her date with Raj, the emails dropped to a dispiriting two or three a week, and it was almost a month before she received anything that sounded even vaguely interesting. Shaam, a fifty-six-year-old Indian divorcee from Calcutta with two grown-up children and an enormous love of food, impressed her with his witty, well-written note, but she was reluctant to pursue anything with him. She preferred to meet men from other cultures, where, at least at first, she felt she was seen as a rough outline of an image. With them, she could determine— to whatever extent it was possible for a woman to determine—how sharp the contours of the image would be, what colors would suffuse or diffuse it, whether it would be abstract or semi-abstract, whether smudges would smear the edges or not. But if she went out with an Indian, she would already be seen as a nearly complete, if not entirely complete picture where the man already had most of the information, regardless of whether that information was accurate or not. He just had to decide if he liked the image or not.

Naina still hadn't told her daughter about her online dating, but one time, Amaya, who had broken up with Nevin, asked her if she wanted to meet on a Friday night; only that was the night of her date with Raj, so Naina declined. She told Amaya she had already made plans with Alannah to see a play.

When the two of them met a few days later at a French bistro, Amaya asked how the play was.

"What play?"

"The play you went to with Alannah," Amaya said, her eyes narrowing.

"Oh . . . Oh that," Naina said, catching herself, jerking her head back. "I . . . I never went . . . Alannah had to go to meet Damien . . . Instead I . . . I went to the MoMA with Shona and then for dinner."

"Hmmm . . ." Amaya said, the pupils in her eyes rapidly enlarging, ready to ensnare the truth. "Are you seeing someone?"

"Seeing someone?" Naina said, her voice sounding high and incredulous. "What are you talking about? Of course not. Don't be silly."

"Are you sure? You seem to have been going out a lot lately."

"Of course I'm sure," Naina said with indignation in her voice.

"You can tell me if you are. I won't tell Karan."

"I'm *not* seeing anyone, Amaya. Men aren't lining up for a fifty-something-year-old, like they are for you . . ."

"All right," Amaya said, shrugging. "You don't have to tell me if you don't want to."

A hush fell over them. Yet, unseen to the human eye, unarticulated feelings and words, filled with hue and weight, swirled slowly in the room on their own accord, eschewing any pattern.

"Amaya, my love" Naina said, clasping Amaya's hand. "Tell me about you. Have you met anyone you like lately? I know how important it is to you to be in a relationship."

Amaya shook her head and now Naina thought she could see invisible lines of worry in her daughter's smooth face, and a deep, dank, quivering pit of fear in those pupils. She squeezed Amaya's hand tighter.

"What's the matter, darling?"

Amaya smoothed back her hair. "There's been no one lately. No one since Nevin. No one. I'm just not meeting anyone." She turned her head to the side, toward the array of French café posters. "Maybe I never will."

"Of course you will, Amaya," Naina insisted. "Of course, you will."

Meanwhile, Naina could feel guilt rearing its ugly head again. How could she be frolicking around with men while her daughter, a beautiful young girl of marriageable age, was struggling to meet a life partner? A mother out meeting new men while her young daughter sat at home alone? Unnatural, horrible, terrible. She should just stop this dating business now, and make sure her daughter was well-settled.

"Amaya," Naina said, feeling an urgency to say what she had to regardless of the consequences. "I know we already talked about this, but really, why don't you try online dating? There are so many men out there Alannah tells me."

"Alannah tells you or do you know firsthand?"

"You're a brilliant, beautiful girl," Naina said. "Any man would be lucky to have you . . . If that's the modern way of meeting people, why must you be so stubborn and resist?"

"Because *that's* who I am. I am not like Alannah . . . Or her friends." She raised her head and shot a direct glance at her mother. "I don't like this gambling style of meeting people. I'm not such a risk taker. I don't want to meet any psychos."

"All right, all right," Naina said. Then she said something that she never expected to say to her daughter. "Sweetheart, if you want to play it safe, I understand . . . Do you want me to talk to some people in New Jersey and see if they know anyone suitable?"

Amaya threw her head back and sniggered, a dark, incredulous snigger. "Well, well, my mom arranging a marriage for me . . . never thought that day would happen. No, thank you. But if things get really dire, I'm more likely to take you up on your offer than go online trolling for men."

CHAPTER THIRTY

ON A WARM spring evening, Naina went to meet Ludwig at a tiny Mexican restaurant, with just four tables and lots of black Oaxacan pottery, in the East Village. Ludwig, in an interesting coincidence, was born on the same day, in the same month and year as she was. According to his profile, he had never been married and worked as a policy advisor in the poverty reduction area of the United Nations Development Program. His job involved frequent travel around the world, particularly Latin America where he had lived for several years. This impressed Naina. Somehow, working for the UN just had a cachet about it. As did world travel.

When Naina, wearing a red summer dress, walked into the restaurant, on time, he was already seated at the table and seemed to be reading something, his glasses firmly fitted on his face. He looked like someone serious. But he did not look German. Noting his broad features, big, lined forehead, thick brown hair speckled with gray, small green eyes and stocky body, Naina thought he looked like a reasonably attractive man from Uzbekistan or Kazakhstan. She studied him for few moments before smoothing her hair and gingerly walking up to him.

Ludwig handled their date casually, taking off the pressure she invariably felt at these things. Dressed in a short white kurta, jeans, and casual sandals he had a confident-yet-unencumbered air about him, fitting the profile of the bourgeois bohemian that he described himself as. Naina didn't quite know what to make of him and couldn't sense what he made of her.

Without sentimentality or nostalgia, Ludwig spoke about the several years he had spent as a hippie, first in Asia and then in Latin America, in the seventies and eighties doing drugs, having sex, more than making up for the twenty-one years of a strict Catholic upbringing in a small Bavarian town. After bumming around for a very long time, he thought he should do something for someone other than himself and worked at an NGO in southeastern Mexico for about ten years. But his selfish impulses asserted themselves again, and he wanted to live in a big city, see plays, go to museums, and take showers everyday with hot water.

"I thought I'd take up a job at the poverty reduction group at the UN to help ease my guilt about leaving the NGO," he said with a big, sardonic smile.

"You don't seem like you have too much guilt," Naina said, smiling.

Ludwig laughed, an easy, baritone laugh that softened his serious persona, and one she found very sexy.

"You're certainly right about that," he said.

Ludwig asked her out again, in his characteristically unfussy manner, for drinks at an Irish pub in Gramercy Park the following week. She dressed in jeans, a black-and-white peasant top, and short heels, the most casually she had ever dressed for a date. They started off talking about a *New York Times* article on class differences in India, but after a drink or two she asked him the questions that had been on her mind, the sort of questions she had never asked a man before. Starting with a tentativeness that gradually dissipated. Had he had many relationships? Had he ever been married? How long had he been online? Had he been on many dates? What brought him online?

As she refreshed her lipstick in the restroom after her barrage of questions, her brow was knit with worry. Were her questions too invasive? Was her tone too pointed? But when she returned to the bar stool (which was quite uncomfortable though she did not voice that), Ludwig remained unflustered and answered her questions with the same directness she had posed them with. He told her that when he left Germany, he wanted to have nothing to do with marriage or any institution. Also, he was a hippie and so much free love was going around, there was really no need for marriage. It was in his late twenties, while he was still a vagabond trapezing around the world, that he experienced his first itch to be in a proper relationship. So he would just get involved with women who were either hippies like he was or nationals of whatever country he was in, but nothing lasted longer than six months. That's as long as he would stay in one place. When he was in Mexico, however, he fell in love with a beautiful Argentine who worked at the NGO with him. They got engaged, the only time in his life that he'd ever been engaged, and she went back to Argentina to prepare for the wedding. Or so she said. She never returned. He called her several times at her parents' house, but she wouldn't take his calls; and he wrote her letters, but she never wrote back. He still didn't know what happened.

Naina listened carefully, trying to read him. It was quite surprising. He spoke of these experiences without any bitterness, without any sadness, as if they had happened a long, long time ago. As if they had barely marked him. As if his body and soul were still smooth like a child's. Unlike her own, which were forever marked by the hole still waiting to hear Harish's gentle, salve-like voice comforting her in the middle of the night one more time and the big, ugly gash made by Jai's stinging, staccato voice, hard like a slap, spurning her in the West Village.

Ludwig continued as their main courses were served. The experience with the Argentine woman turned him off marriage and it was only when he moved to New York that he began to think of relationships again. So far, he'd never met the right woman. He had had three relationships in New York, all of which lasted for about a year, but none worked out for different, undramatic reasons.

So many relationships this man had had. Tasted the fruit of so many women. While she had hardly had any relationships. Why in the world would he find her interesting?

She noticed that he had almost finished his main course while she was still eating her lamb stew slowly, savoring each bite. This man clearly moved faster than she did.

Ludwig said he thought he'd widen his pool of available women by going online; it had now been two years and though he'd met a number of interesting women, it hadn't quite worked out. Such was the case in New York. Again, it was the same tone. Without regret. Without disappointment. He could have been talking about something else. Anything else, really. It was quite intriguing.

People in New York got set in their ways, and, interestingly, got more idealistic as they got older, he said. They, and that included him, thought they had gone through too much of life to settle for anyone less than the person whose image in their mind had become more and more intricate with the years. Instead of becoming murky and indistinct with the waters of time, people's notion of their ideal partner often coagulated. Its edges became so hard and defined that the vision was not even willing to melt a little.

"So, what about you?" Ludwig asked, finishing the last drops of his beer. "What brings you to this chaotic world of online dating?"

Naina twirled a strand of her hair with her forefinger and thought about how to answer. She cocked her head, then smiled mischievously and shrugged with exaggeration. "Maybe the opportunity to meet German bourgeois bohemians who speak fluent Spanish, live in the West Village, help poor people in Peru, like Gerhard Richter and hate Bush in the White House?"

Ludwig laughed that easy baritone laugh. "All right, then we're going make sure that you make the most of that opportunity . . . By the way, that's a very successful evasion of my question."

On their next date, Ludwig stroked the back of her right hand, his feathery touch making her body tingle. It was the end of the evening, they were the only patrons at the bar, the lights had become even dimmer and two bartenders were busy flirting with each other in an African-sounding language. Naina secretly wondered what Ludwig's mouth would taste like. But he did not kiss her. Instead, he kept stroking her forearms. When they said goodbye, he kissed her on both cheeks and invited her to join him for the big Gerhard Richter show at the MoMA the next Saturday. Naina promptly said yes, wondering later if she had sounded too eager. She went home in a taxi, smiling to herself. Ludwig seemed like the kind of man who could pursue pleasure and adventure enthusiastically without being entangled by it, had an ability to do good yet still watched out for himself first, and had a capacity to sail through the moment without being weighed down by regrets or longings. She liked that. Now, when she looked back, she thought about how that smoky air of melancholy often hung around Jai, like an Edith Piaf song. But Ludwig, Ludwig was more like cool jazz.

THE FOLLOWING SATURDAY, Naina was getting ready for the Gerhard Richter opening, meticulously combing her hair in front of her bathroom mirror. Suddenly, she spotted some gray roots near her temples. She was dismayed. She peered more closely. They seemed to be so conspicuous—she didn't know how she could have missed them before. She frowned, wondering what to do. There wasn't enough time to go the salon, where she had had her hair colored just four weeks before, or do it herself at home.

Yes, she could use some root touch-up spray. She scanned her bathroom cabinet. Oh no, she had run out of it. She quickly put on a muumuu housedress and ran to the nearest drugstore only to find, amid the endless walls of hair products, the store had run out of the brand she normally used. This wasn't an evening to try new products. She ran to another drugstore where she found it peeping out from behind a hair conditioner for balding women.

Naina arrived fifteen minutes late, profusely apologizing to Ludwig. Dressed in black slacks and a white shirt with thin pinstripes, he was standing in the museum's bookstore reading a Gerhard Richter book. She had never seen him so formally dressed. This time, he really looked like a serious German, making her tardiness seem even more unseemly. He looked at his watch when he saw her, and then teased her about what a charming bourgeois bohemian she made in her hot pink paisley-patterned maxi dress.

At the show, Naina was impressed by his thorough scrutiny of the work, and his intelligent commentary—he definitely had a lot more to say about Richter than she did. When they were looking at a lively multi-hued abstract painting, they overheard a young woman next to them exclaim about how she had spotted a female body in the work. Ludwig smiled at Naina. As soon as the young woman and the older woman with her were out of earshot, he said, "That's what I love about abstract art. The image does not dictate what you should see, but just incites and intrigues you. It's interesting how human beings try to 'find' things in everything. I guess it's human to look for something even if there's nothing to find."

"True, that's so true," Naina said, nodding. "Very well put."

Ludwig was most excited when he saw Richter's Baader Meinhof paintings, blurry black-and-white images of corpses of members of the Red Army Faction, the infamous German left-wing terrorist group in the seventies. The paintings were based on real newspaper and police photographs, Naina read on the label.

"Gosh, I remember the Red Army Faction so clearly," Ludwig said. "They died just before I left Germany. They were such a big deal . . . all over the newspapers and televisions, people were talking about it all the time . . . my parents loathed them, of course, but for me and many young Germans at the time, they used to be heroes . . . I can't believe I'm finally getting to see these paintings. Wow."

Naina too couldn't take her eyes off them, these haunting, horrifying images.

"They seem to be made without the slightest ounce of sympathy," she said. "Especially that one of the man."

"Ah, it's interesting that you say that. People on the Left tend to say that they aren't sympathetic enough and people on the other side tend to think they are too sympathetic."

"What do you think?"

"I think they are ambiguous . . . I see the works as more of an intellectual exercise to show how much a person's ideological leanings and sympathies influence the way they see things."

"That's very interesting," Naina said. "A study in the always-fascinating subject of perception."

Soon, she was gazing at a painting of a young Ulrike Meinhof, the co-founder of the faction and probably one of the most famous female terrorists in history. Ulrike looked as innocent as a schoolgirl with long hair, sad, pensive eyes and her arms neatly folded on her chest like a well-brought-up girl from St. Therese's Convent.

"It's hard to believe someone as sweet-looking as she could have killed anyone," she said, transfixed by the painting. "They were probably just misguided romantics."

Ludwig nodded and then excused himself to make a phone call. Naina continued looking at the painting and something about Ulrike's thinking eyes made her think of Amaya, always at the back of her mind and casting invisible shadows during her dates. Of course, she had concluded, with the aid of Alannah, that ceasing dating herself would not make Amaya meet anyone faster, and she was convinced that her daughter would eventually meet someone. But still, it disturbed her, disturbed her greatly, that Amaya was by herself and despondent about her romantic prospects while she . . . She would talk to Soma and some people in New Jersey. Maybe they knew of someone.

For dinner, Naina and Ludwig went to a cozy Italian restaurant in Hell's Kitchen where, after a discussion about politics in art, Ludwig stroked the back of her hands, and their intellectual conversation dried up like big, shiny raindrops shriveling up when suddenly exposed to the summer sun. By the end of the night, they were sitting close to each other and his arm reached toward the back of her knee, which he stroked with his feathery touch. She wasn't surprised when he kissed her on the steps of a small church tucked away on the corner of 48th Street and Tenth Avenue before saying goodbye. But she hadn't quite expected him to start muttering endearments in Spanish to her in between kisses; she hadn't quite expected to feel so wanton and impatient when his staccato German-accented English thawed into melodic Spanish rhythms.

Naina and Ludwig would meet almost every Wednesday and Saturday after that night, always it seemed at Ludwig's suggestion—unless Naina heard from Amaya, wanting her mother's company, in which case Naina would make some excuse to Ludwig, who never protested. They attended discussions on democracy in Latin America and Africa, saw plays by Bertolt Brecht and George Bernard Shaw, saw work by German conceptual artists and contemporary Chinese artists, and ate lots of Mexican, Brazilian, and Ethiopian food. Most of the time, she let him choose what they did because, unlike her, he was very specific about what he liked and didn't like. Ludwig was interested in prose, but not poetry; he listened to contemporary classical music, but not traditional Western classical music; he hated watching any type of dance performance, and, of the all the Asian cuisines available in New York, he only liked Vietnamese food.

Naina found these strict preferences amusing and, as the relationship progressed, would tease him by threatening to take him to a Mozart concert, a show on German Romantic art, a Bollywood movie, or eat spicy Thai food. They talked constantly and spiritedly, mostly about ideas, politics, and culture. She admired his incisive, cerebral intellect, exhaustive knowledge about the myriad things he cared about, and his ability to argue his point in a brainy, analytical way. Initially, his intelligence made her want to hide her own in the shade, and she did not express her own ideas much. But she quickly became more loquacious as she came to see that he was more like a tennis player who wanted to bounce a ball back and forth rather than a philosopher wanting to expound his views to the giant sky. In an effort to sound more erudite, she even started reading up on topics that he cared about, dense books on the coup in Brazil in 1964 and about why development assistance to the Third World had failed, books, which after a few pages, bored her to tears. But she kept on.

After covering the highlights in the beginning, they spoke of their personal lives only in passing, as a brief mention preceding another topic, an observation that bolstered the argument for some larger point they were making, or a fleeting interlude. But, one time, as they were eating dinner, following an emotionally charged Iranian film Naina had chosen to see, the topic of marriage, central to the film, came up. At dinner, she initiated a long conversation about her husband and marriage, the first time she had spoken in any detail about this with any man. She was guarded as she spoke, motivated, she found to her surprise, as much by a sense of loyalty to Harish as by a desire not to reveal the intimate details of her life to Ludwig. She painted a picture of their marriage with thin, firm strokes and a few solid colors, a picture that did not reflect the zigzagging strokes and mottled shades that had existed in their marriage. Ludwig, who asked few questions about her marriage, had a grave, earnest expression as she talked, and she sensed he was listening carefully and making sure he had all the information he needed before he knifed it with analysis later on, and added the new data to the mental picture he was constructing of her.

Naina went to Ludwig's immaculate, minimal one-bedroom apartment on the fourth floor of a building on a quiet tree-laden street in the West Village on their eighth date, and she marveled at his collection of books on German philosophers and Latin American history. That night, they made love on Ludwig's sky-blue linens, an act that seemed so natural and inevitable that Naina decided it would be too childish for her to voice any of the hesitation she felt when she realized, sitting on his fawn-colored sofa with his hands inside the band of her skirt, that sex was imminent.

They ended up making love at the end of almost every evening they got together, always on his blue linens and always in front of a big poster of a colorful Gerhard Richter painting. He made love skillfully using feathery caresses to coax the notes out of her body in places that never knew they had any music in them. He taught her how to give oral sex to a man properly; he taught her that a man's nipples could be as sensitive as a woman's; he taught her how to squeeze a man's balls. She enjoyed making love to him, except for one thing—he never gave her oral sex. But she couldn't bring herself to ask for it.

CHAPTER THIRTY-ONE

IT WAS A slow Tuesday evening and Naina shut the gallery's doors promptly at six. She went and sat with Susan on the bulbous black couches in the office area, the still-strong sun making solid rectangles on her bare legs, warming them from the relentless chill they felt in the air-conditioned space. Susan said she had been talking to several of their donors and doing a lot of thinking and, at this point, she was ready to expand the gallery and move to a bigger space, something she and Naina had been discussing for the past few months. And fortuitously, she had found a new space, which was the right size, on the tenth floor of the building opposite them; it was going to become available in the next few months or so. Susan then went on to talk about her plans for shows, panel discussions, conferences, high-profile guest curators, and building a deeper donor base among younger Asian women.

There was an ease between Naina and Susan as they conversed, their eyes sparkling and voices high as they talked about this potential space. After working together and carefully observing each other for a few years, they had a developed a relationship where they sashayed from the intimacy of two friends prattling about their children or gossiping about people in the art world, to their businesslike personas when talking about work. Then the barriers would quickly be erected again and each would step back into their respective roles, like stepping back into formal shoes after casually lounging around barefoot. Naina had accepted Susan becoming exceptionally demanding and exacting a few days before a show, and if something untoward happened during that time, she could be extremely abrasive. Naina knew that Susan had come to terms with the fact that she could sometimes drift off into some faraway world while she was sitting on a desk, and barely register what Susan was telling her. She knew Susan had noticed that she had, at times, forgotten to put whatever she had just folded into the envelope in front of her and disappeared for long coffee breaks.

Susan was overflowing with compliments for Naina today, a rarity, and Naina was relishing every word. She praised Naina for her instrumental role in raising the profile of the gallery and convincing Susan to do projects she was reluctant about, not an easy thing to do. The gallery would have not been the same without her. Naina felt herself smile, feeling proud.

As Susan continued with the praise, Naina started to feel strange. So many compliments, so much praise from Susan of all people. What was going on?

But Susan continued, bringing up the success of Naina's monthly tea tastings. As a result of those tastings, several women from The New York Women Chefs and Restaurateurs Association and the Alliance of Women Furniture Designers had ended up becoming donors. In addition, the number of people attending the tastings was increasing every month.

"So, I've been doing a lot of thinking, like I've said," Susan said, looking at Naina straight in the eye. "And I'd like you to be the associate gallery director."

The words, though not a surprise, slowly settled around Naina, saturating her with a deep purple satisfaction. When she had joined, in a nebulous administrative capacity a few years before, a title like associate gallery director seemed hallowed and unattainable, reserved for those confident people in their stylish clothes, those who breezily spoke of well-known artists, gallerists and curators as "John," "Cindy," "Hans," and "Shahzia," people around whom she had felt like such a gatecrasher during her early Chelsea days.

"Thank you," Naina said, smiling brightly, like a peacock with its feathers out. "I really appreciate it, Susan."

"But," Susan continued, and then paused. Yes, there had to be a *but*. After all those compliments, there had to be. "I know you're the right person for the job, but I need to know that you really want it. I want someone who's hungry for this, Naina. I want to be absolutely sure that you are committed to this . . . there are going to be long hours and lots *more* work starting pretty soon . . . lately, you've seemed distracted."

Naina bent her head. She knew it was true. There had been successive late nights with Ludwig and she was spending too much time thinking about Third World development and the crisis in Darfur.

"I suspect it's something personal," Susan said. "You don't have to tell me, but I need to have someone who is absolutely committed, not just for a short stint, but for the long haul. I hope that person is you, but I need to be absolutely sure. Do you want some time to think about it?"

Naina imagined herself as the associate gallery director in the air-conditioned gallery on balmy summer evenings, thinking about ways to build the gallery's donor base and planning shows and events while her body felt drained, and her brain too cloudy to compose the five emails she had to get out before the end of that day. Meanwhile, the sun would be getting ready to set a block away, its iridescent hues sparkling in the lapping water of the Hudson River below. And instead of lingering to watch the sun set over the water, as she sometimes did these days when she walked along the Hudson River to meet Ludwig on 14th Street, she pictured herself calling Ludwig from the chilly gallery telling him she would be working too late to see him that night. Then, she saw herself getting into the subway once the night had already fallen, eating take-out, watching some silly TV because she had no energy to read, and finally falling asleep, like a felled soldier, alone, on her big bed.

She envisioned calling her travel agent and canceling her trip to Antigua in September, the solitary excursion she had planned months earlier, among the crumbling, poetic ruins of the old Guatemalan city. She imagined not having a lazy, carefree retirement in the next few years where she could get up late, stroll to museums and art galleries, have lunch with Amaya on Saturdays, enjoy the fall foliage in New Jersey, or go to a yoga class. She pictured herself missing winters with Ludwig in Mexico, sipping margaritas and watching the news about some snowstorm in New York from a small TV while the sun kept her warm and the sea breeze kept her cool. She recalled the offhand comment Ludwig had made the week before about retiring in the next few years. He dreamed of dividing his time between Berlin in the summer and fall and Oaxaca in the winter and spring. Before his youth and health slipped away, he wanted to enjoy vagabond freedoms again.

"I'm absolutely sure," Naina finally said. "I want this job and I'm prepared to give it all I've got."

ON A STEAMY September night, after a grueling day at work, Naina dragged her heels up the numerous steps at her subway stop because the escalator was not working, and only paused to check her voicemail to see if Ludwig had called. He hadn't. He probably wasn't going to call tonight as it was already past nine. Now too exhausted to walk the three avenue blocks and two street blocks needed to go home, she opted for a taxi and climbed into one waiting at the curb—not realizing, until someone knocked on the window and pointed to the driver's seat, there was no driver.

She couldn't put her finger on what had gone wrong. Ever since she had met Ludwig, things had gone smoothly even though her feelings for him never reached the blinding, feverish pitch they had reached with Jai—which Alannah said was a good thing. Even Soma, whom she had reluctantly told about her online dating exploits and Ludwig, agreed that hasty highs did not lead to lasting relationships. Naina put her hand out for a cab, but none seemed to be free. She had no choice but to walk home.

Things between her and Ludwig had been stimulating, both intellectually and physically, and she looked forward to seeing him every Wednesday and Saturday with a sustained level of anticipation. But lately, Ludwig had seemed withdrawn and the last time she saw him he was restlessly flipping the pages a book on China's economic and social transformation as he distractedly answered her questions about the Russian film they had seen earlier that evening. When they made love that night, he did not seem interested in kissing her or muttering endearments in Spanish, and simply plunged into her with an icy disengagement. She had found this behavior odd, but not disconcerting, considering, for the most part, he had always been consistent with her. She rationalized it, saying to herself that he might have been tired or preoccupied with something, intuitively understanding how internal preoccupations lifted a mind out of the present. Still, she was curious and wanted to ask him what, if anything, was going on with him. But she did not. When it came to politics, religion, culture, philosophy, she felt free to engage him, but when it came to the muddled shapes of whatever was fluttering inside of him as they argued about the merits and demerits of feminism or communism, she felt a barrier between them, invisible and strong.

After the last time she had seen Ludwig, he had not called her the next day as he normally would do. By eight in the evening, slightly concerned, she called him, but the phone kept ringing and then went to his voicemail. She left him a message saying she was hoping he was having a good Sunday and wondering if he wanted to see a production of August Strindberg's *Miss Julie* at a church on St. Mark's Place on Wednesday. He did not return her call that evening, causing her to toss and turn in bed that night as a feeling of dread rumbled inside her. She did not hear from him the next day either despite making another call, less calm than the first, or the next day, and the rumbling feeling swelled into a storm. It became hard for her to concentrate on work, and she ended up staying at the gallery until nine at night for two consecutive days to get everything done, constantly checking her voicemail and email.

Tonight, after discovering Ludwig still hadn't called, she began to realize that he might never call again. The storm inside her abated and was replaced by a steady downpour of melancholy.

When Naina reached her building, she saw a big sign saying the elevator was not working. Sighing, she sat down on the chocolate-colored sofa in the lobby with her eyes closed, barely registering the building's other residents yelling out expletives at the incompetence of the superintendent before sprinting up the stairs. Ten minutes later, she took off her heels and ambled toward the stairwell, carrying her shoes and her bag, the weight of these items feeling too much. As she climbed those steps, stopping often due to exhaustion, she felt the bulk of her listless body, the tightness in her lower back, and her own fragility compared with the vigor of the thirty-something guy for whom she quickly stepped aside as he bounded up the stairs in gym shorts, looking like some sort of superhero and saying something about the markets.

When she got to her apartment, Naina put on a CD of Pandit Shiv Kumar Sharma's *santoor*, lit some lavender-scented candles, and sprawled on her bed, too tired to even bother heating up some food or ordering something to eat. Little by little, everything that Ludwig had ever said or implied that had to do with age entered her mind, pricking her like thorns. She remembered him telling her how his Argentine girlfriend, who was twelve years younger than he, had the untainted enthusiasm of people in their twenties. She remembered him telling her how his British friends at work teasingly accused him of being a Dorian

Gray. She remembered how, on two separate occasions, he had referred to a homeless woman begging on the street and an elderly woman talking nonstop after a film as "old, old ladies." She remembered how he had quickly shrugged off her question when she asked him if wanted children by saying "It's not something I think about right now" and then quickly changing the subject to something about race relations in South America compared to North America. She remembered how his face had lit up when he had seen a little girl in a beautiful yellow dress practicing how to walk in Central Park with her father, a cheerful-looking man with folds under his eyes suggesting he must have been in his early fifties if not older.

She imagined a woman—liberal, attractive, toned, in her mid-thirties with firm, substantial hips and breasts that exuded a sophisticated fertility—with Ludwig, the two of them looking at child-friendly apartments downtown or in Brooklyn because they could never think of living above 14th Street as they fiercely argued about the benefits of private school versus public school. Meanwhile, Naina would be haplessly and helplessly watching her post-menopausal body inevitably moving further downward, gathering wrinkles, flab, purple veins, and becoming so frail that she would not even be able to climb the five flights of stairs like she had just done. That woman would be becoming a mother for the first time while she would be becoming a grandmother for the first time.

NAINA WOKE UP at two-thirty in the morning huddled on the right side of her comforter in her work clothes, ravenous and desperate to use the bathroom. She microwaved a South Beach Diet pizza, and after hurriedly eating it, felt so full that the thought of going back to bed right away made her queasy. So she sat on her desk with a hot peppermint tea and decided to check email. Maybe her sister-in-law in India, who often sent funny jokes, might have sent her something that would lift her spirits. Before an email that said, "10 More Reasons To Hate Your Ma-in-law" from her sister-in-law, was an email from Ludwig with the simple subject line "Hi."

> Dear Naina,
>   I'm sorry for not calling you. I needed some space to think about what was happening between us and needed to not have any contact with you during that time. I think you are a wonderful person and have really enjoyed spending time with you. But, to be brutally frank, I don't see things between us going any further. We are very different people, and though we have a lot in common, overall, I don't think we are suited for each other. Or maybe, I'm just a fool still looking for perfection. I know the right thing to probably say is that we should try to be friends, but I'm old enough to know that former lovers

can rarely be friends. Take care of yourself and good luck with everything.
Best regards,
Ludwig

Naina read the email just once, recoiling from its nonchalant frostiness. Then she trembled with shock, mystified. How could anyone who had shared a bed with someone and woken up next to them so many times, known that they wore black underwear every single day of their lives, known how their breath smelled after coffee, known how they jumped when they saw a cockroach—how could anyone so neatly and effortlessly sever someone who knew them so intimately from their lives? The act seemed so smooth, so perfected, almost like that of a butcher. Her insides burned. Her skin smarted. Her mind fumed.

She turned off her computer. and paced around her apartment, drinking big, agitated sips of peppermint tea. Everything around her—the fluffy white comforter in a crumpled heap on the edge of her bed; the *Time Out New York* magazine, with an image of a young woman in pink sunglasses sipping a cocktail, on her nightstand; the ticket from the experimental jazz trio at Merkin Concert Hall she and Ludwig had attended the previous week on her glass coffee table; the mustard-colored card from the Vietnamese restaurant they had gone to a few weeks before perched atop a long pillar of restaurant cards she had collected—all seemed absurd. She didn't quite realize it then, but her feelings for Ludwig snapped quite suddenly, severing him from her—though not as quickly and seemingly painlessly as she had been cut off by him.

Naina finally managed to go back to sleep about four a.m. When she woke up at 6:45 in the morning, she could see patches of whitish gray clouds through her window. She was tired, so tired, yet she couldn't go back to sleep. Images of the Yorkshire moors, bleak, brooding expanses of land she had never been to but imagined so many times through *Wuthering Heights*, came to her, pushing out everything else. A quiet sorrow flowed through her.

For the next ninety minutes or so, she remained in bed. She wondered if she was capable of going into work. After tossing the idea around in her head, she decided she would go to work. She had to go to work. She needed to go to work. But she would call Susan and tell her she would be a couple of hours late. Christina, the gallery assistant, was definitely going to be in today.

When Naina emerged from the bed, she craved Turkish coffee. She had brought her ibrik—a brass coffee pot with a wide base, tapered neck, and extra-long handle that Harish used to make Turkish coffee with—to New York, though she had never used it. She took out her little stool and, standing on her tiptoes, tried to see the items in the topmost kitchen cabinet, the items she used the least. There were two orange thermoses, small porcelain teacups, hand-blown whiskey glasses, and Irish beer mugs. On a silver tray was the ibrik decorated with lots of curlicues, like a sleeping relic of the past. Naina pulled it out along with a demitasse cup and got off the stool. They looked dirty and dusty, so she carefully washed them. She made coffee the way she had seen Harish make it. With finely ground coffee beans, cold water, mixing in sugar during the brewing process, and adding some cardamom.

She sat down on her couch, waiting for the coffee to cool. The clouds outside had turned more gray than white, but it didn't look like it was going to rain. Just like it was going to be gloomy for a while. She finally sipped the coffee and frowned. It was awful. Too sweet, too strong, with too little cardamom. She got up and drank a glass of water to drown out the taste. She went back and lay down on her couch, on her stomach, burying her face in a cushion.

Naina thought of Harish's fingers on her forehead checking for fever every time she told him she had a headache; she thought of how he would happily change the kids' diapers after a long day of work if she even remotely suggested she was tired; she thought of how he, even though he hated Mexican food, would bring her takeout from the Mexican place about five miles away from his office a few times a month without reminders. She remembered his voice, always soft and gentle, soothing her during that terrible night when they received that phone call telling them that her father had died in India. And, of course, his Turkish coffee was the best—smooth, sweet, and just the right kind of flavorful.

She craved that cushiony sense of reassurance she had always felt around Harish—that no matter what, as long as he was alive, he would be there for her, solid like those big, heavy, wooden doors in Indian forts, shielding her from pain and danger in the best way he knew how. It was the way arranged marriages, at least those she knew, worked. When two people who typically did not know each other very well sat in front of the wedding fire, muttering vows in Sanskrit they did not understand, they both did clearly understand one thing—they were promising to take care of each other regardless of the vagaries of the future.

Naina opened her scrunchie and let her hair fall over the pillow. It had that unwashed smell and more knots than usual.

She recalled how her sister-in-law's sister's husband, a high-ranking army officer, treated his wife with a quiet tenderness when she, just in her mid-forties, developed a series of health problems that made her exceptionally obese and unable to walk steadily. She recalled how the wife of a close family friend of her parents spent the rest of her life devotedly caring for her sixty-year-old husband, twelve years older than she, when he lost his left leg and the ability to speak coherently after a car accident. She knew if she had been stricken in any way, Harish too would have uncomplainingly and patiently looked after her, and if she had been the same person living with him in New Jersey she would have done the same for him. Though she was quite sure she wouldn't have done it as graciously and cheerfully as Harish or the wife of the family friend.

As the morning progressed, Naina felt like a large, ungainly anachronism who had found herself in a new world order. A jet setting new world order where everything and everyone was disposable; where it was as easy to move from one country to another as it was to move from one set of friends to another, one lover to another, one wife or husband to another; where one felt free to gravitate toward anything or anyone that gave pleasure and away from anything or anyone that caused displeasure. Ludwig was a part of that new world order— he had moved from place to place for most of his life because a new place offered something new or because an old place had become old, and, even now, he was in quest of the perfect place to retire in. But none of these moves involved any commitments, obligations, or attachments to the past. Ludwig glided smoothly, guided by whatever he wanted at the time, like a lithe aquatic creature for whom the world truly was its oyster. If anyone happened to slip on the shiny, capricious surfaces of this new order, then she imagined the Ludwigs of the world would shrug and tell her that it was a small price to pay for opportunity, freedom, and mobility. She wasn't quite sure she liked the codes of this jet setting new world even though she knew that she, herself, in recent years, had more or less followed them. She wasn't sure that people who belonged to this tribe were capable of real love. Was she?

Naina walked into her bedroom. She looked at the empty king-sized bed flattened just on the right side where she slept, and puffy on the left side, and yearned for the erratic pulse of Harish's breathing next to her—essential rhythms of the many vital, unspectacular years of her life, almost as pivotal as the tempo of her own breath. She remembered how Harish would wake up at seven in the morning, mutter *good morning* while she was still in bed, get up, brush his teeth, shave, shower, and then patiently wait for her to prepare cereal and toast for both of them before he went to work. She looked around her room filled with all the lovely things she had chosen for herself without ever having to worry. She thought of how her husband continued to provide for her even after his death and felt tenderness and gratitude course through her like milk. Languidly, moving as if she were in a dream, she sat cross-legged on the edge of her bed, shedding tears that never came. Sometime later, she got under the covers, silently chanting the Mool mantra she had learned in yoga class for about forty minutes before she finally had to get ready and go to work.

CHAPTER THIRTY-TWO

THE CROONER WAS dressed in a long burgundy sequined dress, big sparkling earrings, and an extensive fake diamond-studded necklace that covered her chest and reached deep into her cleavage. She sashayed onto the stage in the melodramatic, excessive hip-swaying manner of Bollywood heroines. She was slightly plump and wearing burgundy lipstick that obviously extended far above and below the confines of her small mouth and bright aquamarine eyeshadow that clashed with her dark skin. But she had a high-spiritedness and a crude mammal warmth that made her appear more attractive than she really was. When she announced in her cheery, husky voice that she would be starting with "Jawane Janeman," a sultry eighties song from a popular Bollywood film where actress Parveen Babi had mesmerized millions with her sizzling performance, the audience clapped with glee, and two or three middle-aged men even whistled, putting to use the skills they had probably perfected thousands of miles away as young men in Indian cinema halls. Naina clapped vigorously while Karan, who didn't remember the song at all, gave his mother an amused, quizzical glance, and Amaya, who vaguely remembered the song, softly applauded.

It was late October and it was the season of Diwali, the Hindu festival of lights marking the triumph of good over evil. Karan had unexpectedly showed up in New York, and now the three of them were having dinner and watching the cultural variety show at Mahaan, a high-end, not particularly fashionable Indian restaurant in midtown Manhattan, that had been around since the seventies.

When Harish was alive, he put aside his usual aversion to the city during Diwali time and loved coming to Mahaan to eat dinner and watch the annual show. When Amaya and Karan were young, they would accompany their parents for this celebration, but as they grew older, they lost interest. Still, Naina and Harish would drive in for the show almost every year, him donning a formal kurta pajama and her in a nice salwar kameez or sari. The last time Naina had been to the restaurant was on Diwali, just a few months before Harish died.

This time, it was Naina's idea to bring the family together at Mahaan for a pre-Diwali celebration. Both her kids seemed to like being there.

The crooner, who introduced herself as Bobby, was singing much too loudly as well as winking a lot, which might have looked sexy on Parveen Babi, but appeared merely comical on Bobby. However, it didn't seem to matter. As

Naina discreetly looked around, every man in the audience seemed to be loving the performance. She knew Harish would have found the excessive winking ridiculous.

Recently, Naina had been thinking of Harish a lot, memories of his every small kind gesture or act of consideration appearing bright and iridescent, sometimes dazzlingly so, as they were further illuminated by the flattering, inflating glow of nostalgia. Meanwhile, all his flaws shrunk to tiny, colorless specks. She felt particularly sympathetic toward him after reading and re-reading a long article on erectile dysfunction in *Time* magazine when she was at the nail salon one day, seriously wondering whether poor Harish had suffered from the condition about which she had previously known very little. She doubted that he, despite being a doctor, would have known much about it either, and, even if he had, he would have probably never imagined he had it. How come it had never occurred to her before? Maybe that's why intimacy between them was so infrequent in the last few years. Maybe that's why he would hide his private parts under the sheets at times and turn crimson like the shyest of brides when the act was not completed. Or maybe there was some other reason. Naina felt a sudden urge to hug Harish's slim, lanky body, and rock it back and forth.

The crooner finished her first set, and Naina watched Karan take a big spoonful of dal in his mouth. She was so happy he was able to join her and Amaya, his last-minute visit was a real treat. He rarely had business on the East Coast, but two of his colleagues who worked with Internet marketing companies in the region had taken ill the week before, and he was asked to attend meetings in their place in New York.

"Good god," Karan said. "What's that on your hair?"

"What? What?" Naina said.

"That white thing. That white stain."

"You're just noticing it," Amaya said. "God, you're slow."

"Oh that," Naina said, feeling relieved. "Just some white hair."

The day before, when Naina had gone for her regular cut and color, Alvina, her hairstylist, had accidentally forgotten to color a chunk of hair. And now, Naina, who had scrupulously dyed her hair every six weeks from the moment she had started graying at thirty-five, had a handful of gray hair near her forehead. A portly Russian woman prone to theatrical outburst, Alvina screamed when she discovered her mistake, holding Naina's hand, apologizing profusely for her mistake, promising her a free blow dry, a free conditioning treatment, free hair care products, or anything else she wanted. But when Naina looked at herself in the mirror and saw the streak of silver-gray shining over her black hair, she told Alvina, "Let it be. I like it. It's elegant. It looks young at heart without looking young."

Alvina stared at her, vigorously shaking her head.

"I think I'm going to keep it . . . What do you think, beta?"

"Hmmm . . . let me see," Karan said, peering at it. "Actually, it looks nice. Very grown-up. Classy."

"Oh, come on, Karan," Amaya said. "It looks so odd . . . a white streak trying to get attention amid all that black. It makes Mom look old-ladyish. Without *that*, she looked so young."

"And why does she have to look *so* young? What happened to aging gracefully?"

"Oh god, Karan, you've turned into such a fuddy duddy uncle."

"All right, stop you two," Naina said, slipping into her *mother* voice. "Your food is getting cold. And the next song is starting soon, so no more arguing. And I'm keeping the white hair."

After the crooner took another break, Karan removed a red velvet box from his pocket and gave it to Naina.

"What is this?"

"Just open it, Mom."

Naina opened the box and gazed at a pendant with a round sapphire—a vivid shade of indigo glistening like a tropical sky at dusk and looking as if it cradled both the earth and infinity within it.

"Oh, beta, thank you," Naina said, unable to take her eyes off the pendant. "This is fabulous. Really . . . You didn't have to."

Karan beamed. "I'm so glad you like it. It's Diwali, isn't it?"

Naina could tell he loved the fact that she loved it. This was the first time he had bought her a gift for Diwali in years, and not a coincidence that it was after she had returned to New Jersey.

"Hey, Am, don't worry, I didn't forget about you," Karan said, whipping out another jewelry box. It contained tiny ruby earrings, and Amaya tried them on while smiling with delight.

"So, I have another surprise," Karan said, leaning forward on the table, his gold cuff links shining on the ends of his black shirt. Where had he got these cuff links from? Naina had never seen him wear gold cuff links before.

"I'm seriously seeing someone," he said, smiling brightly. "Actually, I've been seeing her for just under a year and I didn't want to tell you guys until I was sure."

"That's great, beta," Naina said after taking some time to digest the information. "Who is she? What does she do? And how serious is it?"

Karan patiently answered all her questions. Roopali grew up in Southern California, one of three sisters in a conservative religious and traditional Rajasthani family. But Roopali herself was not that traditional, Karan quickly added. She was twenty-six and worked on the business side of a high-tech company in the Bay Area.

"So how serious is it?" Amaya asked.

"Very serious," Karan said. "You might hear of an engagement within the next few months."

"Really? I'm so happy for you," Naina said, consciously rearranging her features so she looked cheerful.

The truth was that she was worried. He had also been very serious with that awful Arti, the dentist who dumped him for someone whom her parents had chosen. Was her son barking up the wrong tree again?

"So when do we get to meet her?" Naina asked. "Why don't you bring her to New York?"

"Ya, right," Karan said, laughing. "She's a modern girl but not that modern . . . She's not going to travel with me until we're married. You're going to have to come to California to meet her."

"Where do you find these Victorian girls, Karan?" Amaya said, rolling her eyes. "You say she comes from a conservative family. Are you sure she's not one of those who's going to dump you for her parents' chosen groom?"

Karan bent his head. Naina could see that the aftertaste of pain from the Arti incident was still in him, bitter and sour. Her heart reached out to him.

"I'm as sure as I can be, Am," Karan said. "Arti was quite devious and kept me away from her parents. But Roopali, she's not like that. I've met her parents and though they are conservative, they are very nice. Look, they even gave me these gold cuff links."

"I think you guys will like her," Karan added, almost as if he hoped it would be true. "She's gentle, soft, and generous."

"Off to California then, I guess. Congrats, bro." Amaya summoned the waiter to order her dessert.

"So how long did you say you've been dating her?"

"Almost a year."

"Wow, that's pretty quick after . . . after the last one, I mean," Amaya said, and Naina could detect a note of envy in her voice. "You've obviously got the right moves . . . But it's so much easier for a man to find the right person . . ."

Naina could see the despondence in Amaya's drooping brown eyes, in the corners of her turned-down mouth, and it made the blood and bones in her chest wobbly. With the help of some friends in Jersey, she had arranged for Amaya to meet a neurosurgeon and a civil rights attorney. Amaya had reluctantly agreed to being set up, but neither had worked out. Amaya found the neurosurgeon too dull, but was open to giving the civil rights attorney a chance. Unfortunately, he was not interested in her.

"But you've been dating a lot," Karan said.

"Not a lot," Amaya snapped. "Not a lot . . . It's not so easy for me. Not easy at all."

"Gosh, chill out, Amaya. Calm down. You sound so neurotic. My God. Maybe it's true then . . . single women over thirty lose their minds in New York. Like in *Sex and The City.*"

Amaya threw her head back and laughed sarcastically, looking at Karan as if he were just a foolish babe in the woods, not a man just two years younger than she. "Really, Karan? So you think Mom and I have *Sex and the City* lives?

"Amaya, how dare you drag Mom into this conversation?"

"You said single women over thirty in New York. That would include Mom, wouldn't it?"

Naina cringed at the direction this conversation was taking. She clutched the edge of her kameez and clasped her lips together. Although she had given up online dating, she sometimes felt that Amaya sensed that there had been other men in her life. So many times Amaya had looked at her, her pupils enlarging, that psychotherapist look in her face, analyzing everything her mother said and everything she didn't say. Meanwhile Naina, flailing within, had wished she could turn herself opaque. But Amaya rarely probed much and that was probably for the best. Her daughter probably didn't want to know the details any more than Naina wanted to share them. But now to be pulled in this fighting match between her two children like this . . .

Karan's face was red with indignation. "Amaya, stop talking nonsense. Leave Mom out of this. This is about the nuttiness of women in *your* generation. You know very well what I'm talking about."

Before either of her kids said something else, Naina got up and went to the restroom. She stayed there for ten minutes until the crooner came back on stage, sashaying her ample hips with even greater exaggeration than before, and the men started whistling again.

CHAPTER THIRTY-THREE

OVER SEVEN MONTHS had passed since Naina lost five hundred dollars at Aditi and Samesh's Diwali card party in New Jersey, more than reversing the unexpected gain of two hundred dollars at Richa and Naveen's party. The loss had shaken Naina enough to not want to play cards again at any other Diwali party, and she vowed never to gamble again for the rest of her life.

But now, slightly tipsy and alone in a bed in a country cabin in the Finger Lakes a few hours after she had watched the July 4th fireworks explode in a blaze of color over Seneca Lake, she could barely wait the four months for Diwali, imagining the light of fire in jewel-toned clay diyas dancing like liquid gold. And, as much as she hated to admit it, she was eager to hold those cards in her hands again and gamble without restraint during the ebullience of the Hindu festival season. Maybe, if she played cleverly and Goddess Lakshmi smiled at her, she might be able win a lot this year. She imagined those delicious moments of uncertainty when she was just one of two people left in the game and it became heated and feisty because everyone knew only one person was going to get the booty on the table.

A few minutes later, as Naina shut off the light, plunging her cathedral-ceilinged room in the sort of deathly blackness one can only experience in the country, she knew she wouldn't be able to resist the urge to play cards again. She resolved to be more cautious this Diwali. The maximum she could allow herself to lose would be a hundred dollars. Not a penny more.

Naina still felt grateful for the warmth she had received from her old friends in New Jersey, not sure it was entirely deserved. The hostility from some remained, but it had lessened and usually just brushed past her, rarely denting her. It was funny—she was the same person, yet not the same person. She felt completely rooted, yet completely dislocated in her old hometown. Still, there was a comfort in being there, a comfort in passing all those diners, a comfort in driving on near-empty roads (in driving, period), a comfort in seeing the Italian woman in her red-and-white apron still making oven-baked pizzas, a comfort in the buzzing crickets at night, a comfort in watching a ruby-throated hummingbird lapping up nectar from a feeder, a comfort in not having to digest a million sounds at once. So far, the only person in Jersey who had questioned Naina about any romantic liaisons was her friend, Lily, an American fabric designer and part-time innkeeper. As Naina lay sprawled on an antique lightly worn Victorian chaise lounge in Lily's rambling Jersey farmhouse inn, sipping a glass of sherry on a sunny Sunday afternoon, Lily asked, in her typical airy manner, if there might be a special man in Naina's life. And Naina found herself telling Lily about her dating adventures, peppering the anecdotes with comical details, telling the stories in a way that she could only do now—now that enough time had separated her from the trenches of the moment. The two of them had giggled well into the late evening after which Naina drove back to New York in her rented Chevrolet, driving slowly so she could enjoy the wide-open spaces and the steady, noiseless traffic of Jersey.

Once Naina had stopped online dating, she decided to leave her romantic life, if she were to have any, to fate. And fate had not brought her any prospects, but she wasn't too bothered by it. After Ludwig, she no longer craved a man in her life. But Amaya, thankfully, after a long, dry spell, had started meeting men again, and even though no relationship seemed to loom on the horizon, just being asked out by a handful of men had boosted her daughter's spirits.

Despite the long drive to the Finger Lakes, Naina was still not sleepy. She moved her eyes around the cabin, unable to see anything. It was the first time in a long time that she did not have even a single shadow in a room where she slept. This was what her mind needed to be like when she meditated. Devoid of the shadows of thoughts. Although she had tried, she couldn't stop her mind from working all the damn time.

Her mind wandered to the gallery; the last couple of months she had been overwhelmed with work as Susan had fractured her right leg and arm. The economy had slowed, making fund raising doubly difficult, and the last show, something she had helped curate, on the portrayal of the "kitchen" by young female photographers from different countries, had been indifferently received.

For July 4th though, Naina wanted to get away from the relentless burden of work and the ruthless din of the city. She was so, so tired, and desperately in need of a break. But she could find no one to go with. Amaya had already made plans to spend the holiday weekend with a friend at her uncle's ranch in Sedona. And Alannah—who had married Damien in a Catholic Church followed by a boisterous reception where she wore a red-and-gold lehenga, resembling one of those white Bollywood actresses that were gaining popularity—would not travel without her beloved husband. Neither would Lily. And Mara had burrowed into a secret hole, like a desert tortoise, hardly seeing or talking to anyone. And Soma might have left Deepak to join her, but, in a surprising development, she was on her honeymoon in the Bahamas.

One June afternoon, Deepak had taken Soma downtown on the pretext of going to a new South Indian restaurant, but as they walked past City Hall, he knelt down on one knee and took out a big diamond ring and antique Victorian pendant she had been eyeing at a store downtown. He proposed to her by singing an old Bollywood song. Floored, she said yes, and they got married the same day because Deepak had slyly managed to obtain all her documents.

Despite all of his boorishness, Deepak could be quite the romantic. Soma was only the second Indian woman in her fifties, whom she knew, who had gotten married; this was the first time she had heard such a charming story about a man popping the question to an Indian woman of her age.

WHEN NAINA WOKE up after a long, dreamless sleep in her Finger Lakes cabin, sunlight poured through the skylight onto her bed and the wall in front of her, transforming the yellow-orange of the rustic wood into a golden glow and warming her already warm body. She could see the sunlight-mottled waters of Seneca Lake and the light-deluged trees, bright green and copious in the bounty of summer, all quivering because of a strong wind. She smiled as the world outside looked as if it were a bit drunk and dancing with clumsy, careless pleasure.

Alcohol had been on her mind since the Finger Lakes was wine country, a smaller, less reputed cousin of fancy Napa Valley. Located in bucolic upstate New York, the Finger Lakes acquired its unique name because of its long and slender lakes that reminded early mapmakers of the fingers of a hand, and it was known to be more homey and informal with its converted barn houses as tasting rooms, talk of wine in homespun, non-technical language, and two-or three-dollar wine tastings.

As Naina lay in bed, the temperature outside was 68 degrees, requiring her to take a light jacket when she finally went out. But as she stretched her legs and rolled around in soft cotton sheets, enjoying the view of the lake, she was in no rush to go outside. It was her first time in the Finger Lakes region, and so far, after driving for seven hours through holiday traffic, she liked what she had seen. Right now, she felt partial to the lakes—slender, cool blue streams of serene water, so much stiller than the restless, capricious waters of the sea.

Before picking up a travel magazine on her nightstand, she decided to check the time. It was eleven a.m.—much later than she had expected, and way past breakfast time, which, as she had been clearly informed, ended promptly at ten in the main house. Spreading herself diagonally on the bed, she read an article on Zanzibar—she didn't care about missing breakfast or the time. She was actually glad she had come alone, free to follow her own rhythm or no rhythm at all, relieved she did not have to ask anyone else what they wanted to do, grateful she did not have to deflate her own desires . . . and *compromise*. At that moment, the word *compromise* seemed to her like a polite ruse for making something as dreadful as hindering the freedom to do as you pleased sound noble, civilization's cunning attempt to sap the cream of one's pleasures and leave you with a dreary, watery soup.

And best of all, the silence all around her felt like music, so melodiously enveloping she didn't want it to end, and she asked her mind to learn from it.

ON HER THIRD day in the Finger Lakes, Naina was happy to finally find a red wine she liked. Now, after two days of indulging in chilled sweet Rieslings and Gewürztraminers and those wonderful ice wines that were terrible for her figure, she was craving some good room temperature, flavorful red wine that would gently burn her throat in that fine way a white wine never could. But she had found it hard to discover anything good as the reds from the area tended to be rather lackluster. But that day, as the sun was peeping out of the sky for the first time at four o'clock, she tasted the fourth wine on the roster, a diaphanously crimson Cabernet Franc that tasted young and fruity, and glided smoothly on her palate. She knew she was going to take a couple of bottles of the wine back to New York . . . the sudden thought of going back to work in densely packed, frenetic New York where everyone's nerves were always ignited interrupted her enjoyment of the wine, and she put the city out of her mind.

Naina was at an old dairy farm converted into a winery called *Milk of the Gods*. It had a wooded charm with its crisscrossing antique lumber beams, which still had teeth marks from a saw blade, hardwood floors, blond wood bar, big windows in solid maple frames, and stools made of old oak wine casks. After Charlie, the owner of the vineyard, generously gave her a full glass of Cabernet Franc and narrated a story about how the beams were originally from the house of a wounded Italian man who moved to America after his brothers had been brutally killed in World War I, he offered her a local cheese gently spiced with jalapeno peppers, which Naina gladly accepted. She relished big chunks of it, forgetting again about her figure, and smiling furtively as she saw herself sitting in a winery that smelled of wood and wine, sipping wine, eating cheese, and listening to stories from a down-home local. She probably looked like what she imagined Ludwig would refer to as an archetypal bourgeois bohemian. Briefly, she wondered what had happened to him.

At around five o' clock, lots of people poured into the winery. One pair, a young, recently married couple on their honeymoon, loudly introduced themselves as Rhonda and Rod from Binghamton to Charlie and anyone else who was within handshaking distance. When someone asked them when they had gotten married, Rhonda, an animated woman dressed in tight jeans and a fuchsia top, which was precariously held up by four strings on one shoulder, looked as if she had just been waiting for the question. Immediately, she seized the chance to speak at length about their wedding. "Oh my God, it was so, so awesome . . . the church ceremony was perfect, not too short, not too long. The priest was so amazing that my mother and sisters and even my brother who never shows any emotion, like never ever, started crying. Oh yeah. You've got to have the right priest, I tell ya. You should have seen the flowers at the reception, oh my God . . . I think they were as good as the flowers at J.Lo's wedding.

I'm telling ya, you had to see it to believe it. The only issue was my uncle, my mother's brother, who's such an asshole and we would have never invited them if my mom hadn't insisted, but luckily he got drunk really early at the reception, and then my cousin took him to the hotel where he totally passed out. Wo . . . that was such a big relief, let me tell ya." And then Rhonda flashed her gigantic, shiny diamond ring at the bar, and a cluster of people gasped.

Once again, Naina found herself feeling, as she still did after thirty-five years in America, both in awe and disgusted by this distinctive American trait for oversharing. Growing up in India and being surrounded by Indians for most of her life in the US, she had been taught that personal affairs were personal and should be kept guarded, apart from close family or friends—even then, if the information was incriminating in any way, close family or friends could also betray you, opening the door to public humiliation. The nuns at her school had espoused a similar view, and Sister Rosemary likened criticizing one's teachers or family members to sinning. All these years, Naina had rarely shared confidences with anyone, and it was only after befriending Alannah, Mara, and Soma that she had become somewhat comfortable discussing private truths. Yet, even now, when she talked about herself, she had to feel like it was occurring inside a tight cocoon of secrecy—a space where no one came in and no one left.

A few minutes later, a group of women, who had been sitting on the other side of the bar, came and sat closer to Naina so they could get a better view of Seneca Lake. At the same time, an Indian-looking man entered the winery alone, only the second South Asian person she had seen in her three days in the Finger Lakes. He sat on the opposite side of the bar, a spot from where Naina knew he could see her, but not hear her. The group of women, sophisticated, well-dressed, and likely in their thirties, were obviously from New York City. One was a tall, alabaster-skinned woman who might have been mistaken as Scandinavian if it weren't for the charming Southern lilt in her voice. She went on about how she was going to be thirty-nine this year and had still not found anyone despite fifteen years of living in New York. A skinny, ethereal-looking Latina, picked up where the Southern woman left off, narrating her own tale of woe. Her French boyfriend had left her in her mid-thirties despite promising marriage and children. The others chimed in with similar stories.

Naina got up, picked up her poetry book, and went to the deck, even though it was slightly chilly and the sun was staring impotently at the lake. She couldn't take it anymore—she felt the aching-hearted, empty-wombed sorrow of these women suck out the sweet weightlessness she had been feeling on this vacation. She knew the right thing to do was to feel sympathy for them (their troubles reminded her of Amaya's after all), but on this trip, she wanted no space inside herself to be weighed down by such concerns. She felt glad she had already been married and already had her children. She thought of Fermina Daza, the female protagonist of Gabriel García Márquez's *Love in the Time of Cholera,* and the immense sense of freedom Fermina felt after her husband, an excellent husband by any standards of time and place, died. She burnt all the unnecessary clutter in her house, making it feel "large, easy, and all hers."

Naina opened her poetry book, which she hadn't read all day, but then put it back on the railing. She looked up at the sky, which had changed again in the last twenty minutes to a painterly medley of grayish black clouds, frail white clouds, and a feeble sun. A veritable study in the peaceful co-existence of contrasts and inconsistencies in nature. Inviting humans to look and learn.

Then she saw a hummingbird perched on a tree, looking regal as it proudly flashed its bright ruby throat, before furiously flying out of sight. Naina remembered how, in the Andes mountains, these birds were viewed as symbols of resurrection, and now that notion appealed to her even more. Naina did not like the idea that the end was the final conclusion, the ultimate termination, or the non-negotiable period or full stop. For her, it was too pessimistic a view. She much preferred the concept of resurrection or rebirth, but without the entrapment of any religious ideology. There was hope, continuity, and change in rising again, as well as poetry, mystery, and inspiration.

The South Asian-looking man, whom she sensed had been discreetly glancing at her in the tasting room, walked out onto the deck, holding his wine—probably the same Cabernet Franc she was drinking. He was of medium height, had a full head of black hair specked with gray, and an average-built body with a slight paunch. He was wearing jeans and a black long-sleeved shirt. His moderately attractive face had some creases on his forehead and under his eyes—probably an indication of the sizable number of years he had spent on Earth. Yet his eyes, though unremarkable from a physical point of view, were rather striking in their luminosity, large ovals of light illuminating his entire face, making it hard to tell how old he was.

The deck was not very large and he leaned on the wooden railing a few feet away from her, staring at the lake. A short while later, he turned toward her. "Doesn't this winery have the best view in the area?"

"Yes, it does," she said, surprised he had spoken to her. Now, he looked like he could be anywhere from fifty to sixty.

"I noticed you were looking at the sky earlier. It changes so fast here."

Naina nodded.

"Oh, by the way, I forgot to introduce myself," he said, walking closer. "I'm Faisal."

"I'm Naina."

"Naina." He smiled, taking his time to enunciate her name. His voice, neither too deep nor too high, was crackling and earthy, like wooden logs burning on a low, steady fire. It was not bad. Rather nice even. "That means eyes, doesn't it?"

"It does," she replied, smiling. "Are you Indian?"

"No, Pakistani, but there isn't really a difference is there? Just a boundary separating two nations that have always been one."

Ah, an attractive, liberal Pakistani. "Yes, that's true."

"You're Indian, I'm guessing."

"Right." Naina placed her empty glass on the wooden railing. He was wearing the cologne Quorum by Puig, which had been around for years. He smelled of wood, leather, and spice, pleasantly pervading the air with a vintage earthy aroma.

"And where do you live now?" Faisal asked.

"In New York City."

"Wow, what a coincidence," Faisal said, looking genuinely pleased. "It's a small world. So do I . . . here to escape the crazy city, aren't you?"

Faisal noticed Naina's empty glass of wine and offered to get her some more.

"Why not?" he said, when she declined his offer. "C'mon, you're in a winery for God's sake."

"Because I've had enough," she said. And she meant it. By no means was she drunk, but she was close to being tipsy.

"You look too sober to have had much." There was that crackling voice and convincing manner. This man seemed like a charmer.

"Really?" Naina said, cocking her head. "You mean, I've fooled the world?"

Faisal laughed, emitting sparks of joy. Few people laughed as if their laughter came from their belly, tickling every organ on their way up. "Yes, very successfully, I might add. Lots of Indian and Pakistani women are very good at concealing things, aren't they?"

"If you say so." Naina shrugged playfully; she was feeling unrestrained today. The Finger Lakes seemed so far, far away from everything.

"There's some truth to it, isn't there?" Faisal said, smiling. "Years ago, one of my aunts in Pakistan used to have three glasses of whiskey in a navy-blue tumbler so it would look like she was drinking water or a soft drink. If she was drunk, no one except her close family members would know. At the end of the evening, when she'd walk back to her car, she'd always have this mother-of-pearl and sterling silver walking stick with her, which she'd never use except after several drinks."

Naina giggled as she imagined a middle-aged woman like herself or older in a salwar kameez in Pakistan where she had heard of laws prohibiting the sale of alcohol, drinking in this odd way that was more open than clandestine, balancing her tipsiness with social grace by carrying an unnecessary, unreasonably fine walking stick, that traditional symbol of elderly refinement. That comical image quickly filled her head as she pictured this aunt in purple silk, dyed hair, librarian glasses, impeccable social graces, and drunk out of her mind, and she laughed even louder.

Faisal also chuckled.

"God, this is so silly . . . I can't believe we're both cracking up," Naina said, slightly embarrassed as she laughed again.

Now, Naina felt a need to say something substantial, intelligent, or at least somewhat witty so Faisal wouldn't think she was a complete nut.

"Your aunt sounds like a very smart woman. In places like India and Pakistan often the older you look, the less anyone can judge you," Naina said a minute or so later. "Agism works in your favor there, unlike in this youth-obsessed country. The walking stick sounds like a really good idea. Maybe I'll try it sometime."

"I can't imagine that," Faisal said, his lips curling into a smile. "You know, when my aunt would stagger back to the car at night, her driver and the neighbors just thought the poor thing was getting old and needed to see her relatives more at that stage in her life. Little did they know that her brother's house had the best whiskey."

Once again, Naina, despite efforts to suppress herself, chortled and Faisal followed suit. She agreed to another glass of Cabernet Franc. As she picked up her glass to give to Faisal, her book next to it fell to the floor. Once again, she felt stirred by the image of a beautiful Persian-looking woman holding a carafe of wine in a fantastical paradise adorning the cover.

Faisal rushed to pick up the book, and then looked at her, his eyes aglow. "So, you're an Omar Khayyam fan?"

"Oh, yes," Naina said, pleased he sounded so knowing about the eleventh-century Persian poet. "*The Rubaiyat* is one of my favorite books."

"Isn't he great with wine?" Faisal had such a look of mischief in his eyes. Naina imagined he must have been a naughty boy when he was young.

"Ha. There couldn't be anyone better. Have you read him?"

"Me? Many, many times." Faisal was now closer and she could smell more of him. The scent of wood, leather, and spice. It was strong and heady. She shouldn't allow herself to be this close to him. She needed to be able to think straight.

"It's interesting, most people in the West would probably not think that a man from the Muslim world could write some of the most eloquent poetry about wine." Naina arched her back a little. "So which is your favorite poem?"

"Well, I like all of them, but if I had to pick one it would be the one about marrying the daughter of the vine."

"Hmmm . . . which one is that?"

Faisal took the book and showed it to her.

> *You know, my Friends, with what a brave Carouse*
> *I made a Second Marriage in my house;*
> *Divorced old barren Reason from my Bed,*
> *And took the Daughter of the Vine to Spouse.*

"That's excellent," Naina said, breaking into a smile and feeling a small mist of shell pink shyness rising from within her. "Divorced old barren reason . . . very nice."

They continued chatting about Omar Khayyam for the next few minutes, discussing whether the Persian poet's quatrains were simply a celebration of hedonism. Faisal said he once heard it referred to as "The Drunkard's Bible" and they laughed again. Naina said she had heard the poet described as a great mystic, the wine just a metaphor for the divine, and the intoxication a metaphor for sublime rapture. Faisal looked at her carefully as they talked, making her feel her cheeks turn pink as she tidied her hair.

"So he was both a mystic and a hedonist," Faisal said. "That way you don't miss out on anything."

Naina told him about a book called *The Wine of the Mystic* she had recently seen, and he quickly jotted down the title in his phone. Naina noticed that Faisal's fingers were, in fact, quite short and stubby, and did not move particularly gracefully.

The weather, as it was apt to in the Finger Lakes, changed again and the weak sun disappeared, dark clouds diminished, the white clouds proliferated, and a gentle breeze made barely audible sounds.

"Ah, isn't the breeze lovely?" Faisal said. "It's so soft, like a whisper in the wind. Just like a whisper in the wind."

He said the words whisper in the wind so deliberately, so purposefully, that Naina felt the warmth rise instantly in in her cheeks and then spread throughout her body as she recognized her old dating site alias. Such an immediate assumption might be seen as an act of absurd paranoia, but she sensed, in her gut, that she wasn't wrong. Faisal hadn't just strung those words in that emphatic, awkward manner and repeated them by accident.

Faisal cleared his throat and looked at her through blinking eyes. "Do you like whispers in the wind? I very much do."

Naina felt a chill sweep over her along with a wave of heat. Like the flu. She felt her shaking body flinch away from Faisal and tried to steady herself. She put her glass of wine down to avoid any chance of a spill. He definitely knew something more about her than he let on. A part of her was so embarrassed that she wanted to run. But then, what exactly did he know?

"What exactly are you trying to say?" Naina said, her tone sharpening into little nibs. She crossed her arms against her thrumming chest.

"Nothing," Faisal said, his voice faltering. "I was just saying that the breeze is beautiful. See, even though the sun is gone, the weather is so pleasant. Breezes here are really lovely, aren't they?"

He sounded sheepish, and he gazed at the lake while her eyes were fixed on him. She was even more convinced that her hunch was right.

"I don't think that's all you were trying to say," Naina said, her voice even more pointed. "I think you need to tell me what you were trying to say."

Faisal averted his gaze, then looked briefly and almost pleadingly at Naina, before shifting his eyes away again.

"You're right," he finally said. "I was being a coward. I'm sorry. I didn't mean to embarrass you."

"You're being very mysterious," Naina said, as she gripped her upper arms with her sweaty palms. "What do you mean?"

A long, thick pause bobbed between them.

"Naina, I'm really enjoying talking to you and I don't want to spoil it," Faisal said, staring at the vast green expanse of vines framed by the Catskill Mountains. "I apologize I was being a bit dodgy, but I just wanted to see . . . uh . . . whether you were the same woman I had written to on . . . on . . . an Internet site last year and I didn't have the guts to ask you directly."

Again, he glanced almost beseechingly at Naina and then hung his head. "Cowardly and immature, I know, I know . . . When I saw you in the tasting room, I felt I had seen you before, but I couldn't remember where. And then when you went to the deck, I remembered that hazy picture of this South Asian woman with a great profile, both the facial one and the written one. It really made an impression on me, as you can probably tell. I just had this nagging feeling that you were the same woman. But I wasn't sure so I thought I would come out here and talk to you and try to figure it out . . . I know I did it in a caddish way. Please forgive me." He paused. "But I was really intrigued by you. You have no idea how many times I read your profile and stared at your picture."

Naina felt her face bristle with cold-hot antagonism as she struggled to conceal her immense curiosity and embarrassment.

"And then my hunch seemed to be correct when you dropped *The Rubaiyat*," Faisal said. "I remembered how you had said you liked Khayyam in your profile. It's not the most common thing people say . . . Then I became even more curious to know if you were the same woman. Dastardly, dastardly, I know." He put his hands deep inside his pockets and stared at the vineyards, his gaze cryptic and sort of worshipful, as if they might contain succor for him.

"And you found out. Now, is your curiosity satisfied?" Naina could hear the steeliness in her voice, staccato intonations marking every word, making it sound more pronounced.

"I behaved like a juvenile ass and I sincerely apologize for that . . . But, I'm not some sleazy cad, I promise."

"Of course not," Naina shot back. "I'm sure you're not. I've got to go. Have a good evening." She picked up her empty glass and started to walk away.

"Naina, please don't go. I should have asked you directly instead of foolishly insinuating . . . but I was nervous and not thinking straight . . . Everybody's a coward sometimes, everybody makes mistakes . . . I'm sure you have too . . . I'm really embarrassed . . . We were having such a wonderful conversation before this . . ." Faisal shook his head and sighed.

"Yes, we were having a good conversation before this, before I knew what you were up to. I don't remember your profile, but I'm glad, for reasons I don't recall now, that I didn't write to you."

"Ouch, that hurt. But I deserve it, I know . . . Naina, I liked you online, much more than anyone else, and I like you even better in person. I know I didn't behave in the most gentlemanly way, but I want you to know I'm really enjoying being with you and I would very much like to spend more time with you . . ."

With her bag firmly hanging on her shoulder, her empty wine glass in one hand, her poetry book in the other, Naina wavered at the sincerity in his voice and saw what looked like real regret on his warm, cheery face. Her view of him morphed into an Impressionist painting with fluid edges and blurry lines from the hard-edged, firmly delineated forms of a classic realistic portrait. Would she have done the same thing if she had been in his position? Maybe.

"What did you say in your profile?" she finally said.

"Nothing interesting obviously since you never wrote back."

Naina laughed, softening even more. There was something really cute about him.

"Probably not, but maybe you could help refresh my memory. When did you write to me?"

"I doubt you'll remember," Faisal said. "It was a while ago."

"But when did you write?"

"Last summer, I think. Probably didn't even register with you."

Faisal, once again, put his hands in his pockets and looked away. He still looked so sheepish that Naina almost felt sorry for him. Of course, she had made mistakes. Especially one colossal one. But now was not the time to think about it.

"Maybe I will remember and maybe I won't."

"All right, let me brace myself for embarrassment now." Faisal folded his arms. "It was a short profile. I think I mentioned I loved After Eight chocolates and pista kulfi. And Omar Khayyam. And that I didn't like British dramas." She could hear the soft rattling of his keys in his pocket as he moved back and forth. "I don't know if any of this is unique, but I think that whatever else I said was completely dull . . . probably in no way different from what many men I'm sure wrote to you . . . I'm sure you don't remember it."

But she did remember it, vaguely but definitely, an amusing, self-deprecating profile that unlike so many others, did not seem to try too hard. She recalled yearning for pista kulfi, the North Indian pistachio-flavored ice cream after reading the profile, and remembered the After Eight chocolates, those thin British mint chocolates that were all the rage in her family and viciously fought over when anyone came from England. She remembered thinking about how she wanted to curate a show featuring biscuits and chocolates to talk about British colonialism in India, and how that plan never seemed to come together. But she also remembered that, at the time, she was involved with Ludwig and close to deleting her profile on mysoulmate.com.

"I do recall it," Naina said, breaking into a small smile. "It made me very hungry."

Faisal laughed, a hearty chortle that seemed to come from his recesses, and she began to feel her muscles drop their guard.

"I'm glad it left some impression on you," Faisal said, relief visible on his face. "Talking about being hungry, are you hungry?"

"For pista kulfi?"

"Oh come on now. You know I can't find that in the Finger Lakes . . . Would anything else please madam?"

"No," Naina said, shaking her head. "Just pista kulfi."

"Oh, I see you are not easy to please."

She shook her head.

"Ok, how about some great homemade pasta?"

She smiled, but shook her head again.

"How about some great salmon?"

She smiled and shook her head again.

"How about some Thai?"

Naina laughed. "You never give up, do you?" she said, placing her empty glass on the wooden railing and her left hand on her hips.

"It depends," he said. "In this case, I'd kick myself in the shins if I gave up easily."

THAT NIGHT, THEY stayed out until ten-thirty, the last guests to leave the serene open-air Middle Eastern restaurant next to Seneca Lake. Beneath the stars that would momentarily shine and then go into hiding under the nomadic clouds, they first talked about what was on everyone's minds in 2008—the presidential election.

Faisal loved Obama, with his message of hope and change, his potential to be a transformative, uniting figure, and above all, his appeal for public service. But Naina wasn't so sure about him. She liked Obama's passionate oratory, powerful use of language, electrifying charisma, and mixed-race background, but there was something, something she couldn't quite put her finger on, that kept her from trusting him, afraid he might be a chimera too good to be true. Plus, she still had a soft spot for Hillary Clinton, vanquished in the primaries by Obama, who, with her naked ambition, resolute focus on changing the country despite significant public setbacks in her political life, tarnished yet functional marriage, blazing brilliance without any extra helpings of feminine charm, seemed more relatable than Obama with his radical empath image branded flawlessly and effortlessly as if created by a high-end corporation, impeccably designed website, enviable marriage, lean body, and unflappable coolness.

As the evening proceeded, Naina asked Faisal about himself. He was an international business lawyer with a large firm, though he worked part-time now. He was born in Lahore and lived there for sixteen years before going to England for college where he spent about thirty years before moving to New York. A softness crept in her voice when he spoke of London, and she could tell that the city's thoughts still kept his heart warm. He had no children but had been married for several years to a German woman he had met at university. Then he paused, and his luminous eyes receded into some old dark pit with cobwebs and dead bats. His wife had died six years earlier of Alzheimer's disease. Naina did not probe.

Faisal asked Naina questions, but she wasn't in a mood to talk about herself, deflecting or cursorily answering his questions until he seemed to understand her intent. Faisal followed her to her cabin in his car, saying he wanted to make sure she got back safe after all that drinking. Even though it was dark and secluded next to her cabin, he made no attempt to kiss her or do anything even vaguely suggestive, and parted from her by shaking her hand and repeating that he had really a good evening. He did, however, ask her which wineries she planned to visit the next day, her second to last day in the Finger Lakes.

A few seconds after he headed to his car, Naina realized that he, too, had had a fair amount to drink and would be driving alone with no one to keep an eye on him. She ran toward him and asked him to text her to let her know he had reached his hotel. He smiled warmly, and his eyes flickered like fireflies in the cavernous night. He asked for her mobile phone number, teasing her that he would wake her up at seven in the morning, the time he always woke up, regardless of when he slept, after he turned fifty.

Naina went into her cabin and quickly changed and got ready for bed, refusing to yield to her exhaustion until she heard from Faisal.

CHAPTER THIRTY-FOUR

THE NEXT DAY turned out to be gorgeous, a sunny 82 degrees, and Naina decided to wear jeans, a fuchsia-colored sleeveless top, accessorized by earrings made of colored wooden beads. She entered Twilight Waters, a tall sunset-colored winery with asymmetrical elements that had been designed by a young German architect who created structures inspired by the aesthetics of the Bauhaus movement and found Faisal sitting at the bar. He was sipping a glass of wine and reading a book of Sufi poetry. It was just noon, yet Naina somehow sensed he had been there for a long time. The sight of him made her glad. He greeted her warmly, asked her if she had slept well, complimented her necklace, and told her that the Gewürztraminer were good. The air between them was lighter and looser as the shadows of the awkard incident of the previous day receded further. Still, the topic of Internet dating or relationships never came up.

"So did you grow up around a lot of Sufi poetry?" Naina asked. She knew little about Sufi or Middle Eastern poetry besides Khayyam and Rumi.

"No, no way," Faisal said, with a big merry smile, so different from that measly half-smile of Jai. "Some of us Pakistanis grew up just as colonized as you people in India. I did my Senior Cambridge in the late sixties and there was no Brown man's poetry in the syllabus . . . Just poets like that sweet, nature-loving Wordsworth, that tragic Keats, and that Don Juan-loving wanderer Byron."

"Oh my goodness . . . wow," Naina said.

"Yes. Senior Cambridge . . . gosh, I haven't thought of that exam in years . . . I used to love Byron. Do you remember that poem . . . oh, what's it called . . . *She walks in beauty like the night of cloudless climes and starry skies* and . . . and . . ."

"*All that's best of dark and bright meet in her aspect and her eyes.*"

Once again, they erupted in laughter. A grave-looking elderly couple sitting next to them stared with reproachful eyes, and Naina and Faisal grinned at each other like two children caught doing something naughty. They spoke more softly to each other, amplifying everything they were feeling.

"Do you remember Dickens?" said Naina.

"Of course." Faisal made a face. "That miserable writer writing about an even more miserable England. I could never get through that damn *David Copperfield.*"

"Oh, come on," Naina said, cocking up her head. "I loved Dickens. How could anyone not like Dickens? But I preferred *Tale of Two Cities* to *Copperfield*."

"What about the Brontés? Were you also one of those girls who loved the Bronté sisters?"

"Oh, yes. Of course."

They were now outside, on the grounds of the winery, and sitting on a bench. Her legs were crossed while he was perched on the edge with his legs slightly apart. Naina looked up at the sky, which had changed yet again. The sun had disappeared, and the sky now looked like a frothy vanilla milk shake. "I remember reading *Wuthering Heights* in the horribly hot summer of sixty-nine, in the back of the house, and dreaming of those chilly Yorkshire Plains and of Heathcliff."

"Ah Heathcliff, so you liked Heathcliff," Faisal said, a smile on his lips. "My cousins use to be in love with him. One of them used to say she would only marry someone who reminded her of Heathcliff and no one else."

"I think everyone went through that phase," Naina said, tossing her head back and laughing.

"So even *you* wanted to marry a Heathcliff?" he asked, his teasing gaze on her.

Suddenly, Naina, unable to meet his eyes, felt shy. "I was not that different from everybody else," She lifted her hand to her throat and turned the wooden beads on her necklace.

"Now you don't expect me to believe that, do you?" Faisal said, the mirth in his face making it seem even more expansive.

Naina put her hands in her lap, her left wrist limp and exposed, which she stroked with her right hand. "I may have liked Heathcliff then, but I no longer think he's this grand, romantic hero. Heathcliff is downright cruel, and although terrible things happened to him, which one can be sympathetic toward, it does not excuse his being so violent and hateful and so remorseless about it. One time, he killed his wife Isabella's dog . . . I can never forget Heathcliff's words, *The first thing she saw me do, on coming out of the Grange, was to hang up her little dog; and when she pleaded for it, the first words I uttered were a wish that I had the hanging of every being belonging to her, except one: possibly she took that exception for herself.*"

"My goodness . . . cruel is an understatement," Faisal said. "I read the book ages ago and even then I don't think I quite understood why women would swoon over him."

Naina was quiet for a moment, thinking about how she had conflated Heathcliff and Jai together in her head. "So, did your Heathcliff-obsessed cousin actually marry someone like him?"

"No, far from it. But she did initially fall in love with someone who went on raging rampages like Heathcliff. Her parents absolutely refused to let her marry him. When she told him, he was furious and once threw a stone at her father's car. No one was hurt, but it showed her what the man was capable of and she wanted to have nothing to do with him after that. She ended up having an arranged marriage with a neuroscientist and is actually very happy."

"Saved from the likes of Heathcliff by protective parents and ushered into unending joy by an arranged marriage."

Faisal laughed, his eyes glistening. His eyes were really quite remarkable. They made her think of full moons, huge balls of light illuminating the night sky. In Hinduism, full moons were considered harbingers of good fortune and several festivals were held during those days. Of course, in Western culture, full moons were associated with madness—but didn't his eyes seem auspicious and a little mad at the same time?

"You know, even bigger than Heathcliff was Mr. Darcy." Naina looked away from Faisal again. "I think every Indian mother wanted to find good homegrown versions of Mr. Darcy to marry their daughters to."

"Aha," Faisal said. "I think it was the same across the border."

Under the fluttering umbrella of flirtatious signals, Naina and Faisal continued trading stories of their lives in India and Pakistan, narratives in which fact, fantasy, and fiction bled into each other, further jumbled by the muddied lens of memory. He told her how he used to bet on which plane brought the results of the Senior Cambridge exams from England, and she told him how her grandmother never believed their papers were marked in England because she didn't believe the British would spend their time grading papers of Indians. She told him about being glued in front of *The Lucy Show* on a black-and-white TV set in Delhi; he told her about his hero worship of the Beatles and his parents' horror when he first wore orange bell-bottom pants before going to a rock 'n' roll party in Lahore in 1970. He told her about his adolescent curiosity about India where he was told people of more than six religions happily lived together and she told him about her teenage longing for fancy foreign cars that she believed Pakistan had—unlike India, which had only that sad and slow car called Ambassador because of India's anti-import laws.

They were still sitting next to each other on the bench in the vineyard grounds, their bodies curving like vines toward each other, eating dark hazelnut chocolates and sipping Reisling. Though, in many ways, their lives were similar, there were significant differences, and Naina, fascinated by his unusual background, asked him countless questions. To start with, his family sounded much more elite than hers. His father, who came from a family of landowners, was a British-educated lawyer whose favorite sport was polo and he encouraged both his sons to play the sport, the only sport besides cricket that, in his opinion, a gentleman should play. And when Faisal would resist, being no good at controlling horses, his father would beat him with hardbound books of Shakespeare, he said, a wry smile on his lips.

Naina flung her head back and laughed. Somehow the image of Faisal, with his stocky body, slightly protruding belly, unremarkable arms and legs, and movements like those of a kindly bull, simultaneously trying to manage a horse and swing a mallet was just too funny.

"Yes, I know, I know . . . I looked pretty ridiculous playing polo."

"Gosh . . . I'm sorry . . . I wasn't thinking that." Naina covered her mouth, still laughing.

"You know I even fell off the horse a few times."

"Oh no." Naina laughed. "Did you get injured?"

"Just my ego and my not-so-flat behind," he said, with a droll smile. "But that was nothing compared to my father taking me to task."

"Did he really beat you with hardbound books of Shakespeare?" Naina asked, her eyes turning big and incredulous.

Faisal nodded.

"I'm sure it probably hurt, but that has to be one of the most comical things I have ever heard."

"Well, I aim to please, my lady."

Naina felt her eyes sparkling like those of a cat, certain a tint of greenish gold was emerging from the brown. Faisal was a good storyteller like Jai. But there was a difference. Faisal's style was more extemporaneous than Jai's, and when he spoke, his whole face opened and moved, like a hibiscus unfurling its petals and swaying with the wind. Meanwhile, Jai's story remained confined to the modulations and inflections of his rehearsed voice and to the glow in his chocolate-colored eyes, a gleam that compared with Faisal's full moon dazzle, seemed barely a glow at all. Then another analogy jumped up like a monkey from the marshes of Naina's mind, an analogy that made her inwardly blush and reprimand herself for having such obscene thoughts. While telling a story, Faisal's face opened like a liberated woman's legs unafraid of seeking pleasure, whereas Jai's face was like that of a prim and proper girl with her legs crossed, wanting pleasure, flirting with pleasure, but too scared to actually seek it.

"What are you thinking?" Faisal said.

"Nothing," Naina said, moving some strands of her hair from her face. "Tell me more . . . what was your father's relationship with Islam like?"

Repositioning himself closer to Naina, Faisal said his father was also unusual in his virulent opposition to religion, forbidding the family from celebrating Eid or fasting during Ramadan. He would be furious with his wife, a demure woman only educated until the fifth grade, when she tried to secretly fast. The only religious festival the family was allowed to celebrate was Christmas, for which his father would host a big party of a hundred people with a big tree and ensure all the children got grand presents. He liked to read Nietzsche, Marx, Shakespeare, Pope, Dryden, Oscar Wilde, Bernard Shaw, but disdained anything that was not British or European. He passionately detested ghazals, calling the traditional

Urdu poetry set to music something made for "unsophisticated imbeciles" and thought Hindustani classical music sounded like an alarm clock waking up the dead. The family was only allowed to eat with knives and forks, and if anyone dared to ask for something on the table, saying "Can I have that?" his father would give them his fierce look until the person said *may* instead of *can.*

Faisal's mother, though, spoke limited English, a fact that remained a thorn in his father's flesh until he died. He hired British tutors followed by Pakistani women who were fluent in Urdu as well as English, yet she never mastered the language, perpetually putting the verb establishing tense after the active verb or adjective as was the case in Punjabi and Urdu. His mother's first name was Gulab, only the sound of it was so coarse to his father's ears that he called her by its English equivalent "Rose."

Faisal's father also passionately hated America, calling its people bandars (monkeys) with no civilization, corrupting the English language in a way that even the people of the subcontinent had not. All of this made Naina laugh, still it also really surprised her. She had heard about brown sahibs—although never of anyone as extreme as Faisal's father. And what did that make Faisal? An unbearable Anglophile? But then why did he know about Omar Khayyam?

What truly stunned Naina was Faisal's father reaction to his son, the older of only two, marrying a German woman, because no matter how Westernized Indians or Pakistanis were, they generally wanted their offspring to marry within their own community. Instead, his father was thrilled at the prospect of a German daughter-in-law whose family had fled to England from Germany during World War II. His father did not ask Greta to convert to Islam and was delighted to go to England to attend their wedding in a synagogue. He held a grand outdoor reception for them in Lahore and asked Greta to wear a long dress and broad-brimmed hat and not a traditional salwar kameez or lehenga choli, much to the horror of everyone in Pakistan. And his mother, what did his poor mother feel about this marriage, Naina asked, trying to imagine her distress.

Alas, his mother was not happy about it, Faisal said. Sheepishly, he also revealed, that, at the time, he was too young and caught up in himself to have been as sensitive to his mother's feelings as he, in retrospect, should have been.

"That is one of my big regrets," Faisal said, putting his hands in his pockets.

"Does it weigh upon you?"

"I wouldn't say that, not anymore at least. But there's still a residue and I expect that will always remain. But life has to go on."

They sat in silence for a few minutes.

"So how did you go from being this British sahib with a German wife and indoctrination in nothing but Western culture to someone who loves Sufi poetry and Middle Eastern and Pakistani music?" Naina asked, tingling with curiosity. She tilted her head to her left and moved her hair to the side of her neck.

"That's another story," Faisal said, handing her another hazelnut chocolate. "I'll tell you later. First tell me about you and your family. Did they migrate from what is now Pakistan like a lot of Punjabis?"

After declaring that she could not eat any more hazelnut chocolates, Naina told him her story, aware it was not nearly as interesting as his. She told him her grandparents had moved to Delhi from Lahore and that her maternal grandmother spoke of Lahore as a city paved with gold. She spoke about her idealistic, gentle father and described how he was often lost in Urdu ghazals and sentimental Hindi melodies. Her father generally ate with his hands and a spoon—hands for things like roti and tandoori meats—and a spoon for scooping up dal, vegetables, and yogurt. Unlike Faisal's polo-playing father, the closest her father ever got to sports was listening to the cricket scores on the radio and then when television came to India, watching cricket matches. Like his father, her father also drank whiskey, not every day but on special occasions, and even then, he never had more than one glass. As for America, her father knew little about the country except that its charismatic leader Kennedy had been tragically killed, and that it was a wellspring of wealth and opportunity.

By dusk, Naina and Faisal had been to three wineries and drove to an open-air steakhouse on Cayuga Lake for dinner. As soon as their food was served, Naina reminded Faisal to tell her how he came to discover Sufi poetry and Middle Eastern and South Asian music.

It happened about a decade before when he moved to New York, Faisal said between bites of steak au poivre. After living in London for so many years as a British Pakistani, who was more British than Pakistani and married to a German woman, he had grown accustomed with his identity, which seemed unremarkable to him, and one few people around him questioned or even seemed curious about. And, because he had lived in London for so long, he already had his old friends who had known him for a long time. At that point, no one expected him to explain himself or anything about Pakistan.

But when he came to New York, he was instantly confronted with a quintessentially American blaze of questions and unmitigated inquisitiveness. Where was he from? Not England, where he'd lived in for twenty-five years, but originally? What did his language, not English, but the one native to his country, sound like? Would he teach them to say *I love you?* and curse in that musical language? Since Pakistan was so close to India, did they have those long-haired, bearded holy men there too? Did his mother cover her head? What was the significance of that? Did he pray five or six times a day? Could he tell us more about Islam? And then, there were the questions from the more worldly, cultured lot. What did he think of Nusrat Fateh Ali Khan? Was there a big Sufi presence in Pakistan? How was the Islam practiced in Pakistan different from that of other Middle Eastern countries? How did Pakistan see globalization? Had he gone to see the exhibit of such-and-such Pakistani artist in Chelsea?

But Faisal, who knew little about Pakistani culture and Islam and had not even been back to the country since his parents died in the late eighties, felt discombobulated by these questions, unsettled by the expectation that he was supposed to be able to respond knowledgeably to these queries, and bothered by this attempt to bond him to his heritage, a heritage he had never felt particularly aligned with.

"It was all foreign to me, but not foreign enough," Faisal said.

And he was perturbed by his own paucity of understanding—his own lack of awareness about South Asia and the Middle East. So, he started to read Rumi, the thirteenth-century Persian poet, recommended by an American colleague who told him he was one of the most widely read poets in America. He was struck by the beauty, wisdom and ecstasy of Rumi's poetry and it brought back memories of his whiskey-swiveling aunt talking about the poet when he was young. Then he read Omar Khayyam, Hafiz, and Faiz Ahmed Faiz; listened to Nusrat Fateh Ali Khan, Abida Parveen, and Junoon; pored over various books on Sufism, and read the Quran for the first time in its entirety along with books on the architecture of Lahore. He was intrigued and fascinated by everything he was discovering, annoyed it had taken him so long to discover the treasures in his own backyard. Then, he couldn't stop. He devoured the poetry of Kabir, the fifteenth-century mystical North Indian poet, a book on the Hindu temples of Pakistan, and several biographies of Gandhi, Nehru, and Jinnah. During this time, the oud, a Middle Eastern pear-shaped string instrument, became one of his favorite instruments, and he began to love its soulful, melancholy sound as much as he loved the sound of his beloved guitar.

Naina was impressed. Faisal spoke with such passion. The sort of passion that steeped the soul, reddened the blood, and made it surge through the body. A force as vivid as the mad, auspicious light of full moons.

Faisal continued, saying that when September 11 struck, suddenly every unthreatening-looking, clean-cut Muslim by birth was forced into the position of being a spokesman for the entire Islamic world. While September 11 did sadly lead to a widespread demonization of Muslims, there was a small consolation, Faisal said as Naina looked at him with surprise. In a flash, there was an unprecedented interest in Islamic culture in the West, a frenzied effort to at least attempt to understand the world of those who supposedly wanted to destroy them. Faisal felt if he was going to be able to talk somewhat intelligently about the Islamic world, he needed to know more about it.

It was well past ten at night, and they had finished dinner, dessert, and wine more than an hour before. It was extremely dark, and the lighting was not good, yet Naina noticed that Faisal's cheerful face looked tired, that the marks on his face seemed more pronounced, and that the shadows under his eyes looked darker. Unlike a few hours earlier, he now looked like he was in his mid-fifties, which was how old she guessed he was. She didn't want to press him with any more questions, but there was one question she couldn't resist asking, a question that had been tugging at her while he had been talking. Did all this learning make him a more religious Muslim?

"No," he replied, laughing. "Not at all. Enjoying some of the great culture that's come out of the Islamic world is not the same as becoming more Muslim. That's like saying being interested in European culture makes you more Christian." He leaned forward on the table, the corners of his mouth again turned upward in his wry manner. "Not that you've noticed, but I do drink more than I should sometimes, and I'm told I make really good ham sandwiches."

He lifted his eyebrows and smiled mischievously, a smile that melted years off his face. "But there's one aspect of Islam that I really like. The four wives aspect. Now, that sounds really good except that you have to treat them equally. There can't be an iota of difference. Tell me, which man can do that?"

The two of them burst into laughter again, their voices crackling in the quiet of the starless night.

CHAPTER THIRTY-FIVE

NAINA LEFT THE Finger Lakes the next morning, listening to a CD of the Pakistani Sufi singer Nusrat Fateh Ali Khan (one of Faisal's favorite musicians that she found tucked away at the back of her CD binder) as she drove past sun-soaked, scenic rolling hills before embarking on the highway. She felt happy, a quiet joy, like a dew-nuzzled dawn before the world awakens, radiated upward from her gut. She hummed along to "Afreen," a heady, daze-inducing song about a beloved whose greatness is beyond praise, her favorite by Nusrat Fateh Ali Khan and one she played repeatedly.

But there was one thing that kept bothering her, constantly poking her like a shard of glass stuck inside her foot. Faisal was Muslim by birth (even though he was non-practicing) and Pakistani. Typically, something like that would have never perturbed her because she, who prided herself on her open-mindedness, had been friendly with Pakistanis ever since she moved to America. And whenever Harish, whose eldest brother was in the Indian army, would mumble about how Pakistanis were never to be trusted, she would tell him to stop being biased, reminding him that Indians and Pakistanis shared a common language, history, and culture. After September 11, she had felt terrible for all the Muslims that were speciously detained and shuddered when she heard that Afzal Hamid, the soft-spoken Pakistani cashier at her neighborhood juice store in New Jersey, had a strawberry banana smoothie thrown at him along with a volley of insults by a college student. During that time, she had vigorously defended Muslims and Islam to Americans and even to those Hindus in their circle whose latent prejudices against Muslims quickly steamed to the surface, hot and billowy, after the 9/11 attacks.

Naina had insisted that all religions had radical, extremist elements, but that did not mean that all people from that religion were bad. And even at the gallery, she had pushed to show Muslim artists, and arranged panel discussions to foster a more comprehensive view of women in Islam.

But alone in her car now, as the prospect of some sort of relationship with a Pakistani man, even one that seemed as open-minded as Faisal, loomed, she found herself uneasy as sweaty drops of prejudice seeped into her from the swamps of her brain, from a place below her conscious mind, so hot that it melted all reason. Here, in this primal swamp there was just raw sensation and old generational wounds; here, in this place the difference between one and all just became one hot haze; here, in this place, facts, humanity, and compassion could not cleanse the stale, stubborn, stagnant waters still holding on to the refuse of the past. Naina was shocked and disturbed to find this existed inside her.

She remembered her grandmother describing her brother being slaughtered while they were on a train fleeing Pakistan for India during The Partition. "They (Muslims) are brutal, they are animals," her grandmother would say, choking up with grief and rage. "They cut him into pieces. Right in front of our very eyes. Tell me, which human being does that? They slaughter a goat for Bakrid. Slaughter a goat? Now tell me, what kind of religion tells people to do that?"

Naina winced, recalling the faded black-and-white photograph of her great uncle, with his gentle chocolate boy good looks, a photograph that she had seen so many times. To think that he had been slaughtered at twenty-two. She recollected her grandmother describing that gruesome scene to her over and over when Naina was just four or five years old and how it gave her terrible nightmares that made her shriek in the middle of the night.

She pulled over. She couldn't drive like this. But what did any of this have to do with Faisal? She was angry at her feelings, at the prejudices she didn't even know she had, rising from the marshes of her very own self.

Looking out into space, she recalled that even her own mother, who had a close Muslim friend and socialized with her husband's Muslim colleagues, never fully trusted them, insisting that privately all of them were loyal to Pakistan. And no matter how progressive they seemed, they treated women badly, her mother insisted. Growing up, Naina had understood she was to marry a good Hindu, but in the awful circumstance that she transgressed and wanted to marry someone else, it had to be a Sikh, a Parsi, or a Christian. *Anyone* was better than a Muslim. "They will jail you in purdah and go off and marry other women and that will be the end of you," she remembered her mother telling her when she was a young girl and asking her mother why she shouldn't marry a Muslim man.

The song "Afreen" ended again. She turned off the music, preferring the silence. She pulled back on the road.

Slowing down as she approached a toll booth, she recollected, how, at the age of seventeen, she had developed a strong attraction to the handsome, beautifully mannered son of her father's Muslim colleague and spent many nights dreaming about him reading Urdu poetry and singing ghazals to her, the fantasy of it heightened by its impossibility. Fareed, yes, Fareed, that was the boy's name.

No, Naina said to herself, clenching her fists on the steering wheel. *No*. She would not allow the muddy swamps of herself dictate how she should think or feel. She had to let go of the past. The swamp had to be decimated. Reason had to triumph. Otherwise, there was no point in having a mind. Or a will, for that matter.

FAISAL CALLED NAINA a day after he returned to New York and asked her to join him at a qawwali performance by a Karachi troupe called the Ansari Brothers on Saturday. Naina accepted. She dressed carefully, wearing a shapely deep red kurti that covered half her hips, tailored black pants and an intricately carved gold pendant on her neck. She arrived ten minutes after the performance had started and spotted him, dressed in light tan pants and a crisp white shirt, standing at the entrance and anxiously turning his head in every direction. Nervous she might have upset him by being late, she started to almost run toward him, her heels clicking loudly on the pavement, afraid she would slip and fall. His anxious expression melted into a big, broad smile when he saw her, immediately putting her at ease.

He asked her if she was all right, if she needed water, considering the heat. Naina said yes and he quickly got a bottle of water for her. As they walked down the tricky stairs, he warned her to watch her step, and when she dropped the program, he picked it up. All this old-fashioned courtliness was very charming and made Naina feel like a young girl. She felt ashamed of her uncharitable feelings during her drive back from the Finger Lakes. How could she have felt that way? Of course, that didn't make those feelings disappear, but she vowed to pay no attention to them. That way they would either cease existing or cease having any influence on her.

The qawwali was a concert of Sufi devotional music, with the two Ansari brothers as the lead singers. Other musicians played the harmonium or percussion instruments like the tabla and dholak, and some repeatedly clapped their hands. They were all men.

Naina thought it was awful. It was loud, strident, discordant, and often the voices sounded like funereal wails, emitting no feeling of grief, just plenty of noise. And the constant hand clapping—it was getting on her nerves. She tried to contain herself, not to show any signs of her displeasure when Faisal seemed so obviously rapt. During the concert, he whispered in her ear to ask if she was enjoying the music. She replied in the affirmative.

"Are you sure?" he persisted. "We can leave if you don't like it."

"I'm a hundred percent sure."

He quizzically smiled at her. "If you say so."

After the concert, he asked her if she would like to listen to some live jazz and have some soul food. Naina was glad—the thought of jazz sounded soothing after all that jarring noise. Just like in the Finger Lakes, conversation flowed easily between them at dinner; once again they ended up laughing a lot, and by the end of the evening when they were a little tipsy, they started teasing each other.

"You put up a good front pretending to like the concert, well-behaved, convent-educated Miss Naina," Faisal said.

"Oh, how dare you accuse me of deception, sir?" Naina retorted, leaning back on her chair and placing her hands on her hips.

"It's a skilled art form. You seem pretty good at it." The impish grin once again came over his face, making him look so much younger.

She felt her blood turn warm, sweet, and heady like the hot buttered rum she was drinking. "And what proof do you have that I was lying, Mr. Anglo Sufi Prosecutor?"

"Your body was stiff like a stone during the qawwali. Murde ki tarah tha tumhara jism (Your body was like that of a corpse)."

"Who asked you to take me to a such a terrible qawwali anyway, sir?"

Faisal kissed Naina on a quiet spot in the street, his lips tentatively hovering over hers before she could no longer take it and thrust her tongue into his mouth. When he dropped her home in a taxi, he asked her to take him to something related to art, and she invited him for an exhibition of a Vietnamese artist at the Asia Society on Wednesday.

Soon, they were meeting often, as much as three or four times a week. Sometimes, they did things they had planned and sometimes they met for an impromptu coffee, movie, or dinner. He was the only man Naina knew who could enjoy a romantic comedy as much as a woman, and they would go watch the latest summer movies at a theater near her gallery and gorge on popcorn. They also went out dancing to a small club in the East Village with seventies music and decor, with both of them shaking vigorously when any Abba song came on, a major musical force in both their lives during their adolescent years and beyond. Central Park was one of Faisal's favorite spots in New York and they often went there on Sundays, carrying wine, cheese, and grapes. It was there that they read poetry to each other.

Despite the comfort they felt around each other, Naina never felt fully at ease with him when they were out. Every time they went somewhere, she would thoroughly investigate it to check if Amaya or any of her friends were around. She did not want to get caught. She had no intention of telling her daughter, who still did not have a boyfriend, or her son, about Faisal. At least not yet. How awful it would be for Amaya to see her mother find a relationship before her, reversing the natural order of things, the thought chilling Naina as guilt, that chronic illness, showed its grisly, wretched face again. She had already behaved in an unnatural, deviant way before. She did not need to make matters worse.

She briefly explained her behavior when they were out to Faisal who, being South Asian, seemed to understand a widowed mother's unease with telling her children about her romantic relationship. But Naina was worried that Amaya was becoming suspicious. It was there in the way she rolled her eyes and said "uhumm" when Naina gave an elaborate lie about where she had gone; there in her probing eyes when she asked her why she suddenly had so many books on

Pakistani and Middle Eastern poetry; there in the pointed inflection of her voice when she asked why she was suddenly wearing so much green, a color she had previously never shown any favor to until she discovered it was Faisal's favorite color. Not too long after they started seeing each other, Faisal, without any probing from Naina, told her about his marriage to Greta, a sweet geography teacher with whom he found less and less in common with as he grew older.

"I became a glutton for life and she started to live like she was on a diet," Faisal said as they walked, hand in hand, in Central Park. Though it was still warm, the trees' leaves had started to turn orange, red, and gold. It was their last moment of glory that year. Very soon, the leaves would turn the trees brown and bereft, the notion affecting Naina more than usual.

"Did you love her?" Naina asked, looking at him, and then discreetly to her right and left, constantly looking out for Amaya or her friends.

"I think so," Faisal said, his eyes softening, his voice tender like an early morning drizzle. "Absolutely in the beginning. And then, and then, I don't know . . . I always had tons of affection for her. She was a wonderful person . . . it's funny, I thought our relationship would be different because we had a love marriage. But no, I came to realize that that was not the case. There doesn't have to be a huge difference between love and arranged marriages, you know. The result can be the same, but the path is just different."

Naina looked at his pensive face. What an interesting observation.

Shortly after Faisal and Greta moved to New York, Faisal noticed that Greta, typically an organized person, started to repeatedly lose things like her keys and her wallet, struggled to find ordinary words like chair, table, hot, and cold, and once even panicked as she sat holding a five-dollar bill, saying she did not know what to do with this odd piece of paper that had strangely appeared in her hands. He became worried, thinking it had something to do with the move to New York, and tried to take her to a doctor. But Greta, who had an irrational fear of doctors, would not agree until he found her crying in the bathroom late one night, telling him that something horrible had happened to her. She begged him to save her.

Specters moved across Faisal's face, and his eyes looked out in the distance. Naina squeezed his hand.

The next day, he took Greta to a doctor who referred her to a psychiatrist. The psychiatrist said it was an acute case of depression and gave her a strong dose of antidepressants. But they didn't help, and he helplessly watched Greta decline. And then two things happened that convinced him that something much more serious than depression was happening to his wife; she put her blue scarf, a much-cherished gift from her mother, in the fridge, and told a plumber that she was not sure which country she was from in utter seriousness. He took Greta to a series of doctors until one finally told him that he suspected that his wife had Alzheimer's disease at the age of forty-five.

Naina had no words to tell him how dreadful she felt that he had to go through this or how deeply she felt for him. Everything that came to mind seemed trite or contrived. So under an American elm tree, she gave him a big, tight hug, trying to merge both of them. Through his cotton shirt, she could hear the sounds of his heartbeat, robust and fast like a galloping horse. They walked in silence from the Bethesda fountain in Central Park, where lots of people had gathered, to a quiet patch of grass. A few orange leaves were scattered on the ground. Naina picked them up and opened a bag of crackers, cheese, and grapes.

Naina urged Faisal to continue telling her about Greta, feeling he needed talk about it as much as she needed to hear about it. He described how Greta quickly deteriorated, wearing sweaters and hats in the height of summer, crying at the sight of her own reflection in the mirror, shredding tissues in the afternoons, and losing her way after buying toothpaste at a deli next to their apartment. She needed full-time help, so he hired a nurse to look after her for eight hours a day and reduced his work hours so he could spend more time with her. He couldn't bring himself to send her to a nursing home; he didn't know why, and she remained at home even when she was unable to recognize him or eat or go to the toilet by herself.

Faisal was hunched over on the grass, slowly and absently eating grapes. Recently, he had lost some weight and his shoulders were naturally narrow. Underneath the tall, flaming trees and the vast landscape of the park, he looked small. But, in Naina's mind, he loomed large, larger than any man had ever loomed. A man made vast by his capacity for generosity and compassion. She felt grateful to have him in her life.

Greta eventually died because of diabetes-related complications in the early morning of Sept. 11, 2001, before the terrorists flew their planes into the World Trade Center. Faisal remembered New York City turning into a big, public mourning ground after the horrific event with crude posters of photographs, hand-scribbled names of missing people, and makeshift memorials spilling everywhere like blood. He turned to walking the streets aimlessly, his own grief about Greta mingling with the collective grief, each hemorrhaging each other until he couldn't tell them apart.

While Faisal personally never suffered from the backlash against Muslims in America—except for a few unwelcome stares—he was deeply troubled by the secret detentions and offered his services as an interpreter to a well-known immigration attorney. This also provided a distraction for him.

Naina was even more impressed. She sliced a few pieces of cheese, put them on crackers and offered them to him.

It took more than a year, but his appetite for life did return, Faisal said. He decided to take some time off and travel to Pakistan and India for six months. It was then, as time and space magnified without Greta to take care of, that he recognized he was lonely, and had been for years. He found he wanted to be with a woman again, but didn't know how to go about finding someone at his age. He turned to the Internet two years earlier, but that endeavor had not been successful because some women didn't want to go out with a man from Pakistan, some didn't find him interesting, and others he didn't find interesting.

"And then I got lucky," Faisal said, planting a gentle kiss on Naina's cheek that sent a gush through her body.

IT WAS WITH Faisal that Naina learned to fully drop her guard around a man for the first time; it was with him that she became a child that made funny faces and tickled underarms; it was with him that she let the first man since Harish touch her when her legs were not waxed; it was with him that she cried and laughed when she discovered a gray hair in her pubic area.

Naina also found herself revealing facts about herself (and even fictions she would teasingly tell him) and her life in an unfettered, cavalier way. She told him about her marriage with Harish and she sensed that he instinctively understood what she meant without any need for elaborate explanations or disclaimers or need to present information in a particularly cautious and balanced way. She felt thankful she was with a man from her part of the world, someone who intuitively understood the complex texture of arranged marriages, and the potential for both great contentment and great boredom it could breed. Or great love, as in the case of his Heathcliff-loving cousin who was, three decades later, still madly in love with her husband, whom her parents had fixed her up with.

She told him about her own crisis after Harish's death, her one-night stand with John, and her experiences with men on mysoulmate.com, all information he seemed to take in without any judgement. She felt so good about unfurling herself that late one night as they sat in her bed drinking chamomile tea to nurse their coughs, she started to tell him about her obsession with Jai without revealing his name. In the beginning, Faisal gave away nothing as she spoke, but as she kept talking, she noticed the color fading from his face, and his eyes narrowing as the light slowly disappeared from them. She immediately stopped and desperately tried to alleviate the damage by repeating how much she regretted it, how the guilt still lived inside her like an interminable cancer, insisting that she would have never engaged in any sort of relationship with her daughter's boyfriend.

Faisal was obviously appalled, and he kept pressing her with questions, which she refused to answer. Finally and firmly, Naina told him (as she squirmed inside) that she did not want to discuss the subject with him, not now, not ever.

CHAPTER THIRTY-SIX

THAT GRAND MOMENT of peace came when Naina was lying on her daffodil-colored mat during deep relaxation at the end of yoga class, generally a time when she would either fall asleep as she thought about whatever she was planning to do after class, or feel thwarted by the blizzard of thoughts disrupting her earnest endeavor to concentrate on her brow point and her breathing.

Earlier during class that day, her mind had been quite active, mulling over Karan's recent announcement of his engagement to Roopali. Naina had met Roopali on her last trip to San Francisco and, as Karan had said, found her to be sweet and gentle. Maybe a little too straight and narrow for Naina's taste, but suitable for Karan. Nothing like that Arti who had acted like she owned the world. Of course, Roopali too liked jewelry, designer clothes, and the other accoutrements of wealth, but then that was Karan's type.

Amaya had outwardly behaved like she was happy about her brother's engagement, but Naina could feel the frissons of anxiety darting around inside her. Of course, Amaya would find someone soon, Naina told herself yet again, her breath slipping in and out of focus. Her daughter was a great catch. Very soon. It was just a matter of time. And luck. She couldn't help matters by worrying about it herself.

When Naina lay down on her mat at the end of class that day, her mind's garrulousness abated, and she, once again, tried to concentrate on her brow point and her breathing, yet was still ready to be interrupted by a flurry of mental activity. This time, however, the noise slowly, very slowly, receded into the background and she became conscious of nothing except for the continuous whisper of her breath coming in and out of her body and the slight chill on her bare feet from the air conditioning in the room. With no thoughts to intercept or interpret those sensations. For almost two or three minutes, her mind turned into a blank space, an expanse uncrowded by the relentless rapid fire of sparring ideas and the thickening thicket of questions. Unelectrified by the constant currents of crisscrossing thoughts.

Later, when she returned to regular consciousness, she likened her first real experience of meditation to being on a rooftop of the tallest building in Manhattan on a perfect, still, starless night where all she could see was the expanse of the blue-black sky, unobstructed and endless. And hear nothing but the sound of silence. And feel the full, rich presence of absence.

After her class, Naina sauntered out of the yoga center, feeling unusually tranquil and satisfied with herself. It was a cool Sunday afternoon with low-hanging dark clouds, a drizzle dripping from the sky, and streets filled with big puddles from the heavy downpour earlier in the day. Normally, this was the sort of day that Naina hated, but she was feeling so good that nothing bothered her. Instead of taking a subway or taxi to meet Mara, whom she hadn't seen in months, she decided to walk the fifteen blocks and two avenues it would take her to reach Gramercy Park.

She walked past the Garment District, the neighborhood looking like a withered, weathered kilim since most manufacturing of clothing was now done overseas, past the people huddling under umbrellas in Madison Square Park, past the big, trendy, empty restaurants in the Flatiron District. She repeatedly inhaled the invigorating fragrance of the newly washed air. Her newly rinsed mind seemed to possess that same refreshing, renewing quality.

Fifteen minutes and twelve blocks later, the rain came down dramatically, making her clothes wet, the ground treacherously slippery, leaving her unable to walk any further in her wedge-heeled sandals. She took cover under the scaffolding of an up-and-coming organic skin care store. As she stood there shivering, a legion of fire engines stabbed the air with their shrieking, deafening sounds and one of them drenched her sandals as it sped over a big puddle of water. Naina started to feel her exceptional serenity leaking away from her, irritated by its short-livedness. The notion of the impermanence of all things took on an added layer. Everything in life, including the meditative state, was ephemeral, and required a constant renewal of effort.

Now, the gentle, soothing drizzle was transformed into angry white sheets of rain. Naina took off her sodden sandals and stood barefoot on the pavement, regretting she was not carrying anything to read. She smiled as she thought of Faisal. Their love, as Faisal would tell her, was like a mature chicken in good health—it could fly low and for short distances before it came down to the ground, but could keep getting up again and again. Like a chicken, their love was soft; like a chicken, their love liked to nest; like a chicken, their love clucked soothingly; like a chicken, their love could be shrill. But, unlike a chicken, their love could lay no eggs because she was too old, Naina liked to teasingly remind Faisal.

The rain did not last long. Once it stopped, Naina continued walking, carefully and watchfully so she wouldn't trip, carrying the smell and taste of rain, until she reached Madeline's Coffee Place. There, in this converted Victorian carriage house, Naina saw Mara sitting at the back, in front of a large, framed poster of some eighteenth or nineteenth-century painting of a sweet-faced, rosy-cheeked woman wearing a creamy gown and holding a small dog in a lush green, bucolic English garden. A candle, the only candle in the café in the afternoon, flickered on Mara's table, casting a glow on Mara's tight white T-shirt and the dress of the woman in the poster, creating an indefinable link between Mara and that woman. Naina thought how perfect her friend would have been for a portrait like that if she had been alive in that era.

As she came closer, she noticed something different about her friend—an uncharacteristic sharpness in her face, differentiating her from the woman in the poster. She looked like she was forcing herself to smile when she saw Naina. Naina had long suspected that something was wrong with her.

"Mara, what's the matter?" Naina asked, worried, hugging her.

"Sit down." Mara's voice was flat, unlike her usual rounded tones.

Naina quickly obeyed. "What's going on with you? Is everything okay?"

"No," Mara said emphatically. "Nothing is okay . . . Nothing."

Naina was startled by her positive-thinking, new agey friend stringing three negatives in one breath. She leaned on the table, little drops of rain falling from her hair.

"What? What do you mean?"

Mara's pale face became blanched, and she looked like a ghostlike version of herself.

"I'm so confused, Naina," Mara said slowly, putting her hand in a defeated gesture on top of her head. "So confused . . . I feel like such a phony."

Now, Naina was confused, her meditative state and the rain slipping farther and farther from her. What in the world was Mara talking about?

Gradually, in fits and starts, Mara explained. Her old editor had moved to Australia and her new editor, a Turkish woman called Zehra, couldn't stand Mara's new book, *Rekindle Your Soul: The Female Guide to Awakening and Healing Through Ancient Spiritual Practices*. She told Mara she thought her manuscript was superficial, unoriginal, and dumbed down to the point where the spirit of the practices she was talking about—such as connecting with nature, sacred dance, yoga, and tai chi—was totally lost. She said it was exactly like that book *Spirituality for Today's Woman* by the chirpy daytime talk show host Lily Smith. Zehra had expected a lot more from Mara and Green Leaf Press was not going to publish her book.

Naina squeezed Mara's hand, trying to comfort her, quickly saying things that she didn't fully believe, hoping to fill the void gaping out of Mara: the editor was very mean; her book, she was sure, was wonderful and amazing; she should not let any of this get to her; another editor would feel differently and snap the book up—after all, her first book had done so well . . .

Mara stared into space, a glazed expression on her face. An expression Naina knew only too well from her own experience. Her friend's head slumped forward, and her hair fell over her face. The candle was now very close and Naina moved it away from Mara. The flame was still, so still, despite the commotion around it.

"Naina, I've been thinking about it, I've been thinking about it a lot, and Zehra might just be right," Mara said. "When I went to her office, I saw an article called "Microwaveable Nirvana" in *New York* magazine lying open on Zehra's desk . . . After I left her office, I was so upset that I went and bought the magazine to try and figure out what she really thought . . . Do you know what the article said? It said some Americans try to fool people into believing enlightenment can be easily achieved . . . that Americans have made spirituality into a commodity that can be purchased, that Americans don't learn the whole philosophy of any ancient practice, only extract what pleases their fancy, that Americans sometimes misuse spiritual practices to promote materialism and capitalism."

Mara took agitated sips of her tea. Then, with her elbow on the table, she cupped her chin in her palm.

"I just know Zehra shares the view of that columnist . . . I know she thinks I'm one of those Americans." She paused, her face crumbling. "To be honest, the more I've been thinking about it, the more I realize that that article does raise some valid points . . . I'm just a phony. Just a phony."

Naina was disoriented by this whole encounter. Many of the issues raised were legitimate but did not apply to all Americans, by any means. But how much of that should she share with a friend in her distressed state? She couldn't just let someone she cared about disintegrate in front of her, watch pieces of Mara scatter all over the place. How many times had she gone through it herself? Too many times. She took Mara's hands in her own, rubbed them, and said reassuring things, but none of it seemed to help. Mara was buried in her own darkness, impossible to reach.

"The article also said that narcissism is often camouflaged by spirituality in America. As much as I hate to admit it, that's true for me. The whole nature meditation, goddess, belly dance, yoga thing has always been about me." Mara's voice heightened and rumbled with agitation. "I wanted something to hold on to, something to latch onto, some way to feel good about myself, which, of course, is all ego, and it could have been anything. It just happened to be so-called spirituality. I've not reached any higher self-thanks to it . . . I've just put a lid on my aggression and anger with this peaceful mask."

Now Mara was talking so loudly that people turned around and stared. But she did not notice.

"I've never done any service . . . no volunteer work even though I easily could . . . I'm so selfish that I rarely go see my sick mother in Colorado because I hate planes and plus she rattles me and that upsets my peace of mind . . . if she calls me after I've done yoga, dance, or something, I don't even pick up the phone so that it doesn't ruin my peaceful state . . . I've never done a thing to help anyone but myself . . ."

Naina was taken aback by Mara's revelations. This selfish girl was Mara. Sweet, soothing Mara. But then she quickly corrected herself. Neither was it the whole picture. And this was not the time for analysis. Yes, Mara's self-flagellation was sending her spiraling downwards. She wanted to catch Mara from crashing the way she had after she realized she loved Jai, and after Amaya had discovered the truth about her and her boyfriend. She wanted to catch her friend and gather her in her arms, and rock her and tell her that while reflection and insight leading to change were good, there was no point in beating herself up like this, no point in letting reproach smother her until she could no longer breathe. Just the way she wished someone had soothed her. But Mara, sitting just a few feet away from her, seemed too far away to touch, too far away to hear what she had to say. But Naina had to try.

She went around the table and tightly hugged Mara, softly stroking her face. "We are all selfish and narcissistic to some extent. You learn as you go. None of us are perfect. You know about me. Please don't do this to yourself."

"I've not been slightly self-centered, I've been very self-centered," Mara said, shoving Naina away. "I can't even share a room with anyone because I hate being disturbed. I guess it's no surprise that I'm single with that attitude." She looked pleadingly at Naina who reached out again and squeezed her hand.

"I don't know what to do," Mara said, puncturing every word. "I'm so lost . . . nothing makes sense anymore . . . I feel I don't know anything anymore . . . you know this rattly, unsure feeling started creeping up on me over the last year, but, me being me, I didn't pay enough attention to it and diverted myself with all this positive thinking bullshit . . ."

Naina's mind traveled back to the time after Harish's death and all those other times after it. The pool of question marks she had so often been submerged in. Her head constantly bobbing up, desperately searching for an answer, an answer that would put all doubts to rest, offer her the magical key to wisdom and knowledge, and stop the interminable wheel of questions.

"I want to know my path, Naina," Mara said, her voice bubbling with urgency. "I'm tired of being on a seesaw. I don't want to be shaken up anymore . . . I want to find out what my path is . . . there I go on with that me-me narcissism again . . . I want to find out what the right way for a human being to lead his or her life is . . . what is the path? Why am I on earth? What is the purpose of my life? I want some real answers . . . not phony, feel-good answers."

Mara looked so tired, like she hadn't slept for nights. Waves of tenderness rolled out of Naina, light blue and silky.

"What if there are no answers?" Naina said, almost as if she couldn't believe what she was saying. And actually mean it.

Mara recoiled. "That can't be true. There have to be answers. Clear, simple answers."

"But what if life is a constant series of questions with no answers or with many different answers?" Naina said, remembering all the conversations she had had with herself. "What if the questions and answers constantly change with time? What if you have to make up the answers yourself?"

"That's really depressing," Mara said.

"I don't think so. I think it's much more depressing to constantly look for something and never find it."

"Well, I'm going to find the answers. There must be clear-cut, immutable truths out there."

AFTER THE FIRST few months, the delicious flush of togetherness no longer cushioned Naina and Faisal from their differences, and they slowly emerged, bright-colored like a rooster's plumage, sometimes ruffling the feathers of the chicken that was their love.

Whenever they were together, Faisal insisted on watching the pro-Obama MSNBC coverage of the election while Naina, disappointed by Hillary Clinton's defeat in the primaries, lost interest in the election and preferred watching the Travel Channel. One weekend, when they had planned to go and see the experimental jazz trio *Spinning Wheel*, which Naina had first seen with Jai, Faisal dropped out at the last minute because he wanted to go to Pennsylvania to campaign for Obama because the polls had shown a drop-in support for him. This made Naina mad and she let Faisal know it.

Naina liked to make love at night while Faisal, who more often than not started to doze off after eleven p.m., preferred to make love in the morning just before he had breakfast, a time when Naina couldn't even think about sex. Faisal, a very passionate lover, wanted Naina to make sounds of pleasure and intense facial expressions when they were in bed, just like he did, but Naina found this need oppressive, burdening her to express pleasure in a way that he liked. And unlike Ludwig, Faisal loved giving her oral sex, seemed to enjoy it even more than she did, and sometimes went over-the-top with it. He also liked receiving oral sex, but Naina found that she did not particularly enjoy it and, to Faisal's great disappointment, tried her best to avoid it.

Faisal also, Naina discovered, possessed little knowledge or appreciation of art and despite her patient education, gave no sign he would ever improve in this area. And, despite Faisal's attempts to teach Naina to appreciate qawwalis, she still found them harsh and annoying, and refused to let him listen to them while she was around, insisting they gave her a headache.

Naina could spend hours with Faisal silently, reading novels, while Faisal, who almost exclusively read poetry and nonfiction in short bursts, generally wanted to talk to her after fifteen or twenty minutes of silence, disturbing her concentration, and she would end up snapping. He also wanted to see her four or five times a week, but she, after the beginning, wanted to see him no more than two or three times a week.

And then there was the question of friends. Faisal liked hanging out with Soma and Deepak and even got along very well with Deepak, but, for some unknown reason, he and Alannah did not hit it off. She thought he was pretentious, and he thought she was full of herself. So that meant Naina did not get to see Alannah as often as she would have liked, another annoying compromise of being in a relationship.

As for Mara, Faisal never got to meet her. Soon after their conversation at Madeline's Coffee House, Mara left New York for an ashram in the Himalayas. That was all the information she had. Both Naina and Alannah only found this out through a mass email from Mara telling her friends that she had arrived safely and did not want to communicate with anyone until she was ready. But Naina was worried, and repeatedly wrote to her. Mara never wrote back. One night, Naina dreamed that Mara had been raped by some cunning sadhu, and left alone, unconscious on an icy hilltop, the pure white snow turning red as the blood seeped from her body. She shrieked in the middle of the night, and Faisal had to hold her close and massage her forehead, just like Harish used to do when she had had a bad dream. But, unlike Harish, Faisal asked her about her dream, and Naina told him in vivid detail.

"You can't save people from themselves, my love, you can't save people from themselves, my love," he murmured, softly kissing her eyes.

As for her friends in New Jersey, Naina had no intention of telling them about Faisal and he, after putting up a small fuss, consented to being excluded from that part of her life. She continued visiting them whenever she had a chance, mostly alone, but sometimes with Amaya, and always when Karan came to town.

Naina liked most of Faisal's friends, but there was one couple who were very close to Faisal that she just could not stand—Esther and Jonathan. They had lived in Egypt for some years and constantly spoke about the Middle East as if no other topic merited conversation, and that too with an authority that Naina found most irritating. Every time, she dreaded meeting them.

The one thing she and Faisal almost always could agree upon was food. They both liked spicy kebabs, rich curries, spaghetti Bolognese, penne alla vodka, coq au vin, chorizo, blackened catfish, chicken in basil sauce, macaroni and cheese; and whenever they went out together they always got two things they could share. Faisal loved to cook and made excellent ham sandwiches, seekh kebabs, lamb tagines, and chicken pot pies, and at least three or four times a month the two of them would cook together in the roomy, well-equipped kitchen of his sparsely decorated one-bedroom apartment on Riverside Drive with a spectacular view of the Hudson River.

They became so comfortable with each other that just by hearing each other's voices over the phone, they knew if the other wanted to talk or was busy; by observing each other's bodies, they knew if the other was too hot or too cold; by seeing each other's facial expression, they knew if the other liked what he or she was eating or not. But this comfort also came with a price. The balloon of joy that used to be big and glorious whenever they saw each other, withered; the charge that electrified their early interactions lost its potency; the delight that magnified ordinary chores like grocery shopping or chopping vegetables together into something wonderful, dwindled. In Naina's eyes, the rarefied universe of love became ordinary again, populated by mundane tasks, continuous annoyances, compromises borne out of practicality, and sometimes going to bed so tired that there was no energy for romance. While Faisal greeted the quietening of their relationship with a light-hearted acceptance, Naina found herself feeling let down and blue, though she never expressed it to him.

She then understood, with greater clarity, what Soma and Alannah meant when they said that this was the natural course for all relationships, but she still yearned for the chicken that was their love to fly higher and for longer distances. After all, for most of her life, she had nurtured herself, with the aid of romantic novels, on a steady diet of fantasies where the man swept a woman off her feet and the intense, magical love and fervent passion the lovers felt for each other only heightened with the passage of time. Of course, the reality of her actual married life had been completely different, but that had been acceptable because she had known not to expect such grandiosity from an arranged marriage, turning instead to novels and dreams to feed her needs. But now that she was in a relationship (a relationship that had moved past the early stages, unlike her relationship with Ludwig), motivated by a Western-style desire for love, the boundaries between her worlds of fantasy and reality were all blurry.

She had happily welcomed true romantic love, something she had imagined for years, into her life, and knew that her feelings for Faisal came from some deeper place, some place she had never been to before. But she hadn't expected the ordinariness of a regular relationship to intrude into her universe of love. She wanted this relationship to be dissimilar from her marriage with Harish in every way, yet as the relationship progressed, she was reminded of her days with Harish. Maybe Faisal was reminded of his days with Greta too. After all, he had told her that his initial elation about being with Greta gradually dipped to mere affection. Naina also remembered how struck she was when Faisal observed that the outcome of arranged and love marriages might often be quite alike.

After giving the matter much consideration, Naina eventually concluded that no relationship, no matter how good, could rival the magnificence of her long-cultivated dreams. Still, that did not erase her desire for that splendor. She still ached for it and suspected the ache would probably never go away.

AS THEY RAN to catch the E train, Faisal stepped on a greasy plastic bag lying on the subway station like a soiled, broken kite. Naina caught his hand, and he steadied himself. He then pulled Naina close, kissing her eyes. Naina wiggled, embarrassed by this overtly public display of affection. To be behaving like this in public at her age? She must look ridiculous. Then, as she always did, she looked around to see if she could spot Amaya anywhere.

They reached the E train as it was pulling out of the station. They both sighed, knowing that, with the train running so infrequently on weekends, they might have to wait as long as half an hour for another one to come. Naina took out a book, but Faisal talked again about how excited he was about Barack Obama's victory. She gave him a look, eyebrows raised, lips tightly pressed together—a look that told him to be quiet. He said *all right* in a resigned voice.

They were going to Oyster House, a nursing home for elderly people. Faisal— who also did some pro bono legal work for lower-income families of Alzheimer's patients on issues like patients' rights in nursing homes and insurance claims and appeals—had been visiting Oyster House's Alzheimer's unit twice a month for four years to cheer up the patients. Naina wanted to see this part of his life.

It was the last stop in Queens, and they still had a long walk ahead of them. They walked past fast-food restaurants, past Caribbean, South Asian, and South American grocery stores, past an exceptionally beautiful Tudor home, past a large cemetery, past middle-class row houses, past a bend in the road, which led to an empty tract of land overflowing with weeds and smelling of neglect. Next to this dismal piece of land was Oyster House—a small, scruffy brick structure on the edge of Queens, looking as if it had fallen off the earth. Naina was nervous—she hadn't been to Queens in a long time and had never been to this neighborhood. What would this place be like?

Naina gingerly entered the nursing home, her heart beating fast, clasping Faisal's hand, and gazed in astonishment. Around a large circular area, a cluster of old men and women sat in comfortable chairs as a sweet melody, which Naina instantly recognized as Bach, wafted dreamily and long slivers of sunlight quivered on the carpet, giving the room a strangely nostalgic feel. Most of the residents had delicate skin cracking with wrinkles and faces that looked like they might disintegrate any time. One man, wearing a broad-brimmed Panama hat (even though the room was nicely heated), limply held a fat leather-bound book from which Naina could discern the words "World War 1" from afar. His glassy skin was bluish gray, the unsettling color reminding her of her first scary glimpse of Amaya after giving birth. Another woman in a flowery sundress, swayed in gentle, uncoordinated motions in the big brawny arms of a kind-faced man with dreadlocks. Another woman, her fine silver hair tied in a knot at the base of her neck, looked as if she were in deep contemplation about something while she was distractedly eating some kind of semi-solid food fed to her by a young woman. The others were just sitting still in their chairs, with vacant and oddly peaceful expressions on their faces.

The colors in the room were muted but cheerful, a tacky lemon-and-rose colored wallpaper on one wall, and the same lemon coated the opposite wall. The draperies were printed linen, peach with green blossoms, and the upholstery was a soothing sage green. Colorful ceramic plaques—with sayings like "Life is Beautiful," "Let us never know what old age is. Let us know the happiness time brings, not count the years," and "Happiness is in the heart, not in the circumstances"—lined the walls and a big vase of pink carnations sat on a coffee table. The decor was filled with so much light and life that Naina found it only heightened the pungent and heartbreaking smell of death and decay in the room.

No one, except for the two staff members, recognized Faisal. He walked over to the kitchen area where he took out a can of pineapple juice and a bag of soft chocolate chip cookies he had brought, and put the cookies, two each, onto small plates. Naina, standing next to him, felt useless and asked if there was anything she could do. He asked her to get a glass and napkins from the cupboard on the far right. He poured the canned pineapple juice into the glass, whispering in Naina's ear it was for the lady who couldn't eat anything hard like a cookie.

He went up to each one of them, patted their backs and their hands, and gave them their plate of two cookies.

"Hello Farah," he said to the woman in the flowery dress and whistled the tune of "We Wish You A Merry Christmas," and she slowly smiled and touched his cheek. Naina wondered if she just saw a flicker of recognition on her face.

Faisal said, "Good afternoon, Peter" to the man in the Panama Hat, and to Naina's surprise, the man promptly responded, "Good afternoon," and then looked disappointed as he appeared to struggle to recall Faisal's name.

"That hat is great on you," Faisal said.

Peter grinned and mumbled something about how Panama hats were the rage in the twenties.

Faisal motioned to Naina to come near him. "This is my girlfriend," he said, uttering the word "girlfriend" to describe her for the first time.

Naina was taken aback. For her, the word was associated with the young and it had never been used to describe her.

"Ah, girlfriend," Peter mumbled, tipping his hat in an exaggerated gesture of gentlemanliness. "I used to have lotta gals once, lotta gals."

Faisal put on some bhangra music, and the crowd perked up, shaking their bodies in whatever way they could. He held Farah's waist as she jerkily swayed in her flowery dress, then the hands of the pajama-clad man who liked to stamp his feet, and then forced an embarrassed Naina to dance the bhangra with him in front of the group.

Faisal took out a children's book on Mozart's life and read it slowly, deliberately, and theatrically. Except for Peter and the pajama-clad man, who appeared to be able to comprehend something, Naina couldn't tell if anyone else could understand a word of what Faisal was saying. Yet, they seemed rapt.

As she watched him, Naina marveled again at Faisal's capacity for kindness. She, too, had helped educate women about health-related issues, and though she had done her job well, it was never infused with the same compassion as Faisal's. And since she had left Gyan she had not done anything altruistic.

When they left Oyster House, she squeezed Faisal's hand tightly, knowing that her feelings for him had inalterably changed, burrowed deeper into another chamber of her heart. She chided herself for ever having felt uncomfortable about the fact that he was Pakistani or Muslim. This man was so singular, so exceptional, so large that to liken him to any group seemed like an affront. On the long subway journey back, they were mostly silent. Naina was lost in thought and Faisal understood that she didn't want to talk right now. He picked up a copy of *Newsweek* left by someone on the subway and began reading it.

Something else also changed in Naina that day. She started to see that her own life was mostly about her, saw herself as someone who had dug into her own seed and unleashed numerous hidden branches, but also discovered that those same branches had entangled her. They had urged her to meet her own needs, an exhortation that kept her confined in the long and leafy but eventually narrow tree of the self. She also found that she might have gone deep but had not gone wide.

CHAPTER THIRTY-SEVEN

NAINA SHUT HER computer down after checking her personal email at the gallery. It was a cold night and she buttoned her black shearling coat, relief sinking into her. Mara was still alive. She had just received an email from her, after months, simply saying, "Still Alive. Still Searching." That was it. At least she had not been maimed and killed. Though where in the world she was, was anybody's guess.

Sometime later, as Naina was about to step into the subway station, Soma called, asking her if she wanted to join her for dinner; she had just finished some errands in Chelsea. But Naina declined, saying it was past eight and she was really tired. Being the associate gallery director of a bigger space, as Susan had promised, had ended up being a lot of work. She took her time walking down the steps of the subway, much to the chagrin of a young woman behind her, who was exasperatedly clicking her high heels and texting away, but Naina continued her lethargic descent down the steps, pretending she hadn't noticed the woman. Her thoughts turned to her recent conversation with Soma.

Soma had asked her if she planned to tell Amaya and Karan about Faisal. By now, it was obvious they were a couple and seemed likely to stay that way, Soma had said. Would she want her children to find out some other way?

The truth was, Naina didn't know what, if anything, to tell Amaya and Karan. Unbuttoning her coat, she slumped onto a bench on the subway platform. Besides Soma, she didn't know any other Indian woman in a similar situation and had few precedents to draw upon. Soma had told her son, Araan, about Deepak without any hesitation, but Naina knew her situation was different. Araan had grown up in a more unconventional setting, without a mother and father together, seeing traditional notions of gender roles rupture early in his life, and knowing that his mother had sacrificed the company of a man for years because of him. She imagined that Araan might have felt guilty for his mother's sacrifice and solitary years and was probably relieved when he saw his mother with Deepak, glad his existence had not forever blighted his mother's chance for love.

But her own children were different. She ambled onto the train, disappointed that even at this hour she had to hang on to a pole because all the seats were occupied. Amaya and Karan had grown up with parents who had a conventional marriage, with parents quietly filling expected roles, with parents who had little discord between them. Yes, they had American friends whose mothers had boyfriends and fathers had girlfriends, but they so rarely saw that amongst their second-generation Indian immigrant peers. Of Amaya's and Karan's Indian friends, two had lost one parent each in the last few years, and neither had remarried, and, if they had dated, which she highly doubted, it was not openly. The mother of one of Karan's childhood friends moved a few towns closer to her son after her husband passed away, and Amaya's friend's father—who was also on the periphery of hers and Harish's social circle—started to devote all his free time to the temple after his wife died. Karan heartily approved of these choices, and ensured he went to see his friend's widowed mother, Mrs. Varma, whenever he went to Bergen County in Jersey and sang praises about her virtuousness.

Also, Harish was a loving father, an exceptionally loving father who gave his children baths, helped them with their homework, and bought them thoughtful presents, a father whose sudden absence from their lives made the memories of his presence even more precious, beautiful images forever frozen in time. The notion of tarnishing upright, uptight Karan's most cherished family images, which probably always included the four of them, really troubled her. And then there was his fiancé Roopali who came from a conservative family. What would she think of a dating mother-in-law? And the in-your-face idea of his mother having sex, at fifty-six, and that too with a man who was not his father—would that screw Karan up completely? Poor boy, he probably imagined his mother is beyond sex at this age. She briefly smiled to herself and an unknown woman gave her a dirty look.

Naina realized she was leaning her head against the subway pole, taking up too much space. "I'm sorry," she said.

And, Amaya, what about Amaya? Her daughter who had seen her mother fall for her own boyfriend? How would she tell her? She didn't know, she just didn't know, hating the conundrum she had created for herself.

Thankfully though, Amaya was now dating someone, an Indian-American journalist with the *Wall Street Journal*, and she would light up whenever she spoke about him in a way that she hadn't come close to doing since Jai. Naina had even met him.

Mukul was well-spoken, ambitious, a little reserved, and appeared to truly care about Amaya. He did not have as much sparkle in his personality as Jai, but he seemed a lot more grounded. In fact, he seemed so grounded that Naina didn't know if he ever looked up at the sky. He also did not seem like the kind of man who circled around, but someone who moved in a carefully chosen direction. She liked him, but the only thing that made her nervous was that he seemed to be somewhat emotionally restrained, like a plant whose leaves curled inward rather than opened out, a trait that that reminded her of Ludwig. She hesitated to speak to Amaya about her concern, afraid it might be misconstrued.

"I really like Mukul," Naina said to Amaya, trying to strike the right balance between sounding approving and not overly enthusiastic. "He seems like a

smart, together person who seems to genuinely be in love with you. There's just
. . . just . . ."

"What is it, Mom?" Amaya asked.

"Nothing, nothing . . . Mukul seems really wonderful."

"What is it?" Amaya looked straight at her, now speaking in a demanding
tone.

"Nothing . . . nothing . . . just that he seems . . . seems . . ."

"Seems what?"

"Just very . . . self-contained . . . not very expressive . . . but I've just met him
so what do I know?"

Amaya laughed. "That's it, Mom? Here I was preparing myself for you to tell
me that you had seen some inner darkness in him that I had missed. Phew. But
I already know that." Her daughter looked and sounded so sensible and grown-
up. "No one's perfect, Mom. He's a really good person and, so far, I'm happy
with him. If there's ever a problem, I'll deal with it then."

Soma had told Naina that it was finally a good time to tell Amaya, but
Naina refused. So far, everything sounded fine, but it was still new. Mukul
and Amaya were still discovering their feelings for each other, and Naina now
properly understood that Western-style relationships, based on rickety, abstract
criteria like love and getting along, were most vulnerable to cracking in their
early stages when things—such as too many phone calls or too few phone calls;
a lack of common purpose when it came to movies, excessive messiness, or
neatness; a whiny voice; or a couple of lackluster lovemaking experiences—had
the potential to wreck a budding union. Unless Amaya's relationship was on
firmer footing, how could she tell her?

"That's a good idea in theory," Alannah had said. "But what are you going
to do if things don't work between them? How are you going to tell Amaya
then?"

"I don't know. I don't have the faintest idea."

MEANWHILE, NAINA KNEW Faisal was getting impatient and bothered.
Up to that point, Faisal had been understanding about the clandestine nature
of their relationship and had reluctantly accepted being an invisible shadow in
her children's lives. But no more. Every last-minute cancellation Naina made
to be with Amaya, her shushing him if she was talking to Karan, his having to
take away his toothbrush and cologne every time he stayed over was an affront
to their relationship, a kick to his heart and balls, a wallop to the chicken that
was their love, he said. He had included her in every aspect of his life, but she
had not done the same, he said, his face red, glaring at her like she had never
seen before when she had told him, early one Sunday morning, to leave the
apartment because Amaya had unexpectedly called to say she was coming

over. He didn't care about being excluded from her friends in New Jersey, but her children, the significant orbs of her life—he could no longer bear to be shut out.

"But try to understand," Naina had pleaded as Faisal stood at her door in a brown suede jacket, his arms tightly crossed against his chest. "They won't understand. It will hurt them terribly."

"They're grown up, Naina," Faisal had snapped. "Not little children. Of course, they will understand. And if they experience some discomfort, that's life. They're adults, for God's sake. Why should you and I have to hide and suffer so they don't experience an iota of distress? Are they that much more important than us?" Faisal took a deep breath. "You know what I really think . . . I think you're just being a coward."

He slammed the door while Naina sat burying her face in her hands, trying to digest what Faisal had said.

That night, Naina sat up in her bed and pondered over what Alannah had said. That she was not looking at her situation with Faisal clearly, that her residual guilt was like an infection contaminating her vision, distorting the assumed impact on Amaya and Karan to unrealistic, magnified proportions.

"Who knows, maybe Amaya will be glad to know her mother has someone," Alannah said, cracking a devilish smile. "At least that way she would know that her boyfriend is safe from her mother."

"How dare you?" Naina said, her voice sounding like a bark. "How dare you?"

Even as she expressed outrage, Naina couldn't help but wonder if Alannah might possibly be right about the effect on her children. Or did she simply want Alannah to be right? But then, Alannah was Italian American. She couldn't possibly understand these things in an Indian context.

THINGS CAME TO a head during Christmas. Mukul was out of town for the holidays, as were most of Amaya's friends, so Naina wasn't entirely surprised when Amaya asked her what she was doing for Christmas. Nervously moving her hair from her face, Naina told her she was going to Alannah's big Christmas bash, omitting one small fact—that she planned to go with Faisal.

"Can I come too?" Amaya asked. "If it's a big party, it shouldn't matter. I don't want to be alone on Christmas."

"I guess so . . . I guess so. I'll . . . I'll check with Alannah."

"Mom, why are you looking so frightened? I mean if it's some kind of private, exclusive affair I don't have to come. It's not a big deal."

"Frightened? Me? Why, why should I be frightened?"

But of course, Naina was frightened. How could she tell Faisal that she could not spend Christmas with him?

Faisal was angry, but much angrier than she had expected. His body trembled with fury, his blood kicking and screaming, his eyes glowering like ferocious full moons. She was suddenly scared she might lose him forever.

"What am I?" he demanded, his voice crackling like logs in a high fire. "A mistress that needs to be hidden from the wife?"

"No, no, try to understand," Naina said, looking up at him.

"I'm tired of trying to understand," Faisal roared. "Leave, please leave now. Until you can make up your mind to treat me like someone important in your life and be grown-up about it, I don't want to have anything to do with you."

"But, but—"

"No more bloody buts." He pushed the bathroom door open. "And have a merry Christmas."

Breathing in short, jerky bursts, Naina waited by the bathroom door for a couple of minutes before she let herself out and got into the elevator. She wanted to be angry with Faisal, but the feelings just would not come. He had done nothing wrong. All he was demanding was his rightful due.

Naina hated the Christmas party. She arrived with Amaya, barely putting in much effort into her appearance, making forced conversations, detesting the nineties music, and looking out of the big bay windows at the mist-covered Washington Square Park arch in the distance. Alannah gave her an I-told-you-so look while Amaya kept pressing her with questions. No, no, nothing was wrong, she told Amaya. She just wasn't feeling well. That was all. It must be that bug going around.

"Are you sure?" Amaya said again, her eyes narrowing, her pupils enlarging, and her gaze piercing. "I mean really sure?"

Naina licked her lips and smoothed her hair. Perhaps now was the time to tell Amaya? She straightened her back, searching for words. "No darling, nothing's wrong. I'm sure."

Amaya shrugged. "If you say so."

Soon after midnight, Naina left the party while Amaya decided to stay. On an impulse, Naina decided to take a taxi to Faisal's apartment. They had not spoken since that contentious encounter regarding the Christmas party. She missed him so much and wanted things to be normal between them again. Since she had a key to the apartment, she knew she could let herself in.

When she arrived, she peeped at the bottom of his front door and could see light coming from inside. He was home. She froze. What if he asked her to leave like the time before?

And then she slowly, very slowly opened the door, entered the apartment, and saw that the bathroom door was closed. She could hear the sound of water gushing from the tap. Quickly, she took off her clothes, leaving only her lacy black lingerie on, and got inside the sheets.

Faisal walked out of the bathroom and stared at her, his eyes smoky and heavy with alcohol. She rolled the sheets down to expose her bra and her waist. Faisal jumped into bed, softly kissed her eyes, the nape of her neck, her nipples, and then jerked back, his eyes large and glistening with anger.

"No," he said, shaking his head. He got out of bed and purposefully buttoned his pajama shirt. "No. I can't do this. Either you acknowledge me, or we can't continue."

Naina took his hand, worried he might pull it away. "Give me two weeks. Give me two weeks to figure this out. Just two weeks."

"Two weeks," Faisal said, looking at her straight in the eye. "Two weeks."

OVER CAFFE LATTES in a large cafe in the Flatiron district Naina decided to tell Amaya about Faisal; it seemed the perfect place as the cafe was rarely full and the tables were well spaced apart. She hadn't wanted to do it in her apartment—the intimacy of being in such a cocoon frightened her. In between rapid, small sips, averting her eyes and desperately trying to adopt a calm and cool tone, Naina said there was something she wanted to tell her.

Amaya gave her a knowing look. "That there's someone in your life, right?"

"Right . . . how did you know?" Naina said weakly.

Amaya gave her a sardonic smile, and Naina felt as if she were mocking her.

"What kind of fool do you think I am?" Amaya said. "I've known for a while now."

"You have?"

Amaya shook her head. "Gosh, Mom, even an idiot could have figured that out. All those nights out with friends and work stuff? The secret smile on your face sometimes? And a man's leather belt under your bed? The sudden—"

"Stop, stop." Naina put both hands up. A leather belt under her bed? She wanted to curl up in a ball and hide. That was a detail Amaya did not need to know. When could Amaya have seen that? She had been so careful.

Her daughter sounded composed, but something barely audible, barely discernible, underneath the surface roiled away.

"Amaya, are you all right?" Naina asked in a voice she had used to soothe Amaya as a baby.

"I'm fine. Of course, I'm fine." And then she remained silent.

Amaya's coolness was coagulating into something denser and hotter. Her shoulders hunched, her lips pulled taut against each other, and her left forefinger tapped the table. Shadows ran across her face.

"I suppose it's not easy for a daughter to hear such things," Naina said finally, fingering the straps of her handbag, as guilt, that chronic blight, tightly gripped her. She felt herself wince, the swollen threads of her organs coiling into knots.

Why had she told her daughter? Was it the right thing to do? Was she being selfish again?

"No, it's not."

Naina clasped Amaya's hand. "I'm sorry, baby."

Amaya withdrew her hand. She shook her head, as if in frustration. "You don't have to apologize . . . you haven't done anything wrong . . . It's just that . . . just that . . ." She emitted a long sigh and when she spoke, it was in agitated bursts. "I don't know why, don't know why, it's just not easy for me to hear this . . . I mean it's not like it's even news for me considering I've strongly suspected it for so long and I've . . . even wanted you to be with someone . . . but . . . but . . . there's a difference between knowing . . . and actually knowing—"

More shadows ran across her face, faster and darker. Naina cringed again, the consequences of her choice pressing down upon her, the blubbery threads of her organs twisting themselves into tighter knots.

"I'm sorry, Mom," Amaya said, squeezing Naina's hand. "I'm not making any sense and I'm more frustrated with myself than anything else. I'm sorry . . . can we get the check now?"

Naina nodded. They sat in silence before they parted ways.

Right after, Naina went to Faisal's. He held her in his arms, gently kissed her eyes, and caressed her face, reassuring her that she had done the right thing.

A FEW WEEKS later, as Naina continued to feel the sting from her choice to tell her daughter, red and smarting, Amaya asked to meet Faisal. If he was an important person in her life, she wanted to know him. Faisal was ecstatic, but Naina was worried. How did a mother introduce her daughter to her boyfriend and hope for her daughter's approval? The only way she had known things to happen was a child introducing a partner to their parents and hoping for their approval. How did she get into a situation where that natural turn of events was reversed?

The three of them met at an Ethiopian restaurant downtown and Naina was awkward and nervous the whole time. She tightly crossed her legs the entire evening and glared at Faisal whenever he said or did anything that suggested the faintest bit of intimacy between them; when he casually scooped some doro wat off her plate, when he lightly brushed her arm to ask if she remembered the name of the actor who played the writer in the movie *Sophie's Choice* they had recently seen, when he lamented about how long it took for Naina to wash her hair.

Amaya, too, she could sense, felt awkward, at least in the beginning, and, as was her tendency when she felt uncomfortable, became very stiff and formal. At least three times, she disappeared for long bathroom visits. Faisal was the one who seemed most at ease during the dinner, his limbs loose, his arms moving smoothly, a broad smile on his face. He was also the one who initiated the conversation— starting with small talk regarding the weather and New York restaurants—and the one who ended up doing most of the talking. Amaya said the bare minimum to be polite and Naina interjected bits here and there to fill in the gaps. And then Faisal tried some humor. "On my way here, I heard some greasy guy telling a woman with pink hair and high heels, 'You must be from Paris, 'cause you're driving me in-Seine.' And guess what the woman said. 'Are you from Istanbul? Because you sound like a real turkey.'"

Amaya rolled her eyes, the baffled expression on her face, Naina could tell, about to turn into one of her sneers. Naina was annoyed with Faisal for his poor attempt at humor. Amaya, it was obvious, found the joke juvenile, cheesy, and not particularly amusing, a sentiment she shared. Hurriedly, Naina tried to dispel the uncomfortable silence that had settled over them like a fog, by forcing herself to laugh.

"That's so silly, Faisal," she said, attempting a light-hearted tone. "Of all the humorous things one can hear in New York, that's all you found."

And then Amaya, as if catching herself, pried out some chuckles from inside her, chuckles that sounded as false as they likely were.

Faisal did not try any attempts at humor after that. He asked Amaya a lot of interested questions, particularly about her work, which Amaya answered properly and pithily, as if she were at a job interview. Then Faisal revealed that he had read a great deal about mental health issues because his wife, Greta, who had died from Alzheimer's disease several years earlier, was misdiagnosed as having depression or bipolar disorder and put on psychotropic medications. Somehow that bit of self-disclosure in a voice that still trembled from the shadows of those memories seemed to have disarmed Amaya.

"Really?" Amaya said, her eyes wide and open, the stilted tones falling from her voice. "How could the doctors have made such a grave error?"

Faisal talked about Greta and the array of psychiatrists she had seen and the array of diagnoses she had been given, and Amaya listened keenly, asking him multiple questions. The ice had been broken, but Naina could tell how difficult it was for him to open up about this to someone he had just met. He had only told her these details after they had started seeing each other regularly. But she knew he had done it to try to appease Amaya. Her heart, brimming with tenderness, opened and expanded. She wanted to squeeze his hand but did not since Amaya was there.

At the end of the evening, Naina did not leave with Faisal, choosing to take the subway with Amaya instead. She wanted to wait a little while before asking her daughter but could not summon the patience.

"So, what do you think?" she asked as soon as Faisal was out of earshot.

They laughed at the irony of the situation.

"He's all right . . ." Amaya said. "No, no, I mean he's nice. He seems nice. He can talk. Boy, can he talk. Tries too hard though."

"He was only trying to be friendly with you," Naina said, feeling defensive.

"I know, I know. Anyway, you like him and that's what's important. And I think he's really, really into *you*."

Naina felt embarrassed. She looked away to hide the warmth rising in her cheeks and quickly changed the topic.

NAINA WAITED UNTIL she went to San Francisco to tell Karan. She had told Amaya she wanted tell him herself and Amaya quickly acquiesced, looking relieved. At the beginning of her trip she regurgitated—with added emphasis and exposition—her usual lines about how wonderful his father was, how he was such a considerate husband and such a fabulous father, and how she would miss him forever. This time, she added, several times, how she felt so blessed to have been able to create a fulfilling life after his passing.

"You know, he's my hero," Karan said who loved hearing about how great his father was.

Naina could not muster the courage to tell him then.

During her stay, Karan was busy working and when he came home, he was glued to a documentary on the Mumbai terror attacks on an English-language Indian TV channel. In the program, the gruesome spectacle of the attacks were broadcast over and over again—the surviving twenty-year-old terrorist with a ferocious expression and a gun in his hand, the frightening stories of people trapped inside the Taj and Oberoi hotels, the heartrending images of those smiling faces who perished while waiting for a train, eating a meal, or doing their job. And, of course, the documentary went on and on about the tension between India, which blamed Pakistan, its neighbor, for the attack. Naina became even more apprehensive about telling her son.

A day before she left for New York, she resolved she would tell Karan no matter what.

"There's . . . there's . . . something I want to tell you, beta," Naina said, clasping her hands on her lap.

On the wall in front of her was a large family photograph of the four of them at the New Jersey Botanical Gardens, taken more than ten years earlier, big smiles on their faces, their hair blowing in the wind while a ruby-throated hummingbird hovered behind them, lapping up the nectar of newly blossomed petunias. That picture was enough for her to stop, to let her son hold on to that cherished image. But it couldn't be, she determined, yet again. Life changed all the time. One had to learn to move sideways, backward, any which way life demanded—just like that agile hummingbird. Her son was a mature man, soon to be married. He couldn't be protected any more. She looked down at the taupe frieze carpet beneath her.

"Yes, Mom?" Karan turned away from the computer to look at her. His tone was so much more tender after she had started visiting New Jersey. She knew that that was going to change and felt a mounting dread.

"Yes, Mom?" Karan repeated when Naina remained silent. "Is everything okay?"

Naina knew she had to get the words out. The more she thought about it, the more it stalled her.

"You're not going to like what you hear, but I think you need to know," Naina said, crossing and uncrossing her thumbs. "There's someone in my life . . . He's been around for some time and he's a wonderful man and he treats me very well. Please . . . please . . . don't take this to mean I've forgotten your father. I haven't . . . I've just had to . . ."

"*What?*" Karan said, his face contorting with shock and anger. "What the fuck is wrong with you?" His voice was now booming. Naina had never heard him use the word *fuck* before.

Naina bit her lower lip, intent on keeping a lid on her feelings.

"Why do you have keep doing this?" Karan said, forcefully throwing his hands up in the air. "There's something *crazy* going on with you ever since Dad went . . . First, it's ditching everyone in Jersey, then this dressing like a cougar, now this . . . I just don't get it, I just don't get it . . ."

Naina inhaled deeply and shut her eyes. "Karan, beta, I know how hurtful this is for you . . . how hard this is for you . . ."

"You do? Ya right."

His strident voice pulsed with so much bitterness that she could feel its vibrations grating on every cell on her skin.

She folded her arms and clutched her upper arms. "But try to understand, beta . . . I cared deeply for your father, but I have to move on . . . I just have to . . ."

"*Whatever*," Karan said, crossing his arms. "*Whatever*. Do whatever the fuck you want." He picked up a tennis ball and flung it across a wall. "But just do me one favor. If you can that is . . . Don't say anything around Roopali or her family. For heaven's sake. And don't even think about bringing this guy to the wedding."

"Whatever you want, beta."

Karan stared out of the window, seemingly at the Golden Gate Bridge glimmering in the sun.

"So, is he a desi or some white boy you picked up?"

"He's . . . he's . . . a desi." And then she raised her voice a bit. "Karan, you're crossing the line with your language."

"*Whatever.*"

"You're not planning to marry this guy, are you?" Karan said after a long silence had lashed around the room like waves on a surfing beach.

Naina was surprised by this question. "No . . . I don't think so."

"You're worth a decent chunk of change and you don't want make yourself financially vulnerable."

"He's not like that and plus he's got enough. I might be financially okay, but I'm not some super rich woman."

"Still, I don't want anyone to use you."

"He's not using me." Now, Naina felt her temper escalating. Her Faisal was not like that.

"So what part of India is this dude from?"

"He's not from India . . . He's from Pakistan. He lived in London for many years before moving to New York . . . He's very liberal—"

"Pakistan? Pakistan? From that fucking terrorist country that attacked all those innocent people in Mumbai?" Karan snarled, fire spewing out of his eyes.

"Stop it, Karan," Naina said, fuming. "Everyone from Pakistan is not a terrorist."

He emitted a mocking laugh, sounds of steel coming out of his mouth. "I'm *sure*, but a helluva lot of people seem to be these days."

Naina got up from the couch and walked around in small, tight circles. "Karan, you're talking like a bigot," she said in a chastising mother's voice, ashamed of her son. To think that he was made of her, had come out of her body? "Stop it. Is this what your father and I taught you?"

"Don't you dare bring Dad into to this. If you remember correctly, Dad didn't really trust Pakistanis either. Do you remember that Satish Uncle, Dad's father's brother, was in the army and fought in the India Pakistan wars? Or maybe you don't remember?"

"Well, maybe I don't," Naina said, rushing out of the room before she said anything she would regret forever.

CHAPTER THIRTY-EIGHT

THEY HAD BEEN on vacation for three days and still the sun gave no hint that it might actually come out. Ever since Naina and Faisal had got to Montego Bay after long airport delays, the port city's skies had been blanketed by gelatinous, swollen clouds that disintegrated into copious amounts of rainfall by evening. The rain there was not the kind of annoying drip they were used to in New York, but raging showers that lashed out against the soft sand, the hapless palm trees, and the colorful tourist umbrellas. Everything shuddered under the rainfall's might, and Faisal joked that it was just Mother Nature showing who's the boss.

They had rented a home with a pool, a jacuzzi, a garden, and a cook, but Naina had to use her imagination to picture how, in the glow of the sun's rays, the blue water in the pool would have been streaked with gold, the pink of the bougainvillea would have shone in all its vivid glory, the shadows of the jackfruit trees would have been long and dark, and her body would have entered that blissful state that it naturally did in the sun.

It had been Faisal's idea to go to Jamaica; Naina had wanted to go to Montreal to see the jazz festival. But Faisal, in the typical persuasive manner that he used when he wanted something—a trait of his that Naina thought bordered on selfishness—coaxed her into coming to Montego Bay, speaking of the sunshine, the sunbathing, the warm bathtub-like sea water, and the swaying palm trees.

But the weather had been awful, and Jamaica had become much more touristy since the last time Faisal had last been there. But Naina did not complain—she could tell he felt bad enough already and made an extra effort to be nice to her. One day, he walked a mile to buy her a big bouquet of red roses for no reason in particular; every morning he rose early so she would find her café au lait ready when she got up, and one afternoon he gave her a long, vigorous back massage.

The highlight of their trip was their excursion to Dunn's River Falls, a six-hundred-foot waterfall where tourists, holding hands and forming one massive human chain, could climb up. Naina, who had never been sporty, excitedly hopped from one slippery rock to another and brawled with the rushing cascades of water heading downstream.

But Faisal, who boasted of being a good tennis and squash player in his younger years, was scared and it was only when Naina threatened to call him a coward did he agree to climb. They held hands and Naina led the way. She pulled him hard if he deliberated too long on a rock and he splashed lots of water on her if she tried to make him go faster than he wanted to.

That afternoon of the Dunn River Falls, their last day in Jamaica, they returned to the house, exhilarated and exhausted, and took long naps under the cloudy skies and only woke up at dinner time. After they finished a delicious Jamaican dinner prepared for them by their cook, they cuddled on the lounge chairs in the porch with glasses of expensive Bordeaux, something Faisal had bought from a liquor store in Jamaica. The rain was coming down ferociously, as it had every other night, and at one point when Naina was listening to the stamping, stomping rain, as if Mother Nature was throwing a tantrum, Faisal pulled out something from his pocket.

It was a small blue velvet jewelry box.

When Naina saw it, her heart filled with fear as she imagined what it might be. Slowly, very slowly, Faisal opened the box. She was relieved to see a small round pendant with a delicately filigreed gold lotus on a chain of small, sparkling rubies. It was the third piece of jewelry he had given her, and easily the most beautiful. She thanked him profusely, gave him a big hug, and he offered to put the necklace on for her.

Right after he helped her with the necklace, he knelt down on one knee on the damp floor and looked up at her with a beseeching look in his eyes.

"Naina, my darling, I'd hoped to do this under the stars or under bright sunshine, but the weather has not been on my side," Faisal said in a cracking, crackling voice. "So I have to make do with the porch and the rain. Naina, I love you more than anything else in the world and want to make you my wife. I want to wake up next to you every morning, hold you every day, and spend the rest of my life with you."

Naina was stunned. She did not respond. She did not move. She held her breath without realizing it. He slowly got up from the floor, kissed her right cheek, and sat next to her. The intensity of his gaze was too overwhelming for her. She wanted to hide her face in her hands but resisted the urge.

"I realize that this is not a conventional thing to do for desis our age and that there are many things for you to think about, so I'm not asking you for an answer right away. All I ask is for you to think about it. I really love you, Naina. I know you've got kids to think about, but I think they will be fine. They've got their own lives and partners at this stage. And I'm already so fond of Amaya and really think that she is warming up to me. And I'm sure, as time passes, Karan will come around too. I promise you that I will treat them like my own children, but I will also keep as much distance as you want me to."

He put his hand over hers, which was clasping the arm of the lounge chair. "Promise me you'll think about this."

Naina still said nothing. She was astounded by his declaration and she was trying hard to not let it show. She hadn't seen this coming; she hadn't suspected it; she hadn't even imagined it except during her fleeting nighttime reveries. She never expected it to turn into a reality. She heard herself muttering a vague *yes, of course I will, darling.* The surprise continued to sink deeper into her as did the exceptional weight of having to make such a difficult decision.

She saw herself slipping into her own world, absorbing the import of Faisal's words, beginning to contemplate the quandary facing her, and preparing for myriad thoughts and feelings to present themselves. But she stopped herself. Faisal, who was silently slumping, looked fragile and vulnerable. His gray hair appeared pronounced; the shadows under his eyes stood out under the harsh light of the porch; his mouth looked like it was sagging; and his body looked heavy, as if it contained more than the weight of its fifty-seven years. Naina stroked his hair, telling him that she loved him, telling him that she was lucky to have him in her life, telling him that she couldn't imagine her life without him, telling him that she would seriously consider his proposal.

That night, Naina lay tossing and turning as Faisal slept, glad that it was their last night together and, that, tomorrow night, she would be ensconced in her quandary in her own nest. She was vexed and confused, surprised by the size and intensity of her own reaction. She didn't want to get married. Not now. Not ever. Not to Faisal, not to anyone. The thought of living with anyone made her cringe, made her frightened, made her fiercely protective of everything that was hers. All the things in her own little life, small or big, now glowed in her imagination, like fragile, twinkling pleasures in danger of being snuffed out.

She liked sprawling on her bed, her big queen-sized bed, diagonally, with her legs on the right side and her head on the left side, for the three or four nights she slept alone. She liked reading alone, late into the night with her bright bedside lamp on. She liked being the sole owner of her own apartment. She liked her mailbox containing no one else's mail except hers. She liked watching the Travel Channel by herself without arguing about it with anyone. She liked ordering in Chinese food without being told which dishes could be prepared—in the same amount of time it took for delivery— that were much healthier and tastier. She liked spreading her bath and body products all around her tub without being questioned about why she needed so many products. She liked eating achaar from the jar with a spoon and then using the same spoon to put achaar on her plate. She liked coming home to utter silence. She liked not having to always see someone every time she came home, to always feel the weight of their presence fill up the empty space in the apartment. She liked evenings where she didn't have to figure out why the other person was silent or sullen. She liked sometimes retreating into herself without having to explain or defend herself. But, most of all, she liked being in a space where the tentacles of no one else's needs could reach and prey upon her.

The way Naina saw it, marriage or even living together at this point in her or Faisal's life made no sense at all. They had both been married before; they

had both shared a home with someone else; they had both woken up to the
same person for ages; they had both endured another person's presence when
they wanted to be alone; they had both practiced keeping silent and going to
the kitchen when they wanted to scream; they had both eaten food they could
barely swallow while their spouse, eating the same food, smacked his or her lips
with delight.

And, obviously, at their age, there was no question of that business of
procreation and raising a family. Also, for her, marriage would bring unnecessary
complications. Amaya had begun taking to Faisal and her and Mukul occasionally
met up with the two of them, but marriage, the marriage of her mother—how
would Amaya feel about that? As for Karan, he still had not met Faisal, refusing
to even acknowledge him when they spoke, which was not often. And when
they did, Karan's voice was all hard and metallic, ready to shear.

Marriage had conferred respectability when Naina was in her twenties, but
now, at least in the eyes of many Indians, it would be seen as anachronistic,
as a silly way to mimic the crazy ways of American society. Why take on the
added hassle? Once again, she thought of García Márquez's *Love in The Time
of Cholera*, remembering what Fermina Daza's daughter, Ofelia, said about her
seventy-plus-year-old mother having an affair with sweet, pathetic Florentino
Ariza. "Love is ridiculous at our age," Ofelia had said. "But at theirs it is
revolting." Why did she want to open herself to being mocked when she could
easily continue having a clandestine affair? Not that her affair was or could
exactly remain clandestine, but still.

IN THE DAYS that followed Naina's return from Jamaica, reservations
about marriage would make her head would spin for hours. But whenever there
was a lull, she went to an inner cavern where she tasted nothing but a dense,
creamy love for Faisal—love like a chicken soup, a cure for all ills, nourishing
her until she was in the pinkest of pinks of health. During those moments,
all doubts would crumble, and she would be ashamed for having questioned
herself. Life seemed short and she wanted nothing more than to be in Faisal's
arms forever. But then those moments would pass.

But marriage, why did it have to be marriage? Of course, the answer wasn't
that elusive. She knew Faisal only truly enjoyed cooking if there was always
someone else to share the meal with and compliment him on how his spices
were perfectly blended, how his kebabs were so juicy, and how his lamb tagine
was even better than that of Casablanca Café. She surmised he would find the
gleaming azure of the Mediterranean Sea an indifferent blue without someone
to hold hands with, feel unmoved by the glorious sun streaming into his
bedroom unless someone was lying next to him, and find a picturesque car
ride from Rome to Malaga (Naina had recently been reading up on European

travel) tedious unless he could turn around to someone every ten minutes and comment on the rolling hills of Tuscany, the earthy appeal of Marseilles, and the intricate resplendence of the Alhambra. She also knew he was someone who did not like silence and often rushed to fill up its sweet emptiness with long strings of words, various musical recordings, voices from the television, or by opening windows to let in the sounds of the city. Like Florentino Ariza, Faisal too had a cavernous need for love. And that cavern would only be full if she became totally his, literally his wife.

Also, Faisal gave little thought to age unlike her, for whom it was like a twenty-four-hour nightlight, always dimly shining in the background. For him, she guessed, getting married at fifty-seven was the same as getting married at twenty-seven—one wore a smart suit, exchanged vows, went on a honeymoon, and started to build a home together. Perhaps, she wondered, if that sort of attitude came with being a man.

Yet she couldn't cater only to her own needs. As she lay in her bed in her apartment, watching the sunlight-flecked tree careen from her window, she remembered what she had gleaned after her visit to the Oyster House. That she was someone who had dug into her own seed and released many concealed branches, but also that those same branches had ensnared her. They had impelled her to satisfy her own desires, a yearning that kept her mostly restricted in the towering and leafy but ultimately narrow tree of the self.

But how did that apply to the predicament with Faisal? Should she widen the tree to accommodate his needs and not simply hew to her own desires? But how much was too much and how much was too little? What if the tree became so wide and filled with so many branches from a different tree that it no longer resembled the original?

Naina looked out and there was no more sunlight. Even the wind had stopped, and the sparse tree was still. Her head hurt from all that thinking. She lay down, burrowing into her new body pillow. It was so comfortable—she could have stayed like that forever. She thought of Faisal's belly laugh emitting sparkles of delight, and her body turned into a gooey ball of melted caramel.

IT HAD BEEN two weeks since Faisal had asked Naina to consider marrying him, and she still had not been able to come to a decision. Both their stances were valid, and she had no idea how to reconcile them short of coming up with some sort of unconventional arrangement, the kind that the rich, the famous, or the creative had, the kind that got discussed in *O*, Oprah's magazine, or on talk shows like *The View*. But even they did not present her with a satisfactory solution. Maybe they could get married, keep their separate apartments, and spend four or five nights a week together? But wasn't a married couple maintaining two separate places in an expensive city like New York a mad indulgence? Wasn't running two fridges, two toaster ovens, and two televisions bad for the environment? And once she became his wife, would four or five nights a week suffice for him? And would it be too much for her? Maybe they could get a two-bedroom apartment where they could both have their separate bedrooms and bathrooms? But wouldn't that mean that they would argue every night about whether they were going to sleep together or alone? And Faisal being Faisal, wouldn't he just constantly want to be in her room or have her in his? Maybe they could get married, live together but take separate vacations? But wouldn't that mean she would never have her home to herself? And would Faisal want to travel alone?

Both Soma and Alannah sided with Faisal, accusing her of selfishness.

"Selfishness?" Naina said. "Isn't his desire to get married as much about fulfilling his own needs as mine not to get married?"

And then Karan had thrown down the gauntlet. He categorically told Naina that he would never speak to her again if she married Faisal. No ifs, ands, or buts. The thought of losing her son was gut-wrenching, the sort of pain she imagined childless Faisal could not relate to. To carry a child for nine months in her body, nourish them with her milk, see parts of herself grow in them—to cut off ties with that person was beyond painful. But in less emotional moments, she reminded herself that she had dedicated years of her life to being a good mother. There had to be a time to let go. If he, at twenty-nine years of age, could not accept his mother and want her to be happy, then she was not to blame. By now, he was the architect of his own emotional map.

ONE SATURDAY AFTERNOON when it was more cloudy than sunny and the temperature was a pleasant 82 degrees, Naina decided she wasn't going to think about the situation with Faisal for the rest of that day. She got out of work early, happy to have ended the week with sixteen more people buying tickets to attend the gallery's big gala at a rooftop restaurant called The Sky's Balcony with its breathtaking views of Manhattan. There was going to be a fancy three-course Brazilian dinner with Chilean and Argentine wine pairings and a Brazilian jazz band that regularly played in the West Village. She hoped at least another twenty people would buy tickets in the next couple of weeks so they could raise a decent amount of money. After all, the economy was still weak.

As Naina walked crosstown toward her apartment, she found the city unusually hushed—few cars cluttered the streets, even fewer people strolled on them, and those who did were silently going about their business and not screaming the details about their last bad date or the terrible meal they just had, or how they didn't have any money to travel that summer. Even when she entered the Starbucks on 23rd and 8th, typically a crowded place where they played loud blues music, there were only four or five scholarly-looking people poring over newspapers or magazines, and smooth jazz was playing at a comfortable volume. One of the serious-looking women at the Starbucks had her silver hair tied in a knot at the base of her neck, reminding her of a younger version of Edith, the lady at Oyster House, who only ate eat semi-solid food and always appeared like she was pondering a matter of gravitas.

Over the last few months, she and Edith had developed a relationship of sorts. Whenever Naina went to Oyster House, she hugged Edith several times and then held her hand and talked to her about something she had read, seen, or watched on television, making sure her voice, facial expressions, and hand gestures conveyed the idea that she was talking about something serious even if what she was actually saying was neither well-thought out nor well-said. Edith always appeared to be listening intently and always gave her a faint smile in response.

Naina spotted some new dark chocolates at Starbucks when she ordered her coffee and decided to buy ten for her upcoming Oyster House visit. For Edith, she would microwave the chocolates so they melted enough for her to eat.

She continued walking, enjoying the quiet of the city, until she approached Third Avenue. There she heard a jumble of sentimental French songs, hip hop tunes, old Bollywood ballads, and Spanish boleros. Curious, she walked faster, the sounds got louder, and she saw that a big street fair had taken over the avenue.

There were crepes, ready to be filled with Nutella, chocolate, banana, strawberry, and papaya; big chunks of gyro, shwarma, and chicken kebab cooking on long metal skewers; jerk chicken, curried chicken, and Jamaican patties sold by big-breasted women wearing Bob Marley T-shirts and long skirts; biryani, pav bhaji, samosas, and pakoras being sold by teenage South Asian boys; fancy funnel cakes, ice-creams, and fresh fruit in front of which children were protesting the long lines by screaming or throwing tantrums. There were rows of cheap earrings, boxes of fake silver bracelets, necklaces with colorful beads, heaps of underwear and towels, lines of *Made in India* dresses with colorful floral or tropical prints, piles of *Made in China* fake designer handbags and wallets, and mounds of musty dog-eared American classics like *Huckleberry Finn* and *The Scarlet Letter*.

As Naina walked around the fair, eating a Jamaican chicken patty, taking in the visual feast all around her, she felt excited, just like she did every time she was at a street fair. Everything about a street fair reminded her of an Indian bazaar—its makeshift quality, the medley of disparate objects spilling into one another, the teeming, chaotic crowds, the obligatory bargaining, the vendors yelling out lower prices when customers pretended to walk away, and the unapologetic obstruction of traffic. Her longing to go to India, which had been burgeoning within her for some time, assumed an even greater urgency. She thought of her sister-in-law's pictures of their family vacation somewhere in Rajasthan, images of some old palace in the middle of nowhere that had been converted into a hotel—apparently that kind of renovation was all the rage in India these days.

Naina wiped the dust off of the copy of Edith Wharton's *Twilight Sleep* she had just bought and caught a whiff of the unmistakable, piquant odor of henna. She looked around and could not see a stall selling anything that looked like henna. She walked further downtown and saw something that resembled a scene from a henna ceremony at an Indian wedding. Two South Asian women, dressed in saris and sitting on low stools, were painting intricate designs with henna-filled cones on the hands of young women sitting on rugs on the street. Meanwhile, two other South Asian women stood behind a table overflowing with glittering colored glass bangles. They were repeatedly making the case that a woman's hand looked empty unless she wore at least a dozen bangles on each wrist.

"Come, madam, come," one of the henna painters hollered, a plump, sari-clad woman whose partially exposed midriff showed conspicuous stretch marks. Naina walked closer, and the woman smiled brightly and switched to Hindi. "Come, I'll make a special design for you. You are desi—you can appreciate it. Not like these foreigners who come and can't tell the difference between a good and bad design. They just see green on their hands and get excited."

"I don't know if I should get henna," Naina said in Hindi. "I have no special event, so what's the point?"

"No special event? You are desi, madam. In our culture, there's always a special event. Especially marriages. I'm sure someone you know is getting married soon, even if you don't know about it or remember it right now. You know last week, I bought a nice sari in Jackson Heights and my husband asked me where I would wear it. Two days later, we found out that his cousin's daughter-in-law's brother is getting married in three months on Long Island."

Naina smiled and shook her head. "I don't think any special event is going to come up in the next ten days after which point the henna will wear off."

"Then, madam, if you put on the henna, it will attract auspicious events. Is your daughter married yet?"

"No." The question amused Naina. Ah, the daughter's wedding. The event the archetypal Indian mother longs for. Unless her daughter is married, an Indian woman has not fulfilled her motherly duties. But in truth she did want Amaya to get married soon, mostly because her daughter seemed to crave it so badly now.

"Then you must apply henna, madam," the henna painter insisted. "Just see how soon your daughter gets married after that. It's good luck, you know. Why do you think people apply henna before marriage in our culture? C'mon do it, if for nothing else, for your daughter's sake. Arre, you don't want your daughter to end up a spinster because you weren't willing to apply henna to give her good luck. Trust me. See how quickly she becomes a bride after that. And then I'm going to come and apply henna at her wedding and then dance after that. And, madam, don't worry about price, you are the first Indian to come to us today, so I'll do it for fifteen dollars a hand . . . the American rate is twenty dollars a hand, but don't tell anyone. If you want to get just one hand done, that's all right too. Same rate. C'mon sit down. I'll be done with this gori (white woman) in one minute."

Naina left the street fair one hour later with henna on both her palms, the back of her hands, and her wrists. Both her arms were jingling with gold-flecked red bangles. She was colored and painted like a bride, a million miles away from an archetypal Hindu widow in all white, devoid of any color. Except for the few times over the years when she had had just a tiny bit of henna applied to her left hand for weddings, the last time she had such an extensive henna painting and worn so many red-and-gold bangles on each wrist was almost thirty-five years earlier for her own wedding. However, at that time, she had been so preoccupied that she had barely paid any attention to it.

But now, as she stood in front of her apartment building, waiting for someone to open the door so she wouldn't ruin her henna, she slowly sniffed its distinct, bold aroma, leisurely admired the intricate pattern of paisleys and arabesques, enjoyed its cool sensation, and listened to the tinkling of bangles every time she moved her hands. She imagined showing off her new adornments to Faisal when she saw him later that night, but after giving it some thought, decided it might be wiser to take off the bangles before she saw him so he wouldn't misinterpret the numerous red-and-gold bangles and the henna—key ornaments in South Asian weddings—as a sign of her willingness to get married.

The henna started to dry when Naina entered her apartment and she carefully applied some lemon and sugar on it, a concoction her grandmother had told her deepened the natural dye's color. An hour later, the henna started cracking, revealing a rich maroon color, and she scraped it off with a knife. The smell was still pungent, and it pervaded her entire apartment, making it smell like an Indian henna party, an important pre-wedding festivity. She went to her computer to send an email to her sister-in-law to tell her about her henna extravaganza and to ask her if the Bollywood movie *Jab We Met* was any good. When she opened her inbox, she found a two-hour old email from Amaya.

> Dear Mom,
>   I'm sorry it took me so long to write. We've been traveling so much and functioning Internet cafes are not so easy to find. Peru is an amazing country, quite rugged (at least the parts we've been to), and we've been having a good time. Hiking and camping around here is quite an adventure, and I think I'm becoming quite good at it. I think you would like Machu Picchu

even though it's quite touristy. It does feel quite sacred with all
the ruins, the altitude, and the fog. Your kind of place. But it
rained the whole time we were there, and I didn't mind it so
much but Mukul, like you, is a sun-worshipper, and I had to
hear him complain and that wasn't so much fun.

Mom, we've been traveling together for nearly two weeks
and it is our longest trip together. We're getting along really
well, but there's something that's really bothering me. He's
mentioned a couple of times that he thinks marriage has a
greater chance of failure than success. He said he thinks couples
are better off when they are independent though I don't know
exactly what he meant by that and didn't ask. Of course, he's
only talked about this stuff in abstract, hypothetical terms, and
he says this stuff quite casually so I don't know if he's really
serious or what he really thinks. And, right now, we're on a
vacation and frankly I'm too nervous to ask him more. I love him
a lot and know he loves me too but I also want to be married,
wake up next to the same person every day, share a home, share
a mailbox, share a coffee table, share a couch, have children. He
does say he loves children though! I'm almost 32 now. Gosh,
Mom, what a mess! What am I going to do about this? But don't
worry, Mom, I'm fine. I know he loves me. But is that enough for
things to work out?? I hope so.

I'm trying my best not to think about it on the trip and I
know it will all somehow work itself out for the best. At least
that's what I tell myself. Anyway, I better go now because many
people are waiting to use the computer. I hope you and Faisal
had a good trip to Jamaica. As you know, I'll be back Thursday
evening on American Airlines from Lima. I'll send you the flight
number soon.

Love,

Amaya

Naina shut her laptop and sat shaking in her chair. She stared briefly at her
white ceiling before sobbing in soft bursts. Her poor baby. She wanted to take
Amaya in her arms and rock her just like she did when she was a child and woke
up crying.

Naina started to become conscious of the irony of the situation. Their
circumstances were similar except that, in her own case, she was the Mukul and
Faisal was the Amaya. She was resisting marriage, and Amaya was craving it. It
was all too bizarre to digest.

Click-click, clack-clack again went the stiletto heels of the Russian woman
who lived above her, continuing her jarring walk for the next ten or fifteen
minutes. Naina wanted to scream. Instead, she flung a magazine onto the floor.

Her darling daughter deserved to get married, put henna all over her hands and feet and wear a red-and-gold lehenga. She deserved to wake up next to someone every day, cuddle with someone on the couch every night, and eat dinner with someone every evening. She wanted it so badly. Waves of anger toward Mukul lurched through her, but somewhere in the back of her brain, she also realized that she, of all people, didn't have a right to be mad.

Naina sat in her apartment for hours, staring at the ceiling, meditating, and drinking peppermint tea. She kept imagining holding Amaya, rocking her to sleep, and massaging away the creases on her brow.

Why wouldn't a boy like Mukul want marriage? At his age, it seemed like the appropriate thing to do. And then she quickly corrected herself. She should know better than to assume anything about people because of their age.

As for herself, she still had not made up her mind. She still did not want marriage, planned to try her best, in the most delicate yet persuasive manner, to make her case against it. But she knew how stubborn Faisal could be. So if it had to be marriage, she might, just might be willing to give in. But there were certain things she knew, with complete certainty, she would not compromise on. She needed to have a place for long lengths of time where she thought, if she thought about anything at all, about herself, and only herself. A place where she could be as solitary as those wonderful ruby-throated hummingbirds, drinking, hovering, floating forward, backward, and moving in any direction she liked. A place where nobody else's thoughts traversed hers. Regardless of what solution they came up with (and she hoped they came up with a solution), she needed to have this. It was almost as important as her love for Faisal.

She looked at her watch and realized it was almost eight o' clock. She had to meet Faisal at nine. She couldn't wait. After so much silence, she wanted to hear Faisal's long, fragrant garlands of words, his laugh that seemed larger than him, and feel his love that just overflowed like honey without viscosity. She went to the corner of her bedroom wall and picked up a painting of dynamic concentric circles, bluish-green like the color of the ocean lashing against the rocks in Tulum in the afternoon, the color of the Statue of Liberty, the color she most associated with mystery. It was made by a contemporary artist she had recently seen and it made her think of Sufi whirling dervishes, spinning and spinning until their souls were so drunk with ecstasy and their minds were still, so still, that there were no questions, no answers, no past and no future.

Naina had bought the painting as a present for Faisal to add some color and warmth to his sparse walls. She meticulously wrapped it with bubble wrap and acid-free paper, quickly got dressed and ran out the door to meet him, carefully holding on to the painting.

Priya Malhotra grew up in New Delhi, India and and has been a writer and journalist based in New York City for over twenty years. She has a BA in English literature from Kenyon College and a MA in journalism from Columbia University and has contributed to numerous publications including *Newsday, Time Out New York, The Times of India, The Japan Times, Asian Art News, Cosmopolitan* and *News India Times.*

Visit her website at http://www.priyamalhotra.com/

Aim you camera's phone at the code

CPSIA information can be obtained
at www.ICGtesting.com
Printed in the USA
LVHW020427140922
728282LV00001B/1